KIT FIELDING OMNIBUS

Dick Francis has written over forty international best-sellers and is widely acclaimed as one of the world's finest thriller writers. His awards include the Crime Writers' Association's Cartier Diamond Dagger for his outstanding contribution to the crime genre, and an honorary Doctorate of Humane Letters from Tufts University of Boston. In 1996 Dick Francis was made a Mystery Writers of America Grand Master for a lifetime's achievement and in 2000 he received a CBE in the Queen's Birthday Honours list.

Also by Dick Francis in Pan Books

Dick Francis

KIT FIELDING OMNIBUS

Break In
Bolt

PAN BOOKS

Break In first published 1985 by Michael Joseph Ltd
and by Pan Books in 1987
Bolt first published 1986 by Michael Joseph Ltd
and by Pan Books in 1988

This omnibus edition published 2003 by Pan Books
an imprint of Pan Macmillan Ltd
Pan Macmillan, 20 New Wharf Road, London N1 9RR
Basingstoke and Oxford
Associated companies throughout the world
www.panmacmillan.com

ISBN 0 330 41944 7

Printed and bound in Great Britain by
Mackays of Chatham plc, Chatham, Kent

BREAK IN

CHAPTER ONE

Blood ties can mean trouble, chains and fatal obligation. The tie of twins, inescapably strongest. My twin, my bond.

My sister Holly, sprung into the world ten minutes after myself on Christmas morning with bells ringing over frosty fields and hope still wrapped in beckoning parcels, my sister Holly had through thirty years been cot-mate, puppy-companion, boxing target and best friend. Consecutively, on the whole.

My sister Holly came to Cheltenham races and intercepted me between weighing room and parade ring when I went out to ride in a three-mile steeplechase.

'Kit!' she said intensely, singling me out from among the group of other jockeys with whom I walked, and standing four-square and portentously in my way.

I stopped. The other jockeys walked on, parting like water round a rock. I looked at the lines of severe strain in her normally serene face and jumped in before she could say why she'd come.

'Have you any money with you?' I said.

'What? What for?' She wasn't concentrating on my question but on some inner scenario of obvious doom.

'Have you?' I insisted.

'Well . . . but that's not . . .'

'Go to the Tote,' I said. 'Put all you've got on my horse to win. Number eight. Go and do it.'

'But I don't . . .'

'Go and do it,' I interrupted. 'Then go to the bar and with what's left buy yourself a triple gin. Then come and meet me in the winners' enclosure.'

'No, that's not . . .'

I said emphatically, 'Don't put your disaster between me and that winning post.'

She blinked as if awakening, taking in my helmet and the colours I wore beneath my husky, looking towards the departing backs of the other jockeys and understanding what I meant.

'Right?' I said.

'Right.' She swallowed. 'All right.'

'Afterwards,' I said.

She nodded. The doom, the disaster, dragged at her eyes.

'I'll sort it out,' I promised. 'After.'

She nodded dumbly and turned away, beginning almost automatically to open her shoulder bag to look for money. Doing what her brother told her, even after all these years. Coming to her brother, still, for her worst troubles to be fixed. Even though she was four years married, those patterns of behaviour, established in a parentless childhood, still seemed normal to us both.

I'd sometimes wondered what difference it would have made to her if she had been the elder by that crucial ten minutes. Would she have been motherly? Bossy, perhaps. She felt safer, she'd said, being the younger.

I walked on towards the parade ring, putting consciously out of my mind the realization that whatever the trouble this time, it was bad. She had come, for a start, one hundred and fifty miles from Newmarket to see me, and she disliked driving.

I shook my head physically throwing her out. The horse ahead, the taxing job in hand, had absolute and necessary priority. I was primarily no one's brother. I was primarily Kit Fielding, steeplechase jockey, some years champion, some years not, sharing the annual honour with another much like myself, coming out top when my bones didn't break, bowing to fate when they did.

I wore the colours of a middle-aged princess of a dispossessed European monarchy, a woman of powerful femininity whose skin was weathering towards sunset like cracked glaze on porcelain. Sable coat, as usual, swinging from narrow shoulders. Glossy dark hair piled high. Plain gold earrings. I walked towards her across the parade-ring grass; smiled, bowed, and briefly shook the offered glove.

'Cold day,' she said; her consonants faintly thick,

vowel sounds pure English, intonation as always pleasant.

I agreed.

'And will you win?' she asked.

'With luck.'

Her smile was mostly in the eyes. 'I will expect it.'

We watched her horse stalk round the ring, its liver chestnut head held low, the navy rug with gold embroidered crest covering all else from withers to tail. North Face, she'd named it, from her liking for mountains, and a suitably bleak, hard and difficult customer he'd turned out to be. Herring-gutted, ugly, bad-tempered, moody. I'd ridden him in his three-year-old hurdles, his first races, and on over hurdles at four, five and six. I'd ridden him in his novice steeplechases at seven and through his prime at eight and nine. He tolerated me when he felt like it and I knew his every mean move. At ten he was still an unpredictable rogue, and as clever a jumper as a cat. He had won thirty-eight races over the years and I'd ridden him in all but one. Twice to my fury he had purposefully dropped his shoulder and dislodged me in the parade ring. Three times we had fallen together on landing, he each time getting unhurt to his feet and departing at speed with indestructible legs, indestructible courage, indestructible will to win. I loved him and hated him and he was as usual starting favourite.

The princess and I had stood together in such a way in parade rings more often than one could count, as she rarely kept fewer than twenty horses in training and I'd ridden them constantly for ten years. She and I had come to the point of almost monosyllabic but perfectly understood conversation and, as far as I could tell, mutual trust and regard. She called me 'Kit', and I called her 'Princess' (at her request) and we shared a positive and quite close friendship which nevertheless began and ended at the racecourse gates. If we met outside, as occasionally happened, she was considerably more formal.

We stood alone together in the parade ring, as so often, because Wykeham Harlow, who trained North Face, suffered from migraine. The headaches, I'd noticed, occurred most regularly on the coldest days, which might have been a truly physical phenomenon, but also they seemed to develop in severity in direct ratio to the distance between his armchair and the day's racing. Wykeham Harlow trained south of London and very seldom now made the north-westerly traverse to Cheltenham: he was growing old and wouldn't confess he was nervous about driving home in the winter dark.

The signal was given for jockeys to mount, and Dusty, the travelling head lad who nowadays deputized for Wykeham more often than not, removed North Face's rug with a flick and gave me a deft leg-up into the saddle.

The princess said, 'Good luck,' and I said cheerfully, 'Thank you.'

No one in jump racing said 'Break a leg' instead of

'Good luck', as they did in the theatre. Break a leg was all too depressingly possible.

North Face was feeling murderous: I sensed it the moment I sat on his back and put my feet in the irons. The telepathy between that horse and myself was particularly strong always, and I simply cursed him in my mind and silently told him to shut up and concentrate on winning, and we went out on to the windy track with the mental dialogue continuing unabated.

One had to trust that the urge to race would overcome his grouchiness once the actual contest started. It almost always did, but there had been days in the past when he'd refused to turn on the enthusiasm until too late. Days, like this one, when his unfocused hatred flowed most strongly.

There was no way of cajoling him with sweet words, encouraging pats, pulling his ears. None of that pleased him. A battle of wills was what he sought, and that, from me, was what he habitually got.

We circled at the starting point, seven runners in all, while the roll was called and girths were tightened. Waited, with jockeys' faces turning pale blue in the chilly November wind, for the seconds to tick away to start time, lining up in no particular order as there were no draws or stalls in jump races, watching for the starter to raise the tapes and let us go.

North Face's comment on the proceedings took the form of a lowered head and arched back, and a kick like a bronco. The other riders cursed and kept out of his way, and the starter told me to stay well to the rear.

It was the big race of the day, though heavier in prestige than prize money, an event in which the sponsors, a newspaper, were getting maximum television coverage for minimum outlay. The Sunday Towncrier Trophy occurred annually on a Saturday afternoon (naturally) for full coverage in the *Sunday Towncrier* itself the next morning, with self-congratulatory prose and dramatic pictures jostling scandals on the front page. Dramatic pictures of Fielding being bucked off before the start were definitely not going to be taken. I called the horse a bastard, a sod and a bloody pig, and in that gentlemanly fashion the race began.

He was mulish and reluctant and we got away slowly, trailing by ten lengths after the first few strides. It didn't help that the start was in plain view of the stands instead of decently hidden in some far corner. He gave another two bronco kicks to entertain the multitude, and there weren't actually many horses who could manage that while approaching the first fence at Cheltenham.

He scrambled over that fence, came almost to a halt on landing and bucked again before setting off, shying against coercion from the saddle both bodily and clearly in mind.

Two full circuits ahead. Nineteen more jumps. A gap between me and the other runners of embarrassing and lengthening proportions. I sent him furious messages:

Race, you bastard, race, or you'll end up as dogmeat, I'll personally kill you, you bastard, and if you think you'll get me off, think again, you're taking me all the way, you sod, so get on with it, start racing, you sod, you bastard, you know you like it, so get going . . .

We'd been through it before, over and over, but he'd never been worse. He ignored all take-off signals at the second fence and made a mess of it and absolutely refused to gallop properly round the next bend.

Once in the past when he'd been in this mood I'd tried simply not fighting him but letting him sort out his own feelings, and he'd brought himself to a total halt within a few strides. Persevering was the only way: waiting until the demonic fit burned itself out.

He stuck his toes in as we approached the next fence as if the downhill slope there alarmed him, which I knew it didn't; and over the next, the water jump, he landed with his head down by his feet and his back arched, a configuration almost guaranteed to send a jockey flying. I knew his tricks so well that I was ready for him and stayed in the saddle, and after that jolly little manoeuvre we were more than three hundred yards behind the other horses and seriously running out of time.

My feelings about him rose to somewhere near absolute fury. His sheer pigheadedness was again going to lose us a race we could easily have won, and as on other similar occasions I swore to myself that I'd never ride the brute again, never. Not ever. Never. I almost believed I meant it.

As if he'd been a naughty child who knew its tantrums had gone too far, he suddenly began to race. The bumpy uneven stride went smooth, the rage faded away, the marvellous surge of fighting spirit returned, as it always did in the end. But we were a furlong and a half to the rear, and to come from more than three hundred yards behind and still win meant theoretically that one could have won by the same margin if one had tried from the start. A whole mile had been wasted; two left for retrieval. Hopeless.

Never give up, they say.

Yard by flying yard over the second circuit we clawed back the gap, but we were still ten lengths behind the last tired and trailing horse in front as we turned towards the final two fences. Passed him over the first of them. No longer last, but that was hardly what mattered. Five horses in front, all still on their feet after the long contest, all intent on the final uphill battle.

All five went over the last fence in front of North Face. He must have gained twenty feet in the air. He landed and strode away with smooth athletic power as if sticky bronco jumps were the peccadillo of another horse altogether.

I could dimly hear the crowd roaring, which one usually couldn't. North Face put his ears back and galloped with a flat, intense, bloody-minded stride, accelerating towards the place he knew was his, that he'd so wilfully rejected, that he wanted in his heart.

I flattened myself forward to the line of his neck to cut the wind resistance; kept the reins tight, my body still, my weight steady over his shoulders, all the urging a matter of mind and hands, a matter of giving that fantastic racing creature his maximum chance.

The others were tiring, the incline slowing them drastically, as it did always to so many. North Face swept past a bunch of them as they wavered and there was suddenly only one in front, one whose jockey thought he was surely winning and had half dropped his hands.

One could feel sorry for him, but he was a gift from heaven. North Face caught him at a rush a bare few strides from the winning post, and I heard his agonized cry as I passed.

Too close for comfort, I thought, pulling up. Reprieved on the scaffold.

There was nothing coming from the horse's mind: just a general sort of haze that in a human one would have interpreted as smugness. Most good horses knew when they'd won: filled their lungs and raised their heads with pride. Some were definitely depressed when they lost. Guilt they never felt, nor shame nor regret nor compassion: North Face would dump me next time if he could.

The princess greeted us in the unsaddling enclosure with starry eyes and a flush on her cheeks. Stars for success, I diagnosed, and the flush from earlier embarrassment. I unbuckled the girths, slid the saddle over my arm and paused briefly before going to weigh in, my head near to hers.

'Well done,' she said.

I smiled slightly. 'I expected curses.'

'He was especially difficult.'

'And brilliant.'

'There's a trophy.'

'I'll come right out,' I said, and left her to the flocking newsmen, who liked her and treated her reverently, on the whole.

I passed the scales. The jockey I'd beaten at the last second was looking ashamed, but it was his own fault, as well he knew. The Stewards might fine him. His owners might sack him. No one else paid much attention either to his loss or to my win. The past was the past: the next race was what mattered.

I gave my helmet and saddle to the valet, changed into different colours, weighed out, put the princess's colours back on, on top of those I would carry in the next race, combed my hair and went out dutifully for the speeches. It always seemed a shame to me when the presentation photographs were taken with the jockey not wearing the winner's colours, and for owners I cared for I did whenever possible appear with the right set on top. It cost me nothing but a couple of minutes, and it was more satisfactory, I thought.

The racecourse (in the shape of the chairman of directors) thanked the *Sunday Towncrier* for its generosity and the *Sunday Towncrier* (in the shape of its proprietor, Lord Vaughnley) said it was a pleasure to support National Hunt racing and all who sailed in her.

Cameras clicked.

There was no sign anywhere of Holly.

The proprietor's lady, thin, painted and good-natured, stepped forward in smooth couturier clothes to give a foot-high gilded statue of a towncrier (medieval version) to the princess, amid congratulation and hand shaking. The princess accepted also a smaller gilt version on behalf of Wykeham Harlow, and in my turn I received the smile, the handshake, the congratulations and the attentions of the cameras, but not, to my surprise, my third set of golden towncrier cufflinks.

'We were afraid you might win them again,' Lady Vaughnley explained sweetly, 'so this year it's a figure like the others,' and she pressed warmly into my hands a little golden man calling out the news to the days before printing.

I genuinely thanked her. I had more cufflinks already than shirts with cuffs to take them.

'What a finish you gave us,' she said, smiling. 'My husband is thrilled. Like an arrow from nowhere, he said.'

'We were lucky.'

I looked automatically to her shoulder, expecting to greet also her son, who at all other Towncriers had accompanied his parents, hovering around and running errands, willing, nice-natured, on the low side of average for brains.

'Your son isn't with you?' I asked.

Most of Lady Vaughnley's animation went into eclipse. She glanced swiftly and uncomfortably across to her husband, who hadn't heard my remark, and said unhappily, 'No, not today.'

'I'm sorry,' I said; not for Hugh Vaughnley's absence, but for the obvious row in the family. She nodded and turned away, blinking, and I thought fleetingly that the trouble must be new and bad, near the surface of tears.

The princess invited Lord and Lady Vaughnley to her box and they happily accepted.

'You as well, Kit,' she said.

'I'm riding in the next race.'

'Come after.'

'Yes. Thank you.'

Everyone left their trophies on the presentation table to be taken away for engraving and I returned to the changing room as the princess moved away with the Vaughnleys.

She always asked me to her box because she liked to discuss her horses and what they'd done, and she had a loving and knowledgeable interest in all of them. She liked most to race where she rented a private box, namely at Cheltenham, Ascot, Sandown and Lingfield, and she went only to other courses where she had standing invitations from box-endowed friends. She was not democratic to the point of standing on the open stands and yelling.

I came out in the right colours for the next race and found Holly fiercely at my elbow immediately.

'Have you collected your winnings?' I asked.

'I couldn't reach you,' she said disgustedly. 'All those officials, keeping everyone back, and the crowds . . .'

'Look, I'm sorry. I've got to ride again now.'

'Straight after, then.'

'Straight after.'

My mount in that race, in contrast to North Face, was unexciting, unintelligent and of only run-of-the-mill ability. Still, we tried hard, finished third, and seemed to give moderate pleasure to owners and trainer. Bread and butter for me: expenses covered for them. The basic fabric of jump racing.

I weighed in and changed rapidly into street clothes, and Holly was waiting when I came out.

'Now, Kit . . .'

'Um,' I said. 'The princess is expecting me.'

'No! Kit!' She was exasperated.

'Well . . . it's my job.'

'Don't come to the office, you mean?'

I relented. 'OK. What's the matter?'

'Have you seen this?' She pulled a page torn from a newspaper called the *Daily Flag* out of her shoulder bag. 'Has anyone said anything in the weighing room?'

'No and no,' I said, taking the paper and looking

where she was pointing with an agitated stabbing finger. 'I don't read that rag.'

'Nor do we, for God's sake. Just look at it.'

I glanced at the paragraph which was boxed by heavy red lines on a page entitled 'Intimate Details', a page well known to contain information varying from stale to scurrilous and to be intentionally geared to stirring up trouble.

'It's yesterday's,' I said, looking at the date.

'Yes, yes. Read it.'

I read the piece. It said:

Folk say the skids are under Robertson (Bobby) Allardeck (32), racehorse-trainer son of tycoon Maynard Allardeck (50). Never Daddy's favourite (they're not talking), Bobby's bought more than he can pay for, naughty boy, and guess who won't be coming to the rescue. Watch this space for more.

Robertson (Bobby) Allardeck (32) was my sister Holly's husband.

'It's libellous,' I said. 'Bobby can sue.'

'What with?' Holly demanded. 'We can't afford it. And we might not win.'

I looked at the worry in her normally unlined face.

'Is it true, then?' I said.

'No. Yes. In a way. Of course he's bought things he can't pay for. Everyone does. He's bought horses. It's

15

yearling sale time, dammit. Every trainer buys yearlings he can't pay for. It's natural, you know that.'

I nodded. Trainers bought yearlings at auction for their owners, paying compulsorily for them on the spot and relying on the owners to reimburse them fairly soon. Sometimes the owners backed out after a yearling had been bought; sometimes trainers bought an extra animal or two to bring on themselves and have ready for a later sale at a profit. Either way, at sale time, it was more common than not to borrow thousands short-term from the bank.

'How many has Bobby bought that he can't sell?' I asked.

'He'll sell them in the end, of course,' she said, staunchly.

Of course. Probably. Perhaps.

'But now?'

'Three. We've got three.'

'Total damage?'

'More than a hundred thousand.'

'The bank paid for them?'

She nodded. 'It's not that it won't be all right in the end, but where did that disgusting rag get the information from? And why put it in the paper at all? I mean, it's pointless.'

'And what's happened?' I asked.

'What's happened is that everyone we owe money to has telephoned demanding to be paid. I mean, horrible threats, really, about taking us to court. All day yesterday . . . and this morning the feed-merchant rang and said he wouldn't deliver any more feed unless we paid our bill and we've got thirty horses munching their heads off, and the owners are on the line non-stop asking if Bobby's going to go on training or not and making veiled hints about taking their horses away.'

I was sceptical. 'All this reaction from that one little paragraph?'

'Yes.' She was suddenly close to tears. 'Someone pushed the paper through the letter box of half the tradesmen in Newmarket, open at that page with that paragraph outlined in red, just like this. The blacksmith showed me. It's his paper. He came to shoe some of the horses and made us pay him first. Made a joke of it. But all the same, he meant it. Not everyone's been so nice.'

'And I suppose you can't simply just pay everyone off and confound them?'

'You know we can't. The bank manager would bounce the cheques. We have to do it gradually, like we always do. Everyone will get paid, if they wait.'

Bobby and Holly lived in fairly usual fashion at permanent full stretch of their permitted overdraft, juggling the incoming cheques from the owners with the outgoing expenses of fodder, wages, overheads and taxes. Owners sometimes paid months late, but the horses had to be fed and the lads' wages found to the minute. The cash flow tended to suffer from air locks.

'Well,' I said, 'go for another triple gin while I talk to the princess.'

CHAPTER TWO

The Princess Casilia, Mme de Brescou (to give her her full style), had as usual asked a few friends to lunch with her to watch the races, and her box contained, besides herself and the Vaughnleys, a small assortment of furs and tweeds, all with inhabitants I'd formerly met on similar occasions.

'You know everyone, don't you?' the princess said, and I nodded 'Yes', although I couldn't remember half their names.

'Tea?' she asked.

'Yes, thank you.'

The same waitress as usual smoothly gave me a full cup, smiling. No milk, no sugar, slice of lemon, as always.

The princess had had a designer decorate her boxes at the racecourses and they were all the same: pale peach hessian on the walls, coffee-coloured carpet and a glass-topped dining table surrounded by comfortable chairs. By late afternoon, my habitual visiting time, the table had been pushed to one side and bore not lunch but plates of sandwiches, creamy pastries, assorted alcohol, a box of cigars. The princess's friends tended to linger long after the last races had been run.

One of the women guests picked up a plate of small delicious-looking cakes and offered it to me.

'No, thank you,' I said mildly. 'Not this minute.'

'Not ever,' the princess told her friend. 'He can't eat those. And don't tempt him. He's hungry.'

The friend looked startled and confused. 'My dear, I never thought. And he's so tall.'

'I eat a lot,' I said. 'But just not those.'

The princess, who had some idea at least of the constant struggle I had to stay down at a body weight of ten stone, gave me a glimmering look through her eyelashes, expressing disbelief.

The friend was straightforwardly curious. 'What do you eat most of,' she asked, 'if not cake?'

'Lobster, probably,' I said.

'Good heavens.'

Her male companion gave me a critical glance from above a large moustache and long front teeth.

'Left it a bit late in the big race, didn't you, what?' he said.

'I'm afraid so, yes.'

'Couldn't think what you were doing out there, fiddling about at the back. You nearly bungled it entirely, what? The princess was most uncomfortable, I can tell you, as we all had our money on you, of course.'

The princess said, 'North Face can behave very

badly, Jack. I told you. He has such a mind of his own. Sometimes it's hard to get him to race.'

'It's the jockey's job to get him to race,' Jack said to me with a touch of belligerence. 'Don't you agree, what?'

'Yes,' I said. 'I do agree.'

Jack looked fractionally disconcerted and the princess's lips twitched.

'And then you set him alight,' said Lord Vaughnley, overhearing. 'Gave us a rousing finish. The sort of thing a sponsor prays for, my dear fellow. Memorable. Something to talk about, to refer to. North Face's finish in the Towncrier Trophy. Splendid, do you see?'

Jack saw, chose not to like it, drifted away. Lord Vaughnley's grey eyes looked with bonhomie from his large bland face and he patted me with kindly meant approval on the shoulder.

'Third time in a row,' he said. 'You've done us proud. Would you care, one Saturday night, to see the paper put to bed?'

'Yes,' I said, surprised. 'Very much.'

'We might print a picture of you watching a picture of yourself go through the presses.'

More than bonhomie, I thought, behind the grey eyes: a total newspaperman's mentality.

He was the proprietor of the *Towncrier* by inheritance, the fiftyish son of one of the old-style newspaper barons who had muscled on to the scene in the nineteen thirties and brought new screaming life to millions of breakfasts. Vaughnley Senior had bought a dying provincial weekly and turned it into a lusty voice read nationwide. He'd taken it to Fleet Street, seen the circulation explode, and in due course had launched a daily version which still prospered despite sarcastic onslaughts from newer rivals.

The old man had been a colourful buccaneering entrepreneur. The son was quieter, a manager, an advertising man at heart. The *Towncrier*, once a raucous newsheet, had over the last ten years developed Establishment leanings, a remarkable testimony of the hand-over from the elder personality to the younger.

I thought of Hugh Vaughnley, the son, next in the line: the sweet-tempered young man without strength, at present at odds, it appeared, with his parents. In his hands, if it survived at all, the *Towncrier* would soften to platitude, waffle and syrup.

The *Daily Flag*, still at the brassiest stage, and among the *Towncrier*'s most strident opposition, had been recently bought, after bitter financial intrigues, by a thrusting financier in the ascendant, a man hungry, it was said, for power and a peerage, and taking a well-tried path towards both. The *Flag* was bustling, go-getting, stamping on sacrosanct toes and boasting of new readers daily.

Since I'd met Lord Vaughnley several times at various racing presentation dinners where annual honours were dished out to the fortunate (like champion jockeys, leading trainers, owners-of-the-year, and so on) and with Holly's distress sharp in my mind, I asked him if he knew who was responsible for 'Intimate Details' in the *Flag*.

'Responsible?' he repeated with a hint of holier-than-thou distaste. 'Irresponsible, more like.'

'Irresponsible, then.'

'Why, precisely?' he asked.

'They've made an unprovoked and apparently point-less attack on my brother-in-law.'

'Hm,' Lord Vaughnley said. 'Too bad. But, my dear fellow, pointless attacks are what the public likes to read. Destructive criticism sells papers, back-patting doesn't. My father used to say that, and he was seldom wrong.'

'And to hell with justice,' I said.

'We live in an unkind world. Always have, always will. Christians to the lions, roll up, buy the best seats in the shade, gory spectacle guaranteed. People buy newspapers, my dear fellow, to see victims torn limb from limb. Be thankful it's physically bloodless, we've advanced at least that far.' He smiled as if talking to a child. 'Intimate Details, as you must know, is a com-posite affair, with a whole bunch of journalists digging out nuggets and also a network of informants in hospi-tals, mortuaries, night clubs, police stations and all sorts of less savoury places, telephoning in with the dirt and collecting their dues. We at the *Towncrier* do the same sort of thing. Every paper does. Gossip columns would be non-starters, my dear fellow, if one didn't.'

'I'd like to know where the piece about my brother-in-law came from. Who told who, if you see what I mean. And why.'

'Hm.' The grey eyes considered. 'The editor of the *Flag* is Sam Leggatt. You could ask him of course, but even if he finds out from his staff, he won't tell you. Head against brick wall, I'm afraid, my dear fellow.'

'And you approve,' I said, reading his tone. 'Closing ranks, never revealing sources, and all that.'

'If your brother-in-law has suffered real positive harm,' he nodded blandly, 'he should get his solicitor to send Sam Leggatt a letter announcing imminent prosecution for libel unless a retraction and an apology are published immediately. It sometimes works. Failing that, your brother-in-law might get a small cash settlement out of court. But do advise him, my dear fellow, against pressing for a fully fledged libel action with a jury. The *Flag* retains heavyweight lawyers and they play very rough. They would turn your brother-in-law's most innocent secrets inside out and paint them dirty. He'd wish he'd never started. Friendly advice, my dear fellow, I do assure you.'

I told him about the paragraph being outlined in red and delivered by hand to the houses of tradespeople.

Lord Vaughnley frowned. 'Tell him to look for the informant on his own doorstep,' he said. 'Gossip column items often spring from local spite. So do stories about vicars and their mistresses.' He smiled briefly.

'Good old spite. Whatever would the newspaper industry do without it!'

'Such a confession!' I said with mockery.

'We clamour for peace, honesty, harmony, common sense and equal justice for all,' he said. 'I assure you we do, my dear fellow.'

'Yes,' I said. 'I know.'

The princess touched Lord Vaughnley's arm and invited him to go out on to the balcony to see the last race. He said, however, that he should return to the *Towncrier*'s guests whom he had temporarily abandoned in a sponsors' hospitality room, and, collecting his wife, he departed.

'Now, Kit,' said the princess, 'while everyone is outside watching the race, tell me about North Face.'

We sat, as so often, in two of the chairs, and I told her without reservation what had happened between her horse and myself.

'I do wish,' she said thoughtfully, at the end, 'that I had your sense of what horses are thinking. I've tried putting my head against their heads,' she smiled almost self-consciously, 'but nothing happens. I get nothing at all. So how do you do it?'

'I don't know,' I said. 'I don't think head to head would work, anyway. It's just when I'm riding them, I seem to know. It's not in words, not at all. It's just there. It just seems to come. It happens to very many riders. Horses are telepathic creatures.'

She looked at me with her head on one side. 'But

you, Kit, you're telepathic with people as well as horses. Quite often you've answered a question I was just going to ask. Quite disconcerting. How do you do it?'

I was startled. 'I don't know how.'

'But you know you do?'

'Well . . . I used to. My twin sister Holly and I were telepathic between ourselves at one time. Almost like an extra way of talking. But we've grown out of it, these last few years.'

'Pity,' she said. 'Such an interesting gift.'

'It can't logically exist.'

'But it does.' She patted my hand. 'Thank you for today, although you and North Face between you almost stopped my heart.'

She stood up without haste, adept from some distant training at ending a conversation gracefully when she wished, and I stood also and thanked her formally for her tea. She smiled through the eyelashes, as she often did with everybody: not out of coquetry but in order, it seemed to me, to hide her private feelings.

She had a husband to whom she went home daily; Monsieur Roland de Brescou, a Frenchman of aristocratic lineage, immense wealth and advanced age. I had met him twice, a frail white-haired figure in a wheelchair with an autocratic nose and little to say. I asked after his health occasionally: the princess replied always that he was well. Impossible ever to tell from her voice or demeanour what she felt about him: love, anxiety, frustration, impatience, joy . . . nothing showed.

'We run at Devon and Exeter, don't we?' she said.

'Yes, Princess. Bernina and Icicle.'

'Good. I'll see you there on Tuesday.'

I shook her hand. I'd sometimes thought, after a win such as that day's, of planting a farewell kiss on her porcelain cheek. I liked her very much. She might consider it the most appalling liberty, though, and give me the sack, so in her own disciplined fashion I made her merely a sketch of a bow, and went away.

'You've been a hell of a long time,' Holly complained. 'That woman treats you like a lap dog. It's sickening.'

'Yeah . . . well . . . here I am.'

She had been waiting for me on her feet outside the weighing room in the cold wind, not snugly in a chair in the bar. The triple gin anyway had been a joke because she seldom drank alcohol, but that she couldn't even sit down revealed the intensity of her worry.

The last race was over, the crowds streaming towards the car parks. Jockeys and trainers, officials and valets and pressmen bade each other goodnight all around us although it was barely three-forty in the afternoon and not yet dusk. Time to go home from the office. Work was work, even if the end product was entertainment. Leisure was a growth industry, so they said.

'Will you come home with me?' Holly asked.

I had known for an hour that that was what she would want.

27

'Yes,' I said.

Her relief was enormous but she tried to hide it with a cough, a joke and a jerky laugh. 'Your car or mine?'

I'd thought it over. 'We'll both go to the cottage. I'll drive us in your car from there.'

'OK.' She swallowed. 'And Kit . . .'

'Save it,' I said.

She nodded. We'd had an ancient pact: never say thank you out loud. Thanks came in help returned, unstintingly and at once, when one needed it. The pact had faded into abeyance with her marriage but still, I felt, existed: and so did she, or she wouldn't have come.

Holly and I were more alike in looks than many fraternal twins, but nowhere near the identical Viola and Sebastian: Shakespeare, most rarely, got it wrong. We each had dark hair, curly. Each, lightish brown eyes. Each, flat ears, high foreheads, long necks, easily tanned skin. We had different noses and different mouths, though the same slant to the bone above the eye socket. We had never had an impression of looking into a mirror at the sight of the other, although the other's face was more familiar to us than our own.

When we were two years old our young and effervescent parents left us with our grandparents, went for a winter holiday in the Alps, and skied into an avalanche. Our father's parents, devastated, had kept us and brought us up and couldn't in many ways have been better, but Holly and I had turned inward to each other more than might have happened in a normal family. We had invented and spoken our own private language, as many such children do, and from there had progressed to a speechless communication of minds. Our telepathy had been more a matter of knowing what the other was thinking rather than of deliberately planting thoughts in the other's head. More reception than transmission, one might say: and it happened also without us realizing it, as over and over again when we'd been briefly apart we had done things like writing in the same hour to our Australian aunt, getting the same book out of the library, and buying identical objects on impulse. We had both, for instance, one day gone separately home with roller skates as a surprise birthday present for the other and hidden them in our grandmother's wardrobe. Grandmother herself by that time hadn't found it strange as we'd done similar things too often, and she'd said that right from when we could talk if she asked, 'Kit, where's Holly?' or, 'Holly, where's Kit?' we would always know, even if logically we couldn't.

The telepathy between us had not only survived the stresses and upheavals of puberty and adolescence but had actually become stronger: also we were more conscious of it, and used it purposely when we wanted, and grew in young adulthood into a new dimension of friendship. Naturally we put up a front to the world of banter, sarcasm and sibling rivalry, but underneath we were solid, never doubting our private certainty.

When I'd left our grandparents' house to buy a place

of my own with my earnings, Holly had from time to time lived there with me, working away in London most of the time but returning as of right whenever she wished, both of us taking it for granted that my cottage was now her home also.

That state of affairs had continued until she fell in love with Bobby Allardeck and married him.

Even before the wedding the telepathy had begun to fade and fairly soon afterwards it had more or less stopped. I wondered for a while if she had shut down deliberately, and then realized it had been also my own decision: she was off on a new life and it wouldn't have been a good idea to try to cling to her, or to intrude.

Four years on, the old habit had vanished to such an extent that I hadn't felt a flicker of her present distress, where once I would somehow have had it in my mind and would have telephoned to find out if she was all right.

On our way out to the car park I asked her how much she'd won on North Face.

'My God,' she said, 'you left that a bit late, didn't you?'

'Mm.'

'Anyway, I went to put my money on the Tote but the queues were so long I didn't bother and I went down on to the lawn to watch the race. Then when you were left so far behind I was glad I hadn't backed you. Then those bookies on the rails began shouting five to one North Face. Five to one! I mean, you'd started at odds-on. There was a bit of booing when you came past the stands and it made me cross. You always do your best, they didn't have to boo. So I walked over and got one of the bookies to take all my money at fives. It was a sort of gesture, I suppose. I won a hundred and twenty-five, which will pay the plumber, so thanks.'

'Did the plumber get Intimate Details?'

'Yes, he did.'

'Someone knows your life pretty thoroughly,' I said.

'Yes. But who? We were awake half the night wondering.' Her voice was miserable. 'Who could hate us that much?'

'You haven't just kicked out any grievance-laden employees?'

'No. We've a good lot of lads this year. Better than most.'

We arrived at her car and she drove me to where mine was parked.

'Is that house of yours finished yet?' she asked.

'Getting on.'

'You're bizarre.'

I smiled. Holly liked things secure, settled and planned in advance. She thought it crazy that I'd bought on impulse the roofless shell of a one-storey house from a builder who was going broke. He'd been in the local pub one night when I'd gone in for a steak: leaning on the bar and morosely drowning his sorrows in beer.

He'd been building the house for himself, he said, but he'd no money left. All work on it had stopped.

I'd ridden horses for him in his better-off days and had known him for several years, so the next morning I'd gone with him to see the house; and I'd liked its possibilities and bought it on the spot, and engaged him to finish it for me, paying him week by week for work done. It was going to be a great place to live and I was going to move into it, finished or not, well before Christmas, as I'd already exchanged contracts on my old cottage and would have to leave there willy nilly.

'I'll follow you to the cottage,' Holly said. 'And don't drive like you won the Towncrier.'

We proceeded in sedate convoy to the racehorse-training village of Lambourn on the Berkshire Downs, leaving my car in its own garage there and setting off together on the hundred miles plus to the Suffolk town of Newmarket, headquarters of the racing industry.

I liked the informality of little Lambourn. Holly and Bobby swam easily in the grander pond. Or had done, until a pike came along to snap them up.

I told her what Lord Vaughnley had said about demanding a retraction from the *Flag*'s editor but not suing, and she said I'd better tell Bobby. She seemed a great deal more peaceful now that I was actually on the road with her, and I thought she had more faith in my ability to fix things than I had myself. This was a lot different from beating up a boy who pinched her bottom twice at school. A little more shadowy than making a salesman take back the rotten car he'd conned her into buying.

She slept most of the way to Newmarket and I had no idea at all what I was letting myself in for.

We drove into the Allardeck stableyard at about eight o'clock and found it ablaze with lights and movement when it should have been quiet and dark. A large horsebox was parked in the centre, all doors open, loading ramp down. Beside it stood an elderly man watching a stable-lad lead a horse towards the ramp. The door of the place where the horse had been dozing the night away shone as a wide open oblong of yellow behind him.

A few steps away from the horsebox, lit as on a stage, were two men arguing with fists raised, arms gesticulating, voices clearly shouting.

One of them was my brother-in-law, Bobby. The other . . .?

'Oh my God,' Holly said. 'That's one of our owners. Taking his horses. And he owes us a fortune.'

She scrambled out of the car almost before I'd braked to a halt, and ran towards the two men. Her arrival did nothing, as far as I could see, to cool the flourishing row, and to all intents they simply ignored her.

My calm-natured sister was absolutely no good at stalking into any situation and throwing her weight about. She thought privately that it was rather pleasant to cook and keep house and be a gentle old-fashioned woman: but then she was of a generation for whom that way was a choice, not a drudgery oppressively imposed.

I got out of the car and walked across to see what could be done. Holly ran back to meet me.

'Can you stop him?' she said urgently. 'If he takes the horses, we'll never get his money.'

I nodded.

The lad leading the horse had reached the ramp but the horse was reluctant to board. I walked over to the lad without delay, stood in his way, on the bottom of the ramp, and told him to put the horse back where he'd brought it from.

'What?' he said. He was young, small, and apparently astonished to see anyone materialize from the dark.

'Put it back in the box, switch off the light, close the door. Do it now.'

'But Mr Graves told me . . .'

'Just do it,' I said.

He looked doubtfully across to the two shouting men.

'Do you work here?' I said. 'Or did you come with the horsebox?'

'I came with the horsebox.' He looked at the elderly man standing there who had so far said and done nothing. 'What should I do, Jim?'

'Who are you?' I asked him.

'The driver,' he said flatly. 'Keep me out of it.'

'Right,' I said to the lad. 'The horse isn't leaving. Take it back.'

'Are you Kit Fielding?' he said doubtfully.

'That's right. Mrs Allardeck's brother. Get going.'

'But Mr Graves...'

'I'll deal with Mr Graves,' I said. 'His horse isn't leaving tonight.'

'Horses,' the boy said, correcting me. 'I loaded the other one already.'

'OK,' I said. 'They're both staying here. When you've put back the one you're loading, unload the first one again.'

The boy gave me a wavering look, then turned the horse round and began to plod it back towards its rightful quarters.

The change of direction broke up the slanging match at once. The man who wasn't Bobby broke away and shouted to the lad across the yard, 'Hey, you, what the shit do you think you're doing? Load the horse this minute.'

The lad stopped. I walked fast over to him, took hold of the horse's head-collar and led the bemused animal back into its own home. The lad made no move at all to stop me. I came out. Switched off the light. Shut and bolted the door.

Mr Graves (presumably) was advancing fast with flailing arms and an extremely belligerent expression.

'Who the shit do you think you are?' he shouted. 'That's my horse. Get it out here at once!'

I stood, however, in front of the bolted door, leaning my shoulders on it, crossing one ankle over the other, folding my arms. Mr Graves came to a screeching and disbelieving halt.

'Get away from there,' he said thunderously, stabbing the night air with a forefinger. 'That's my horse. I'm taking it, and you can't stop me.'

His pudgy face rigid with obstinacy, he stood about five feet five from balding crown to polished toecaps. He was perhaps fifty, plump, already out of breath. There was no way whatever that he was going to shift my five feet ten by force.

'Mr Graves,' I said calmly, 'you can take your horses away when you've paid your bill.'

His mouth opened speechlessly. He took a step forward and peered at my face, which I dare say was in shadow.

'That's right,' I said. 'Kit Fielding. Holly's brother.'

The open mouth snapped shut. 'And what the shit has all this to do with you? Get out of my way.'

'A cheque,' I said. 'You do have your chequebook with you?'

His gaze grew calculating. I gave him little time to slide out.

I said, 'The *Daily Flag* is always hungry for tit-bits for its Intimate Details. Owners trying to sneak their horses away at dead of night without paying their bills would be worth a splash, don't you think?'

'That's a threat!' he said furiously.

'Quite right.'

'You wouldn't do that.'

'Oh yes, I certainly would. I might even suggest that if you can't pay this one bill, maybe you can't pay others. Then all your creditors would be down like vultures in a flash.'

'But that's . . . that's . . .'

'That's what's happening to Bobby, yes. And if Bobby has a cash-flow problem, and I'm only saying if, then it's partly due to you yourself and others like you who don't pay when you should.'

'You can't talk to me like that,' he said furiously.

'I don't see why not.'

'I'll report you to the Jockey Club.'

'Yes, you do that.'

He was blustering, his threat a sham. I looked over his shoulder towards Bobby and Holly, who had been near enough to hear the whole exchange.

'Bobby,' I said, 'go and fetch Mr Graves's account. Make sure every single item he owes is on it, as you may not have a second chance.'

Bobby went at a half-run, followed more tentatively by Holly. The lad who had come with the horsebox retreated with the driver into the shadows. Mr Graves and I stood as if in a private tableau, waiting.

While a horse remained in a trainer's yard the trainer had a good chance of collecting his due, because the law firmly allowed him to sell the horse and deduct from the proceeds what he was owed. With the horse whisked away his prospects were a court action and a lengthy wait, and if the owner went bankrupt, nothing at all.

Graves's horses were Bobby's security, plain and simple.

Bobby eventually returned alone bringing a lengthy bill which ran to three sheets.

'Check it,' I said to Graves, as he snatched the pages from Bobby's hand.

Angrily he read the bill through from start to finish and found nothing to annoy him further until he came to the last item. He jabbed at the paper and again raised his voice.

'Interest? What the shit do you mean, interest?'

'Um,' Bobby said, 'on what I've had to borrow because you hadn't paid me.'

There was a sudden silence. Respectful, on my part. I wouldn't have thought my brother-in-law had it in him.

Graves suddenly controlled his anger, pursed his lips, narrowed his eyes, and delved into an inner pocket for his chequebook. Without any sign of fury or haste he carefully wrote a cheque, tore it out, and handed it to Bobby.

'Now,' he said to me. 'Move.'

'Is it all right?' I asked Bobby.

'Yes,' he said as if surprised. 'All of it.'

'Good,' I said, 'then go and unload Mr Graves's other horse from the horsebox.'

CHAPTER THREE

'Do what?' Bobby said, astonished.

I remarked mildly, 'A cheque is only a piece of paper until it's been through the bank.'

'That's slander!' Graves said furiously, all his earlier truculence reappearing.

'It's an observation,' I said.

Bobby shoved the cheque quickly into his trouser pocket as if fearing that Graves would try to snatch it back, not an unreasonable suspicion in view of the malevolence facing him.

'Once the cheque's been cleared,' I said to Graves, 'you can come and pick up the horses. Thursday or Friday should do. Bobby will keep them for nothing until then, but if you haven't removed them by Saturday he will begin charging training fees again.'

Bobby's mouth opened slightly and shut purposefully, and he walked without more ado towards the horsebox. Graves scuttled a few steps after him, protesting loudly, and then reversed and returned to me, shouting and practically dancing up and down.

'I'll see the Stewards hear about this!'

'Most unwise,' I said.

'I'll stop that cheque.'

'If you do,' I said calmly, 'Bobby will have you put on the forfeit list.'

This most dire of threats cut off Graves's ranting miraculously. A person placed on the Jockey Club's forfeit list for non-payment of training fees was barred in disgrace from all racecourses, along with his horses. Mr Graves, it seemed, was not quite ready for such a social blight.

'I won't forget this,' he assured me viciously. 'You'll regret you meddled with me, I'll see to that.'

Bobby had succeeded in unloading Graves's first horse and was leading it across to its stable, while the lad and the driver closed the ramp and bolted it shut.

'Off you go, then, Mr Graves,' I said. 'Come back in the daytime and telephone first.'

He gave me a bullish stare and then suddenly went into the same routine as earlier: pursed his mouth, narrowed his eyes and abruptly quietened his rage. I had guessed, the first time, watching him write his cheque without further histrionics, that he had decided he might as well write it because he would tell his bank not to cash it.

It looked very much now as if he were planning something else. The question was, what?

I watched him walk calmly over to the horsebox and wave an impatient hand at the lad and the driver, telling

41

them to get on board. Then he himself climbed clumsily up into the cab after them and slammed the door.

The engine started. The heavy vehicle throbbed, shuddered, and rolled away slowly out of the yard, Graves looking steadfastly ahead as if blinkered.

I detached myself from the stable door and walked across towards Bobby.

'Thanks,' he said.

'Be my guest.'

He looked round. 'All quiet. Let's go in. It's cold.'

'Mm.'

We walked two steps and I stopped.

'What is it?' Bobby asked, turning.

'Graves,' I said. 'He went too meekly.'

'He couldn't have done much else.'

'He could have gone shouting and kicking and uttering last-minute threats.'

'I don't know what you're worrying about. We've got his cheque and we've got his horses ... er, thanks to you.'

His horses.

The breath in my lungs went out in a whoosh, steaming in a vanishing plume against the night sky.

'Bobby,' I said, 'have you any empty boxes?'

'Yes, there are some in the fillies' yard.' He was puzzled. 'Why?'

'We might just put Graves's horses in them, don't you think?'

'You mean ... he might come back?' Bobby shook

his head. 'I'd hear him. I heard him before, though I admit that was lucky because we should have been out at a party, but we were too worried about things to go.'

'Could Graves have known you would be out?' I asked.

He looked startled. 'Yes, I suppose he could. The invitation is on the mantelpiece in the sitting room. He came in there last Sunday for a drink. Anyway, I'd hear a horsebox coming back. Couldn't miss it.'

'And if it parked at three in the morning on that strip of grass along from your gate, and the horses were led out in rubber boots to deaden the noise of their hooves?'

Bobby looked nonplussed. 'But he wouldn't. Not all that. Would he?'

'He was planning something. It showed.'

'All right,' Bobby said. 'We'll move them.'

On my way back to fetch the horse I'd been guarding I reflected that Bobby was uncommonly amenable to advice. He usually considered any suggestion from me to be criticism of himself and defensively found sixteen reasons for not doing what I'd mentioned: or at least not until I was well out of sight and wouldn't know. This evening things were different. Bobby had to be very worried indeed.

We walked Graves's horses round to Bobby's second yard behind the main quadrangle and installed them there in two empty boxes, which happened (all to the good, I thought) not to be side by side.

'Does Graves know his horses by sight?' I asked Bobby; which was not by any means a stupid question, as many owners didn't.

'I don't know,' he said dubiously. 'It's never come up.'

'In other words,' I said, 'he always knows them because they're where he expects to see them?'

'Yes. I should think so. But it's not certain. He might know them better than I think.'

'Well . . . in that case, how about rigging some sort of alarm?'

Bobby didn't say certainly not, it wasn't necessary, he said, 'Where?'

Incredible.

'On one of the boxes they are normally in,' I said.

'Yes. I see. Yes.' He paused. 'What sort of alarm? I haven't any electric gadgets here. If I need any special tight security before a big race I hire a man with a dog.'

I did a quick mental review of his house and its contents. Saucepan lids? Metal trays? Something to make a noise.

'The bell,' I said. 'Your old school bell.'

'In the study.' He nodded. 'I'll fetch it.'

Bobby's study contained shelves of tidily arranged mementoes of his blameless early life: cricket caps, silver cups won at school sports, team photographs, a rugger ball . . . and the hand bell which as a prefect he had rung noisily through his House to send the younger boys to bed. Bobby had been the sort of steadfast team-spirited boy that made the British public school system work: that he had emerged complacent and slightly pompous was probably owing to his many good qualities being manifest to all, including himself.

'Bring a hammer,' I said. 'And some staples if you have any. Nails, if not. And some heavy-duty string.'

'Right.'

He went away and in due course returned carrying the bell quietly by its clapper in one hand and a toolbox in the other. Between us we installed the bell as near to Bobby's house as possible and rigged it in such a way that a good tug to the string tied to its handle would send it toppling and jangling. Then we led the string through a long line of staples to the usual home of one of Graves's horses, and fastened the end of it out of sight to the top of the closed door.

'OK,' I said. 'Go into the house. I'll open this door and you see if you can hear the bell.'

He nodded and went away, and after a fair interval I opened the stable door. The bell fell with a satisfying clamour and Bobby came back saying it would wake the dead. We returned it to its precarious pre-toppling position and with rare accord walked together into the house.

There had been Fieldings and there had been Allardecks in racing further back than anyone could remember: two families with some land and some money and a bitter mutual persisting hatred.

There had been a Fielding and an Allardeck knifing each other for favour with King Charles II when he held court not in London but in Newmarket, thereby making foreign ambassadors travel wearily north-east by coach to present their credentials.

There had been an Allardeck who had wagered three hundred sovereigns on a two-horse race on Queen Anne's own racecourse on Ascot Heath and lost his money to a Fielding, who had been killed and robbed before he reached home.

There had been a Mr Allardeck in the Regency years who had challenged a Mr Fielding to a cross-country contest over fearsome jumps, the winner to take the other's horse. Mr Allardeck (who lost) accused Mr Fielding (an easy victor) of taking a cheating short cut, and the dispute went to pistols at dawn, when they each shot carefully at the other and died of their wounds.

There had been a Victorian gentleman rider named Fielding with a wild moustache and a wilder reputation, and an Allardeck who had fallen off, drunk, at the start of the Grand National. Fielding accused Allardeck of being a coward, Allardeck accused Fielding of seducing his (Allardeck's) sister. Both charges were true: and those two settled their differences by fisticuffs on New-market Heath, Fielding half killing the (again) drunk and frightened Allardeck.

By Edwardian times the two families were inextricably locked into inherited hostility and would accuse each other of anything handy. A particularly aggressive Fielding had bought an estate next door to the Allardecks on purpose to irritate, and bitter boundary disputes led to confrontations with shotguns and (more tamely) writs.

Bobby's great-grandfather burned down Great-grandfather Fielding's hay-barn (Great-grandfather Fielding having built it where it most spoiled the Allardeck's view) only to find his favourite hunter shot dead in its field a week later.

Bobby's grandfather and Grandfather Fielding had naturally been brought up to hate each other, the feud in their case extending later to bitter professional rivalry, as each (being a second son and not likely to inherit the family estate) had decided to set up as a licensed racehorse trainer. They each bought training stables in Newmarket and paid their lads to spy and report on the other. They cockily crowed when their horses won and seethed when the other's did, and, if coming first and second in the same race, lodged objections against each other almost as a matter of course.

Holly and I, being brought up in Grandfather Fielding's tempestuous household, were duly indoctrinated with the premise that all Allardecks were villainous madmen (or worse) who were to be cut dead at all times in Newmarket High Street.

Bobby and I, I dare say, each having been taught from birth to detest the other, might in our turn have come to fists or fire, were it not for my father dying, and Bobby's father leaving Newmarket with his family and going off into property and commodities. Not that Bobby's father, Maynard, could bear even the mention of the word Fielding: and the reason he was not speaking to Bobby (as truthfully noted in Intimate Details) was because Bobby Allardeck had dared, despite a promise of disinheritance, to defy his father's fury and walk up the aisle with Holly Fielding.

When Holly was thirteen her one absolute heroine had been Juliet in *Romeo and Juliet*. She learned almost the whole play by heart, but Juliet's part particularly, and became hopelessly romantic about the dead young lovers uniting the warring families of Montague and Capulet. Bobby Allardeck, I reckoned, was her Romeo, and she had been powerfully predisposed to fall in love with him, even if he hadn't been, as he was, tall, fair-haired and good-looking.

They had met by chance (or did she seek him out?) in London after several years of not seeing each other, and within a month were inseparable. The marriage had succeeded in its secret purpose to the extent that Bobby and I were now almost always polite to each other and that our children, if we had any, could, if they would, be friends.

Bobby and Holly had returned to Newmarket, Bobby hoping to take over as trainer in his by then ailing grandfather's yard, but the quarrelsome old man, calling his grandson a traitor to the family, had made him pay full market price for the property, and had then died, not leaving him a penny.

Bobby's current financial troubles were not simple. His house and yard (such small part of it as was free from mortgage) would as a matter of course be held by the bank as security for the extra loans they'd made him for the buying of yearlings. If the bank called in the loans, he and Holly would be left with no home, no livelihood, and an extremely bleak future.

As in many racing houses, a great deal of life went on in the kitchen, which in Holly and Bobby's case was typically furnished with a long dining table and a good number of comfortable chairs. A friendly room, with a lot of light pine, warmly lit and welcoming. When Bobby and I went in from the yard Holly was whisking eggs in a bowl and frying chopped onions and green peppers in a large pan.

'Smells good,' I said.

'I was starving.' She poured the eggs over the onions and peppers. 'We must all be.'

We ate the omelette with hot French bread and wine and talked of nothing much until we had finished.

Then Holly, making coffee, said, 'How did you get Jermyn Graves to go?'

'Jermyn? Is that his name? I told him if he stopped the cheque Bobby would put him on the forfeit list.'

'And don't think I haven't thought of it,' Bobby said.

'But of course it's a dead loss from our point of view really.'

I nodded. The Jockey Club would refrain from putting an owner on the forfeit list if he (or she) paid all training fees which had been owing for three months or more. Unfortunately, though, the forfeit list leverage applied to basic training fees only, and not to vets' or blacksmiths' fees or to the cost of transporting horses to race meetings. Bobby had had to pay out for all those things already for Graves's horses, and putting the owner on the forfeit list wouldn't get them reimbursed.

'Why is he in such a hurry to take his horses away?' I asked.

'He's just using our troubles as an excuse,' Holly said.

Bobby nodded. 'He's done something like this to at least two other trainers. All young and trying to get going, like us. He runs up big bills and then one day the trainer comes home and finds the horses gone. Then Graves pays the bare training fees to avoid the forfeit list, and the trainer's left with no horses as security and all the difficulties and expense of going to court to try to get what he's owed, and of course it's seldom worth it, and Graves gets away with it.'

'Why did you accept his horses in the first place?' I said.

'We didn't know about him, then,' Holly said gloomily. 'And we're not exactly going to turn away people who ask us to take two horses, are we?'

'No,' I said.

'Anyway,' Holly said, 'Jermyn's just another blow. The worst crisis is the feed-merchant.'

'Give him Graves's cheque,' I said.

Holly looked pleased but Bobby said dubiously, 'Our accountant doesn't like us doing that sort of thing.'

'Yeah, but your accountant hasn't got thirty hungry horses on his doorstep staring at him reproachfully.'

'Twenty-nine, really,' Holly said.

'Twenty-seven,' Bobby sighed, 'when Graves's have gone.'

'Does that include the three unsold yearlings?' I asked.

'Yes.'

I rubbed my nose. Twenty-four paying inmates were basically a perfectly viable proposition, even if in his grandfather's day there had been nearer forty. They were, moreover, just about to enter their annual rest period (as Bobby trained only on the Flat) and would no longer be incurring the higher expenses of the season.

Conversely they could not until the following March win any prize money, but then nor would they be losing any bets.

Winter, in flat-racing stables, was time for equilibrium, for holidays, for repainting, and for breaking in the yearlings, sold or not.

'Apart from the unsold yearlings, how much do you owe?' I asked.

I didn't think Bobby would tell me, but after a pause, reluctantly, he did.

I winced.

'But we can pay everything,' Holly said. 'At our own pace. We always do.'

Bobby nodded.

'And it's so unfair about the yearlings,' my sister said passionately. 'One of our owners told Bobby to go up to fifty thousand to get one particular yearling, and Bobby did, and now the owner's telephoned to say he's very sorry he can't afford it after all; he just hasn't got the money. And if we send it back to the next sale, we'll make a loss. It's always that way. People will think there's something wrong with it.'

'I'll probably be able to syndicate it,' Bobby said. 'Sell twelve equal shares. But it takes time to do that.'

'Well,' I said, 'surely the bank will give you time.'

'The bank manager's panic-stricken by that damned newspaper.'

'Did someone deliver it to him too?' I asked.

Holly said gloomily, 'Someone did.'

I told Bobby what Lord Vaughnley had said about the *Flag*'s informant being someone local with a grudge.

'Yes, but who?' Bobby said. 'We really haven't any enemies.' He gave me a sidelong look in which humour was definitely surfacing. 'Once upon a time it would have been a Fielding.'

'Too true.'

'Grandfather!' Holly said. 'It couldn't be him, could it? He's never forgiven me, but surely . . . he wouldn't?'

We thought of the obstinate old curmudgeon who still trained a yardful of horses half a mile away and bellowed at his luckless lads on the Heath every morning. He was still, at eighty-two, a wiry, vigorous, cunningly intelligent plotter whose chief regret these days was that Bobby's grandfather was no longer alive to be outsmarted.

It was true that Grandfather Fielding had been as outraged as Grandfather Allardeck by the unthinkable nuptials, but the man who brought us up had loved us in his own testy way, and I couldn't believe he would actively try to destroy his granddaughter's future. Not unless old age was warping him into malice, as it sadly could sometimes.

'I'll go and ask him,' I said.

'Tonight?' Holly looked at the clock. 'He'll be in bed. He goes so early.'

'In the morning.'

'I don't want it to be him,' Holly said.

'Nor do I.'

We sat over the coffee for a while, and at length I said, 'Make a list of all the people who you know had the *Flag* delivered to them with that paragraph marked, and I'll go and call on some of them tomorrow. All I can get to on a Sunday.'

'What for?' Bobby said. 'They won't change their

minds. I've tried. They just say they want their money at once. People believe what they read in newspapers. Even when it's all lies, they believe it.'

'Mm,' I said. 'But apart from telling them again that they'll be paid OK I'll ask them if any of them saw the paper being delivered. Ask them what time it came. Get a picture of what actually went on.'

'All right,' Holly said. 'We'll make the list.'

'And after that,' I said, 'work out who could possibly know who you deal with. Who could have written the same list. Unless, of course,' I reflected, 'dozens of other people who you don't owe money to got the paper delivered to them as well.'

'I've no idea,' Holly said. 'We never thought of that.'

'We'll find out tomorrow.'

Bobby yawned. 'Scarcely slept last night,' he said.

'Yes. Holly told me.'

There was suddenly a loud clanging from outside, a fierce and urgent alarm, enough to reawaken all the houses, if not the dead.

'God!' Bobby leapt to his feet, crashing his chair over backwards. 'He came back!'

We pelted out into the yard, all three of us, intent on catching Jermyn Graves in the act of trying to steal away his own property; and we did indeed find an extremely bewildered man holding open a stable door.

It was not, however, Jermyn Graves, but Nigel,

Bobby's ancient head lad. He had switched on the light inside the empty box and turned his weatherbeaten face to us as he heard us approach, the light carving deep canyons in his heavy vertical wrinkles.

'Sooty's gone,' he said anxiously. 'Sooty's gone, guv'nor. I fed him myself at half-six, and all the doors were shut and bolted when I went home.' There was a detectable tinge of defensiveness in his voice which Bobby also heard and laid to rest.

'I moved him,' he said easily. 'Sooty's fine.'

Sooty was not the real name of Graves's horse, but the real names of some horses tended to be hopeless mouthfuls for their attendant lads. It was hard to sound affectionate when saying (for instance) Nettleton Manor. Move over Nettleton Manor. Nettleton Manor, you old rogue, have a carrot.

'I was just taking a last look round,' Nigel said. 'Going home from the pub, like.'

Bobby nodded. Nigel, like most head lads, took the welfare of the horses as a personal pride. Beyond duty, their horses could be as dear to head lads as their own children, and seeing they were safely tucked up last thing at night was a parental urge that applied to both species.

'Did you hear a bell ring?' Holly said.

'Yes.' He wrinkled his forehead. 'Near the house.' He paused. 'What was it?'

'A new security system we're trying out,' Bobby said.

'The bell rings to tell us someone's moving about the yard.'

'Oh?' Nigel looked interested. 'Works a treat then, doesn't it?'

CHAPTER FOUR

Work a treat the bell might, but no one came in the small hours to tug it again to its sentinel duty. I slept undisturbed in jeans and sweater, ready for battle but not called, and Bobby went out and disconnected the string before the lads arrived for work in the morning.

He and Holly had written out the list of *Flag* recipients, and after coffee, when it was light, I set off in Holly's car to seek them out.

I went first, though, as it was Sunday and early, to every newsagent, both in the town and within a fair radius of the outskirts, asking if they had sold a lot of copies of the *Flag* to any one person two days ago, on Friday, or if anyone had arranged for many extra copies to be delivered on that morning.

The answer was a uniform negative. Sales of the *Flag* on Friday had been the same as Thursday, give or take. None of the shops, big or small, had ordered more copies than usual, they said, and no one had sold right out of the *Flag*. The boys had done their regular delivery rounds, nothing more.

Dead end to the first and easiest trail.

I went next to seek out the feed-merchant, who was not the one who supplied my grandfather. I had been struck at once, in fact, by the unfamiliarity of all the names of Bobby's suppliers, though when one thought about it, it was probably only to be expected. Bobby, taking over from his grandfather, would continue to use his grandfather's suppliers: and never, it seemed, had the lifelong antagonists used the same blacksmith, the same vet, the same anything. Each had always believed the other would spy on him, given the slightest opportunity. Each had been right.

No feed-merchant in Newmarket, with several thousand horses round about, would find it strange to have his doorbell rung on his theoretical day of rest. The feed-merchant who waved me into the brick office annexe to his house was young and polished; and in an expensive accent and with crispness he told me it was not good business to allow accounts to run on overdue, he had his own cash-flow to consider, and Allardeck's credit had run out.

I handed him Jermyn Graves's cheque, duly endorsed by Bobby on the back.

'Ah,' said the feed-merchant, brightening. 'Why ever didn't you say so?'

'Bobby hoped you might wait, as usual.'

'Sorry. No can do. Cash on delivery from now on.'

'That cheque is for more than your account,' I pointed out.

'So it is. Right then. Bobby shall be supplied until this runs out.'

'Thank you,' I said, and asked him if he had seen his copy of the *Flag* delivered.

'No. Why?'

I explained why. 'This was a large scale and deliberate act of spite. One tends to want to know who.'

'Ah.'

I waited. He considered.

'It must have been here fairly early Friday morning,' he said finally. 'And it was delivered here to the office, not to the house, as the papers usually are. I picked it up with the letters when I came in. Say about eight-thirty.'

'And it was open at the gossip page with the paragraph outlined in red?'

'That's right.'

'Didn't you wonder who'd sent it?'

'Not really . . .' He frowned. 'I thought someone was doing me a good turn.'

'Mm,' I said. 'Do you take the *Flag* usually?'

'No, I don't. *The Times* and the *Sporting Life*.'

I thanked him and left, and took Holly's winnings to the plumber, who greeted me with satisfaction and gave me some of the same answers as the feed-merchant. The *Flag* had been inside his house on the front door mat by seven o'clock, and he hadn't seen who brought it. Mr Allardeck owed him for some pipe-work done way back in the summer, and he would admit, he said, that he had telephoned and threatened him pretty strongly with a county court action if he didn't pay up at once.

Did the plumber take the *Flag* usually?

Yes, he did. On Friday, he got two.

'Together?' I asked. 'I mean, were they both there on the mat at seven?'

'Yes. They were.'

'Which was on top of the other?'

He shrugged, thought, and said, 'As far as I remember, the one marked in red was underneath. Funny, I thought it was, that the boy had delivered two. Then I saw the paragraph, and I reckoned one of my neighbours was tipping me off.'

I said it was all very hard on Bobby.

'Yes, well, I suppose so.' He sniffed. 'He's not the only bad payer, by a long shot.' He gave me the beginnings of a sardonic smile. 'They pay up pretty quick when their pipes burst. Come a nice heavy freeze.'

I tried three more creditors on the list. Still unpaid, they were more brusque and less helpful, but an overall pattern held good. The marked papers had been delivered before the newsboys did their rounds and no one had seen who delivered them.

I went back to the largest of the newsagents and asked the earliest time their boys set out.

'The papers reach us here by van at six. We sort them into the rounds, and the boys set off on their bicycles before six-thirty.'

'Thanks,' I said.

They nodded. 'Any time.'

Disturbed by the stealth and thoroughness of the operation I drove finally to see my grandfather in the house where I'd been brought up: a large brick-built place with gables like comic eyebrows peering down at a barbed-wire-topped boundary fence.

The yard was deserted when I drove in, all the horses in their boxes with the top doors closed against the cold. On the day after the last day of the Flat season, no one went out to gallop on the Heath. Hibernation, which my grandfather hated, was already setting in.

I found him in his stable office, typing letters with concentration, the result, I surmised, of the departure of yet another beleaguered secretary.

'Kit!' he said, glancing up momentarily. 'I didn't know you were coming. Sit down. Get a drink.' He waved a thin hand. 'I won't be long. Damned secretary walked out. No consideration, none at all.'

I sat and watched while he hammered the keys with twice the force necessary, and felt the usual slightly exasperated affection for him, and the same admiration.

He loved horses beyond all else. He loved Grandmother next best and had gone very silent for a while the winter she'd died, the house eerily quiet after the years they'd spent shouting at each other. Within a few months he had begun shouting at Holly and me instead, and later, after we'd left, at the secretaries. He didn't intend to be unkind. In an imperfect world he was a perfectionist irritated by minor incompetencies, which meant most of the time.

The typing stopped. He stood up, the same height as myself, white-haired, straight and trim in shirt, tie and excellently cut tweed jacket. Casual my grandfather was not, not in habits or manners or dress, and if he was obsessive by nature it was probably just that factor which had brought him notable success over almost sixty years.

'There's some cheese,' he said, 'for lunch. Are you staying tonight?'

'I'm, er, staying with Holly.'

His mouth compressed sharply. 'Your place is here.'

'I wish you'd make it up with her.'

'I talk to her now,' he said, 'which is more than can be said for that arrogant Maynard with his rat of a son. She comes up here some afternoons. Brings me stews and things sometimes. But I won't have him here and I won't go there, so don't ask.' He patted my arm, the ultimate indication of approval. 'You and I, we get along all right, eh? That's enough.'

He led the way to the dining room where two trays lay on the table, each covered with a cloth. He removed one cloth to reveal a carefully laid single lunch: cheeses, biscuits under clingfilm, pats of butter, dish of chutney, a banana and an apple with a silver fruit knife. The other tray was for dinner.

'New housekeeper,' he said succinctly. 'Very good.'

Long may she last, I thought. I removed the clingfilm and brought another knife and plate, and the two of us sat there politely eating very little, he from age, I from necessity.

I told him about the paragraph in the *Flag* and knew at once with relief that he'd had no hand in it.

'Nasty,' he said. 'Mind you, my old father could have done something like that, if he'd thought of it. Might have done it myself,' he chuckled, 'long ago. To Allardeck.' Allardeck, to Grandfather, was Bobby's grandfather, Maynard's father, the undear departed. Grandfather had never in my hearing called him anything but plain Allardeck.

'Not to Holly,' my grandfather said. 'Couldn't do it to Holly. Wouldn't be fair.'

'No.'

He looked at me searchingly. 'Did she think it might be me?'

'She said it couldn't be, and also that she very much didn't want it to be you.'

He nodded, satisfied and unhurt. 'Quite right. Little Holly. Can't think what possessed her, marrying that little rat.'

'He's not so bad,' I said.

'He's like Allardeck. Just the same. Smirking all over his face when his horse beat mine at Kempton two weeks ago.'

'But you didn't lodge an objection, I noticed.'

'Couldn't. No grounds. No bumping, boring or

crossing. His horse won by three lengths.' He was disgusted. 'Were you there? I didn't see you.'

'Read it in the paper.'

'Huh.' He chose the banana. I ate the apple. 'I saw you win the Towncrier yesterday on television. Rotten horse, full of hate. You could see it.'

'Mm.'

'You get people like that, too,' he observed. 'Chockful of ability and too twisted up to do anything worthwhile.'

'He did win,' I pointed out.

'Just. Thanks to you. And don't argue about that, it's something I enjoy, watching you ride. There never was an Allardeck anywhere near your class.'

'And I suppose that's what you said to Allardeck himself?'

'Yes, of course. He hated it.' Grandfather sighed. 'It's not the same since he's gone. I thought I'd be glad, but it's taken some of the point out of life. I used to enjoy his sour looks when I got the better of him. I got him barred from running his horse in the St Leger once, because my spies told me it had ringworm. Did I tell you that? He would have killed me that day if he could. But he'd stolen one of my gullible lady owners with a load of lies about me never entering her horses where they could win. They didn't win for him either, as I never let him forget.' He cut the peeled banana into neat pieces and sat looking at them. 'Maynard, now,' he said, 'Maynard hates my guts too, but he's not worth the ground Allardeck stood on. Maynard is a power-hungry egomaniac, just the same, but he's also a creeper, which his father never was, for all his faults.'

'How do you mean, a creeper?'

'A bully to the weak but a boot-licker to the strong. Maynard boot-licked his way up every ladder, stamping down on all the people he passed. He was a hateful child. Smarmy. He had the cheek to come up to me once on the Heath and tell me that when he grew up he was going to be a lord, because then I would have to bow to him, and so would everyone else.'

'Did he really?'

'He was quite small. Eight or nine. I told him he was repulsive and clipped his ear. He snitched to his father, of course, and Allardeck sent me a stiff letter of complaint. Long ago, long ago.' He ate a slice of banana without enthusiasm. 'But that longing for people to bow to him, he's still got it, I should think. Why else does he take over all those businesses?'

'To win,' I said. 'Like we win, you and I, if we can.'

'We don't trample on people doing it. We don't want to be bowed to.' He grinned. 'Except by Allardecks, of course.'

We made some coffee and while we drank I telephoned some of Grandfather's traditional suppliers, and his vet and blacksmith and plumber. All were surprised at my question, and no, none of them had received a marked copy of the *Flag*.

'The little rat's got a traitor right inside his camp,'

Grandfather said without noticeable regret. 'Who's his secretary?'

'No one. He does everything himself.'

'Huh. Allardeck had a secretary.'

'You told me about fifty times Allardeck had a secretary only because you did. You boasted in his hearing that you needed a secretary as you had so many horses to train, so he got one too.'

'He never could bear me having more than he did.'

'And if I remember right,' I said, 'you were hopping up and down when he got some practice starting stalls, until you got some too.'

'No one's perfect.' He shrugged dismissively. 'If the little rat hasn't got a secretary, who else knows his life inside out?'

'That,' I said, 'is indeed the question.'

'Maynard,' Grandfather said positively. 'That's who. Maynard lived in that house, remember, until long after he was married. He married at eighteen . . . stupid, I thought it, but Bobby was on the way. And then he was in and out for at least another fifteen years, when he was supposed to be Allardeck's assistant, but was always creeping off to London to do all those deals. Cocoa! Did you ever hear of anyone making a fortune out of cocoa? That was Maynard. Allardeck smirked about it for weeks, going on and on about how smart his son was. Well, my son was dead, as I reminded him pretty sharply one day, and he shut up after that.'

'Maynard wouldn't destroy Bobby's career,' I said.

'Why not? He hasn't spoken to him since he took up with Holly. Holly told me if Maynard wants to say anything to Bobby he gets his tame lawyer to write, and all the letters so far have been about Bobby repaying some money Maynard lent him to buy a car when he left school. Holly says Bobby was so grateful he wrote his father a letter thanking him and promising to repay him one day, and now Maynard's holding him to it.'

'I can't believe it.'

'Absolutely true.'

'What a bastard.'

'The one thing Maynard is actually not,' Grandfather said dryly, 'is a bastard. He's got Allardeck's looks stamped all over him. The same sneer. The same supercilious smirk. Lanky hair. No chin. The little rat's just like them, too.'

Bobby, the little rat, was to any but a Fielding eye a man with a perfectly normal chin and a rather pleasant smile, but I let it pass. The sins and shortcomings of the Allardecks, past and present, could never be assessed impartially in a Fielding house.

I stayed with Grandfather all afternoon and walked round the yard with him at evening stables at four-thirty, the short winter day already darkening and the lights in the boxes shining yellow.

The lads were busy, as always, removing droppings, carrying hay and water, setting the boxes straight. The long-time head lad (at whom Grandfather never shouted) walked round with us, both of them briefly discussing details of each of the fifty or so horses. Their voices were quiet, absorbed and serious, and also in a way regretful, as the year's expectations and triumphs were all over, excitement put away.

I dreaded the prospect of those excitements being put away for ever: of Grandfather ill or dying. He wouldn't retire before he had to, because his job was totally his life, but it was expected that at some point not too very far ahead I would return to live in that house and take over the licence. Grandfather expected it, the owners were prepared for it, the racing world in general thought it a foregone conclusion; and I knew that I was far from ready. I wanted four more years, or five, at the game I had a passion for. I wanted to race for as long as my body was fit and uninjured and anyone would pay me. Jump jockeys never went on riding as long as flat jockeys because crunching to the ground at thirty miles an hour upwards of thirty times a year is a young man's sport, but I'd always thought of thirty-five as approximately hanging-up-the-boots time.

By the time I was thirty-five, Grandfather would be eighty-seven, and even for him ... I shivered in the cold air and thrust the thought away. The future would have to be faced, but it wasn't upon me yet.

To Grandfather's great disgust I left him after stables and went back to the enemy house, to find the tail end of the same evening ritual still in progress. Graves's horses were still in the fillies' yard, and Bobby was feeling safer because Nigel had told him that Graves had at least twice mistaken other horses for his own when he'd called to see them on Sunday mornings.

I watched Bobby with his horses as he ran his hand down their legs to feel for heat in strained tendons, and peered at the progress of minor skin eruptions, and slapped their rumps as a friendly gesture. He was a natural-born horseman, there was no doubt, and the animals responded to him in the indefinable way that they do to someone they feel comfortable with.

I might find him a bit indecisive sometimes, and not a razor-brain, but he was in truth a good enough fellow, and I could see how Holly could love him. He had, moreover, loved her enough himself to turn his back on his ancestors and estrange himself from his powerful father, and it had taken strength, I reckoned, to do that.

He stood up from feeling a leg and saw me watching him, and with an instinct straight from the subconscious stretched to his full height and gave me a hawk-like look of vivid antagonism.

'Fielding,' he said flatly, as if the word itself was an accusation and a curse: a declaration of continuing war.

'Allardeck,' I replied, in the same way. I grinned slightly. 'I was thinking, as a matter of fact, that I liked you.'

'Oh!' He relaxed as fast as he'd tensed, and looked confused. 'I don't know . . . for a moment . . . I felt . . .'

'I know,' I said, nodding. 'Hatred.'

'Your eyes were in shadow. You looked ... hooded.'

It was an acceptable explanation and a sort of apology; and I thought how irrational it was that the deep conditioning raised itself so quickly to the surface, and in myself on occasions just the same, however I might try to stop it.

He finished the horses without comment and we walked back towards the house.

'I'm sorry,' he said then, with a touch of awkwardness. 'Back there ...' He waved a hand. 'I didn't mean it.'

I asked curiously, 'Do you ever think of Holly in that way? As a Fielding? If her eyes are in shadow, does she seem a menace?'

'No, of course not. She's different.'

'How is she different?'

He glanced at my face and seemed to find it all right to explain. 'You,' he said, 'are strong. I mean, in your mind, not just muscles. No one who's talked to you much could miss it. It makes you ... I don't know ... somehow people notice when you're there, like in the weighing room, or somewhere. People would be able to say if you'd been at a particular race meeting or not, or at a party, even though you don't try. I suppose I'm not making sense. It's what's made you a champion jockey, I should think, and it's totally *Fielding*. Well, Holly's not like that. She's gentle and calm and she hasn't an ounce of aggressiveness or ambition, and she doesn't want to go out and beat the world on horses, so she isn't really a Fielding at heart.'

'Mm.' It was a dry noise from the throat more than a word. Bobby gave me another quick glance. 'It's all right,' I said. 'I'll plead guilty to my inheritance, and also exonerate her from it. But she does have ambition.'

'No.' He shook his head positively.

'For you,' I said. 'For you to be a lasting success. For you both to be. To prove you were right to get married.'

He paused with his hand on the knob of the door which led from the yard to the kitchen. 'You were against it, like all the others.'

'Yes, for various reasons. But not now.'

'Not on the actual day,' he said with fairness. 'You were the only one that turned up.'

'She couldn't walk up that aisle by herself, could she?' I said. 'Someone had to go with her.'

He smiled as instinctively as before he'd hated.

'A Fielding giving a Fielding to an Allardeck,' he said. 'I wondered at the time if there would be an earthquake.'

He opened the door and we went in. Holly, who bound us together, had lit the log fire in the sitting room and was trying determinedly to be cheerful.

We sat in armchairs and I told them about my morning travels, and also assured them of Grandfather's non-involvement.

'The marked copies of the *Flag* were on people's mats at least by six,' I said, 'and they came from outside, not from Newmarket. I don't know what time the papers get to the shops in Cambridge, but not a great deal before five, I shouldn't think, and there couldn't have been much time for anyone to buy twenty or so papers in Cambridge and deliver them, folded and marked, to addresses all over Newmarket, twenty miles away, before the newsboys here started on their rounds.'

'London?' Holly said. 'Do you think someone brought them up direct?'

'I should think so,' I nodded. 'Of course that doesn't necessarily mean that it wasn't someone from here who arranged it, or even did it personally, so we're not much further ahead.'

'It's all so pointless,' Holly said.

'No one seems to have been looking out of their windows by six,' I went on. 'You'd think someone would be, in this town. But no one that I asked had seen anyone walking up to anyone's door with a newspaper at that time. It was black dark, of course. They said they hardly ever see the newsboys themselves, in winter.'

The telephone on the desk beside Bobby's chair rang, and Bobby stretched out a hand to pick up the receiver with a look of apprehension.

'Oh . . . hello, Seb,' he said. There was some relief in his voice, but not much.

'Friend,' Holly said to me. 'Has a horse with us.'

'You saw it, did you?' Bobby made a face. 'Someone

sent you a copy...' He listened, then said, 'No, of course I don't know who. It's sheer malice. No, of course it's not true. I'm here in business to stay, and don't worry, your mare is very well and I was just now feeling her tendon. It's cool and firm and doing fine. What? Father? He won't guarantee a penny, he said so. Yes, you may well say he's a ruthless swine ... No, there's no hope of it. In fact on the contrary he's trying to squeeze out of me some money he lent me to buy a car about fourteen years ago. Yes, well ... I suppose it's that sort of flint that's made him rich. What? No, not a fortune, it was a second-hand old banger, but my first. I suppose I'll have to pay him in the end just to get his lawyers off my back. Yes, I told you, everything's fine. Pay no attention to the *Flag*. Sure, Seb, any time. Bye.'

He put down the receiver, his air nowhere near as confident as his telephone voice.

'Another owner full of doubt. Load of rats. Half of them are thinking of leaving without waiting to see if the ship will sink. Half of them, as well, haven't paid their last month's bills.'

'Has Seb?' asked Holly.

Bobby shook his head.

'He's got a cheek, then.'

'That wretched paragraph reached him by post yesterday: just the Intimate Details column. A clipping, he said, not the whole paper. In an ordinary brown envelope, typed. From London, like the others.'

'Did all the owners get a clipping?' I asked.

'It looks like it. Most of them have been on the phone. I haven't exactly rung the rest to ask.'

We sat around for a while, and I borrowed the telephone to pick up my messages from the answering machine in the cottage, and to call in return a couple of trainers who'd offered rides during the week, and to talk to a couple of jockeys who lived in Newmarket, asking for a lift down to Plumpton in Sussex for racing the next day. Two of them were already going together, they said, and would take me.

'Will you come back here?' Holly said, when all was fixed.

I looked at the anxiety in her face and the lack of opposition in Bobby's. I wouldn't have expected him to want me even in the first place, but it seemed I was wrong.

'Stay,' he said briefly, but with invitation, not grudge.

'I haven't been much help.'

'We feel better,' Holly said, 'with you here.'

I didn't much want to stay because of practical considerations. I was due to ride in Devon on the Tuesday, and one reason I preferred to live in Lambourn, not Newmarket, was that from Lambourn one could drive to every racecourse in England and return home on the same day. Lambourn was central.

I said apologetically, 'I'll have to get a lift back to Lambourn from Plumpton, because I need my car to go to Devon on Tuesday. When I get back to Lambourn on Tuesday evening, we'll see how things are here.'

Holly said, 'All right,' dispiritedly, not attempting to persuade.

I looked at her downcast face, more beautiful, as often, in sorrow than in joy. A thought came unexpectedly into my head and I said without reflection, 'Holly, are you pregnant?'

CHAPTER FIVE

Bobby was dumbstruck.

Holly gave me a piercing look from the light brown eyes in which I read both alarm and stimulation.

'Why did you say that?' Bobby demanded.

'She's only a short while overdue. We haven't had any tests done yet,' Bobby said; and to Holly, 'You must have told him.'

'No, I haven't.' She shook her head. 'But I was thinking just then how happy I was first thing on Friday, when I woke up feeling sick. I was thinking how ironic it would be. All those months of trying, and the first time it may really have happened, we are in such trouble that the very last thing we need is a baby.'

Bobby frowned. 'You must have told him,' he repeated, and he sounded definitely upset, almost as if he were jealous.

'Well, no, I didn't,' Holly said uncertainly.

'On the way back here yesterday,' he insisted.

'Look,' I said. 'Forget I said it. What does it matter?'

Bobby looked at me with resentment and then more

forgivingly at Holly, as if some thought had struck him. 'Is this the sort of thing you meant,' he said doubtfully, 'when you told me once about you and Kit reading each other's minds when you were kids?'

She reluctantly nodded. 'We haven't done it for years, though.'

'It doesn't happen nowadays,' I agreed. 'I mean, this was just a one-off. A throw-back. I don't suppose it will happen again.'

And if it did happen again, I thought, I would be more careful what I said. Stray thoughts would be sieved.

I understood Bobby's jealousy perfectly well because I had felt it myself, extraordinarily strongly, when Holly first told me she had fallen in love. The jealousy had been quickly overlaid by a more normal dismay when she'd confessed just who it was she'd set her heart on, but I still remembered the sharpness of not wanting to share her, not wanting my status as her closest friend to be usurped by a stranger.

I'd been slightly shocked at my jealousy and done a fair amount of soul-searching, never before having questioned my feelings for my sister: and I'd made the reassuring but also rueful discovery that she could sleep with Bobby all she liked and leave me undisturbed: it was the mental intimacy I minded losing.

There had been sexual adventures of my own, of course, both before and after her marriage, but they had been short-lived affairs with no deep involvement, nothing anywhere approaching Holly's commitment to Bobby. Plenty of time, I thought, and maybe, one of these days; and platitudes like that.

Bobby made at least a show of believing that telepathy between me and Holly wouldn't happen again, although both she and I, giving each other the merest flick of a glance, guessed differently. If we chose to tune in, so to speak, the old habit would come back.

The three of us spent the evening trying not to return over and over to the central questions of who and why, and in the end went wearily to bed without any possible answers. I lay down again in jeans, jersey and socks in case Graves should return, but I reckoned that if he'd ever planned it, he had had second thoughts.

I was wrong.

The bell woke me with a clatter at three-thirty-five in the morning, and I was into my shoes, out of the house and running down the drive, in the strategy that Bobby and I had discussed the night before, almost before it stopped ringing.

Out of the open gateway, turn left; and sure enough, on a stretch of roadside grass that sometimes accommodated gypsies, stood the wherewithal for shifting horses. A car, this time, towing a two-horse trailer. A trailer with its rear ramp lowered; ready, but not yet loaded.

I ran straight up to the car and yanked open the driver's door, but there was no one inside to be taken by surprise. Just keys in the ignition; unbelievable.

I lifted up the trailer's ramp and bolted it shut, then

climbed into the car, started up, and drove a couple of hundred yards to a side road. I turned into there, parked a short way along, left the keys in the ignition as before, and sprinted back to Bobby's yard.

The scene was almost a repeat of the time before, at least as far as the lights, the shouting and obscenity went. Bobby and Jermyn Graves were standing outside the empty box where the alarm had been rigged and had all but come to blows. A thin boy of perhaps sixteen stood a short distance away, holding a large carrier bag, shifting from foot to foot and looking unhappy.

'Give me my property,' Graves yelled. 'This is stealing.'

'No, it's not,' I said in his ear. 'Stealing is an intention permanently to deprive.'

'What?' He swung round to glare at me. 'You again!'

'If you're talking law,' I said, 'it is within the law to withhold property upon which money is owed, until the debt is discharged.'

'I'll ruin you,' he said vindictively. 'I'll ruin you both.'

'Be sensible, Mr Graves,' I said. 'You're in the wrong.'

'Who the shit cares. I won't have some pipsqueak jockey and some bankrupt little trainer get the better of me, I'll tell you that.'

The attendant boy said nervously, 'Uncle . . .'

'You shut up,' Graves snapped.

The boy dropped the carrier and and fell over his feet picking it up.

'Go away, Mr Graves,' I said. 'Calm down. Think it over. Come and fetch your horses when your cheque's been cleared, and that'll be the end of it.'

'No, it won't.'

'Up to you,' I said, shrugging.

Bobby and I watched him try to extricate himself without severe loss of face, which could hardly be done. He delivered a few more threats with a good deal of bluster, and then finally, saying 'Come on, come on' irritably to his nephew, he stalked away down the drive.

'Did you immobilize his horsebox?' Bobby asked.

'It was a car and a trailer, and the key was in it. I just drove it out of sight round the nearest corner. Wonder if they'll find it.'

'I suppose we needn't have bothered,' Bobby said. 'As Graves went to the alarm box first.'

We had thought he might go to his other horse's box first, find it empty, think he had the wrong place, and perhaps remove one of the horses from either side. We thought he might have brought more men. In the event, he hadn't done either. But the precaution, all the same, might have been worth it.

We closed the empty stable and Bobby kicked against something on the ground. He bent to pick it up, and held it out for me to see: a large piece of thick felt with pieces of velcro attached. A silencer for a hoof. Fallen out of the carrier, no doubt.

'Not leather boots,' Bobby said, grimly. 'Home-made.'

He switched off the yard lights and we stood for a while near the kitchen door, waiting. We would hear the car and trailer drive off, we thought, in the quiet night. What we heard instead, however, were hesitant footsteps coming back into the yard.

Bobby turned the lights on again, and the boy stood there, blinking and highly embarrassed.

'Someone's stolen Uncle's car,' he said.

'What's your name?' I asked.

'Jasper.'

'Graves?'

He nodded and swallowed. 'Uncle wants me to ring the police and get a taxi.'

'If I were you,' I said, 'I'd go out of the gate here, turn left, take the first turn to the left along the road a bit, and use the public telephone box you'll find down there.'

'Oh,' he said. 'All right.' He looked at us almost beseechingly. 'It was only supposed to be a lark,' he said. 'It's all gone wrong.'

We gave him no particular comfort, and after a moment he turned and went away again down the drive, his footsteps slowly receding.

'What do you think?' Bobby said.

'I think we should rig the bell so that anyone coming up the drive sets it off.'

'So do I. And I'll disconnect it first thing when I get up.'

We began to run a blackened string tightly across the drive at knee level, and heard Graves's car start up in the distance.

'He's found it,' Bobby said. He smiled. 'There's no telephone box down that road, did you know?'

We finished the elementary alarm system and went yawning indoors to sleep for another couple of hours, and I reflected, as I lay down, about the way a feud could start, as with Graves, and continue through centuries, as with Allardecks and Fieldings, and could expand into political and religious persecutions on a national scale, permanently persisting as a habit of mind, a destructive hatred stuck in one groove. I would make a start in my own small corner, I thought sardonically, drifting off, and force my subconscious to love the Allardecks, of which my own sister, God help her, was one.

Persistence raised its ugliest head first thing in the morning.

I answered the telephone when it rang at eight-thirty because Bobby was out exercising his horses and Holly was again feeling sick: and it was the feed-merchant calling in his Etonian accent to say that he had received a further copy of the *Daily Flag.*

'I've just picked it up,' he said. 'It's today's paper. Monday. There's another piece outlined in red.'

'What does it say?' I asked, my heart sinking.

'I think . . . well . . . you can come and fetch it, if you like. It's longer, this time. And there's a picture of Bobby.'

'I'll be there.'

I drove straight round in Holly's car and found the feed-merchant in his office as before. Silently he handed me the paper, and with growing dismay I looked at the picture which made Bobby seem a grinning fool, and read the damage in Intimate Details.

Money troubles abound for Robertson (Bobby) Allardeck (32), still training a few racehorses in his grandfather's once-bustling stables in Newmarket. Local traders threaten court action over unpaid bills. Bobby weakly denies the owners of the remaining horses should be worried, although the feed-merchant has stopped deliveries. Where will it end?

Not with manna from heaven from Daddy.

Maynard 'Moneybags' Allardeck (50), cross with Bobby for marrying badly, won't come to the rescue.

Maynard, known to be fishing for a knighthood, gives all his spare cash to charity.

Needy Bobby's opinion? Unprintable.

Watch this space for more.

'If Bobby doesn't sue for libel,' I said, 'his father surely will.'

'Greater the truth, greater the libel,' the feed-merchant said dryly, and added, 'Tell Bobby his credit's good with me again. I've been thinking it over. He's always paid me regularly, even if always late. And I don't like being manipulated by muck like that.' He pointed to the paper. 'So tell Bobby I'll supply him as before. Tell him to tell his owners.'

I thanked him and went back to Bobby's house, and read Intimate Details again over a cup of coffee in the kitchen. Then I pensively telephoned the feed-merchant.

'Did you,' I said, 'actually tell anyone that you intended to stop making deliveries to Bobby?'

'I told Bobby.' He sounded equally thoughtful. 'No one else.'

'Positive.'

'Not even your secretary? Or your family?'

'I admit that on Friday I was very annoyed and wanted my money immediately, but no one overheard my giving Bobby a talking to about it, I'm quite certain. My secretary doesn't come in until eleven on Fridays, and as you know, my office is an annexe. I was alone when I telephoned him, I assure you.'

'Well, thanks,' I said.

'The informant must be at Bobby's end,' he insisted.

'Yes. I think you're right.'

We disconnected and I began to read the *Daily Flag*

from start to finish, which I'd never done before,
seeking enlightenment perhaps on what made a newspaper suddenly attack an inoffensive man and aim to
destroy him.

The *Flag*'s overall and constant tone, I found, was
of self-righteous spite, its message a sneer, its aftertaste
guaranteed to send a reader belligerently out looking
for an excuse to take umbrage or to spread ill will.

Any story that would show someone in a poor light
was in. Praise was out. The put-down had been
developed to a minor art, so that a woman, however
prominent or successful, did not 'say'; instead she
'trilled', or she 'shrilled', or she 'wailed'. A man
'chortled', or he 'fumed', or he 'squeaked'.

The word 'anger' appeared on every single page. All
sorts of things were 'slammed', but not doors. People
were reported as denying things in a way that interpreted 'deny' as 'guilty but won't own up'; and the
word 'claims', in the *Flag*'s view, as, for instance, in 'He
claims he saw . . .' was synonymous with 'He is lying
when he says he saw . . .'

The *Flag* thought that respect was unnecessary, envy
was normal, all motives were loved; and presumably
it was what people wanted to read, as the circulation
(said the *Flag*) was increasing daily.

On the premise that a newspaper ultimately
reflected the personality of its owner, as the *Towncrier*
did Lord Vaughnley's, I thought the proprietor of the
Daily Flag to be destructive, calculating, mean-spirited

and dangerous. Not a good prospect. It meant one couldn't with any hope of success appeal to the *Flag*'s better nature to let up on Bobby, because a better nature it didn't have.

Holly came downstairs looking wan but more cheerful, Bobby returned from the Heath with reviving optimism, and I found the necessity of demolishing their fragile recovery just one more reason to detest the *Flag*.

Holly began to cry quietly and Bobby strode about the kitchen wanting to smash things, and still there was the unanswerable question: Why?

'This time,' I said, 'you consult your lawyer, and to hell with the cost. Also this time we are going to pay all your worst bills at once, and we are going to get letters from all your creditors saying they have been paid, and we'll get those letters photocopied by the dozen, and we'll send a set of them out to everyone who got a copy of the *Flag*, and to the *Flag* itself, to Sam Leggatt, the editor, special delivery, and to all the owners, and to anyone else we can think of, and we'll accompany these with a letter of your own saying you don't understand why the *Flag* is attacking you but the attacks have no foundation, the stable is in good shape and you are certainly not going out of business.'

'But,' Holly said, gulping, 'the bank manager won't honour our cheques.'

'Get the worst bills,' I said to Bobby, 'and let's have a look at them. 'Specially the blacksmith, the vets and the transport people. We'll pay those and any others that are vital.'

'What with?' he said irritably.

'With my money.'

They were both suddenly still, as if shocked, and I realized with a thrust of pleasure that that plain solution simply hadn't occurred to them. They were not askers, those two.

Holly couldn't disguise her upsurge of hope, but she said doubtfully, 'Your new house, though. It must be taking you all you've saved. You haven't been paid for the cottage yet.'

'There's enough,' I assured her. 'And let's get started because I'll have to be off to Plumpton pretty soon.'

'But we can't . . .' Bobby said.

'Yes, you must. Don't argue.'

Bobby looked pole-axed but he fetched the bunch of accounts and I made out several cheques.

'Take these round yourself this morning and get watertight receipts, and in a minute we'll write the letter to go with them,' I said. 'And see if you can get them all photocopied and clipped into sets in time to catch this afternoon's post. I know it's a bit of a job, but the sooner very much the better, don't you think?'

'And one set to Graves?' Bobby asked.

'Certainly to Graves.'

'We'll start immediately,' Holly said.

'Don't forget the feed-merchant,' I said. 'He'll write

you something good. He didn't like being made use of by the *Flag*.'

'I don't like to mention it . . .' Holly began slowly.

'The bank?' I asked.

She nodded.

'Leave the bank for now. Tomorrow maybe you can go to the manager with a set of letters and see if he will reinstate you. He darned well ought to. His bank's making enough out of you in interest, especially on the yearling loans. And you do still have the yearlings as security.'

'Unfortunately,' Bobby said.

'One step at a time,' I said.

'I'll telephone my solicitor straight away,' he said, picking up the receiver and looking at his watch. 'He'll be in by now.'

'No, I shouldn't,' I said.

'But you said . . .'

'You've got an informant right inside this house.'

'What do you mean?'

'Your telephone,' I said, 'I should think.'

He looked at it with disgusted understanding and in a half-groan said, 'Oh, God.'

'It's been done before,' I said: and there had in fact been a time in Lambourn when everyone had been paranoid about being overheard and had gone to elaborate lengths to avoid talking on their home telephones. Illegal it might well be to listen uninvited, but it was carried on nevertheless, as everyone knew.

Without more ado we unscrewed all the telephones in the house, but found no limpet-like bugs inside. Horses, however, not electronics, were our speciality, and Bobby said he would go out to a public box and ring up the telephone company and ask them to come themselves to see what they could find.

It happened at one point that Bobby was on his knees by the kitchen wall screwing together the telephone junction there and Holly and I were standing side by side in the centre of the room, watching him, so that when the newcomer suddenly arrived among us unannounced it was my sister and I that he saw first.

A tall man with fair hair fading to grey, immensely well brushed. Neat, good-looking features, smoothly shaven rounded chin; trim figure inside a grey City suit of the most impeccable breeding. A man of fifty, a man of power whose very presence filled the kitchen, a man holding a folded copy of the *Daily Flag* and looking at Holly and me with open loathing.

Maynard Allardeck; Bobby's father.

Known to me, as I to him, as the enemy. Known to each other by frequent sight, by indoctrination, by professional repute. Ever known, never willingly meeting.

'Fieldings,' he said with battering hate; and to me directly, 'What do you think you're doing in this house?'

'I asked him,' Bobby said, straightening up.

His father turned abruptly in his direction, seeing

his son for the first time closely face to face for more than four years.

They stared at each other for a long moment as if frozen, as if relearning familiar features, taking physical stock. Seeing each other perhaps as partial strangers, freshly. Whatever any of us might have expected or wished for in the way of reconciliation, it turned out to be the opposite of what Maynard had in mind. He had come neither to help nor even to commiserate, but to complain.

Without any form of greeting he said, 'How dare you drag me into your sordid little troubles.' He waved his copy of the *Flag*. 'I won't have you whining to the Press about something that's entirely your own fault. If you want to marry into a bunch of crooks, take your consequences and keep me out of it.'

I imagine we all blinked, as Bobby was doing. Maynard's voice was thick with anger and his sudden onslaught out of all proportion, but it was his reasoning above all which had us stunned.

'I didn't,' Bobby said, almost rocking on his feet. 'I mean, I haven't talked to the Press. I wouldn't. They just wrote it.'

'And this part about me refusing you money? How else would they know, if you hadn't told them? Answer me that.'

Bobby swallowed. 'You've always said . . . I mean, I thought you meant it, that you wouldn't.'

'Of course I mean it.' His father glared at him. 'I

won't. That's not the point. You've no business snivel-
ling about it in public and I won't have it. Do you
hear?'

'I haven't,' Bobby protested, but without conviction.

I thought how much father and son resembled each
other in looks, and how little in character. Maynard
had six times the force of Bobby but none of his sense
of fair play. Maynard could make money work for him,
Bobby worked to be paid. Maynard could hold a
grudge implacably for ever, Bobby could waver and
crumble and rethink. The comparative weaknesses in
Bobby, I thought, were also his strength.

'You must have been blabbing.' Maynard was
uncompromisingly offensive in his tone, and I thought
that if Bobby ever wanted to announce to the whole
world that his father would let him sink, he would have
every provocation and every right.

Bobby said with a rush, 'We think someone may
have been tapping our telephone.'

'Oh, you do, do you?' Maynard said ominously,
casting an angry look at the silent instrument. 'So it's
on the telephone you've been bleating about me, is it?'

'No,' Bobby said, half stuttering. 'I mean, no I
haven't. But one or two people said ask your father for
money, and I told them I couldn't.'

'And this bit,' Maynard belted the air furiously with
the newspaper, 'about me fishing for a knighthood. I
won't have it. It's a damned lie.'

It struck me forcibly at that point, perhaps because

of an undisguisable edge of fear in his voice, that it was the bit about the knighthood which lay at the real heart of Maynard's rage.

It was no lie, I thought conclusively. It was true. He must indeed be trying actively to get himself a title. Grandfather had said that Maynard at nine had wanted to be a lord. Maynard at fifty was still the same person, but now with money, with influence, with no doubt a line to the right ears. Maynard might be even then in the middle of delicate but entirely unlawful negotiations.

Sir Maynard Allardeck. It certainly rolled well off the tongue. Sir Maynard. Bow down to me, you Fieldings. I am your superior, bow low.

'I didn't say anything about a knighthood,' Bobby protested with more force. 'I mean, I didn't know you wanted one. I never said anything about it. I never thought of it.'

'Why don't you sue the newspaper?' I said.

'You keep quiet,' he said to me vehemently. 'Keep your nose out.' He readdressed himself to Bobby. 'If you didn't mention a knighthood on the telephone, how did they get hold of it? Why did they write that . . . that damned lie? Answer me that.'

'I don't know,' Bobby said, sounding bewildered. 'I don't know why they wrote any of it.'

'Someone has put you up to stirring up trouble against me,' Maynard said, looking hard and mean and deadly in earnest.

We all three stared at him in amazement. How anyone could think that was beyond me.

Bobby said with more stuttering, 'Of course not. I mean, that's stupid. It's not you that's in trouble because of what they wrote, it's me. I wouldn't stir up trouble against myself. It doesn't make sense.'

'Three people telephoned me before seven this morning to tell me there was another paragraph in today's *Flag*,' Maynard said angrily. 'I bought a copy on my way here. I was instantly certain it was your poisonous brother-in-law or his pig of a grandfather who was at the back of it, it's just their filthy sort of thing.'

'No,' Holly said.

Maynard ignored her as if she hadn't spoken.

'I came in here to tell you it served you right,' he said to Bobby, 'and to insist on your forcing the Fieldings to get a full retraction printed in the paper.'

'But,' Bobby said, shaking his head as if concussed, 'it wasn't Kit. He wouldn't do that. Nor his grand-father.'

'You're soft,' Maynard said contemptuously. 'You've never understood that someone can smile into your face while they shove a knife through your ribs.'

'Because of Holly,' Bobby insisted, 'they wouldn't.'

'You're a naive fool,' his father said. 'Why shouldn't they try to break up your marriage? They never wanted it, any more than I did. They're a wily, shifty, vengeful family, the whole lot of them, and if you trust any one of them, you deserve what you get.'

Bobby gave me a quick glance in which I read only discomfort, not doubt. Neither Holly nor I offered any sort of defence because mere words wouldn't dent the opinions that Maynard had held all his life, and nor would hitting him. Moreover we had heard the same sort of invective too often from Grandfather on the subject of the Allardecks. We were more or less immune, by then, to violent reaction. It was Bobby, interestingly, who protested.

'Kit and Holly care what becomes of me,' he said. 'You don't. Kit came to help, and you didn't. So I'll judge as I find, and I don't agree with what you say.'

Maynard looked as if he could hardly believe his ears, and nor, to be honest, could I. It wasn't just that what Bobby was expressing was a heretical defection from his upbringing, but that he also had the courage to stand up to his father and say it to his face.

He looked, as a matter of fact, slightly nervous. Maynard, it was said, inspired wholesale nervousness in the boardroom of any business his eye fell on, and as of that morning I understood why. The unyielding ruthlessness in him, clearly perceptible to all three of us, was central to his success, and for us at least he made no attempt to disguise it or dress it with a façade of charm.

Bobby made a frustrated gesture with both hands, walked over to the sink and began to fill the kettle.

'Do you want any coffee?' he said to his father.

'Of course not.' He spoke as if he'd been insulted. 'I've a committee meeting at the Jockey Club.' He looked at his watch, and then at me. 'You,' he said, 'have attacked me. And you'll suffer for it.'

I said calmly but distinctly, 'If I hear you have said in the Jockey Club that a Fielding is responsible for what has appeared in the *Flag*, I will personally sue you for slander.'

Maynard glared. He said, 'You're filth by birth, you're not worth the fuss that's made of you, and I'd be glad to see you dead.'

I felt Holly beside me begin to spring forward in some passionate explosion of feeling and gripped her wrist tight to stop her. I was actually well satisfied. I had read in Maynard's eyes that he was inclined to take me seriously, but he didn't want me to know it, and I understood also, for the first time, and with unease, that the very fact of my being successful, of being champion, was to him, in his obsession, intolerable.

Along at the Jockey Club, which had its ancient headquarters in Newmarket's main street, and where he had been one of its members for four or five years, Maynard would with luck now pass off the whole *Flag* thing with a grouchy joke. There, in the organization which ruled the racing industry, he would show all courtesy and hide the snarl. There, where he served on dogsbody committees while he made his determined way up that particular ladder, aiming perhaps to be a Steward, one of the top triumvirate, before long, he would now perhaps be careful to say nothing that could get back to my ears.

There were no active professional jockeys in the Jockey Club, nor any licensed trainers, though a few retired practitioners of both sorts sprinkled the ranks. There were many racehorse owners, among whom I had real friends. The approximately 140 members, devoted to the welfare of racing, were self-perpetuating, self-elected. If Maynard had ever campaigned quietly to be chosen for membership it might have helped him to be a member of an old-established racing family, and it might have helped him to be rich, but one thing was certain: he would never have unsheathed for the civilized inspection of his peers the raw, brutal anti-Fielding prejudice he had given spleen to in the kitchen. Nothing alienated the courteous members more than ill-mannered excess.

The preserving of Maynard's public good manners was very much my concern.

He went as he'd come, private manners non-existent, walking out of the kitchen without a farewell. We listened to the firm footsteps recede and to the distant slam of a car door, and his engine starting.

'Do you realize,' Bobby said to me slowly, 'that if he's made a Steward and you're still a jockey . . . you'd be horribly vulnerable . . .?'

'Mm,' I said dryly. 'Very nasty indeed.'

CHAPTER SIX

I rode at Plumpton. A typical day of four rides; one win, one third, one nowhere, one very nearly last, with owner reactions to match.

Far more people than in the previous week seemed to have seen the pieces in Intimate Details, and I spent a good deal of the day assuring all who asked that, no, Bobby wasn't bankrupt, and yes, I was certain, and no, I couldn't say for sure what Bobby's father's intentions were in any respect.

There was the usual small scattering of racing journalists at the meeting, but no one from the *Flag*. The racing column in the *Flag* was most often the work of a sharp young man who wrote disparagingly about what was to come and critically of what was past, and who was avoided whenever possible by all jockeys. On that day, however, I would have been satisfied enough to see him, but had to make do with his equivalent on the *Towncrier*.

'You want to know about the *Flag*? Whatever for? Disgusting rag.' Large and benevolent, Bunty Ireland,

the *Towncrier*'s man, spoke with the complacency of a
more respectful rag behind him. 'But if you want to
know if the parts about your brother-in-law are the
work of our sharp-nosed colleague, then no, I'm pretty
sure they're not. He was at Doncaster on Friday and
he didn't know at first what was in the gossip column.
Slightly put out, he was, when he found out. He said
the gossip people hadn't consulted him and they should
have done. He was his usual endearing sunny self.'
Bunty Ireland beamed. 'Anything else?'

'Yes,' I said. 'Who runs Intimate Details?'

'Can't help you there, old son. I'll ask around, if you
like. But it won't do Bobby much good, you can't just
go and bop us fellows on the nose, however great the
provocation.'

Never be too sure, I thought.

I cadged a lift home to Lambourn, ate some lobster
and an orange, and thought about telephoning Holly.

Someone, it was certain, would be listening in on
the line. Someone had probably been listening in
on that line for quite a long period. Long enough to
make a list of people Bobby dealt with in Newmarket,
long enough to know where he banked, long enough
to know how things stood between him and his father.
The owner who had telephoned to say he couldn't
afford to pay fifty thousand for his yearling must have
been listened to, and so must Bobby's unsuccessful
attempts to sell it to anyone else.

Someone must indeed have listened also to Bobby's

racing plans and to his many conversations with owners and jockeys. There was no trainer alive who wouldn't in the fullness of time have passed unflattering or down-right slanderous opinions about jockeys to owners and vice versa, but nothing of that nature had been used in the paper. No 'inside' revelations of betting coups. No innuendoes about regulations broken or crimes committed, such as giving a horse an easy race, a common practice for which one could be fined or even have one's licence suspended if found out. The target hadn't in fact been Bobby's training secrets, but his financial status alone.

Why?

Too many whys.

I pressed the necessary buttons and the bell rang only once at the other end.

'Kit?' Holly said immediately.

'Yes.'

'Did you try earlier?'

'No,' I said.

'That's all right, then. We've left the receiver off for most of the day, the calls were so awful. But it just occurred to me that you might be trying to ring, so I put it back less than a minute ago . . .' Her voice faded away as she realized what she was saying. 'We've done it again,' she said.

'Yes.'

She must have heard the smile in my voice, because it was in hers also when she replied.

'Look,' she said. 'I've been thinking . . . I've got to go out, now. I'll ring you later, OK?'

'Sure,' I said.

'Bye.'

'Bye,' I said, and disconnected. I also waited, wondering where she would go. Where she'd planned. She called back within fifteen minutes and it was unexpectedly from the feed-merchant's office. The feed-merchant, it appeared, had let her in, switched on the heater, and left her in private.

'He's been terribly good,' Holly explained. 'I think he'd been feeling a bit guilty, though he's no need to really. Anyway I told him we thought our telephone might be bugged and he said he thought it highly possible, and I could come in here and use the phone whenever I liked. I said I'd like to ring you this evening . . . and anyway, here I am.'

'Great,' I said. 'How are things going?'

'We spent the whole day doing those letters and we're frankly bushed. Bobby's asleep on his feet. Everyone took your cheque without question and gave us paid-in-full letters, and we photocopied those and also the rebuttal letter we all wrote before you went to Plumpton, and by the time we'd finished putting everything in the envelopes the last post was just going, and in fact the postman actually waited at the post office while I stuck on the last ten stamps, and I saw him take the special delivery one to the editor of the *Flag*, so with luck, with luck, it will be all over.'

'Mm,' I said. 'Let's hope so.'

'Oh, and Bobby went to see the solicitor, who said he would write a strong letter of protest to the editor and demand a retraction in the paper, like Lord Vaughnley told you, but Bobby says he isn't sure that that letter will have gone today, he says the solicitor didn't seem to think it was frantically urgent.'

'Tell Bobby to get a different solicitor.'

Holly almost laughed. 'Yes. OK.'

We made plans and times for me to talk to her again the next evening after I got home from Devon, but it was at eight in the morning when my telephone rang and her voice came sharp and distressed into my ear.

'It's Holly,' she said. 'Get a copy of the *Flag*. I'll be along where I was last night. OK?'

'Yes,' I said.

She disconnected without another word, and I drove to the village for the paper.

The column would have been printed during the past night. The special delivery envelope wouldn't reach the editor until later in the present morning. I thought in hindsight it would have been better for Bobby to have driven the letter to London and specially delivered it himself, which might just possibly have halted the campaign.

The third broadside read:

Don't pity Robertson (Bobby) Allardeck (32), strapped for cash but still trying to train racehorses in Newmarket. It's the small trader who suffers when fat cats run up unpaid bills.

In his luxury home yesterday Bobby refused to comment on reports he came to blows with the owner of one of the horses in the stable, preventing the owner taking his horse away by force. 'I deny everything,' Bobby fumed.

Meanwhile Daddy Maynard ('Moneybags') Allardeck (50) goes on record as prize skinflint of the month. 'My son won't get a penny in aid from me,' he intoned piously. 'He doesn't deserve it.'

Instead Moneybags lavishes ostentatious handouts on good deserving charities dear to the Government's heart. Can knighthoods be bought nowadays? Of course not!

Bobby wails that while Daddy lashes out the loot on the main chance, he (Bobby) gets threatening letters from Daddy's lawyers demanding repayment of a fourteen-year-old loan. Seems Moneybags advanced a small sum for 18-year-old Bobby to buy a banger on leaving school. With the wheels a long-ago memory on the scrapheap, Daddy wants his money back. Bobby's opinion of Daddy? 'Ruthless swine.'

Can stingy Maynard be extorting interest on top? Watch this space.

Thoughtfully I got the feed-merchant's number from directory enquiries and pressed the buttons: Holly was waiting at the other end.

'What are we going to do?' she said miserably. 'They're such pigs. All those quotes . . . they just made them up.'

'Yes,' I said. 'If you could bear to put together another batch of those letters you sent yesterday, it might do some good to send them to the editors of the other national newspapers, and to the *Sporting Life*. None of them likes the *Flag*. A spot of ridicule from its rivals might make the *Flag* shut up.'

'Might,' Holly said, unconvinced.

'Doing everything one can think of is better than doing nothing,' I said. 'You never know which pellet might kill the bird when you loose off the shot.'

'Poetic,' Holly said sardonically. 'All right. We'll try.'

'And what about the solicitor?' I asked.

'Bobby says he'll find a better one today. Not local. In a London firm. High powered.'

'Some of his owners may know who's best,' I said. 'If not, I could get him a name from one of the people I ride for.'

'Great.'

'But do you know something?' I said.

'What?'

'I'm not so sure that Maynard was very far wrong. All this aggro is aimed as much at him as at Bobby.'

'Yes,' Holly said slowly. 'When we read today's bit of dirt, that's what Bobby thought too.'

'I wouldn't mind betting,' I said, 'that a fair few copies of Intimate Details, episodes one, two and three,

103

will find their way to the attention of the Honours'
Secretary in Downing Street. And that this was chiefly
what was at the bottom of Maynard's anger yesterday.
If Maynard is really being considered for a knighthood,
Intimate Details could have put the lid on his chances,
at least for just now.'

'Do you think it would? Just a few words in a paper?'

'You never know. The whole Honours thing is so
sensitive. Anyway it's about now that they send out
those ultra-secret letters asking Mr Bloggs if he would
accept a medal if invited. They'll be drawing up the
New Year's Honours' List at this moment. And the
sixty-four dollar question is, if you were the Honours'
Secretary drawing up a list for the Prime Minister's
approval, would you put Maynard on it?'

'But we don't know that anything like that is happening.'

'No, we sure don't.'

'It's probably just the *Flag* being its typically vicious,
mean, destructive self.'

'Perhaps,' I said.

'You know how nasty the Press can be, if they want
to. And the *Flag* seems to want to, all the time, as a
matter of policy.'

'Mm,' I said. 'Maybe you're right.'

'But you don't think so?'

'Well . . . It would make more sense if we could see
a purpose behind these attacks, and stopping Maynard
getting a knighthood would be a purpose. But why

they'd want to stop it, and how they got to hear of it . . . hell alone knows.'

'They didn't hear about any knighthood from our telephone,' Holly said positively. 'So perhaps they're just making it up.'

'Everything else in those stories is founded on things that have happened or been said,' I pointed out. 'They've taken the truth and distorted it. Shall I write to the Honours' Secretary and ask if Maynard's on his provisional list?'

'Yes, yes, funny joke.'

'Anyway,' I said. 'How did Bobby get on with the telephone people?'

'They said they would look into it. They said telephone tapping is illegal as of 1985. They didn't send anyone here yesterday looking for bugs. They said something about checking our exchange.'

'The exchange? I didn't know people could tap into an exchange.'

'Well, apparently they can.'

'So no actual bugs?'

'We told them we couldn't find any and they said we probably didn't know where to look.'

'Well, at least they're paying attention.'

'They said a lot of people think they're being bugged when they aren't,' Holly said. 'All the same, they did say they would look.'

'Keep them up to it.'

'I'll ring you this evening when I get back from

Devon,' I said. 'If I don't get back... I'll ring sometime.'

'Yes,' she said. 'Take care of yourself.'

'Always do,' I said automatically; and both she and I knew it was impossible. If a steeplechase jockey took too much care of himself, he didn't win races, and there were days occasionally when one couldn't drive oneself home. I was superstitious to the extent of not making binding commitments for the evenings of race days, and like most other jump jockeys accepted invitations with words like 'If I can' and 'With luck'.

I drove the two hours to the Devon and Exeter meeting with my mind more on Holly and Bobby and Maynard than on the work ahead. None of the five horses I was due to ride posed the problems of North Face, and I'd ridden all of them often enough to know their little quirks and their capabilities. All I had to do was help them turn in the best they could do on the day.

The Devon and Exeter racecourse lay on the top of Halden Moor, a majestic sweep of bare countryside with the winds blowing vigorously from the Channel to the Atlantic. The track itself, with its long circuit of almost two miles, stretched away as a green undulating ribbon between oceans of scrub and heather, its far deserted curves as private a place as one could imagine for contest of horse and man.

Unfashionable in Ascot terms, distant geographically, drawing comparatively small crowds, it was still one of my favourite courses; well run, well kept, with welcoming locals, nice people.

The princess liked to go there because friends of hers maintained one of the few private boxes, friends who had a house down by a Devon beach and who invited her to stay regularly for the meetings.

She was there, lunched, fur-coated and discreetly excited, in good time for the first race, accompanied in the parade ring by a small bunch of the friends. Three friends, to be exact. The couple she stayed with, and a young woman.

The princess made introductions. 'Kit . . . you know Mr and Mrs Inscombe . . .' We shook hands. ' . . . And my niece. Have you met my niece, Danielle?'

No, I hadn't. I shook the niece's hand.

'Danielle de Brescou,' the niece said. 'Hi. How're you doing?' And in spite of her name she was not French but audibly American.

I took in briefly the white wool short coat, the black trousers, the wide band of what looked like flowered chintz holding back a lot of dark hair. I got in return a cool look of assessment; half interest, half judgement deferred, topped by a bright smile of no depth.

'What shall we expect?' the princess asked. 'Will Bernina win?'

Wykeham, naturally, had not made the journey to Devon. Moreover he had been vague when I'd talked to him on the telephone, seeming almost unclear as to Bernina's identity, let alone her state of readiness, and it had been Dusty, when I'd handed him my saddle to put on to the mare before the race, who had told me she was 'jumping out of her skin and acting up something chronic'.

'She's fit and ready,' I said to the princess.

'And Wykeham's riding instructions?' Mr Inscombe enquired genially. 'What are those?'

Wykeham's instructions to me were zero, as they had been for several years. I said diplomatically, 'Stay handy in fourth place or thereabouts and kick for home at the second last hurdle.'

Inscombe nodded benevolent approval and I caught the ghost of a grin from the princess, who knew quite well that Wykeham's instructions, if any, would have taken the form of 'Win if you can', an uncomplicated declaration of honesty by no means universal among trainers.

Wykeham produced his horses fighting fit from a mixture of instinct, inherited wisdom, and loving them individually as athletes and children. He knew how to bring them to a peak and understood their moods and preferences, and if nowadays he found the actual races less interesting than the preparation, he was still, just, one of the greats.

I had been his retained jockey for the whole of the main part of my career and he frequently called me by the name of my predecessor. He quite often told me I would be riding horses long dead. 'Polonium in the big race at Sandown,' he would say, and, mystified, I would ask who owned the horse as I'd never heard of it. 'Polonium? Don't be stupid. Big chestnut. Likes mints. You won on him last week.' 'Oh ... Pepperoni?' 'What? Yes, Pepperoni, of course, that's what I said. Big race at Sandown.'

He was almost as old as my grandfather, and gradually, through their eyes, I was coming to see the whole of racing as a sort of stream that rolled onwards through time, the new generations rising and the old floating slowly away. Racing had a longer history than almost any other sport and changed less, and sometimes I had a powerful feeling of repeating in my own person the experience of generations of jockeys before me and of being a transient speck in a passing pageant; vivid today, talked about, fêted, but gone tomorrow, a memory fading into a footnote, until no one alive had seen me race or cared a damn whether I'd won or lost.

Dead humbling, the whole thing.

Bernina, named after the mountain to the south of St Moritz, had by four years old produced none of the grandeur of the Alps, and to my mind was never going to. She could, however, turn in a respectable performance in moderate company, which was all she was faced with on this occasion, and I hoped very much to win on her, as much for the princess's sake as my own. I understood very well that she liked to be able to please the various hosts around the country who offered her multiple invitations, and was always slightly anxious for her horses to do well where she felt they might contribute to her overnight bread and butter. I thought that if people like the Inscombes didn't enjoy her company for its own sake they wouldn't keep on asking her to stay. The princess's inner insecurities were sometimes astonishing.

Bernina, without any of the foregoing complications of intent, took me out of the parade ring and down to the start in her best immoderate fashion which included a display of extravagant head-shaking and some sideways dancing on her toes. These preliminaries were a good sign: on her off days she went docilely to the starting gate, left it without enthusiasm and took her time about finishing. Last time out she'd had me hauled in front of the Stewards and fined for not trying hard enough to win, and I'd said they should have understood that a horse that doesn't want to race won't race; and that mares have dull days like anyone else. They listened, unimpressed. Pay the fine, they said.

The princess had insisted on reimbursing me for that little lot, where other owners might have raged. 'If she wouldn't go, she wouldn't go,' she'd said with finality. 'And she's my horse, so I'm responsible for her debts.' Owners didn't come more illogical or more generous than the princess.

I'd told her never to let her friends back Bernina on the days she went flat-footed to the start, and she'd acknowledged the advice gravely. I hoped, sitting on top of the bravura performance going on in Devon, that she, the Inscombes and the niece would all be at that moment trekking to the bookmakers or the Tote. The mare was feeling good, and, beyond that, competitive.

The event was a two-mile hurdle race, which meant eight jumps over the sort of fencing used for penning sheep: hurdles made of wood and threaded with gorse or brushwood, each section unattached to the hurdle on either side, so that if a horse hit one, it could be knocked over separately. Good jumpers flowed over hurdles easily, rising little in the air but bending up their forelegs sharply; the trick was to get them to take off from where the hurdle could be crossed in mid-stride.

Bernina, graciously accepting my guidance in that matter, went round the whole course without touching a twig. She also attacked the job of beating her opponents with such gusto that one mightn't have blamed the Stewards this time for testing her for dope, such was the contrast.

She would, if she'd had serious talent, have won by twenty lengths, especially as the chief danger had fallen in a flurry of legs about halfway round. As it was, she made enough progress, when I gave her an encouraging kick between the last two hurdles, to reach the last jump upsides of the only horse still in front, and on the run-in she produced a weak burst of speed for just long enough to pass and demoralize her tiring opponent.

Accepting my congratulatory pats on her victorious neck as totally her due, she pulled up and pranced back to the winners' enclosure, and skittered about there restlessly, sweating copiously and rolling her eyes, up on a high like any other triumphant performer.

The princess, relieved and contented, kept out of the way of the powerful body as I unbuckled the girths and slid my saddle off on to my arm. She didn't say much herself as the Inscombes were doing a good deal of talking, but in any case she didn't have to. I knew what she thought and she knew I knew: we'd been through it all a couple of hundred times before.

The niece said, 'Wow,' a little thoughtfully.

I glanced briefly at her face and saw that she was surprised: I didn't know what she was surprised at, and didn't have time to find out as there was the matter of weighing in, changing, and weighing out for the next race. Icicle, the princess's other runner, didn't go until the fourth race, but I had two other horses to ride before that.

Those two, undisgraced, finished fifth and second, and were both for a local trainer who I rode for when I could: besides Wykeham I also often rode for a stable in Lambourn, and when neither of them had a runner, for anyone else who asked. After, that is, having looked up the offered horse in the form book. Constant fallers I refused, saying Wykeham wouldn't give his approval. Wykeham was a handy excuse.

Icicle, like his name, was the palest of greys; also long-backed, angular and sweet-natured. He had been fast and clever over hurdles, the younger horses' sport, but at a mature eight years and running over bigger fences, was proving more cautious than carefree, more dependable than dazzling, willing but no whirlwind.

I went out to the parade ring again in the princess's colours and found her and the friends deep in a discussion that had nothing to do with horses but which involved a good deal of looking at watches.

'The train from Exeter is very fast,' Mrs Inscombe was saying comfortingly; and the niece was giving her a bright look of stifled impatience.

'Most unfortunate,' Mr Inscombe said in a bluff voice. 'But the train, that's the thing.'

The princess said carefully as if for the tenth time, 'But my dears, the train goes too late . . .' She broke off to give me an absent-minded smile and a brief explanation.

'My niece Danielle was going to London by car with friends but the arrangement has fallen through.' She paused. 'I suppose you don't know anyone who is driving straight from here to London after this race?'

'Sorry, I don't,' I said regretfully.

I looked at the niece: at Danielle. She looked worriedly back. 'I have to be in London by six-thirty,' she said. 'In Chiswick. I expect you know where that is? Just as you reach London from the west?'

I nodded.

'Could you possibly ask,' she waved a hand towards the busy door of the weighing room, 'in there?'

'Yes, I'll ask.'

'I have to be at work.'

I must have showed surprise, because she added, 'I work for a news bureau. This week I'm on duty in the evenings.'

Icicle stalked methodically round the parade ring with two and a half miles of strenuous jumping ahead of him. After that, in the fifth race, I would be riding another two miles over hurdles.

After that . . .

I glanced briefly at the princess, checking her expression, which was benign, and I thought of the fine she'd paid for me when she didn't have to.

I said to Danielle, 'I'll take you myself straight after the fifth race . . . if, er, that would be of any use to you.'

Her gaze intensified fast on my face and the anxiety cleared like sunrise.

'Yes,' she said decisively. 'It sure would.'

Never make positive commitments on race days . . .

'I'll meet you outside the weighing room, after the fifth, then,' I said. 'It's a good road. We should get to Chiswick in time.'

'Great,' she said, and the princess seemed relieved that we could now concentrate on her horse and the immediate future.

'Kind of you, Kit,' she said, nodding.

'Any time.'

'How do you think my old boy will do today?'

'He's got bags of stamina,' I said. 'He should run well.'

114

She smiled. She knew 'bags of stamina' was a euphemism for 'not much finishing speed'. She knew Icicle's ability as well as I did, but like all owners, she wanted good news from her jockey.

'Do your best.'

'Yes,' I said.

I mounted and took Icicle out on to the track.

To hell with superstition, I thought.

CHAPTER SEVEN

It wasn't Icicle I had trouble with.

Icicle jumped adequately but without inspiration and ran on doggedly at one pace up the straight, more by good luck than anything else hanging on to finish second.

'Dear old slowcoach,' the princess said to him proudly in the unsaddling enclosure, rubbing his nose. 'What a gentleman you are.'

It was the hurdler afterwards that came to grief: an experienced racer but unintelligent. The one horse slightly ahead and to the right of us hit the top of the second hurdle as he rose to the jump and stumbled on to his nose on landing, and my horse, as if copying, promptly did exactly the same.

As falls went, it wasn't bad. I rolled like a tumbler on touching the ground, a circus skill learned by every jump jockey, and stayed curled, waiting for all the other runners to pass. As standing up in the middle of a thundering herd was the surest way to get badly injured, staying on the ground, where horses could more easily avoid one, was almost the first lesson in survival. The bad thing about falls near the start of hurdle races, however, was that the horses were going faster than in steeplechases, and were often bunched up together, with the result that they tended not to see a fallen rider until they were on top of him, by which time there was nowhere else to put their feet.

I was fairly used to hoof-shaped bruises. In the quiet that came after the buffeting I stood slowly and stiffly up with the makings of a new collection, and found the other fallen jockey doing the same.

'You all right?' I said.

'Yeah. You?'

I nodded. My colleague expressed a few obscene opinions of his former mount and a car came along to pick us up and deliver us to the ambulance room to be checked by the doctor on duty. In the old days jockeys had got away easily with riding with broken bones, but nowadays the medical inspections had intensified to safeguard the interests not altogether of the men injured but of the people who bet on them. Appeasing the punter was priority stuff.

Bruises didn't count. Doctors never stopped one from riding for those, and in any case bruises weren't visible when very new. I proved to the local man that all the bits of me that should bend, did, and all the bits that shouldn't bend, didn't, and got passed fit to ride again from then on.

One of the two volunteer nurses went to answer a

knock on the door and came back slightly bemused to say I was wanted outside by a woman who said she was a princess.

'Right,' I said, thanking the doctor and turning to go.

'Is she?' the nurse asked dubiously.

'A princess? Yes. How often do you come to race meetings?'

'Today's my first.'

'She's been leading owner three times in the past six jumping seasons, and she's a right darling.'

The young nurse grinned. 'Makes you sick.'

I went outside to find the right darling looking first worried and then relieved at my reappearance. She was certainly not in the habit of enquiring after my health by waiting around outside ambulance room doors, and of course it wasn't my actual well-being which mattered at that point, but my being well enough to drive the niece to work.

The niece was also there and also relieved and also looking at her watch. I said I would change into street clothes and be ready shortly, and the princess kissed the niece and patted my arm, and went away saying she would see me at Newbury on the morrow.

I changed, found the niece waiting outside the weighing room, and took her to my car. She was fairly fidgeting with an impatience which slightly abated when she found the car was a Mercedes, but changed to straight anxiety when she saw me wince as I edged into the driving seat.

'Are you OK? You're not going to pass out, or anything, are you?' she said.

'I shouldn't think so.'

I started the car and extricated ourselves from the close-packed rows. A few other cars were leaving, but not enough to clog the entrance or the road outside. We would have a clear run, barring accidents.

'I guess I thought you'd be dead,' the niece said without emotion. 'How does anyone survive being trampled that way by a stampede?'

'Luck,' I said succinctly.

'My aunt was sure relieved when you stood up.'

I made an assenting noise in my throat. 'So was I.'

'Why do you do it?' she said.

'Race?'

'Uh-huh.'

'I like it.'

'Like getting trampled?'

'No,' I said. 'That doesn't happen all that often.'

We swooped down the hill from the moor and sped unhindered along roads that in the summer were busy with holiday crises. No swaying overloaded caravans being towed that day, no children being sick at the roadside, no radiators boiling and burst, with glum groups on the verges waiting for help. Devon roads in November were bare and fast and led straight to the motorways which should take us to Chiswick with no problems.

'Tell me truthfully,' she said, 'why do you do it?'

I glanced at her face, seeing there a quality of interest suitable for a newsgatherer. She had also large grey eyes, a narrow nose, and a determined mouth. Good-looking in a well-groomed way, I thought.

I had been asked the same question many times by other newsgatherers, and I gave the standard answer.

'I do it because I was born to it. I was brought up in a racing stable and I can't remember not being able to ride. I can't remember not wanting to ride in races.'

She listened with her head on one side and her gaze on my face.

'I guess I never met a jockey until now,' she said reflectively. 'And we don't have much jump racing in America.'

'No,' I agreed. 'In England there are probably more jump races than Flat. Just as many, anyway.'

'So why do you do it?'

'I told you,' I said.

'Yeah.'

She turned her head away to look out at the passing fields.

I raced, I thought fancifully, as one might play a violin, making one's own sort of music from coordinated muscles and intuitive spirit. I raced because the partnership with horses filled my mind with perfections of cadence and rhythmic excitement and intensities of communion: and I couldn't exactly say aloud such pretentious rubbish.

'I feel alive,' I said, 'on a horse.'

She looked back, faintly smiling. 'My aunt says you read their thoughts.'

'Everyone close to horses does that.'

'But some more than others?'

'I don't really know.'

She nodded. 'That makes sense. My aunt says you read the thoughts of people also.'

I glanced at her briefly. 'Your aunt seems to have said a lot.'

'My aunt,' she said neutrally, 'wanted me to understand, I think, that if I went in your car I should arrive unmolested.'

'Good God.'

'She was right, I see.'

'Mm.'

Molesting Danielle de Brescou, I thought, would be my quickest route to unemployment. Not that in other circumstances and with her willing cooperation I would have found it unthinkable. Danielle de Brescou moved with understated long-legged grace and watched the world from clear eyes, and if I found the sheen and scent of her hair and skin fresh and pleasing, it did no more than change the journey from a chore to a pleasure.

Between Exeter and Bristol, while dusk dimmed the day, she told me that she had been in England for three weeks and was staying with her uncle and aunt while she found herself an apartment. She had come because she'd been posted to London by the national broadcasting company she worked for: she was the bureau coordinator, and as it was only her second week there it was essential not to be late.

'You won't be late,' I assured her.

'No ... Do you always drive at eighty miles an hour?'

'Not if I'm in a real hurry.'

'Very funny.'

She told me Roland de Brescou, the princess's husband, was her father's eldest brother. Her father had emigrated to California from France as a young man and had married an American girl, Danielle being their only child.

'I guess there was a family ruckus when Dad left home, but he never told me the details. He's been sending greetings cards lately though, nostalgic for his roots, I guess. Anyway, he told Uncle Roland I was coming to London and the princess wrote me to say come visit. I hadn't met either of them before. It's my first trip to Europe.'

'How do you like it?'

She smiled. 'How would you like being cosseted in a sort of mansion in Eaton Square with a cook and maids and a butler? And a chauffeur. All last week the chauffeur drove me to work and picked me up after. Same thing yesterday. Aunt Casilia says it's not safe here after midnight on the subway, the same as it isn't in New York. She fusses worse than my own mother. But I can't live with them for too long. They're both sweet to me. I like her a lot and we get along fine. But I need a place of my own, near the office. And I'll get a car. I guess I'll have to.'

'How long will you be in England?' I asked.

'Don't know. Three years, maybe. Maybe less. The company can shift you around.'

She said I didn't need to tell her much about myself on account of information from her aunt.

She said she knew I lived in Lambourn and came from an old racing family and had a twin sister married to a racehorse trainer in Newmarket. She said she knew I wasn't married. She left the last observation dangling like a question mark, so I answered the unasked query.

'Not married. No present girlfriend. A couple in the past.'

I could feel her smile.

'And you?' I asked.

'Same thing.'

We drove for a good while in silence on that thought, and I rather pensively wondered what the princess would say or think if I asked her niece out to dinner. The close but arms-length relationship I'd had with her for so many years would change subtly if I did, and perhaps not for the better.

Between Bristol and Chiswick, while we sped with headlights on up the M4 motorway, Danielle told me about her job, which was, she said, pretty much a matter of logistics: she sent the camera crews and interviewers to wherever the news was.

'Half the time I'm looking at train schedules and road maps to find the fastest route, and starting from when we did, and taking the road we're on right now, I expected to be late.' She glanced at the speedometer. 'I didn't dream of ninety.'

I eased the car back to eighty-eight. A car passed us effortlessly. Danielle shook her head. 'I guess it'll take a while,' she said. 'How often do you get speeding tickets?'

'I've had three in ten years.'

'Driving like this every day?'

'Pretty much.'

She sighed. 'In dear old US of A we think seventy is sinful. Have you ever been there?'

'America?' I nodded. 'Twice. I rode there once in the Maryland Hunt Cup.'

'That's an amateurs' race,' she said without emphasis, careful, it seemed, not to appear to doubt my word.

'Yes. I started as an amateur. It seemed best to find out if I was any good before I committed my future to what I do.'

'And if it hadn't worked out?'

'I had a place at college.'

'And you didn't take it?' she said incredulously.

'No. I started winning, and that was what I wanted

most. I tried for the place at college only in case I couldn't make it as a jockey. Sort of insurance.'

'What subject?'

'Veterinary science.'

It shocked her. 'You mean you passed up being a veterinarian to be a jockey?'

'That's right,' I said. 'Why not?'

'But ... but ...'

'Yeah,' I said. 'All athletes ... sportsmen ... whatever ... find themselves on the wrong side of thirty-five with old age staring them point-blank in the face. I might have another five years yet.'

'And then?'

'Train them, I suppose. Train horses for others to ride.' I shrugged. 'It's a long way off.'

'It came pretty close this afternoon,' Danielle said.

'Not really.'

'Aunt Casilia says the Cresta Run is possibly more dangerous than the life of a jump jockey. Possibly. She wasn't sure.'

'The Cresta Run is a gold medal or the fright of a lifetime, not a career.'

'Have you been down it?'

'Of course not. It's dangerous.'

She laughed. 'Are all jockeys like you?'

'No. All different. Like princesses.'

She took a deep breath, as if of sea air. I removed my attention from the motorway for a second's inspection of her face, for whatever her aunt might think of my ability to read minds I never seemed to be able to do it with any young woman except Holly ... I was aware also that I wanted to, that without it, any loving was incomplete. I thought that if I hadn't had Holly I might have married one of the two girls I'd most liked: as it was, I hadn't reached the living-in stage with either of them.

I hadn't wanted to marry Holly, nor to sleep with her, but I'd loved her more deeply. It seemed that sex and telepathy couldn't co-exist in me, and until or unless they did, I probably would stay single.

'What are you thinking?' Danielle asked.

I smiled wryly. 'About not knowing what you were thinking.'

After a pause she said, 'I was thinking that when Aunt Casilia said you were exceptional, I can see what she meant.'

'She said what?'

'Exceptional. I asked her in what way, but she just smiled sweetly and changed the subject.'

'Er ... when was that?'

'On our way down to Devon this morning. She's been wanting me to go racing with her ever since I came over, so today I did, because she'd arranged that ride back for me, although she herself was staying with the Inscombes tonight for some frantically grand party. She hoped I would love racing like she does, I think. Do you think sometimes she's lonesome, travelling all those miles to racemeets with just her chauffeur?'

'I don't think she felt lonesome until you came.'

'Oh!'

She fell silent for a while, and eventually I said prosaically, 'We'll be in Chiswick in three minutes.'

'Will we?' She sounded almost disappointed. 'I mean, good. But I've enjoyed the journey.'

'So have I.'

My inner vision was suddenly filled very powerfully with the presence of Holly, and I had a vivid impression of her face, screwed up in deep distress.

I said abruptly to Danielle, 'Is there a public telephone anywhere near your office?'

'Yeah, I guess so.' She seemed slightly puzzled by the urgency I could hear in my voice. 'Sure . . . use the one on my desk. Did you remember something important?'

'No . . . er, I . . .' I drew back from the impossibility of rational explanation. 'I have a feeling,' I said lamely, 'that I should telephone my sister.'

'A feeling?' she asked curiously. 'You looked as if you'd forgotten a date with the President, at least.'

I shook my head. 'This is Chiswick. Where do we go from here?'

She gave me directions and we stopped in a parking space labelled 'Staff Only' outside a warehouse-like building in a side street. Six-twenty on the clock; ten minutes to spare.

'Come on in,' Danielle said. 'The least I can do is lend you a phone.'

127

I stood up stiffly out of the car, and she said with contrition, 'I guess I shouldn't have let you drive all this way.'

'It's not much further than going home.'

'You lie in your teeth. We passed the exit to Lambourn fifty miles back.'

'A bagatelle.'

She watched me lock the car door. 'Seriously, are you OK?'

'It's nothing that a hot bath won't put right.'

She nodded and turned to lead the way into the building, which proved to have glass entrance doors into a hallway furnished with armchairs, potted plants and a uniformed guard behind a reception desk. She and he signed me into a book, gave me a pass to clip to my clothes, and ushered me through a heavy door that opened to an electronic buzz.

'Sorry about the fortress syndrome,' Danielle said. 'The company is currently paranoid about bombs.'

We went down a short corridor into a wide open office inhabited by six or seven desks, mostly with people behind them showing signs of packing up to go home. There was also a sea of green carpet, a dozen or so computers, and on one long wall a row of television screens above head height, all showing different programmes and none of them emitting a sound.

Danielle and the other inhabitants exchanged a few 'Hi's, and 'How're you doing's, and no one questioned my presence. She took me across the room to her own domain, an area of two large desks set at right angles with a comfortable-looking swivelling chair serving both. The desk tops bore several box files, a computer, a typewriter, a stack of newspapers and a telephone. On the wall behind the chair there was a large chart on which things could be written in chinagraph and rubbed off: a chart with columns labelled along the top as SLUG, TEAM, LOCATION, TIME, FORMAT.

'Sit down,' Danielle said, pointing to the chair. She picked up the receiver and pressed a lighted button on the telephone. 'OK. Make your call.' She turned to look at the chart. 'Let's see what's been happening in the world since I left it.' She scanned the segments. Under SLUG someone had written 'Embassy' in large black letters. Danielle called across the room, 'Hank, what's this embassy story?' and a voice answered, 'Someone painted "Yanks Go Home" in red on the US embassy steps and there's a stink about security.'

'Good grief.'

'You'll need to do a follow-up for *Nightline*.'

'Right . . . has anyone interviewed the Ambassador?'

'We couldn't reach him earlier.'

'Guess I'll try again.'

'Sure. It's your baby, baby. All yours.'

Danielle smiled vividly down at me, and I recognized with some surprise that her job was of far higher status than I'd guessed, and that she herself came alive also when she was working.

'Make your call,' she said again.

'Yes.'

I pressed the buttons and at the first ring Holly picked up the receiver.

'Kit,' she said immediately, full of stress.

'Yes,' I said.

Holly's voice had come explosively out of the telephone, loudly enough to reach Danielle's ears.

'How did she know?' she asked. Then her eyes widened. 'She was waiting ... you knew.'

I half nodded. 'Kit,' Holly was saying. 'Where are you? Are you all right? Your horse fell ...'

'I'm fine. I'm in London. What's the matter?'

'Everything's worse. Everything's terrible. We're going to lose ... lose the yard ... everything ... Bobby's out walking somewhere ...'

'Holly, remember the telephone,' I said.

'What? Oh, the bugs? I simply don't care any more. The telephone people are coming to look for bugs in the morning, they've promised. But what does it matter? We're finished ... It's over.' She sounded exhausted. 'Can you come? Bobby wants you. We need you. You hold us together.'

'What's happened?' I asked.

'It's the bank. The new manager. We went to see him today and he says we can't even have the money for the wages on Friday and they're going to make us sell up ... he says we haven't enough security to cover all we owe them ... and we're just slipping further into debt because we aren't making enough profit to pay the interest on the loan for those yearlings, and do you know how much he's charging us for that now? Seven per cent over base rate. Seven. That's about seventeen per cent right now. And he's adding the interest on, so now we're paying interest on the interest . . . it's like a snowball . . . it's monstrous . . . it's bloody unfair.'

A shambles, I thought. Banks were never in the benefaction business.

'He admitted it was because of the newspaper articles,' Holly said wretchedly. 'He said it was unfortunate . . . unfortunate! . . . that Bobby's father wouldn't help us, not even a penny . . . I've caused Bobby all this trouble . . . it's because of me . . .'

'Holly, stop it,' I said. 'That's nonsense. Sit tight and I'll come. I'm at Chiswick. It will take me an hour and a half.'

'The bank manager says we will have to tell the owners to take their horses away. He says we're not the only trainers who've ever had to sell up . . . he says it happens, it's quite common . . . he's so hard-hearted I could kill him.'

'Mm,' I said. 'Well, don't do anything yet. Have a drink. Cook me some spinach or something, I'm starving. I'll be on my way . . . See you soon.'

I put down the receiver with a sigh. I didn't really want to drive on to Newmarket with stiffening bruises and an echoingly empty stomach, and I didn't really want to shoulder all the Allardeck troubles again, but a pact was a pact and that was the end of it. My twin, my bond, and all that.

'Trouble?' Danielle said, watching.

I nodded. I told her briefly about the attacks in the *Flag* and their dire financial consequences and she came swiftly to the same conclusion as myself.

'Bobby's father is crass.'

'Crass,' I said appreciatively, 'puts it in a nutshell.'

I stood up slowly from her chair and thanked her for the telephone.

'You're in no shape for all this,' she said objectively.

'Never believe it.' I leaned forward and kissed her fragrant cheek. 'Will you come racing again, with your aunt?'

She looked at me straightly. 'Probably,' she said.

'Good.'

Bobby and Holly were sitting in silence in the kitchen, staring into space, and turned their heads towards me apathetically when I went in.

I touched Bobby on the shoulder and kissed Holly and said, 'Come on, now, where's the wine? I'm dying of various ills and the first thing I need is a drink.'

My voice sounded loud in their gloom. Holly got heavily to her feet and went over to the cupboard where they kept glasses. She put her hand out towards it and then let it fall again. She turned towards me.

'I had my test results since you phoned,' she said

blankly. 'I definitely am pregnant. This should have been the happiest night of our lives.' She put her arms around my neck and began quietly to cry. I wrapped my arms round her and held her, and Bobby stayed sitting down, too defeated, it seemed, to be jealous.

'All right,' I said. 'We'll drink to the baby. Come on, loves, businesses come and go, and this one hasn't gone yet, but babies are for ever, God rot their dear little souls.'

I disentangled her arms and picked out the glasses while she silently wiped her eyes on the sleeve of her jersey.

Bobby said dully, 'You don't understand,' but I did, very well. There was no fight in him, the deflation was too great; and I'd had my own agonizing disappointments now and then. It could take a great effort of will not to sit around and mope.

I said to Holly, 'Put on some music, very loud.'

'No,' Bobby said.

'Yes, Bobby. Yes,' I said. 'Stand up and yell. Stick two fingers up at fate. Break something. Swear your guts out.'

'I'll break your neck,' he said with a flicker of savagery.

'All right, then, do it.'

He raised his head and stared at me and then rose abruptly to his feet, power crowding back into his muscles and vigour and exasperation into his face.

'All right then,' he shouted, 'I'll break your fucking Fielding neck.'

'That's better,' I said. 'And give me something to eat.'

Instead he went over to Holly and enfolded her and the two of them stood there half weeping, half laughing, entwined in privacy and back with the living. I resignedly dug in the freezer for something fast and unfattening and transferred it to the microwave oven, and I poured some red wine and drank it at a gulp.

Over the food Bobby admitted that he'd been too depressed to walk round at evening stables, so after coffee he and I both went out into the yard for a last inspection. The night was windy and cold and moonlit behind scurrying clouds. Everything looked normal and quiet, all the horses dozing behind closed doors, scarcely moving when we looked in on them, checking.

The boxes that had contained Jermyn Graves's horses were still empty, and the string which led to the bell had been detached from the door and hung limply from its last guiding staple. Bobby watched while I attached it to the door again.

'Do you think it's still necessary?' he asked dubiously.

'Yes, I do,' I said positively. 'The feed-merchant will have paid in Graves's cheque yesterday, but it won't have been cleared yet. I wouldn't trust Graves out of sight and I'd rig as many strings to the bell as we can manage.'

'He won't come back again,' Bobby said, shaking his head.

'Do you want to risk it?'

He stared at me for a while and then said, 'No.'

We ran three more strings, all as tripwires across pathways, and made sure the bell would fall if any one of them was tugged. It was perhaps not the most sophisticated of systems, but it had twice proved that it worked.

It worked for the third time at one in the morning.

CHAPTER EIGHT

My first feeling, despite what I'd said to Bobby, was of incredulity. My second, that springing out of bed was a bad idea, despite the long hot soaking I'd loosened up with earlier; and I creaked and groaned and felt sore.

As I took basic overnight things with me permanently in a bag in the car – razor, clean shirt, toothbrush – I was sleeping (as usual in other people's houses) in bright blue running shorts. I would have dressed, I think, if I'd felt more supple. Instead I simply thrust my feet into shoes and went out on to the landing, and found Bobby there, bleary-eyed, indecisive, wearing the top half of his pyjamas.

'Was that the bell?' he said.

'Yes. I'll take the drive again. You take the yard.'

He looked down at his half-nakedness and then at mine.

'Wait.' He dived back into his and Holly's bedroom and reappeared with a sweater for me and trousers for himself, and, struggling into these garments en route, we careered down the stairs and went out into the windy night. There was enough moonlight to see by, which was as well, as we hadn't brought torches.

At a shuffle more than a run I hurried down the drive, but the string across that route was still stretched tight. If Graves had come, he hadn't come that way.

I turned back and went to help Bobby in the yard, but he was standing there indecisively in the semi-darkness, looking around him, puzzled. 'I can't find Graves,' he said. 'Do you think the bell just blew off in the wind?'

'It's too heavy. Have you checked all the strings?'

'All except the one across the gate from the garden. But there's no one here. No one's come that way.'

'All the same . . .' I set off down the path to the gate to the garden, Bobby following: and we found the rustic wooden barrier wide open. We both knew it couldn't have blown open. It was held shut normally with a loop of chain, and the chain hung there on the gatepost, lifted off the gate by human hands.

We couldn't hear much for the wind. Bobby looked doubtfully back the way we had come and made as if to return to the yard.

I said, 'Suppose he's in the garden.'

'But what for? And how?'

'He could have come through the hedge from the road into the paddock, and over the paddock fence, and then down this path, and he'd have missed all the strings except this one.'

'But it's pointless. He can't get horses out through the garden. There are walls all round it. He wouldn't try.'

I was inclined to agree, but all the same, someone had opened the gate.

The walled garden of Bobby's house was all and only on one side, with the drive, stable yard and outhouses wrapping round the other three; and apart from the gate where we now stood, the only way into the garden was through French windows from the drawing room of the house.

Maybe Bobby was struck by the same unwelcome thought as myself. In any case he followed me instantly through the gate and off the paving-stone path inside on to the grass which would be quieter underfoot.

We went silently, fast, the short distance towards the French windows, but they appeared shut, the many square glass frames reflecting the pale light from the sky.

We were about to go over to try them to make sure they were still locked when a faint click and a rattle reached my ears above the breeze, followed by a sharp and definite 'Bugger'.

Bobby and I stood stock still. We could see no one, even with eyes fast approaching maximum night vision.

'Get down,' a voice said. 'I don't like it.'

'Shut up.'

Feeling highly visible in my long bare legs and electric blue shorts I moved across the grass in the direction of the shadows which held the voices, and as policemen will tell you, you should not do that; one should go indoors and telephone the force.

We found, Bobby and I, a man standing at the bottom of a ladder, looking upwards. He wore no mask, no hood, simply an ordinary suit – incongruous as a burglar kit.

He was not Jermyn Graves, and he was not the nephew, Jasper.

He was under forty, dark haired, and a stranger.

He didn't see us at all until we were near him, so firmly fixed upwards was his attention, and when I said loudly, 'What the hell do you think you're doing?' he jumped a foot.

Bobby made a flying rugby tackle at his knees and I took hold of the ladder and pushed it sideways. There was a yell from above and a good deal of clattering, and a second stranger tumbled down from the eaves and fell with a thud on to an uninhabited flower bed.

I pounced on that one and pushed his face down into the November mud and with one hand tried to search his pockets for a weapon, with him heaving and threshing about beneath me, and then when I found no weapon, for some sort of identification, for a diary or a letter, for anything. People who came to burgle dressed as for going to the office might not have taken all suitable precautions.

I couldn't get into his pockets – it was too dark and there was too much movement – but somehow I found myself grasping the collar of his jacket, and I pulled it backwards and downwards with both hands, temporarily fastening his arms to his sides. He plunged and kicked and managed to throw my weight off his back, but I held fiercely on to the jacket, which was entangling his arms and driving him frantic.

To get loose he slid right out of the jacket, leaving it in my hands, and before I could do anything he was up from his knees to his feet, and running.

Instead of chasing him I turned towards Bobby, who was rolling on the ground exchanging short jabbing blows and breathless grunts with the man who'd been holding the ladder. Throwing the jacket into the deep shadow against the house wall I went to Bobby's help, and between the two of us we managed to pin the intruder face down on to the grass, Bobby astride his legs and I with a foot on his neck. Bobby delivered several meaningful blows to the kidneys, designed to hurt.

'Something to tie him with,' he said.

I bent down, gripped the collar of that jacket also, and pulled it as before backwards over the burglar's shoulders, pinning his arms, and then yanking it right off, I took my foot off the neck and said to Bobby, 'That's enough.'

'What? Don't be stupid.'

The intruder rolled under him still full of fight. Bobby punched him wickedly on the ear and again in the small of his back.

I shoved a hand into an inside pocket of the jacket and drew out a wallet.

'See,' I said to Bobby, pushing it under his nose. He shook his head, ignoring it, not wanting to be deterred.

I put the wallet back into the jacket and threw that jacket too into the shadows, and for a second watched Bobby and the now shirt-sleeved intruder tearing at each other and punching again, half standing, half falling, the one trying to cling on and hit, the other to escape.

Bobby was tall and strong and angry at having his house attacked, and no doubt erupting also with the suppressed and helpless fury of the past traumatic days: in any case he was hitting his adversary with tangible hatred and very hard, and I thought with spurting sudden alarm that it was too much, he was beating the man viciously and murderously and not merely capturing a burglar.

I caught Bobby's raised wrist and pulled his bunched fist backwards, upsetting his balance, and his victim twisted out of his grasp and half fell on his knees, coughing, retching, clutching his stomach.

Bobby shouted 'You bugger' bitterly and hit me instead, and the intruder got unsteadily to his feet and staggered towards the gate.

Bobby tried to follow and when I grasped at him to stop him he jabbed his fist solidly into my ribs, calling me a bloody Fielding, a bloody sod, a fucking bastard.

'Bobby . . . Let him go.'

I got a frightful cuff on the head and another clout in the ribs along with some more obscene opinions of my character and ancestors, and he didn't calm down, he kicked my shin and shoved me off him, tearing himself away with another direct hit to my head which rattled my teeth.

I caught him again in a couple of strides and he swung at me, swearing and increasingly violent, and I said to him, 'For God's sake, Bobby . . .' and just tried to hang on to his lethal fists and parry them and survive until the fireball had spent itself.

The generations were all there in his intent face: Allardecks and Fieldings fighting with guns and swords and bare knuckles in malice and perpetuity. He had transferred the intruder-born fury on to the older enemy and all rational restraints had vanished. It was me, his blood's foe, that he was at that point trying to smash, I the focus of his anger and fear and despair.

Locked in this futile archaic struggle we traversed the lawn all the way to the gate; and it was there, when I was wedged against the heavy post and finally in serious trouble, that the killing rage went out of his hands from one second to the next, and he let them fall, the passion dying, the manic strength draining away.

He gave me a blank look, his eyes like glass reflecting the moonlight, and he said 'Bastard', but without much force, and he turned and walked away along the path to the yard.

I said 'God Almighty' aloud, and took a few deep

breaths of rueful and shaky relief, standing for a while
to let my hammering heart settle before shoving off
the gatepost to go and fetch the burglars' coats. Bobby's
fists hadn't had the same weight as the hurdlers' hooves,
but I could well have done without them. Heigh ho, I
thought, in about twelve hours I would ride three tricky
jumpers at Newbury.

The coats lay where I had thrown them, in the angle
of the empty flower bed and the brick wall of the house.
I picked them up and stood there looking at the silvery
ladder which had reached high up the wall, and then
at the wall itself, which stretched in that section right
to the roof, smooth and unbroken.

No windows.

Why would burglars try to break into a house at a
point where there were no windows?

I frowned, tipping my head back, looking upwards.
Beyond the line of the roof, above it, rising like a
silhouette against the night sky, there was a sturdy brick
chimney, surmounted by a pair of antique pots. It was,
I worked out, the chimney from the fireplace in the
drawing room. The fireplace was right through the wall
from where I stood.

Irresolutely I looked from the ladder to the chimney
pots and shivered in the wind. Then, shrugging, I put
the jackets back into the shadow, propped the ladder
up against the eaves, rooted its feet firmly in the flower
bed, and climbed.

The ladder was aluminium, made in telescopic sections. I hoped none of them would collapse.

I didn't much like heights. Halfway up I regretted the whole enterprise. What on earth was I doing climbing an unsteady ladder in the dark? I could fall and hurt myself and not be able to race. It was madness, the whole thing. Crazy.

I reached the roof. The top of the ladder extended beyond that, four or five more rungs going right up to the chimney. On the tiles of the roof lay an opened tool kit, a sort of cloth roll with spanners, screwdrivers, pliers and so on, all held in stitched pockets. Beside it lay a coil of what looked like dark cord, with one end leading upwards to a bracket on the chimney.

I looked more closely at the chimney and almost laughed. One takes so many things for granted, sees certain objects day by day and never consciously sees them at all. Fixed to the chimney was the bracket and mounted on the bracket were the two terminals of the telephone wires leading to Bobby's house. I had seen them a hundred times and never noticed they were fixed to the chimney.

The wire itself stretched away into darkness, going across the telephone pole out on the road; the old above-ground wiring system of all but modern housing.

Attached to the telephone bracket, at the end of the dark cord leading from the coil, there appeared to be a small square object about the size of a sugar cube, with a thin rod about the length of a finger extending downwards. I stretched out a hand precariously to touch it and found it wobbled as if only half attached.

The moon seemed to be going down just when I needed it most. I fumbled around the small cube and came to what felt like a half-undone screw. I couldn't see it, but it turned easily anti-clockwise and in a few moments slipped out into my hand.

The cube and the rod fell straight off the bracket, and I would have lost them in the night if it hadn't been for the coil of stiff cord attached to them. Some of the cord unwound before I caught it, but not a great deal, and I put the coil, the cube and the rod on to the row of tools and rolled up the canvas kit and fastened it with its buckle.

The flower bed, I thought, wouldn't hurt the tool kit, so I dropped the rolled bundle straight below, and went down the ladder as slowly as I'd gone up, careful to balance and not to fall. There was no doubt I felt more at home on horses.

Retrieving the jackets and the tool kit but leaving the ladder, I went out of the garden and walked along the path and round to the kitchen door. Holly in a dressing gown and with wide frightened eyes was standing there, shivering with cold and anxiety.

'Thank goodness,' she said when I appeared. 'Where's Bobby?'

'I don't know. Come on in. Let's make a hot drink.'

We went into the kitchen where it was always

warmest and I put the kettle on while Holly looked
out of the window for her missing husband.

'He'll come soon,' I said. 'He's all right.'

'I saw two men running . . .'

'Where did they go?'

'Over the fence into the paddock. One first, then
the other a bit later. The second one was . . . well . . .
groaning.'

'Mm,' I said. 'Bobby hit him.'

'Did he?' She sounded proud. 'Who were they? They
weren't Jermyn. Did they come for his horses?'

'Which do you want,' I asked, 'coffee, tea or
chocolate?'

'Chocolate.'

I made chocolate for her and tea for myself and
brought the steaming cups to the table.

'Come and sit down,' I said. 'He'll be back.'

She came reluctantly and then watched with awakening curiosity while I unbuckled and unrolled the tool
kit.

'See that?' I said. 'That tiny little box with its rod
and its coil of cord? I'll bet anything that that's what's
been listening to your telephone.'

'But it's minute.'

'Yes. I wish I knew more. Tomorrow we'll find out
just how it works.' I looked at my watch. 'Today, I
suppose one should say.' I told her where I'd found the
bug, and about Bobby and me disturbing the intruders.

She frowned. 'These two men . . . Were they fixing this to our telephone?'

'Taking it away, perhaps. Or changing its battery.'

She reflected. 'I did say to you this evening on the telephone that the telephone people were coming tomorrow to look for bugs.'

'So you did.'

'So perhaps if they heard that, they thought . . . those two men . . . that if they took their bug away first, there wouldn't be anything to find, and we'd never know for sure.'

'Yes,' I said. 'I think you're right.' I picked up the first of the jackets and went through the pockets methodically, laying the contents on the table.

Holly, watching in amazement, said, 'They surely didn't leave their coats?'

'They didn't have much choice.'

'But all those things . . .'

'Dead careless,' I said. 'Amateurs.'

The first jacket produced a notepad, three pens, a diary, a handkerchief, two toothpicks and the wallet I had shown to Bobby in the garden. The wallet contained a moderate amount of money, five credit cards, a photograph of a young woman, and a reminder to go to the dentist. The name on the credit cards was Owen Watts. The diary not only gave the same name but also an address (home) and telephone number (office). The pages were filled with appointments and memos, and spoke of a busy and orderly life.

'Why are you purring like a cat with cream?' Holly said.

'Take a look.'

I pushed Owen Watts's belongings over to her and emptied the pockets of the second jacket. These revealed another notepad, more pens, a comb, cigarettes, throwaway lighter, two letters and a chequebook. There was also, tucked into the outside breast pocket, a small plastic folder containing a gold-coloured card announcing that Mr Jay Erskine was member number 609 of The Press Club, London EC4A 3JB; and Mr Jay Erskine's signature and address were on the back.

Just as well to make absolutely certain, I thought.

I telephoned to Owen Watts's office number, and a man's voice answered immediately.

'*Daily Flag*,' he said.

Satisfied, I put the receiver down without speaking.

'No answer?' Holly said. 'Not surprising, at this hour.'

'The *Daily Flag* neither slumbers nor sleeps. The switchboard, anyway, was awake.'

'So those two really are . . . those pigs.'

'Well,' I said. 'They work for the *Flag*. One can't say if they actually wrote those pieces. Not tonight. We'll find out in the morning.'

'I'd like to smash their faces.'

I shook my head. 'You want to smash the face of whoever sent them.'

'Him too.' She stood up restlessly. 'Where is Bobby? What's he doing?'

'Probably making sure that everything's secure.'

'You don't think those men came back?' she said, alarmed.

'No, I don't. Bobby will come in when he's ready.'

She was worried, however, and went to the outside door and called him, but the wind snatched her voice away so that one could scarcely have heard her from across the yard.

'Go and look for him, will you?' she said anxiously. 'He's been out there so long.'

'All right.' I collected the bugging device, the tools and the pressmen's things together on the table. 'Could you find a box for these, and put them somewhere safe.'

She nodded and began to look vaguely about, and I went out into the yard on the unwelcome errand. Wherever Bobby was, I was probably the last person he wanted to have come after him. I thought that I would simply set about rigging the alarm bell again, and if he wanted to be found, he would appear.

I rigged the bell and got back some night vision, and came across him down by the gate into the garden. He had brought the ladder out so that it lay along the path, and he was simply standing by the gatepost, doing nothing.

'Holly's wondering where you've got to,' I said easily.

He didn't answer.

'Do you think you can hear the bell from here?' I

said. 'Would you climb up someone's house if you'd heard an alarm bell?'

Bobby said nothing. He watched in flat calm while I found the string and shut the gate, fastening everything as before so that the bell would fall on the far side of the house if the gate was opened.

Bobby watched but did nothing. Shrugging, I opened the gate.

One could hear the bell if one was listening for it. On a still night it would have been alarming, but in the breeze the intruders had ignored it.

'Let's go in,' I said. 'Holly's anxious.'

I turned away to walk up the path.

'Kit,' he said stiffly.

I turned back.

'Did you tell her?' he asked.

'No.'

'I'm sorry,' he said.

'Come on in. It doesn't matter.'

'Yes, it does matter.' He paused. 'I couldn't help it. That makes it worse.'

'Tell you what,' I said, 'let's go in out of this bloody cold wind. My legs are freezing. If you want to talk, we'll talk tomorrow. But it's OK. Come on in, you old bugger, it's OK.'

I put the journalists' belongings under my bed for safety before I went achingly back to sleep, but their owners seemed to make no attempt to break in to get them back. I derived a great deal of yawning pleasure from picturing their joint states of mind and body, and thought that anything that had happened to them served them very well right.

Owen Watts and Jay Erskine. Jay Erskine, Owen Watts.

They were going to be, I decided hazily, trying to find an unbruised area to lie on, the lever with which to shift the world. Careless, sneaky, callous Owen Watts, battered half unconscious by Bobby, and stupid, snooping, flint-hearted Jay Erskine, fallen off his ladder with his face pressed into the mud. Served them bloody well right.

I dreamed of being run over by a tractor and felt like it a bit when I woke up. The morning after falls like the day before's were always a bore.

It was nearly nine when I made it to the kitchen, but although the lights were on against the grey morning, there was no one else there. I heated myself some coffee and began to read Bobby's daily paper, which was the *Towncrier*, not the *Flag*.

On page seven, which was wholly devoted to the Wednesday comments and opinions of a leading and immensely influential lady columnist, the central headline read:

WHAT PRICE FATHERLY LOVE?

And underneath, in a long spread unmissable by any *Towncrier* reader, came an outline of Maynard Allardeck's upwardly thrusting career.

He had journeyed from commodity broker, she said, to multi-storey magnate, sucking in other people's enterprises and spitting out the husks.

His *modus operandi*, she explained, was to advance smilingly towards an over-extended business with offers of loans of life-saving cash. Easy terms, pay when you can, glad to help. His new partners, the journalist said, welcomed him with open arms and spoke enthusiastically of their benefactor. But oh, the disillusionment! Once the business was running smoothly, Maynard would very pleasantly ask for his money back. Consternation! Disaster! Impossible to pay him without selling up and closing. The workforce redundant. Personal tragedies abounding. Can't have that, Maynard agreed genially. He would take the business instead of the money, how was that? Everyone still had their job. Except, hard luck, the proprietor and the managing director. Maynard presently would sell his now financially stable newly acquired business at a comfortable profit to any big fish looking out for manageable minnows: and so back, one might say, to the start, with Maynard appreciably richer.

How do I know all this? the lady journalist asked; and answered herself; less than three weeks ago on the TV programme *How's Trade*, Maynard himself told us. Classic takeover procedure, he smugly called it.

Anyone could do the same. Anyone could make a fortune the same way that he had.

It now seemed, she wrote, that one particular over-extended business in dire need of easy-terms cash was the racehorse training enterprise of Maynard's own and only son, Robertson (32).

Maynard was on record in this one instance as obstinately refusing to offer help.

My advice to someone in Robertson's (known as Bobby) position, said the lady firmly, would be to not touch Daddy's money with a bargepole. To count his rocky blessings. Daddy's fond embrace could find him presently sweeping the streets. Don't forget, she said, this parent is still grasping for car money he lent his son as a kid.

Is Maynard, she asked finally, worth a knighthood for services to industry? And she answered herself again: in her own opinion, definitely not.

There was a photograph of Maynard, polished and handsome, showing a lot of teeth. The word 'shark' sprang to mind. Maynard, I thought, would be apoplectic.

Bobby's first lot of horses clattered back into the yard from their morning exercise on the Heath, and Bobby himself came into the kitchen looking intensely depressed. He fixed himself a cup of coffee and wouldn't look at me, and drank standing by the window, staring out.

'How's Holly?' I asked.

'Sick.'

'Your father's in the paper,' I said.

'I don't want to read it.' He put down his cup. 'I expect you'll be going.'

'Yes. I'm riding at Newbury.'

'I meant . . . because of last night.'

'No, not because of that.'

He came over to the table and sat down, looking not at me but at his hands. There were grazes on the knuckles of both fists, red-raw patches where he'd smashed off his own skin.

'Why didn't you fight?' he said.

'I didn't want to.'

'You could have hurt me to hell and gone. I know that now. Why didn't you? I could have killed you.'

'Over my dead body,' I said dryly.

He shook his head. I looked at his face, at the downcast blue eyes, seeing the trouble, the self-doubt, the confusion.

'What I fight,' I said, 'is being brainwashed. Why should we still jump to that old hate? It was a Fielding you were trying to kill. Any Fielding. Not me, Kit, your brother-in-law who actually likes you, though I can't quite see why after last night. I'll fight my indoctrination, I'll fight my bloody ancestors, but I won't fight you, my sister's husband, with whom I have no quarrel.'

He sat for a while without speaking, still looking at his hands, then in a low voice he said, 'You're stronger than me.'

'No. If it makes you feel better, I don't know what I'd have done if I'd been through all you have in the past week and there had been an Allardeck handy to let it all out on.'

He raised his head, the very faintest of glimmers reappearing. 'Truce, then?' he said.

'Yeah,' I agreed; and wondered if our subconscious minds would observe it.

CHAPTER NINE

The vans swept into the yard as if conducting a race; one red, one yellow. Out of each emerged more slowly a man in dark clothes carrying, from the red van, the day's letters, and from the yellow, a clipboard. The Royal Mail and British Telecom side by side.

Bobby went to the door, accepted the letters, and brought the phone company man back with him into the kitchen.

'Bug-hunting,' the latter said heartily, as the red van roared away again outside. 'Got termites in the tele-phone, have you? Been hearing clicking noises on the line? No end of people hear them. False alarms, you know.'

He was large, moustached, and too full of unnecessary bonhomie. Bobby, making a great effort, offered tea or coffee, and I went upstairs to fetch the non-imaginary equipment from the chimney.

I could hear the phone man's voice long before I could see him on my way back.

'You get your M15, of course, but your average left-wing militant, they call us in regular. In Cambridge, now, false alarms all the time.'

'This is not,' Bobby said through gritted teeth, 'a false alarm.'

'We found this,' I said calmingly, putting the tool kit on the table, unrolling it, and producing for inspection the small metal cube with its rod and its coil of attached stiff cord.

'Ah now,' the telephone man's interest came to life, 'now you know what this is, don't you?'

'A bug,' I said.

'Now that,' he said, 'is your transformer stroke transmitter and your earth. Where's the rest?'

'What rest?'

He looked at us with pity. 'You got to have the tap itself. Where did you get this little lot?'

'From the chimney stack, where the phone wires reach the house.'

'Did you now.' He blew down his nose. 'Then that's where we'd better look.'

We took him outside the house rather than through the drawing room, walking down the path from the yard and through the gate. The telescopic aluminium ladder still lay on the path, but the phone man, eyeing the height of the chimney, decided against its fragile support and went back to his van for much sturdier rungs. He returned also with a busy tool-belt buckled round his rotund middle.

Planting and extending his workmanlike ladder he

lumbered up it as casually as walking. To each his own expertise.

At the top, with his stomach supported, he reached out to where the telephone wire divided to the two terminals, and with tools from his belt spent some time clamping, clipping and refastening before returning unruffled to earth.

'A neat little job,' he said appreciatively. 'Superior bit of wire-tapping. Looks like it's been in place for a couple of weeks. Grimy, but not too bad, see? Been up there just a while in the soot and rain.'

He held out a large palm on which rested a small cylinder with two short wires leading from it.

'See, this picks up the currents from your phone wire and leads them into that transformer you took down last night. See, voice frequencies run at anywhere between fifty Hertz and three kiloHertz, but you can't transmit that by radio, you have to transform it up to about three thousand megaHertz. You need an amplifier which modulates the frequency to something a microwave transmitter can transmit.' He looked at our faces. 'Not exactly electronics experts, are you?'

'No,' we said.

With complacent superiority he led the way back to the yard, carrying his heavy ladder with ease. In the kitchen he put the newly gathered cylinder alongside the previous night's spoils and continued with the lecture.

'These two wires from the cylinder plug into the transformer and this short little rod is the aerial.'

'What's all that cord?' I asked.

'Cord?' He smiled largely. 'That's not cord, it's wire. See? Fine wire inside insulation. That's an earth wire, to complete the circuit.'

We looked no doubt blank.

'If you'd have closely inspected your brickwork below your chimney these last weeks you'd have seen this so-called cord lying against it. Running through clips, even. Going down from the transmitter into the earth.'

'Yes,' Bobby said. 'We're never out there much this time of the year.'

'Neat little job,' the telephone man said again.

'Is it difficult to get?' I asked. 'This sort of equipment.'

'Dead easy,' he said pityingly. 'You can send for it from your electronic mail order catalogue any day.'

'And what then?' I asked. 'We've got the tap and the transmitter. Where would we find the receiver?'

The phone man said judiciously, 'This is a low-powered transmitter. Has to be, see, being so small. Runs on a battery, see? So you'd need a big dish-receiver to pick up the signals. Line of sight. Say a quarter-mile away? And no buildings to distort things. Then I'd reckon you'd get good results.'

'A big dish-receiver a quarter of a mile away?' I repeated. 'Everyone would see it.'

'Not inside a van, they wouldn't.' He touched the cube transmitter reflectively. 'Nice high chimney you've got there. Most often we find these babies on the poles out on the road. But the higher you put the transmitter, of course, the further you get good reception.'

'Yes,' I said, understanding that at least.

'This is an unofficial bit of snooping,' he said, happy to instruct. 'Private. You won't get no clicks from this, neither. You'd never know it was there.' He hitched up his tool-belt. 'Right then, you just sign my sheet and I'll be off. And you want to take your binoculars out there now and then and keep a watch on your chimney and your pole in the road, and if you see any more little strangers growing on your wires, you give me a ring and I'll be right back.'

Bobby signed his sheet and thanked him and saw him out to his van; and I looked at the silent bug and wondered vaguely whose telephone I could tap with it, if I learned how.

Holly came in as the yellow van departed, Holly looking pale in jeans and sloppy sweater, with hair still damp from the shower.

'Morning sickness is the pits,' she said. 'Did you make any tea?'

'Coffee in the pot.'

'Couldn't face it.' She put the kettle on. 'What happened out there last night between you and Bobby? He said you would never forgive him, but he wouldn't say what for. I don't think he slept at all. He was up walking round the house at five. So what happened?'

'There's no trouble between us,' I said. 'I promise you.'

She swallowed. 'It would just be the end if you and Bobby quarrelled.'

'We didn't.'

She was still doubtful but said no more. She put some bread in the toaster as Bobby came back, and the three of us sat round the table passing the marmalade and thinking our own thoughts, which in my case was a jumble of journalists, Bobby's bank manager, and how was I going to warm and loosen my muscles before the first race.

Bobby with apprehension began opening the day's letters, but his fears were unfounded. There was no blast from the bank and no demands for payment with menaces. Three of the envelopes contained cheques.

'I don't believe it,' he said, sounding stunned. 'The owners are paying.'

'That's fast,' I said. 'They can only have got those letters yesterday. Their consciences must be pricking overtime.'

'Seb's paid,' Bobby said. He mentally added the three totals and then pushed the cheques across to me. 'They're yours.'

I hesitated.

'Go on,' he said. 'You paid our bills on Monday. If

those cheques had come on Monday you wouldn't have had to.'

Holly nodded.

'What about the lads' wages this Friday?' I asked.

Bobby shrugged frustratedly. 'God knows.'

'What did your bank manager actually say?' I said.

'Sadistic bully,' Bobby said. 'He sat there with a smirk on his prim little face telling me I should go into voluntary liquidation immediately. Voluntary! He said if I didn't, the bank would have no choice but to start bankruptcy proceedings. No choice! Of course they have a choice. Why did they ever lend the money for the yearlings if they were going to behave like this five minutes later?'

The probable answer to that was because Bobby was Maynard's son. Maynard's millions might have seemed security enough, before the *Flag* fired its broadside.

'Isn't there any trainer in Newmarket who would buy the yearlings from you?' I said.

'Not a chance. Most of them are in the same boat. They can't sell their own.'

I pondered. 'Did the bank manager say anything about bailiffs?'

'No,' Bobby said, and Holly, if possible, went paler.

We might have a week, I thought. I didn't know much about liquidation or bankruptcy: I didn't know the speed of events. Perhaps we had no time at all. No one, however, could expect Bobby to be able to sell all his property overnight.

'I'll take the cheques,' I said, 'and I'll get them cashed. We'll pay your lads this week out of the proceeds and keep the rest for contingencies. And don't tell the bank manager, because he no doubt thinks this money belongs to the bank.'

'They lent it to us quick enough,' Holly said bitterly. 'No one twisted their arm.'

It wasn't only Maynard, I thought, who could lend with a smile and foreclose with a vengeance.

'It's hopeless,' Bobby said. 'I'll have to tell the owners to take their horses. Sack the lads.' He stopped abruptly. Holly, too, had tears in her eyes. 'It's such a mess,' Bobby said.

'Yeah ... well ... hold tight for a day or two,' I said.

'What's the point?'

'We might try a little fund-raising.'

'What do you mean?'

I knew only vaguely what I meant and I didn't think I would discuss it with Bobby. I said instead, 'Don't break up the stable before the dragon's breathing fire right in the yard.'

'St George might come along,' Holly said.

'What?' Bobby looked uncomprehending.

'In the story,' Holly said. 'You know. Kit and I had a pop-up book where St George came along and slew the dragon. We used to read it with a torch under the bedclothes and scare ourselves with shadows.'

'Oh.' He looked from one of us to the other, seeing

163

dark-haired twins with a shared and private history. He may have felt another twinge of exclusion because he smothered some reaction with a firming of the mouth, but after a while, with only a hint of sarcasm and as if stifling any hope I might have raised, he came up with an adequate reply. 'OK, St George. Get on your horse.'

I drove to Newbury and solved the stiff muscle problem by borrowing the sauna of a local flat race jockey who spent every summer sweating away his body in there and had thankfully come out for the winter. I didn't like water-shedding in saunas as a daily form of weight-control (still less diuretics), but after twenty minutes of its hot embrace on that cold morning I did feel a good deal fitter.

My first two mounts were for the Lambourn stable I normally rode for, and, given a jockey with smooth-ly working limbs, they both cleared the obstacles efficiently without covering themselves with either mud or glory. One could say to the hopeful owners after-wards that yes, their horses would win one day; and so they might, when the weights were favourable and the ground was right and a few of the better opponents fell. I'd ridden duds I wouldn't have taken out of the stable and had them come in first.

My final mount of the day belonged to the princess, who was waiting, alone as usual, for me to join her in the parade ring. I was aware of being faintly disappointed that Danielle wasn't with her, even though I hadn't expected it: most illogical. The princess, sable coat swinging, wore a pale yellow silk scarf at her neck with gold and citrine earrings, and although I'd seen her in them often before I thought she was looking exceptionally well and glowing. I made the small bow; shook her hand. She smiled.

'How do you think we'll do today?' she said.

'I think we'll win.'

Her eyes widened. 'You're not usually so positive.'

'Your horses are all in form. And . . .' I stopped.

'And what?'

'And . . . er . . . you were thinking, yourself, that we would win.'

She said without surprise, 'Yes, I was.' She turned to watch her horse walk by. 'What else was I thinking?'

'That . . . well . . . that you were happy.'

'Yes.' She paused. 'Do you think the Irish mare will beat us? Several people have tipped it.'

'She's got a lot of weight.'

'Lord Vaughnley thinks she'll win.'

'Lord Vaughnley?' I repeated, my interest quickening. 'Is he here?'

'Yes,' she said. 'He was lunching in a box near mine. I came down the stairs with him just now.'

I asked her if she remembered which box, but she didn't. I said I would like to talk to him, if I could find him.

'He'll be glad to,' she said, nodding. 'He's still

delighted about the Towncrier Trophy. He says literally hundreds of people have congratulated him on this year's race.'

'Good,' I said. 'If I ask him a favour, I might get it.'

'You could ask the world.'

'Not that much.'

The signal came for jockeys to mount, and I got up on her horse to see what we could do about the Irish mare: and what we did was to start out at a fast pace and maintain it steadily throughout, making the mare feel every extra pound she was carrying every stride of the way, and finally to beat off her determined challenge most satisfactorily by a length and a half.

'Splendid,' the princess exclaimed in the winners' enclosure, sparkling. 'Beautiful.' She patted her excited 'chaser. 'Come up to the box, Kit, when you've changed.' She saw my very faint and stifled hesitation and interpreted it. 'I saw Lord Vaughnley up there again. I asked him to my box also.'

'You're amazingly kind.'

'I'm amazingly pleased with winning races like this.'

I changed into street clothes and went up to her familiar box high above the winning post. For once she was there alone, not surrounded by guests, and she mentioned that she was on her way back from Devon, her chauffeur having driven her up that morning.

'My niece telephoned yesterday evening from her bureau to say she had arrived promptly,' the princess said. 'She was most grateful.'

I said I'd been very pleased to help. The princess offered tea, pouring it herself, and we sat on adjacent chairs, as so often, as I described the past race to her almost fence by fence.

'I could see,' she said contentedly. 'You were pushing along just ahead of the mare all the way. When she quickened, you quickened, when she took a breather down the bottom end, so did you. And then I could see you just shake up my horse when her jockey took up his whip . . . I knew we'd win. I was sure of it all the way round. It was lovely.'

Such sublime confidence could come crashing down on its nose at the last fence, but she knew that as well as I did. There had been times when it had. It made the good times better.

She said, 'Wykeham says we're giving Kinley his first try over hurdles at Towcester tomorrow. His first ever race.'

'Yes,' I nodded. 'And Dhaulagiri's taking his first start at a novice 'chase. I rode both of them schooling at Wykeham's last week, did he tell you? They both jumped super. Er . . . will you be there?'

'I wouldn't miss it.' She paused. 'My niece says she will come with me.'

I lifted my head. 'Will she?'

'She said so.'

The princess regarded me calmly and I looked straight back, but although it would have been useful I couldn't read what she was thinking.

'I enjoyed driving her,' I said.

'She said the journey went quickly.'

'Yes.'

The princess patted my arm non-committally, and Lord and Lady Vaughnley appeared in the doorway, looking in with enquiring faces and coming forward with greetings. The princess welcomed them, gave them glasses of port, which it seemed they liked particularly on cold days, and drew Lady Vaughnley away with her to admire something out on the viewing balcony, leaving Lord Vaughnley alone inside with me.

He said how truly delighted he'd been with everyone's response to last Saturday's race, and I asked if he could possibly do me a favour.

'My dear man. Fire away. Anything I can.'

I explained again about Bobby and the attacks in the *Flag*, which by now he himself knew all about.

'Good Lord, yes. Did you see the comment page in our own paper this morning? That woman of ours, Rose Quince, she has a tongue like a rattlesnake, but when she writes, she makes sense. What's the favour?'

'I wondered,' I said, 'if the *Towncrier* would have a file of clippings about Maynard Allardeck. And if you have one, would you let me see it.'

'Good Lord,' he said. 'You'll have a reason, no doubt?'

I said we had concluded that Bobby had been a casualty in a campaign mainly aimed at his father. 'And it would be handy to know who might have enough of a grudge against Maynard to kill off his chance of a knighthood.'

Lord Vaughnley smiled benignly. 'Such as anyone whose business was pulled from beneath them?'

'Such as,' I agreed. 'Yes.'

'You're suggesting that the *Flag* could be pressured into mounting a hate campaign?' He pursed his mouth, considering.

'I wouldn't have thought it would take much pressure,' I said. 'The whole paper's a hate campaign.'

'Dear, dear,' he said with mock reproof. 'Very well. I can't see how it will directly help your brother-in-law, but yes, I'll see you get access to our files.'

'That's great,' I said fervently. 'Thank you very much.'

'When would suit you?'

'As soon as possible.'

He looked at his watch. 'Six o'clock?'

I shut my mouth on a gasp. He said, 'I have to be at a dinner in the City this evening. I'll be dropping into the *Towncrier* first. Ask for me at the front desk.'

I duly asked at his front desk in Fleet Street and was directed upwards to the editorial section on the third floor, arriving, it seemed, at a point of maximum bustle as the earliest editions of the following day's papers were about to go to press.

Lord Vaughnley, incongruous in tweed jacket, dress

trousers, stiff shirt and white tie, stood at the shoulder of a coatless man seated at a central table, both of them intent on the newspaper before them. Around them, in many bays half separated from each other by shoulder-high partitions, were clumps of three or four desks, each bay inhabited by telephones, typewriters, potted plants and people in a faint but continuous state of agitation.

'What do you want?' someone said to me brusquely as I hovered, and when I said Lord Vaughnley, he merely pointed. Accordingly I walked over to the centre of the activity and said neutrally to Lord Vaughnley, 'Excuse me . . .'

He raised his eyes but not his head. 'Ah yes, my dear chap, be with you directly,' he said, and lowered the eyes again, intently scanning what I saw to be tomorrow's front page, freshly printed.

I waited with interest while he finished, looking around at a functional scene which I guessed hadn't changed much since the days of that rumbustious giant, the first Lord Vaughnley. Desks and equipment had no doubt come and gone, but from the brown floor to the yellowing cream walls the overall impression was of a working permanence, slightly old-fashioned.

The present Lord Vaughnley finished reading, stretched himself upwards and patted the shirt-sleeved shoulder of the seated man, who was, I discovered later, that big white chief, the editor.

'Strong stuff, Marty. Well done.'

The seated man nodded and went on reading. Lord Vaughnley said to me, 'Rose Quince is here. You might like to meet her.'

'Yes,' I said, 'I would.'

'Over here.' He set off towards one of the bays, the lair, it proved, of the lady of the rattlesnake tongue who could nevertheless write sense, and who had written that day's judgement on Maynard.

'Rose,' said the paper's proprietor, 'take care of Kit Fielding, won't you?' and the redoubtable Rose Quince assured him that yes, she would.

'Files,' Lord Vaughnley said. 'Whatever he wants to see, show him.'

'Right.'

To me he said, 'We have a box at Ascot. The *Town-crier* has, I mean. I understand from the princess that you'll be riding there this Friday and Saturday. No point, I suppose, my dear chap, in asking you to lunch with me on Saturday, which is the day I'll be there, but do come up for a drink when you've finished. You'll always be welcome.'

I said I'd be glad to.

'Good. Good. My wife will be delighted. You'll be in good hands with Rose, now. She was born in Fleet Street the same as I was, her father was Conn Quince who edited the old *Chronicle*; she knows more of what goes on than the Street itself. She'll give you the gen, won't you, Rose?'

Rose, who looked to me to be bristling with

reservations, agreed again that yes, she would; and Lord Vaughnley, with the nod of a man who knows he's done well, went away and left me to her serpent mercies.

She did not, it is true, have Medusa snakes growing out of her head, but whoever had named her Rose couldn't have foreseen its incongruity.

A rose she was not. A tiger-lily, more like. She was tall and very thin and fifteen to twenty years older than myself. Her artfully tousled and abundant hair was dark but streaked throughout with blonde, the aim having clearly been two contrasting colours, not overall tortoiseshell. The expertly painted sallow face could never have been pretty but was strongly good-looking, the nose masculine, the eyes noticeably pale blue; and from several feet away one could smell her sweet and heavy scent.

A quantity of bracelets, rings and necklaces decorated the ultimate in fashionable outlines, complemented by a heavy bossed and buckled belt round the hips, and I wondered if the general overstatement was a sort of stockade to frighten off the encroachment of the next generation of writers, a battlement against time.

If it was, I knew how she felt. Every jump jockey over thirty felt threatened by the rising nineteen-year-olds who would supplant them sooner or later. Every jockey, every champion had to prove race by race that he was as good as he'd ever been, and it was tough at the top only because of those hungry to take over one's saddle. I didn't need bangles, but I pulled out grey hairs when they appeared.

Rose Quince looked me up and down critically and said, 'Big for a jockey, aren't you?' which was hardly original, as most people I met said the same.

'Big enough.'

Her voice had an edge to it more than an accent, and was as positive as her appearance.

'And your sister is married to Maynard Allardeck's son.'

'Yes, that's right.'

'The source of Daddy's disapproval.'

'Yes.'

'What's wrong with her? Was she a whore?'

'No, a Capulet.'

Rose took barely three seconds to comprehend, then she shook her head in self-disgust.

'I missed an angle,' she said.

'Just as well.'

She narrowed her eyes and looked at me with her head tilted.

'I watched the Towncrier Trophy on television last Saturday,' she said. 'It would more or less have been treason not to.' She let her gaze wander around my shoulders. 'Left it a bit late, didn't you?'

'Probably.'

She looked back to my face. 'No excuses?'

'We won.'

'Yes, dammit, after you'd given everyone cardiac

arrest. Did you realize that half the people in this building had their pay packets on you?'

'No, I didn't.'

'The Sports Desk told us you couldn't lose.'

'Bunty Ireland?'

'Precisely, Bunty Ireland. He thinks the sun shines out of your arse.' She shook an armful of baubles to express dismissal of Bunty's opinions. 'No jockey is that smart.'

'Mm,' I said. 'Could we talk about Maynard?'

Her dark eyebrows rose. 'On first name terms, are you?'

'Maynard Allardeck.'

'A prize shit.'

'Olympic gold.'

She smiled, showing well-disciplined teeth. 'You read nothing in the paper, buddy boy. Do you want to see the tape?'

'What tape?'

'The tape of *How's Trade*. It's still here, downstairs. If you want to see it, now's the time.'

'Yes,' I said.

'Right. Come along. I've got the unexpurgated version, the one they cut from to make the programme. Ready for the rough stuff? It's dynamite.'

CHAPTER TEN

She had acquired, it appeared, both the ten-minute edition which had been broadcast as well as the half-hour original.

'Did you see the programme on the box?' Rose said.

I shook my head.

'You'd better see that first, then.'

She had taken me to a small room which contained a semi-circle of comfortable chairs grouped in front of a television set. To each side of the set various makes of video machine sat on tables, with connecting cables snaking about in apparent disorder.

'We get brought or sent unsolicited tapes of things that have happened,' Rose explained casually. 'All sorts of tapes. Loch Ness monsters by the pailful. Mostly rubbish, but you never know. We've had a scoop or sixteen this way. The big white chief swears by it. Then we record things ourselves. Some of our reporters like to interview with video cameras, as I do sometimes. You get the flavour back fresh if you don't write the piece for a week or so.'

While she talked she connected a couple of wandering cable ends to the back of the television set and switched everything on. Her every movement was accompanied by metallic clinks and jingles, and her lily scent filled the room. She picked up a tape cassette which had been lying on the table behind one of the video machines and fed it into the slot.

'Right. Here we go.'

We sat in two of the chairs, she sprawling sideways so she could see my face, and the screen sprang immediately to life with an interesting arrangement of snow. Total silence ensued for ten seconds before the Maynard segment of *How's Trade* arrived in full sharp colour with sound attached. Then we had the benefit of Maynard looking bland and polished through a voice-over introduction, with time to admire the hand-sewn lapels and silk tie.

The interviewer asked several harmless questions, Maynard's slightly condescending answers being lavishly interrupted by views of the interviewer nodding and smiling. The interviewer himself, unknown as far as I was concerned, was perhaps in his mid-thirties, with forgettable features except for calculating eyes of a chilling detachment. A prosecutor, I thought; and disliked him.

In reply to a question about how he got rich Maynard said that 'once or twice' he had come to the rescue of an ailing but basically sound business, had set it back on its feet with injections of liquidity and had

176

subsequently acquired it to save it from closure when it had been unable to repay him. To the benefit, he suavely insisted, of all concerned.

'Except the former owners?' the interviewer asked; but the question was put as merely fact-finding, without bite.

Maynard's voice said that generous compensation was of course paid to the owners.

'And then what?' asked the interviewer, in the same way.

Naturally, Maynard said, if a good offer came along, he would in his turn sell: he could then lend the money to rescue another needy firm. The buying, selling and merging of businesses was advisable when jobs could be saved and a sensible profit made. He had done his modest best for industry and had ensured employment for many. It had been most rewarding in human terms.

Neither Maynard nor the interviewer raised his voice above a civilized monotone, and as an entertainment it was a drag. The segment ended with the interviewer thanking Maynard for a most interesting discussion, and there was a final shot of Maynard looking noble.

The screen, as if bored silly, reverted to black and white snow.

'Allardeck the philanthropist,' Rose said, jangling the bracelets and recrossing her long legs. 'Have you met him?'

'Yes.'

'Well, now for Allardeck the rapacious bully.'

'I've met him too,' I said.

She gave me a quizzical look and watched me watch the snowstorm until we were suddenly alive again with Maynard's charm and with the introduction and the first few harmless questions. It wasn't until the interviewer started asking about takeovers that things warmed up; and in this version the interviewer's voice was sharp and critical, designed to raise a prickly defensive response.

Maynard had kept his temper for a while, reacting self-righteously rather than with irritation, and these answers had been broadcast. In the end however his courtesy disintegrated, his voice rose and a forefinger began to wag.

'I act within the law,' he told the interviewer heavily. 'Your insinuations are disgraceful. When a debtor can't pay, one is entitled to take his property. The state does it. The courts enforce it. It's the law. Let me tell you that in the horse racing business, if a man can't pay his training fees, the trainer is entitled to sell the horse to recover his money. It's the law, and what's more, it's natural justice.'

The interviewer mentioned villainous mortgage holders who foreclosed and evicted their tenants. Hadn't Maynard, he asked, lent money to a hard-pressed family business that owned a block of flats which was costing more to maintain than the rental income, and couldn't afford the repairs required by the authorities? And after the repairs were done, hadn't

Maynard demanded his money back? And when the family couldn't pay, hadn't he said he would take the flats instead, which were a loss to the family anyway? And after that, hadn't mysterious cracks developed in the fabric, so that the building was condemned and all the poor tenants had to leave? And after that, hadn't he demolished the flats and sold the freehold land to a development company for ten times his original loan for repairs?

The inquisitional nature of the interviewer was by now totally laid bare, and the questions came spitting out as accusations, to which Maynard answered variously with growing fury:

'It's none of your business.'

'It was a long time ago.'

'The building subsided because of underground trains.'

'The family was glad to be rid of a millstone liability.'

'I will not answer these questions.'

The last statement was practically a shout. The interviewer made calming motions with his hand, leaning back in his chair, appearing to relax, all of which cooling behaviour caused Maynard to simmer rather than seethe. A mean-looking scowl, however, remained in place. Nobility was nowhere to be seen.

The interviewer with subterranean cunning said pleasantly, 'You mentioned racehorses. Am I right in thinking your own father was a racehorse trainer and that you at one time were his assistant?'

Maynard said ungraciously, 'Yes.'

'Give us your opinion of investing in bloodstock.'

Maynard said profits could be made if one took expert advice.

'But in your case,' the interviewer said, 'you must be your own expert.'

Maynard shrugged. 'Perhaps.'

The interviewer said very smoothly, 'Will you tell us how you acquired your racehorse Metavane?'

Maynard said tightly, 'I took him in settlement of a bad debt.'

'In the same way as your other businesses?'

Maynard didn't answer.

'Metavane proved to be a great horse, didn't he? And you syndicated him for at least four million pounds ... which must be your biggest coup ever – bigger than the Bourne Brothers' patents. Shall we talk about those two enterprises? First, tell me how much you allow either Metavane's former owners or the Bourne Brothers out of the continuing fruits of your machinations.'

'Look here,' Maynard said furiously, 'if you had a fraction of my business sense you'd be out doing something useful instead of sitting here green with envy picking holes.'

He stood up fiercely and abruptly and walked decisively off the set, tearing off the microphone he had been wearing on his tie and flinging it on the ground. The interviewer made no attempt to stop him. Instead he faced the camera and with carefully presented distaste said that some of the other businesses, big and small, known to have benefited from Mr Allardeck's rescue missions were Downs and Co. (a printing works), Benjy's Fast Food Takeout, Healthy Life (sports goods manufacturers), Applewood Garden Centre, Purfleet Electronics and Bourne Brothers (light engineers).

The Bourne Brothers' assets, he said, had proved to include some long overlooked patents for a special valve which had turned out to be just what industry was beginning to need. As soon as it was his, Maynard Allardeck had offered the valve on a royalty basis to the highest bidder, and had been collecting handsomely ever since. The Bourne Brothers? The interviewer shook his head. The Bourne Brothers hadn't realized what they'd owned until they'd irrevocably parted with it. But did Maynard Allardeck know what he was getting? Almost certainly yes. The interviewer smiled maliciously and pushed the knife right in. If Allardeck had told the Bourne Brothers what they owned, collecting dust in a file, they could have saved themselves several times over.

The interviewer's smugly sarcastic face vanished into another section of blizzard, and Rose Quince rose languidly to switch everything off.

'Well?' she said.

'Nasty.'

'Is that all?'

'Why didn't they show the whole tape on *How's Trade*? They obviously meant to needle Maynard. Why did they smother the results?'

'I thought you'd never ask.' Rose hitched a hip on to one of the tables and regarded me with acid amusement. 'I should think Allardeck paid them not to show it.'

'What?'

'Pure as a spring lamb, aren't you? That interviewer and his producer have before this set up a pigeon and then thoroughly shot him down, but without the brawl ever reaching the screen. One politician, I know for certain, was invited by the producer to see his hopelessly damaging tape before it was broadcast. He was totally appalled and asked if there was any way he could persuade the producer to edit it. Sure, the producer said, the oldest way in the world, through your wallet.'

'How do you know?'

'The politician told me himself. He wanted me to write about it, he was so furious, but I couldn't. He wouldn't let me use his name.'

'Maynard,' I said slowly, 'has a real genius for acquiring assets.'

'Oh, sure. And nothing illegal. Not unless he helped the trains to shake the block of flats' foundations.'

'One could never find out.'

'Not a chance.'

'How did the interviewer rake all that up?'

Rose shrugged. 'Out of files. Out of archives. Same as we all do when we're on a story.'

'He'd done a great deal of work.'

'Expecting a great deal of pay-off.'

'Mm,' I said, 'if Maynard was already angling for a knighthood, he'd have paid the earth. They could probably have got more from him than they did.'

'They'll curl up like lemon rind now that they know.' The idea pleased Rose greatly.

'How did you get this tape?' I asked curiously.

'From the producer himself, sort of. He owed me a big favour. I told him I wanted to do a shredding job on Allardeck, and asked to see the interview again, uncut if possible, and he was as nice as pie. I wouldn't tell him I knew about his own little scam, now would I?'

'I suppose,' I said slowly, 'that I couldn't have a copy?'

Rose gave me a long cool look while she considered it. Her eyelids, I noticed, were coloured purple, dark contrast to the pale blue eyes.

'What would you do with it?' she said.

'I don't know yet.'

'It's under copyright,' she said.

'Mm.'

'You shouldn't have it.'

'No.'

She bent over the video machine and pressed the eject button. The large black cassette slid quietly and smoothly into her hand. She slotted it into its case and held it out to me, gold chains tinkling.

'Take this one. This is a copy. I made it myself. The originals never left the building, they're hot as hell about that in that television company, but I'm fairly quick with these things. They left me alone in an editing room to view, with some spare tapes stacked in a corner, which was their big mistake.'

I took the box, which bore a large white label saying 'Do not touch'.

'Now listen to me, buddy boy, if you're found with this, you don't get me into trouble, right?'

'Right,' I said. 'Do you want it back?'

'I don't know why I trust you,' she said plaintively. 'A goddamn jockey. If I want it back I'll ask. You keep it somewhere safe. Don't leave it lying about, for God's sake. Though I suppose I should tell you it won't play on an ordinary video. The tape is professional tape three-quarters of an inch wide, it gives better definition. You'll need a machine that takes that size.'

'What were you going to do with it yourself?' I asked.

'Wipe it off,' she said decisively. 'I got it yesterday morning and played it several times here to make sure I didn't put the uncut version's words into Allardeck's mouth in the paper. I don't need suing. Then I wrote my piece, and I've been busy today ... but if you'd come one day later, it would all have been wiped.'

'Lucky,' I said.

'Yes. What else? Files? There's more on the tape, but Bill said files, so files you can have.'

'Bill?'

'Bill Vaughnley. We worked together when we were young. Bill started at the bottom, the old Lord made him. So did I. You don't call someone sir when you've shared cigarette butts on a night stint.'

They had been lovers, I thought. It was in her voice.

'He says I have a tongue like a viper,' she said without offence. 'I dare say he told you?'

I nodded. 'Rattlesnake.'

She smiled. 'When he's a pompous fool, I let him know it.'

She stood up, tawny and tinkling like a mobile in a breeze, and we went out of the television room, down a corridor, round a few corners, and found ourselves in an expanse like a library with shelves to the ceiling bearing not books but folders of all sorts, the whole presided over by a severe looking youth in spectacles who signed us in, looked up the indexing and directed us to the section we needed.

The file on Maynard Allardeck was, as Rose had said, less informative than the tape. There were sundry photographs of him, black and white glossy prints, chiefly taken at race meetings, where I supposed he was more accessible. There were three, several years old now, of him leading in his great horse Metavane after its win in the 2000 Guineas, the Goodwood Mile and the Champion Stakes. Details and dates were on flimsy paper strips stuck to the back of the prints.

There were two bunches of newspaper clippings, one from the *Towncrier*, one from other sources such as the *Financial Times* and the *Sporting Life*. Nothing critical had been written, it seemed, before the onslaught in the *Flag*. The paragraphs were mainly dull: Maynard, from one of the oldest racing families ... Maynard, proud owner ... Maynard, member of the Jockey Club ... Maynard, astute businessman ... Maynard, supporter of charity ... Maynard the great and good. Approving adjectives like bold, compassionate, far-sighted and responsible occurred. The public persona at its prettiest.

'Enough to make you puke,' Rose said.

'Mm,' I said. 'Do you think you could ask your producer friend why he hit on Maynard as a target?'

'Maybe. Why?'

'Someone's got it in for Maynard. That TV interview might be an attack that didn't work, God bless bribery and corruption. The attack in the *Flag* has worked well. You've helped it along handsomely yourself. So who got to the *Flag*, and did they also get to the producer?'

'I take it back,' she said. 'Some jockeys are smarter than others.'

'Very few are dumb.'

'They just talk a different language?'

'Dead right.'

She returned the file to its place. 'Anything else? Any dinky little thing?'

'Yes,' I said. 'How would I get to talk to Sam Leggatt, who edits the *Flag*?'

She let out a breath, a cross between a cough and a laugh. 'Sam Leggatt? You don't.'

'Why not?'

'He walks around in a bullet-proof vest.'

'Seriously?'

'Metaphorically.'

'Do you know him?'

'Sure, I know him. Can't say I like him. He was political correspondent on the *Record* before he went to the *Flag*, and he's always thought he was God's gift to Fleet Street. He's a mocker by nature. He and the *Flag* are soulmates.'

'Could you reach him on the telephone?' I asked.

She shook her head over my naivety. 'They'll be printing the first edition by now, but he'll be checking everything again for the second. Adding stuff. Changing it round. There's no way he'd talk to Moses let alone a . . . a jumping bean.'

'You could say,' I suggested, 'that you were your editor's secretary, and it was urgent.'

She looked at me in disbelief. 'And why the hell should I?'

'Because you trade in favours.'

'Jee-sus.' She blinked the pale blue eyes.

'Any time,' I said. 'I'll pay. I took it for granted that this . . .' I held up the tape, 'was on account.'

'The telephone,' she said, 'makes it two favours.'

'All right.'

She said with amusement, 'Is this how you win your races?' She turned without waiting for an answer and led the way back roughly to where we had started from but ending in a small, bare little room furnished only with three or four chairs, a table and a telephone.

'Interview room,' Rose said. 'General purposes. Not used much. I'm not having anyone hear me make this call.'

She sat on one of the chairs looking exotically sensuous and behaving with middle-class propriety, the baroque façade for frighteners, the sensible woman beneath.

'You'll have about ten seconds, if that,' she said, stretching out the bracelets for the telephone. 'Leggatt will know straight away you're not our editor. Our editor comes from Yorkshire and still sounds like it.'

I nodded.

She got an outside line and with long red nails tapped in the *Flag*'s number, which she knew by heart; and within a minute, after out-blarneying the Irish, she handed me the receiver silently.

'Hello, Martin, what goes?' an unenthusiastic voice said.

I said slowly and clearly, 'Owen Watts left his credit cards in Bobby Allardeck's garden.'

'What? I don't see . . .' There was a sudden silence. 'Who is this?'

'Jay Erskine,' I said, 'left his Press Club card in the same place. To whom should I report these losses? To the Press Council, the police or my member of parliament?'

'Who is that?' he asked flatly.

'I'm speaking from a telephone in the *Towncrier*. Will you talk to me in your office, or shall I give the *Towncrier* a scoop?'

There was a long pause. I waited. His voice then said, 'I'll ring you back. Give me your extension.'

'No,' I said. 'Now or never.'

A much shorter pause. 'Very well. Come to the front desk. Say you're from the *Towncrier*.'

'I'll be there.'

He crashed the telephone down as soon as I'd finished speaking, and Rose was staring at me as if alarmed for my wholeness of mind.

'No one speaks to editors like that,' she said.

'Yeah . . . well, I don't work for him. And somewhere along the way I've learned not to be afraid of people. I was never afraid of horses. People were more difficult.'

She said with a touch of seriousness, 'People can harm you.'

'They sure can. But I'd get nowhere with Leggatt by being soft.'

'Where do you want to be?' she asked. 'What's this scoop you're not giving the *Towncrier*?'

'Nothing much. Just some dirty tricks the *Flag* indulged in to get their Allardeck story for Intimate Details.'

She shrugged. 'I doubt if we'd print that.'

'Maybe not. What's the limit journalists will go to to get a story?'

'No limit. Up Everest, into battlefields, along the gutters, anywhere a scandal leads. I've done my crusading time in rotten health farms, corrupt local governments, nutty religions. I've seen more dirt, more famine, more poverty, more tragedy than I need. I've sat through nights with parents of murdered children and I've been in a village of lifeboatmen's widows weeping for their dead. And then some damn fool man expects me to go sit on a prissy gilt chair and swoon over skirt lengths in some goddam Paris salon. I've never been a women's writer and I'm bloody well not starting now.'

She stopped, smiled twistedly, 'My feminism's showing.'

'Say you won't go,' I said. 'If it's a demotion, refuse it. You've got the clout. No one expects you to write about fashion, and I agree with you, you shouldn't.'

She gave me a long look. 'I wouldn't be fired, but he's new, he's a chauvinist, he could certainly make life difficult.'

'You,' I said, 'are one very marketable lady. Get out the famous poison fangs. A little venom might work wonders.'

She stood up, stretching tall, putting her hands on her heavily belted hips. She looked like an Amazon equipped for battle but I could still sense the indecision inside. I stood also, to the same height, and kissed her cheek.

'Very brotherly,' she said dryly. 'Is that all?'

'That's all you want, isn't it?'

'Yes,' she said, mildly surprised. 'You're goddam right.'

The *Daily Flag*, along Fleet Street from the *Towncrier*, had either been built much later or had been done over in Modern Flashy.

There was a fountain throwing out negative ions in the foyer and ceiling-wide chandeliers of thin vertical shimmering glass rods, each emitting light at its downward tip. Also a marble floor, futuristic seating and a security desk populated by four large men in intimidating uniforms.

I told one of them I'd come from the *Towncrier* to see Mr Leggatt and half expected to be thrown out bodily into the street. All that happened, however, was that after a check against a list on the desk I was directed upwards with the same lack of interest as I'd met with on friendlier territory.

Upstairs the decorative contrast continued. Walls in the *Flag* were pale orange with red flecks, the desks shining green plastic, the floor carpeted with busy

orange and red zigzags, the whole a study in unrestful-
ness. Anger on every page, I thought, and no wonder.

Sam Leggatt's office had an opaque glass door
marked 'editor' in large lower-case white letters, followed some way below by smaller but similar letters
telling callers to ring bell and wait.

I rang the bell and waited, and presently with a buzz
the door swung inwards a few inches. Sam Leggatt
might not actually wear a bullet-proof vest but his
defences against people with grievances were
impressive.

I pushed the door open further and went in to
another brash display of rotten taste: black plastic desk,
red wallpaper flecked in a geometric pattern, and a
mottled green carpet, which as a working environment
would have sent me screaming to the bottle.

There were two shirt-sleeved men in there, both
standing, both apparently impervious to their surroundings. One was short, stubby and sandy-haired, the other
taller, stooped, bespectacled and going bald. Both
about fifty, I thought. A third man, younger, sat in a
corner, in a suit, watchful and quiet.

'Mr Leggatt?' I said.

The short sandy-haired one said, 'I'm Leggatt. I'll
give you five minutes.' He inclined his head towards
the taller man beside him. 'This is Tug Tunny, who
edits Intimate Details. That is Mr Evans from our legal
department. So who are you, and what do you want?'

Tug Tunny snapped his fingers. 'I know who he is,'

he said. 'Jockey. That jockey.' He searched for the name in his memory and found it. 'Fielding. Champion jockey.'

I nodded, and it seemed to me that they all relaxed. There was a trace of arrogance all the same in the way Leggatt stood, and a suggestion of pugnaciousness, but not more, I supposed, than his eminence and the circumstances warranted, and he spoke and behaved without bluster throughout.

'What do you want?' Leggatt repeated, but lacking quite the same tension as when I'd entered; and it crossed my mind as he spoke that with his passion for security they would be recording the conversation, and that I was speaking into an open microphone somewhere out of sight.

I said carefully, 'I came to make arrangements for returning the property of two of your journalists, Owen Watts and Jay Erskine.'

'Return it then,' Leggatt said brusquely.

'I would be so glad,' I said, 'if you would tell me why they needed to climb a ladder set against Bobby Allardeck's house at one in the morning.'

'What's it to you?'

'We found them, you understand, with telephone tapping equipment. Up a ladder, with tools, at the point where the telephone wires enter the Allardecks' house. What were they doing there?'

There was a pause, then Tunny flicked his fingers again.

'He's Allardeck's brother-in-law. Mrs Allardeck's brother.'

'Quite right,' I said. 'I was staying with them last night when your men came to break in.'

'They didn't break in,' Leggatt said. 'On the contrary, they were, I understand, quite savagely attacked. Allardeck should be arrested for assault.'

'We thought they were burglars. What would you think if you found people climbing a ladder set against your house at dead of night? It was only after we'd chased them off that we found they weren't after the silver.'

'Found? How found?'

'They left their jackets behind, full of credit cards and other things with their names on.'

'Which you propose to return.'

'Naturally. But I'd like a proper explanation of why they were there at all. Wire-tapping is illegal, and we disturbed them in the act of removing a tap which had been in place for at least two weeks, according to the telephone engineer who came this morning to complete the dismantling.'

They said nothing, just waited with calculating eyes.

I went on. 'Your paper mounted an unprovoked and damaging attack on Bobby Allardeck, using information gleaned by illegal means. Tell me why.'

They said nothing.

I said, 'You were sent, Mr Leggatt, a special delivery letter containing proof that all of Bobby Allardeck's creditors had been paid and he was not going bankrupt. Why don't you now try to undo a fraction of the misery you've caused him and my sister? Why don't you print conspicuously in Intimate Details an apology for mis-representing Bobby's position? Why don't you outline the paragraph in red and get your two busy nocturnal journalists to scoot up to Newmarket with the edition hot off the presses like before, and while the town is asleep deliver a copy personally to every recipient who was on their earlier round? And why don't you send a red-inked copy to each of Bobby's owners, as before? That would be most pleasing, don't you think?'

They didn't looked pleased in the slightest.

'It's unfortunate,' I said mildly, 'that it's one's duty as a citizen to report illegal acts to the relevant authorities.'

Without any show of emotion Sam Leggatt turned his head towards the silent Mr Evans. After a pause Mr Evans briefly nodded.

'Do it,' Sam Leggatt said to Tunny.

Tunny was thunderstruck. 'No.'

'Print the apology and get the papers delivered.'

'But . . .'

'Don't you know a barrel when you see one?' He looked back at me. 'And in return?'

'Watts's credit cards and Erskine's Press Club pass.'

'And you'll still have . . .?'

'Their jackets, a chequebook, photos, letters, note-books, a diary and a neat little bugging system.'

195

He nodded. 'And for those?'

'Well,' I said slowly, 'how about if you asked your lawyers what you would be forced to pay to Bobby if the wire-tapping came to court? If you cared to compensate him at that level now we would press no charges and save you the bad publicity and the costs and the penalties of a trial.'

'I have no authority for that.'

'But you could get it.'

He merely stared, without assent or denial.

'Also,' I said, 'the answer to why the attack was made. Who suggested it? Did you direct your journalists to break the law? Did they do it at their own instigation? Were they paid to do it, and if so by whom?'

'Those questions can't be answered.'

'Do you yourself know the answers?'

He said flatly, 'Your bargaining position is strong enough only for the apology and the delivery of the apology, and you shall have those, and I will consult on the question of compensation. Beyond that, nothing.'

I knew a stone wall when I saw one. The never-reveal-your-sources syndrome at its most flexible. Leggatt was telling me directly that answering my questions would cause the *Flag* more trouble than my reporting them for wire-tapping, which being so I would indeed get nothing else.

'We'll settle for the compensation,' I said. 'We would have to report the wire-tapping quite soon. Within a few days.' I paused. 'When a sufficient apology appears in the paper on Friday morning, and I've checked on the Newmarket deliveries, I'll see that the credit cards and the Press Club pass reach you here at your front desk.'

'Acceptable,' Leggatt said, smothering a protest from Tunny. 'I agree to that.'

I nodded to them and turned and went out through the door, and when I'd gone three steps felt a hand on my arm and found Leggatt had followed me.

'Off the record,' he said, 'what would you do if you discovered who had suggested the Allardeck attacks?'

I looked into sandy brown eyes, at one with the hair. At the businesslike outward presentation of the man who daily printed sneers, innuendo, distrust and spite, and spoke without showing a trace of them.

'Off the record,' I said, 'bash his face in.'

CHAPTER ELEVEN

I didn't suppose an apology printed in the *Flag* would melt Bobby's bank manager's cash register heart, and I was afraid that the *Flag*'s compensation, if they paid it, wouldn't be enough, or soon enough, to make much difference.

I thought with a sigh of the manager in my own bank, who had seen me uncomplainingly through bad patches in the past and had stuck out his neck later to lend me capital for one or two business excursions, never pressing prematurely for repayment. Now that I looked like being solvent for the foreseeable future he behaved the same as ever, friendly, helpful, a generous source of advice.

Getting the apology printed was more a gesture than an end to Bobby's troubles, but at least it should reassure the owners and put rock back under the quick-sands for the tradespeople in Newmarket. If the stable could be saved, it would be saved alive, not comatose.

I'd got from Sam Leggatt a tacit admission that the *Flag* had been at fault, and the certainty that he knew the answers to my questions. I needed those answers immediately and had no hope of unlocking his tongue.

With a sense of failure and frustration I booked into a nearby hotel for the night, feeling more tired than I liked to admit and afraid of falling asleep on the seventy dark miles home. I ordered something to eat from room service and made a great many telephone calls between yawns.

First, to Holly.

'Well done, today,' she said.

'What?'

'Your win, of course.'

'Oh, yes.' It seemed a lifetime ago. 'Thanks.'

'Where are you?' she said. 'I tried the cottage.'

'In London.' I told her the hotel and my room number. 'How are things?'

'Awful.'

I told her about the *Flag* promising to print the apology, which cheered her a little but not much.

'Bobby's out. He's gone walking on the Heath. It's all dreadful. I wish he'd come back.'

The anxiety was raw in her voice and I spent some time trying to reassure her, saying Bobby would certainly return soon, he would know how she worried; and privately wondering if he wasn't sunk so deep in his own despair that he'd have no room for imagining Holly's.

'Listen,' I said after a while. 'Do something for me, will you?'

'Yes. What?'

'Look up in the form books for Maynard's horse Metavane. Do you remember, it won the 2000 Guineas about eight years ago?'

'Vaguely.'

'I want to know who owned it before Maynard.'

'Is it important?' She sounded uninterested and dispirited.

'Yes. See if you can find out, and ring me back.'

'All right.'

'And don't worry.'

'I can't help it.'

No one could help it, I thought, disconnecting. Her unhappiness settled heavily on me as if generated in my own mind.

I telephoned Rose Quince at the home number she had given me on my way out, and she answered breathlessly at the eighth ring saying she had just that minute come through the door.

'So they didn't throw you to the presses?' she said.

'No. But I fear I got bounced off the flak jacket.'

'Not surprising.'

'All the same, read Intimate Details on Friday. And by the way, do you know a man called Tunny? He edits Intimate Details.'

'Tunny,' she said. 'Tug Tunny. A memory like a floppy disc, instant recall at the flick of a switch. He's been in the gossip business all his life. He probably pulled the wings off butterflies as a child and he's ful-filled if he can goad any poor slob to a messy divorce.'

'He didn't look like that,' I said dubiously.

'Don't be put off by the parsonage exterior. Read his column. That's *him*.'

'Yes. Thanks. And what about Owen Watts and Jay Erskine?'

'The people who left their belongings in your sister's garden?'

'That's right.'

'Owen Watts I've never heard of before today,' Rose said. 'Jay Erskine ... if it's the same Jay Erskine, he used to work on the *Towncrier* as a crime reporter.'

There were reservations in her voice, and I said persuasively, 'Tell me about him.'

'Hm.' She paused, then seemed to make up her mind. 'He went to jail some time ago,' she said. 'He was among criminals so much because of his job, he grew to like them, like policemen sometimes do. He got tried for conspiracy to obstruct the course of justice. Anyway, if it's the same Jay Erskine, he was as hard as nails but a terrific writer. If he wrote those pieces about your brother-in-law, he's sold out for the money.'

'To eat,' I said.

'Don't get compassionate,' Rose said critically. 'Jay Erskine wouldn't.'

'No,' I said. 'Thanks. Have you been inside the *Flag* building?'

'Not since they did it up. I hear it's gruesome. When

Pollgate took over he let loose some decorator who'd been weaned on orange kitchen plastic. What's it like?'

'Gruesome,' I said, 'is an understatement. What's Pollgate like himself?'

'Nestor Pollgate, owner of the *Flag* as of a year ago,' she said, 'is reported to be a fairly young upwardly mobile shit of the first water. I've never met him myself. They say a charging rhinoceros is safer.'

'Does he have editorial control?' I asked. 'Does Sam Leggatt print to Pollgate's orders?'

'In the good old days proprietors never interfered,' she said nostalgically. 'Now, some do, some still don't. Bill Vaughnley gives general advice. The old Lord edited the *Towncrier* himself in the early years, which was different. Pollgate bought the *Flag* over several smarting dead bodies and you'll see old-guard *Flag* journalists weeping into their beer in Fleet Street bars over the whipped-up rancour they have to dip their pens in. The editor before Sam Leggatt threw in the sponge and retired. Pollgate has certainly dragged the *Flag* to new heights of depravity, but whether he stands over Leggatt with a whip, I don't know.'

'He wasn't around tonight, I don't think,' I said.

'He spends his time putting his weight about in the City, so I'm told. Incidentally, compared with Pollgate, your man Maynard is a babe in arms with his small takeovers and his saintly front. They say Pollgate doesn't give a damn what people think of him, and his financial bullying starts where Maynard's leaves off.'

'A right darling.'

'Sam Leggatt I understand,' she said. 'Pollgate I don't. If I were you I wouldn't twist the *Flag*'s tail any further.'

'Perhaps not.'

'Look what they did to your brother-in-law,' she said, 'and be warned.'

'Yes,' I said soberly. 'Thank you.'

'Any time.'

She said goodbye cheerfully and I sat drinking a glass of wine and thinking of Sam Leggatt and the fearsome manipulator behind him: wondering if the campaign against Maynard had originated from the very top, or from Leggatt or from Tunny, or from Watts and Erskine, or from outside the *Flag* altogether, or from one of Maynard's comet-trail of victims.

The telephone rang and I picked up the receiver, hearing Holly's voice saying without preamble, 'Maynard got Metavane when he was an unraced two-year-old, and I couldn't find the former owners in the form book. But Bobby has come back now, and he says he thinks they were called Perryside. He's sure his grandfather used to train for them, but they seem to have dropped right out of racing.'

'Um,' I said. 'Have you got any of those old *Racing Who's Who*s? They had pages of owners in them, with addresses. I've got them, but they're in the cottage, which isn't much good tonight.'

'I don't think we've got any from ten years ago,' she

said doubtfully, and I heard her asking Bobby. 'No, he says not.'

'Then I'll ring up Grandfather and ask him. I know he's kept them all, back to the beginning.'

'Bobby wants to know what's so important about Metavane after all these years.'

'Ask him if Maynard still owns any part of Metavane.'

The murmuring went on and the answer came back. 'He thinks Maynard still owns one share. He syndicated the rest for millions.'

I said, 'I don't know if Metavane's important. I'll know tomorrow. Keep the chin up, won't you?'

'Bobby says to tell you the dragon has started up the drive.'

I put the receiver down smiling. If Bobby could make jokes he had come back whole from the Heath.

Grandfather grumbled that he was ready for bed but consented to go downstairs in his pyjamas. 'Perryside,' he said, reading, 'Major Clement Perryside, The Firs, St Albans, Hertfordshire, telephone number attached.' Disgust filled the old voice. 'Did you know the fella had his horses with Allardeck?'

'Sorry, yes.'

'To hell with him, then. Anything else? No? Then goodnight.'

I telephoned to the Perryside number he'd given me and a voice at the other end said, Yes, it was The Firs, but the Perrysides hadn't lived there for about seven years. The voice had bought the house from Major and Mrs Perryside, and if I would wait they might find their new address and telephone number.

I waited. They found them. I thanked them; said goodnight.

At the new number another voice said, No, Major and Mrs Perryside don't live here any more. The voice had bought the bungalow from them several months back. They thought the Perrysides had gone into sheltered housing in Hitchin. Which sheltered housing? They couldn't say, but it was definitely in Hitchin. Or just outside. They thought.

Thank you, I said, sighing, and disconnected.

Major and Mrs Perryside, growing older and perhaps poorer, knowing Maynard had made millions from their horse: could they still hold a grievance obsessional enough to set them tilting at him at this late stage? But even if they hadn't, I thought it would be profitable to talk to them.

If I could find them; in Hitchin, or outside.

I telephoned to my answering machine in the cottage and collected my messages: four from various trainers, the one from Holly, and a final unidentified man asking me to ring him back, number supplied.

I got through to Wykeham Harlowe first because he, like my grandfather, went early to bed, and he, too, said he was in his pyjamas.

We talked for a while about that day's runners and those for the next day and the rest of the week, normal more or less nightly discussions. And as usual nowadays he said he wouldn't be coming to Towcester tomorrow, it was too far. Ascot, he said, on Friday and Saturday. He would go to Ascot, perhaps only on one day, but he'd be there.

'Great,' I said.

'You know how it is, Paul,' he said. 'Old bones, old bones.'

'Yes,' I said. 'I know. This is Kit.'

'Kit? Of course you're Kit. Who else would you be?'

'No one,' I said. 'I'll ring you tomorrow night.'

'Good, good. Take care of those novices. Goodnight, then, Paul.'

'Goodnight,' I said.

I talked after that with the three other trainers, all on the subject of the horses I'd be riding for them that week and next, and finally, after ten o'clock and yawning convulsively, I got through to the last, unidentified, number.

'This is Kit Fielding,' I said.

'Ah.' There was a pause, then a faint but discernible click. 'I'm offering you,' said a civilized voice, 'a golden opportunity.'

He paused. I said nothing. He went on, very smoothly, 'Three thousand before, ten thousand after.'

'No,' I said.

'You haven't heard the details.'

I'd heard quite enough. I disconnected without

saying another word and sat for a while staring at walls I didn't see.

I'd been propositioned before, but not quite like that. Never for such a large sum. The before-and-after merchants were always wanting jockeys to lose races to order, but I hadn't been approached by any of them seriously for years. Not since they'd tired of being told no.

Tonight's was an unknown voice, or one I hadn't heard often enough to recognize. High in register. Education to match. Prickles wriggled up my spine. The voice, the approach, the amount, the timing, all of them raised horrid little suggestions of entrapment.

I sat looking at the telephone number I'd been given.

A London number. The exchange 722. I got through to the operator and asked whereabouts in London one would find exchange 722, general information printed in London telephone directories. Hold on, she said, and told me almost immediately; 722 was Chalk Farm stroke Hampstead.

I thanked her. Chalk Farm stroke Hampstead meant absolutely nothing, except that it was not an area known for devotion to horse racing. Very much the reverse, I would have thought. Life in Hampstead tended to be intellectually inward-looking, not raucously open-air.

Why Hampstead . . .

I fell asleep in the chair.

*

After a night spent at least half in bed I drank some coffee in the morning and went out shopping, standing in draughty doorways in Tottenham Court Road, waiting for the electronic wizards to unbolt their steel-mesh shutters.

I found a place that would re-record Rose's professional three-quarter-inch tape of Maynard on to a domestic size to fit my own player, no copyright questions asked. The knowingly obliging youth who performed the service seemed disgusted and astounded that the contents weren't pornographic, but I cheered him up a little by buying a lightweight video-recording camera, a battery pack to run it off and a number of new tapes. He showed me in detail how to work everything and encouraged me to practise in the shop. He could point me to a helpful little bachelor club, he said, if I needed therapy.

I declined the offer, piled everything in the car, and set off north to Hitchin, which was not exactly on the direct route to Towcester but at least not in a diametrically opposite direction.

Finding the Perrysides when I got there was easy: they were in the telephone book. Major C. Perryside, 14 Conway Retreat, Ingle Barton. Helpful locals pointed me to the village of Ingle Barton, three miles outside the town, and others there explained how to find number 14 in the retirement homes.

The houses themselves were several long terraces of small one-storey units, each with its own brightly painted front door and strip of minute flower bed. Paths alone led to the houses: one had to park one's car on a tarmac area and walk along neatly paved ways between tiny segments of grass. Furniture removal men, I thought, would curse the lay-out roundly, but it certainly led to an air of unusual peace, even on a cold damp morning in November.

I walked along to number 14, carrying the video camera in its bag. Pressed the bell push. Waited.

Everywhere was quiet, and no one answered the door. After two or three more unsuccessful attempts at knocking and ringing I went to the door of the right-hand neighbour and tried there.

An old lady answered, round, bright-eyed, interested.

'They walked round to the shop,' she said.

'Do you know how long they'll be?'

'They take their time.'

'How would I know them?' I asked.

'The Major has white hair and walks with a stick. Lucy will be wearing a fishing hat, I should think. And if you're thinking of carrying their groceries home for them, young man, you'll be welcomed. But don't try to sell them encyclopaedias or life insurance. You'll be wasting your time.'

'I'm not selling,' I assured her.

'Then the shop is past the car park and down the lane to the left.' She gave me a sharp little nod and retreated behind her lavender door, and I went where she'd directed.

I found the easily recognizable Perrysides on the point of emerging from the tiny village stores, each of them carrying a basket and moving extremely slowly. I walked up to them without haste and asked if I could perhaps help.

'Decent of you,' said the Major gruffly, holding out his basket.

'What are you selling?' Lucy Perryside said suspiciously, relinquishing hers. 'Whatever it is, we're not buying.'

The baskets weren't heavy: the contents looked meagre.

'I'm not selling,' I said, turning to walk with them at the snail's pace apparently dictated by the Major's shaky legs. 'Would the name Fielding mean anything to you?'

They shook their heads.

Lucy under the battered tweed fishing hat had a thin imperious-looking face, heavily wrinkled with age but firm as to mouth. She spoke with clear upper-class diction and held her back ramrod straight as if in defiance of the onslaughts of time. Lucy Perryside, in various guises and various centuries, had pitched pride against bloody adversity and come through unbent.

'My name is Kit Fielding,' I said. 'My grandfather trains horses in Newmarket.'

The Major stopped altogether. 'Fielding. Yes. I remember. We don't like to talk about racing. Better keep off the subject, there's a good chap.'

I nodded slightly and we moved on as before, along the cold little lane with the bare trees fuzzy with the foreboding of drizzle; after a while Lucy said, 'That's why he came, Clement, to talk about racing.'

'Did you?' asked the Major apprehensively.

'I'm afraid so, yes.'

This time, however, he went on walking, with, it seemed to me, resignation; and I had an intense sense of the disappointments and downward adjustments he had made, swallowing his pain and behaving with dignity, civil in the face of disasters.

'Are you a journalist?' Lucy asked.

'No . . . a jockey.'

She gave me a sweeping glance from head to foot. 'You're too big for a jockey.'

'Steeplechasing,' I said.

'Oh.' She nodded. 'We didn't have jumpers.'

'I'm making a film,' I said. 'It's about hard luck stories in racing. And I wondered if you would help with one segment. For a fee, of course.'

They glanced at each other, searching each other's reactions, and in their private language apparently decided not to turn down the offer without listening.

'What would we have to do?' Lucy asked prosaically.

'Just talk. Talk to my camera.' I indicated the bag I

was carrying along with the baskets. 'It wouldn't be difficult.'

'Subject?' the Major asked, and before I could tell him he sighed and said, 'Metavane?'

'Yes,' I said.

They faced up to it as to a firing squad, and Lucy said eventually, 'For a fee. Very well.'

I mentioned an amount. They made no audible comment, but it was clear from their nods of acceptance that it was enough, that it was a relief, that they badly needed the money.

We made our slow progress across the car park and down the path and through their bright blue front door, and at their gestured invitation I brought out the camera and fed in a tape.

They grouped themselves naturally side by side on the sofa whose chintz cover had been patched here and there with different fabrics. They sat in a room unexpectedly spacious, facing large sliding windows which let out on to a tiny secluded paved area where in summer they could sit in the sun. There was a bedroom, Lucy said, and a kitchen and a bathroom, and they were comfortable, as I could see.

I could see that their furniture, although sparse, was antique, and that apart from that it looked as if everything saleable had been sold.

I adjusted the camera in the way I'd been taught and balanced it on a pile of books on a table, kneeling behind it to see through the viewfinder.

'OK,' I said, 'I'll ask you questions. Would you just look into the camera lens while you talk?'

They nodded. She took his hand: to give courage, I thought, rather than to receive.

I started the camera silently recording and said, 'Major, would you tell me how you came to buy Metavane?'

The Major swallowed and blinked, looking distinguished but unhappy.

'Major,' I repeated persuasively, 'please do tell me how you bought Metavane.'

He cleared his throat. 'I er . . . we . . . always had a horse, now and then. One at a time. Couldn't afford more, do you see? But loved them.' He paused. 'We asked our trainer . . . he was called Allardeck . . . to buy us a yearling at the sales. Not too expensive, don't you know. Not more than ten thousand. That was always the limit. But at that price we'd had a lot of fun, a lot of good times. A few thousand for a horse every four or five years, and the training fees. Comfortably off, do you see.'

'Go on, Major,' I said warmly as he stopped. 'You're doing absolutely fine.'

He swallowed. 'Allardeck bought us a colt that we liked very much. Not brilliant to look at, rather small, but good blood lines. Our sort of horse. We were delighted. He was broken in during the winter and during the spring he began to grow fast. Allardeck said we shouldn't race him then until the autumn, and of course we took his advice.' He paused. 'During the summer he developed splendidly and Allardeck told us he was very speedy and that we might have a really good one on our hands if all went well.'

The ancient memory of those heady days lit a faint glow in the eyes, and I saw the Major as he must have been then, full of boyish enthusiasm, inoffensively proud.

'And then, Major, what happened next?'

The light faded and disappeared. He shrugged. He said, 'Had a bit of bad luck, don't you know.'

He seemed at a loss to know how much to say, but Lucy, having contracted for gain, proved to have fewer inhibitions.

'Clement was a member of Lloyd's,' she said. 'He was in one of those syndicates which crashed ... many racing people were, do you remember? He was called upon, of course, to make good his share of the losses.'

'I see,' I said, and indeed I did. Underwriting insurance was fine as long as one never actually had to pay out.

'A hundred and ninety-three thousand pounds,' the Major said heavily, as if the shock was still starkly fresh, 'over and above my Lloyd's deposit, which was another twenty-five. Lloyd's took that, of course, straight away. And it was a bad time to sell shares. The market was down. We cast about, do you see, to know what to do.' He paused gloomily, then went on, 'Our house was already mortgaged. Financial advisers, you understand, had always told us it was best to mortgage one's house and use the money for investments. But the investments had gone badly down ... some of them never recovered.'

The flesh on his old face drooped at the memory of failure. Lucy looked at him anxiously, protectively stroking his hand with one finger.

'It does no good to dwell on it,' she said uneasily. 'I'll tell you what happened. Allardeck got to hear of our problems and said his son Maynard could help us, he understood finance. We'd met Maynard once or twice and he'd been charming. So he came to our house and said if we liked, as we were such old owners of his father, he would lend us whatever we needed. The bank had agreed to advance us fifty thousand on the security of our shares, but that still left a hundred and forty. Am I boring you?'

'No, you are not,' I said with emphasis. 'Please go on.'

She sighed. 'Metavane was going to run in about six weeks and I suppose we were clutching at straws, we hoped he would win. We needed it so badly. We didn't want to have to sell him unraced for whatever we could get. If he won he would be worth very much more. So we were overwhelmed by Maynard's offer. It solved all our problems. We accepted. We were overjoyed. We banked his cheque and Clement paid off his losses at Lloyd's.'

Sardonic bitterness tugged at the corners of her mouth, but her neck was still stretched high.

'Was Maynard charging you interest?' I asked.

'Very low,' the Major said. 'Five per cent. Damned good of him, we thought.' The downward curve of his mouth matched his wife's. 'We knew it would be a struggle, but we were sure we would get back on our feet somehow. Economize, do you see. Sell things. Pay him back gradually. Sell Metavane, when he'd won.'

'Yes,' I said. 'What happened next?'

'Nothing much for about five weeks,' Lucy said. 'Then Maynard came to our house again in a terrible state and told us he had two very bad pieces of news for us. He said he would have to call in some of the money he had just lent us as he was in difficulties himself, and almost worse, his father had asked him to tell us that Metavane had lamed himself out at exercise so badly that the vet said he wouldn't be fit to run before the end of the season. It was late September by then. We'd counted on him running in October. We were absolutely, completely shattered, because of course we couldn't afford any longer to pay training fees for six months until racing started again in March, and worse than that, a lame unraced two-year-old at the end of the season isn't worth much. We wouldn't be able to sell him for even what we'd paid for him.'

She paused, staring wretchedly back to the heartbreak.

'Go on,' I said.

She sighed. 'Maynard offered to take Metavane off our hands.'

'Is that how he put it?'

'Yes. Exactly. Take him off our hands is what he said. He said moreover he would knock ten thousand off our debt, just as if the colt was still worth that much. But, he said, he desperately needed some cash, and couldn't we possibly raise a hundred thousand for him at once.' She looked at me bleakly. 'We simply couldn't. We went through it all with him, explaining. He could see that we couldn't pay him without borrowing from a moneylender at a huge interest and he said in no way would he let us do that. He was understanding and charming and looked so worried that in the end we found ourselves comforting him in his troubles, and assuring him we'd do everything humanly possible to repay him as soon as we could.'

'And then?'

'Then he said we'd better make it all legal, so we signed papers transferring ownership of Metavane to him. He changed the amount we owed him from a hundred and forty to a hundred and thirty thousand, and we signed a banker's order to pay him regularly month by month. We were all unhappy, but it seemed the best that could be done.'

'You let him have Metavane without contingencies?' I asked. 'You didn't ask for extra relief on your debt if the horse turned out well?'

Lucy shook her head wearily. 'We didn't think about

217

contingencies. Who thinks about contingencies for a lame horse?'

'Maynard said he would have to put our interest payments up to ten per cent,' the Major said. 'He kept apologizing, said he felt embarrassed.'

'Perhaps he was,' I said.

Lucy nodded. 'Embarrassed at his own wickedness. He went away leaving us utterly miserable, but it was nothing to what we felt two weeks later. Metavane ran in a two-year-old race at Newmarket and won by three lengths. We couldn't believe it. We saw the result in the paper. We telephoned Allardeck at once. And I suppose you'll have guessed what he said?'

I half nodded.

'He said he couldn't think why we thought Metavane was lame. He wasn't. He never had been. He had been working brilliantly of late on the Heath.'

CHAPTER TWELVE

'You hadn't thought, I suppose,' I said gently, 'to ask to see the vet's report? Or even to check with Allardeck?'

Lucy shook her head. 'We took Maynard's word.'

The Major nodded heavily. 'Trusted him. Allardeck's son, do you see.'

Lucy said, 'We protested vigorously, of course, that Maynard had told us a deliberate lie, and Maynard said he hadn't. He just denied he'd ever told us Metavane wouldn't run before spring. Took our breath away. Clement complained to the Jockey Club, and got nowhere. Maynard charmed them too. Told them we had misunderstood. The Stewards were very cool to Clement. And do you know what I think? I think Maynard told them we were trying to screw yet more money out of him, when he'd been so generous as to help us out of a dreadful hole.'

They were both beginning to look distressed and I had a few twinges of conscience of my own. But I said, 'Please tell me the state of your debt now, and how much Maynard shared with you out of his winnings and the syndication of Metavane as a stallion.'

They both stared.

The Major said as if surprised, 'Nothing.'

'How do you mean, nothing?'

'He didn't give us a farthing.'

'He syndicated the horse for several millions,' I said.

The Major nodded. 'We read about it.'

'I wrote to him,' Lucy said, her cheeks slightly pink. 'I asked him to at least release us from what we owed him.'

'And?'

'He didn't answer.'

'Lucy wrote twice,' the Major said uncomfortably. 'The second time, she sent it special delivery, to be handed to him personally, so we know he must have received it.'

'He didn't reply,' Lucy said.

'We borrowed the money and that's that,' the Major said with resignation. 'Repayments and interest take most of our income, and I don't think we will ever finish.'

Lucy stroked his hand openly. 'We are both eighty-two, you see,' she said.

'And no children?' I asked.

'No children,' Lucy said regretfully. 'It wasn't to be.'

I packed away the camera, thanking them and giving them the cash I'd collected for paying Bobby's lads, proceeds of cashing one of Bobby's cheques with my valet at Newbury. My valet, a walking bank, had found the service routine and had agreed to bring cash for the other cheques to Towcester.

The Major and Lucy accepted the money with some embarrassment but more relief, and I wondered if they had feared I might not actually pay them once I'd got what I wanted. They'd learned in a hard school.

I looked at my watch and asked if I could make a quick credit card call on their telephone. They nodded in unison, and I got through to the manager where I banked.

'John,' I said.

'Kit.'

'Look, I'm in a hurry, on my way to ride at Towcester, but I've been thinking ... It's true, isn't it, that money can be paid into my account without my knowing?'

'Yes, by direct transfer from another bank, like your riding fees. But you'd see it on your next statement.'

'Well,' I said, 'except for my riding fees, could you see to it that nothing gets paid in? If anything else arrives, can you refuse to put it into my account?'

'Yes, I can,' he said doubtfully, 'but why?'

'Someone offered me a bribe last night,' I said. 'It felt too much like a set-up. I don't want to find I've been sneakily paid by a back door for something I don't intend to do. I don't want to find myself trying to tell the Stewards I didn't take the money.'

He said after a short pause, 'Is this one of your intuitions?'

'I just thought I'd take precautions.'

'Yes,' he said. 'All right. If anything comes, I'll check with you before crediting your account.'

'Thanks,' I said. 'Until further notice.'

'And perhaps you would drop me a line putting your instructions in writing? Then you would be wholly safe, if it came to the Stewards.'

'I do not know,' I said, 'what I would do without you.'

I said goodbye to the Perrysides and drove away, reflecting that it was their own total lack of sensible precautions which had crystallized in me the thought that I should prudently take my own.

They should have insured in the first place against a catastrophic loss at Lloyd's and they should have brought in an independent vet to examine Metavane. It was easy to see these things after the event. The trick for survival was to imagine them before.

Towcester was a deep-country course, all rolling green hills sixty miles to the north-west of London. I drove there with my mind on anything except the horses ahead.

Mostly I thought about precautions.

With me in the car, besides my overnight bag, I had the tapes of Maynard, the tape of the Perrysides, the video camera and a small hold-all of Holly's containing the jackets and other belongings of Jay Erskine and Owen Watts. Without all those things I would not be able to get any sort of compensation or future for Bobby and Holly, and it occurred to me that I should make sure that no one stole them.

Sam Leggatt or anyone else at the *Flag* would see that repossessing the journalists' belongings would be a lot cheaper and less painful than coughing up cash and printing and distributing humble apologies.

Owen Watts and Jay Erskine were bound to be revengeful after the damage they had suffered, and they could be literally anywhere, plotting heaven knew what.

I was driving to a time and place printed in more than half the daily newspapers: my name plain to see on the racing pages, declared overnight for the one-thirty, two o'clock, three o'clock and three-thirty races.

If I were Jay Erskine, I thought, I would be jemmying open Kit Fielding's Mercedes at one-thirty, two o'clock, three o'clock or three-thirty.

If I were Owen Watts, perhaps at those times, I would be breaking into Kit Fielding's cottage in Lambourn.

They might.

They might not.

I didn't think a little active breaking and entering would disturb their consciences in the least, especially as the current penalties for a conviction for wire-tapping ran to a two thousand pound fine or up to two years in prison, or both.

I didn't know that I would recognize them from the mêlée in the dark. They could however make it their business to know me. To watch for my arrival in the jockeys' car park. To note my car.

It took forty-five minutes to drive from the Perrysides' village to Towcester racecourse and for half the journey I thought I was being unnecessarily fanciful.

Then abruptly I drove into the centre of the town of Bletchley and booked myself into an old and prosperous looking hotel, the Golden Lion. They took an impression of my credit card and I was shown to a pleasant room, where I hung Watt's and Erskine's jackets in the closet, draped my night things around the bathroom and stowed everything else in a drawer. The receptionist nodded pleasantly and impersonally when I left the key at the desk on my way out, and no one else took any notice; and with a wince at my watch but feeling decidedly safer I broke the speed limit to Towcester.

The princess's novices were the first and last of my booked rides, with another for Wykeham and one for the Lambourn trainer in between.

The princess was waiting with her usual lambent patina in the parade ring when I went out there, and so was Danielle, dressed on that damp day in a blazing red shiny coat over the black trousers. I suppose my pleasure showed. Certainly both of them smiled down their noses in the way women do when they know they're admired, and Danielle, instead of shaking my hand, gave me a brief peck of a kiss on the cheek, a half touch of skin to skin, unpremeditated, the sensation lingering surprisingly in my nerve endings.

She laughed. 'How're you doing?' she said.

'Fine. And you?'

'Great.'

The princess said mildly, 'What do we expect from Kinley, Kit?'

I had a blank second of non-comprehension before remembering that Kinley was her horse. The one I was about to ride: three years old, still entire, a dappled grey going to the starting gate as second favourite for the first race of his life. High time, I thought, that I concentrated on my job.

'Dusty says he's travelled well; he's excited but not sweating,' I said.

'And that's good?' Danielle asked.

'That's good,' said the princess, nodding.

'He's mature for three, he jumps super at home and I think he's fast,' I said.

'And it all depends, I suppose, on whether he enjoys it today.'

'Yes,' I said. 'I'll do my best.'

'Enjoys it?' Danielle asked, surprised.

'Most horses enjoy it,' I said. 'If they don't, they won't race.'

'Do you remember Snowline?' the princess said. I

nodded, and she said to Danielle, 'Snowline was a mare I had a long time ago. She was beautiful to look at and had won two or three times on the Flat, and I bought her to be a hurdler, partly, I must confess, because of her name, but she didn't like jumping. I kept her in training for two years because I had a soft spot for her, but it was a waste of money and hope.' She smiled. 'Wykeham tried other jockeys, do you remember, Kit? For the second of those she wouldn't even start. I learned a great lesson. If a horse doesn't like racing, cut your losses.'

'What became of Snowline?' Danielle said.

'I sold her as a brood mare. Two of her foals have been winners on the Flat.'

Danielle looked from her aunt to me and back again. 'You both totally love it, don't you?'

'Totally,' said the princess.

'Totally,' I agreed.

I got up on Kinley and walked him slowly up past the stands to let him take in the sounds and smells, and then down towards the start, giving him a long close look at a flight of hurdles, letting him stand chest-high, almost touching, looking out over the top. He pricked his ears and extended his nostrils, and I felt the instinct stir in him most satisfactorily, the in-bred compulsion that ran in the blood like a song, the surging will to race and win.

You, Kinley, I thought, know all I've been able to teach you about jumping, and if you mess it up today you'll be wasting all those mornings I've spent with you on the schooling grounds this autumn.

Kinley tossed his head. I smoothed a hand down his neck and took him on to the start, mingling there with two or three other complete novices and about ten who had run at least once before but never won. The youngest a horse was allowed to go jump racing in Britain was in the August of its three-year-old year, and Kinley's was a two-mile event for three-year-olds who hadn't yet won.

Some jockeys avoided doing schooling sessions, but I'd never minded, on the basis that if I'd taught the horse myself I'd know what it could and wouldn't do. Some trainers sent green horses to crash around race-courses with only the haziest idea of how to meet a jump right, but Wykeham and I were in accord: it was no good expecting virtuoso jumping in public without arpeggios at home.

Wykeham was in the habit of referring to Kinley as Kettering, a horse he'd trained in the distant past. It was amazing, I sometimes thought, that the right horses turned up at the meetings: Dusty's doing, no doubt.

Kinley circled and lined up with only an appropriate amount of nervousness and when the tapes went up, set off with a fierce plunge of speed. Everything was new to him, everything unknown; nothing on the home gallops ever prepared a horse for the first rocketing reality. I settled him gradually with hands and mind, careful not to do it too much, not to teach him that what he was really feeling was wrong but just to control it, to keep it simmering, to wait.

He met the first hurdle perfectly and jumped it cleanly and I clearly felt his reaction of recognition, his increase in confidence. He let me shorten his stride a little approaching the second hurdle so as to meet it right and avoid slowing to jump, and at the third flight he landed so far out on the other side that my spirits rose like a bird. Kinley was going to be good. One could tell sometimes right from the beginning, like watching a great actor in his first decent role.

I let him see every obstacle clearly, mostly by keeping him to the outside. Technically the inside was the shortest way, but also the more difficult. Time for squeezing through openings when he could reliably run straight.

Just keep it going, Kinley old son, I told him; you're doing all right. Just take a pull here, that's right, to get set for the next jump, and now go for it, go for it ... dear bloody hell, Kinley, you'll leave me behind, jumping like that, just wait while I get up here over your shoulders, I don't see why we can't kick for home, first time out, why not, it's been done, get on there, Kinley, you keep jumping like that and we'll damned near win.

I gave him a breather on the last uphill section and he was most aggrieved at my lack of urging, but once round the last bend, with one jump left before the run-in, I shook him up and told him aloud to get on with it, squeezing him with the calves of my legs, sending him rhythmic messages through my hands, telling him OK, my son, now fly, now run, now stretch out your bloody neck, this is what it's all about, this is your future, take it, embrace it, it's all yours.

He was bursting with pride when I pulled him up, learning at once that he'd done right, that the many pats I gave him were approval, that the applause greeting his arrival in the winners' enclosure was the curtain call for a smash hit. Heady stuff for a novice; and I reckoned that because of that day he would run his guts out to win all his life.

'He enjoyed it,' the princess said, glowing with pleasure.

'He sure did.'

'Those jumps . . .'

I unbuckled my saddle and drew it off on to my arm.

'He's very good,' I said. 'You have seriously got a good horse.'

She looked at me with speculation, and I nodded. 'You never know. Too soon to be sure.'

'What on earth are you talking about?' Danielle demanded.

'The Triumph Hurdle,' said her aunt.

I went to weigh in, change and weigh out and go through the whole rigmarole again with Wykeham's second runner, which didn't belong to the princess but to a couple in their seventies who cared just as much.

They owned only the one horse, an ageing 'chaser who'd been retired once and had pined until he'd been sent back into training, and I was truly pleased for them when, because of his experience, he stood up throughout the three miles as others fell, and against all the odds thundered along insouciantly into first place.

Wykeham might not go to the meetings, I thought, gratefully pulling up, he might have his mental grooves stuck in the past, but he sure as hell could still train winners.

I watched the next race after that from the jockeys' stand, and won the one after for the Lambourn trainer. One of those days, I thought contentedly. A treble. It happened once or twice a season, not much more.

It occurred to me as I was unbuckling my saddle in the winners' enclosure that Eric Olderjohn, the owner of the horse, who was present and quietly incandescent with delight, was something to do with the Civil Service on a high level, a fact I knew only because he occasionally lamented that government business would keep him away from seeing his pride and joy run.

I asked him on an impulse if I could talk to him for a few minutes after I'd weighed in and changed for the next race, and rather in the Vaughnley mould he said 'Anything' expansively, and was waiting there as promised when I went out.

We talked for a bit about his win, which was uppermost in his mind, and then he asked what I wanted. I wanted, I said, the answers to a couple of questions, and I wondered if he could – or would – get them for me.

'Fire away,' he said. 'I'm listening.'

I explained about the newspaper attacks on Bobby and Maynard, and to my surprise he nodded.

'I've heard about this, yes. What are your questions?'

'Well, first, whether Maynard was in fact being considered for a knighthood, and second, if he was, who would have known?'

He half laughed. 'You don't want much, do you?' He shook his head. 'Patronage is not my department.' He looked up at the sky and down at the colours I wore, which were by then the princess's. 'What good would it do you to find out?'

'I don't know,' I said frankly. 'But someone ought to make reparation to Bobby and my sister.'

'Hm. Why don't they ask these questions themselves?'

I said blankly, 'But they wouldn't.'

'They wouldn't, but you would.' His eyes were half assessing, half amused.

'Those newspaper articles were maliciously unfair,' I said positively. 'Bobby and my sister Holly are gentle well-intentioned people trying to make a success of training and doing no harm to anyone.'

'And the newspaper attack on them makes you angry?'

'Yes, it does. Wouldn't it you?'

He considered it. 'An attack on my daughter would, yes.' He nodded briefly. 'I don't promise, but I'll ask.'

'Thank you very much,' I said.

He smiled, turned to go and said, 'Win for me again next time out.'

I said I hoped to, and wondered why I'd described Bobby as gentle when the marks of his fists lay scattered on my body among the dark red attentions of the hurdlers. Bobby was brother to the wind, the seed of the tornado dormant in the calm.

I went back into the changing room for my helmet and stick and then out to the parade ring again for the sixth and last race of the day, the two-mile novice 'chase.

'Totally awesome,' Danielle said, standing there.

'What is?' I asked.

'We went down in the medic's car to one of the fences. We stood right by there watching you jump. That speed . . . so fast . . . you don't realize, from the stands.'

'In the three-mile 'chase,' the princess said, nodding.

'The medic said you were all going over there at better than thirty miles an hour. He says you're all crazy. He's right.'

The princess asked me if I thought I'd be making it four for the day, but I thought it unlikely: this one, Dhaulagiri, hadn't as much talent as Kinley.

'There's a woman riding in this race,' Danielle observed, watching the other jockeys standing in groups with the owners. She looked at me without archness. 'What do you think if you're beaten in a race by a woman?'

'That she had a faster horse,' I said.

'Ouch.'

The princess smiled but made no comment. She knew I didn't like racing against the very few women who rode professionally over jumps, not for fear of a male ego-battering, but because I couldn't rid myself of protectiveness. A male opponent could take his bumps, but I'd never learned to ride ruthlessly against a female; and moreover I didn't like the idea of what falls and horses' hooves could do to their faces and bodies. The women jockeys despised my concern for them, and took advantage of it if they could.

Dhaulagiri was looking well, I thought, watching him walk round. Better than when I'd schooled him the previous week. Tauter. A new lean line of muscle on the haunch. Something in the carriage of the head.

'What is it, Kit?' the princess asked.

I looked from the horse to her enquiring face. 'He's improved since last week,' I said.

'Wykeham said he seemed to like jumping fences better than hurdles.'

'Yes, he did.'

Her eyes smiled. 'Do you think, then . . .?'

'It would be nice, wouldn't it?'

'Exquisite,' she said.

I nodded and went away on Dhaulagiri to the start,

and in some odd way it seemed a jaunt to the horse as much as to me. Three winners raised my spirits euphorically. Dhaulagiri could jump. So why not, why bloody not make it four. Dhaulagiri took the mood from his jockey, as all horses do. I reckon Dhaulagiri on that afternoon would have light-heartedly jumped off a cliff if I'd asked him.

It wasn't the most advisable tactic for a horse running for the first time over the bigger fences and I dared say Wykeham would have deplored it, but Dhaulagiri and I went round the whole two miles in friendly, fully stretched recklessness, and at the winning post I thought for nearly the thousandth time in my life that there was nothing in existence comparable to the shared intense joy of victory. Better perhaps, but comparable, no. I was laughing aloud when we pulled up.

The exhilaration lasted all the way back to the changing room and in and out of the shower, and only marginally began to abate when my valet handed me a zipped webbing belt stuffed full of Bobby's money. Jockeys' valets washed one's breeches and took one's saddles and other belongings from racecourse to racecourse, turning up with everything clean every day. Besides that they were the grapevine, the machine oil, the comforters and the bank. My valet said he was lending me the money-belt he used himself on holidays, as he didn't like the idea of me walking around with all those thousands in my pockets.

Bobby, I thought, sighing. I would drive to Bletchley and collect my stuff from the Golden Lion, and then go on to Newmarket to give the money to Bobby so he could pay his lads at the normal time the next day and stack the rest away in his safe. I would sleep there and go direct to Ascot in the morning.

I strapped the belt against my skin and buttoned my shirt over it, the valet nodding approval. It didn't show, he said.

I thanked him for his thoughtfulness, finished dressing, and went out for a briefer than usual talk with the princess, whose eyes were still sparkling behind the sheltering lashes.

Vague thoughts I'd had of asking Danielle to help celebrate my four winners over dinner disintegrated when she said she was again due at her bureau at six-thirty, and they would be leaving for London at any moment.

'Do you work at weekends?' I asked.

'No.'

'Could . . . er, could I ask you out on Saturday evening?'

She glanced at her aunt, and so did I, but as usual one could tell nothing from the princess's face that she didn't want one to see. I felt no withdrawal, though, coming from her mind, and nor, it seemed, did her niece.

'Yes,' Danielle said, 'you could. I'll be coming to Ascot. After the races, we might make plans.'

235

Extraordinary, I thought. She understood. She had of course come close to seeing her ride from Devon to London evaporate at the third hurdle two days ago. Two days. That too was extraordinary. I seemed to have known her for longer.

'Tomorrow at Ascot,' the princess said to me, shaking my hand in goodbye. 'How long can we go on winning?'

'Until Christmas.'

She smiled. 'Christmas Fielding.'

'Yes.'

Danielle said, 'What do you mean, Christmas Fielding?'

'It's my name,' I said.

'What? I mean, I know it says C. Fielding on the number boards, but I took it for granted that Kit was for Christopher.'

I shook my head. 'We were born on Christmas morning. Christmas and Holly. No accounting for parents.'

There was warmth in her eyes as well as in the princess's. I left them saying their thanks to their hosts for the day before starting home, and with swelling contentment walked out to my own car.

At the sight of it most of the contentment vanished into anger. All four tyres were flat, the window on the driver's side was broken, and the lid of the boot hovered halfway open.

I said aloud and precisely about four obscene words

and then shrugged and turned to go back into the racecourse to telephone. The AA could deal with it. I could hire another car. The things I'd feared losing were safe in the Golden Lion and if that was what the vandals had been looking for, they were out of luck.

Most people had already left, but there were still a few cars in the park, still a person or two moving about. I was thinking chiefly of inconvenience and paying little attention to anything else, and very suddenly there was a voice at my left ear saying, 'Stand still, Fielding', and another man crowding against my right elbow with the same message.

I did stand still, too taken by surprise to think of doing anything else.

From each side the message reached me clearly.

Reached through my jacket, through my shirt and into my skin, somewhere above the money-belt.

'That's right,' said the one who'd spoken before. 'We've come to repossess some property. You don't want to get cut, do you?'

CHAPTER THIRTEEN

I certainly didn't.

'See that grey Ford over there right by the road,' said the man on my left. 'We're going to get into it, nice and easy. Then you'll tell us where to go for some jackets and the things in the pockets. We'll be sitting one each side of you on the back seat, and we're going to tie your hands, and if you make any sudden moves we'll slice your tendons so you won't stand again, never mind ride horses. You got that?'

Dry mouthed, I nodded.

'You've got to learn there's people you can't push around. We're here to teach you. So now walk.'

They were not Owen Watts and Jay Erskine. Different build, different voices, older and much heavier. They underlined their intentions with jabs against my lower ribs, and I did walk. Walked stiff-legged towards the grey Ford.

I would give them what they wanted: that was simple. Owen Watts's credit cards and Jay Erskine's Press Club pass weren't worth being crippled for. It was what would happen after the Golden Lion that seized up the imagination and quivered in the gut. They weren't going to release me with a handshake and a smile. They had as good as said so.

There was a third man, a driver, sitting in the Ford. At our approach he got out of the car and opened both rear doors. The car itself was pointing in the direction of the way out to the main road.

There seemed to be no one within shouting distance. No one near enough to help. I decided sharply and suddenly that all the same I wouldn't get into the car. I would run. Take my chances in the open air. Better under the sky than in some little dark corner; than on the back seat of a car with my hands tied. I would have given them the jackets but their priority was damage, and their intention of it was reaching me like shock waves.

It came to the point of now or never, and I was already tensing my muscles for it to be now, when a large quiet black car rolled along the road towards the racecourse exit and stopped barely six feet away from where I stood closely flanked. The nearside rear window slid down and a familiar voice said, 'Are you in trouble, Kit?'

I never was more pleased to see the princess in all my life.

'Say no,' the man on the left directed into my ear, screwing his knife round a notch. 'Get rid of them.'

'Kit?'

'Yes,' I said.

The princess's face didn't change. The rear door of her Rolls swung widely open and she said economically, 'Get in.'

I leapt. I jumped. I dived into her car head first, landing on my hands as lightly as possible across her ankles and Danielle's, flicking from there to the floor.

The car was moving forward quite fast even before the princess said, 'Drive on, Thomas' to her chauffeur, and I saw the angry faces of my three would-be captors staring in through the windows, heard their fists beating on the glossy bodywork, their hands trying to open the already centrally locked doors.

'They've got knives,' Danielle said in horror. 'I mean . . . *knives*.'

Thomas accelerated further, setting the heavy men running alongside and then leaving them behind, and I fumbled my way up on to one of the rear-facing folding seats and said I was sorry.

'Sorry!' Danielle exclaimed.

'For involving you in such a mess,' I said to the princess. I rubbed my hand across my face. 'I'm very sorry.'

Thomas said without noticeable alarm, 'Madam, those three men are intending to follow us in a grey Ford car.'

I looked out through the tinted rear window and saw that he was right. The last of them was scrambling in, fingers urgently pointing.

'Then we'd better find a policeman,' the princess said calmly; but as on every other racing day the police had left the racecourse as soon as the crowds had gone. There was no one at the racecourse gate directing traffic, since there was no longer any need. Thomas slowed and turned in the direction of London and put his foot smoothly on the accelerator.

'If I might suggest, madam?' he said.

'Yes. Go on.'

'You would all be safer if we kept going. I don't know where the police station is in Stony Stratford, which is the first town we come to. I would have to stop to ask directions.'

'If we go to a police station,' Danielle said anxiously, 'they'll keep us there for ages, taking statements, and I'll be terribly late.'

'Kit?' the princess asked.

'Keep going,' I said. 'If that's all right.'

'Keep going then, Thomas,' said the princess, and Thomas, nodding, complied. 'And now, Kit,' she said, 'tell us why you needed to be rescued in such a melodramatic fashion.'

'They had knives on him,' Danielle said.

'So I observed. But why?'

'They wanted something I've got.' I took a deep breath, trying to damp down the incredible relief of not being a prisoner in the car behind, trying to stop myself trembling. 'It started with some newspaper articles about my brother-in-law, Bobby Allardeck.'

She nodded. 'I heard about those from Lord Vaughnley yesterday, after you'd gone.'

'I've got blood on my leg,' Danielle said abruptly. 'How did I get . . .' She was looking down at her ankles, and then lifted her head suddenly and said to me, 'When you flew in like an acrobat, were you bleeding? Are you still bleeding?'

'I suppose so.'

'What do you mean, you suppose so? Can't you feel it?'

'No.' I looked inside my jacket, right and left.

'Well?' Danielle demanded.

'A bit,' I said.

Maybe the heavies hadn't expected me to jump with their knives already in. Certainly they'd reacted too slowly to stop me, ripping purposefully, but too late. The sting had been momentary, the aftermath ignorable. A little blood, however, went a long way.

The princess said resignedly, 'Don't we carry a first-aid box, Thomas?'

Thomas said 'Yes, madam' and produced a black box from a built-in compartment. He held it over his shoulder, and I took it, opened it, and found it contained useful-sized padded absorbent sterile dressings and all manner of ointments and sticky tapes. I took out one of the thick dressings and found two pairs of eyes watching.

'Excuse me,' I said awkwardly.

'You're embarrassed!' Danielle said.

'Mm.'

I was embarrassed by the whole situation. The princess turned her head away and studied the passing fields while I groped around under my shirt for somewhere to stick the dressing. The cuts, wherever they were, proved to be too far round for me to see them.

'For heaven's sake,' Danielle said, still watching, 'let me do it.'

She removed herself from the rear seat facing me to the folding seat by my side, took the dressing out of my hand and told me to hold my shirt and jacket up so that she could see the action. When I did she lifted her head slowly and looked at me directly.

'I simply don't believe you can't feel that.'

I smiled into her eyes. Whatever I felt was a pinprick to what I'd been facing. 'Stick the dressing on,' I said.

'All right.'

She stuck it on, and we changed places so she could do the other one, on my left. 'What a mess,' she said, wiping her hands and returning to the rear seat while I tucked my shirt untidily into my trousers. 'That first cut is long and horribly deep and needs stitches.'

The princess stopped staring out of the window and looked at me assessingly.

'I'll be all right for racing tomorrow,' I said.

Her mouth twitched. 'I would expect you to say that, if you had two broken legs.'

'I probably would.'

'Madam,' Thomas said, 'we're approaching the motorway and the grey Ford is still on our tail.'

The princess made an indecisive gesture with her hands. 'I suppose we'd better go on,' she said. 'What do you think?'

'On,' Danielle said positively, and Thomas and I nodded.

'Very well. On to London. And now, Kit, tell us what was happening.'

I told them about Bobby and me finding the journalists dismantling their wire-tap, and about removing their jackets before letting them go.

The princess blinked.

I said I had offered to return the jackets if the *Flag* would print an apology to Bobby and also pay some compensation. I explained about finding my car broken into, and about the suddenness with which my assailants had appeared.

'They wanted those jackets,' I said. 'And although I'd thought about robbery, I hadn't expected violence.' I couldn't think why not, after the violence of Bobby's assault on Owen Watts. I paused. 'I can't thank you enough.'

'Thank Thomas,' the princess said. 'Thomas said you were in trouble. I wouldn't have known.'

'Thank you, Thomas.'

'You could see it a mile off,' he said.

'You were pretty quick getting away.'

'I went to a lecture once about how not to get your employer kidnapped.'

'Thomas!' said the princess. 'Did you really?'

He said seriously, 'I wouldn't want to lose you, madam.'

The princess was moved and for once without an easy surface answer. Thomas, who had driven her devotedly for years, was a large quiet middle-aged Londoner with whom I talked briefly most days in racecourse car parks, where he sat and read books in the Rolls. I'd asked him once long ago if he didn't get bored going to the races every day when he wasn't much interested in horses and didn't gamble, and he'd said no, he liked the long journeys, he liked his solitude and most of all he liked the princess. He and I both, in many ways opposites, would I dare say have died for the lady.

I thought, all the same, that she wouldn't much care for the alarms of the continuing present. I looked back to the grey car still steadfastly following and began to consider what to do to vanish. I was thinking about perhaps diving down into thick undergrowth once we'd left the motorway, when the car behind suddenly swerved dangerously from the centre lane, cut across the slow lane to a wild blowing of horns and disappeared down a side road.

Thomas made a sort of growl in his throat and said with relief, 'They've gone into the service station.'

'You mean we've lost them?' Danielle said, twisting to look back.

'They peeled off.' To telephone, I supposed, a no-success story.

The princess said 'Good' as if that ended the matter entirely, and, greatly released, began to talk of her horses, of the day's triumphs, of more pleasing excitements, tracking with intent and expertise away from the alien violent terror of maiming steel back to the safe familiar danger of breaking one's neck.

By the time we reached central London she had returned the atmosphere to a semblance of full normality, behaving as if my presence in her car were commonplace, the tempestuous entrance overlooked. She would have gone with good manners to the scaffold, I thought, and was grateful for the calm she had laid upon us.

Within the last mile home, with dusk turning to full night, the princess asked Thomas if he would drive her niece to Chiswick as usual and return for her when she'd finished work.

'Certainly, madam.'

'Perhaps,' I said, 'I could fetch Danielle instead? Save Thomas the trip.'

'At two in the morning?' Danielle said.

'Why not?'

'OK.'

The princess made no comment, showed no feeling. 'It seems you have the night off, Thomas' was all she said; and to me, 'If you are wanting to go to the police, Thomas will drive you.'

I shook my head. 'I'm not going to the police.'

'But,' she said doubtfully, 'those horrid men . . .'

'If I go to the police, you will be in the newspapers.'

She said 'Oh' blankly. Cavorting about saving her jockey from a bunch of knife-wielding heavies was not the sort of publicity she yearned for. 'Do what you think best,' she said faintly.

'Yes.'

Thomas braked to a halt outside her house in Eaton Square and opened the car door for us to disembark. On the pavement I thanked the princess for the journey. Politeness conquered all. With the faintest gleam of amusement she said she would no doubt see me at Ascot, and as on ordinary days held out her hand for a formal shake, accepting the sketch of a bow.

'I don't believe it,' Danielle said.

'If you get the form of things right,' the princess said to her sweetly, 'every peril can be tamed.'

I bought a shirt and an anorak and booked into a hotel for the night, stopping in the lobby to rent a car from an agency booth there.

'I want a good one,' I said. 'A Mercedes, if you have one.'

They would try, they assured me.

Upstairs I changed from the slashed bloodstained

shirt and jacket into the new clothes, and began another orgy of telephoning.

The Golden Lion via directory enquiries said there was no problem, they would hold my room for another day, they had my credit card number, too bad I'd been unexpectedly detained, my belongings would be perfectly safe.

The AA said not to worry, they would rescue my car from Towcester racecourse within the hour. If I phoned in the morning, they would tell me where they'd taken it for repairs.

My answering system in the cottage had been hard-worked with please-ring-back messages from the police, my neighbour, my bank manager, Rose Quince, three trainers and Sam Leggatt.

My neighbour, an elderly widow, sounded uncommonly agitated, so I called her back first.

'Kit, dear, I hope I did right,' she said. 'I saw a strange man moving about in your cottage and I told the police.'

'You did right,' I agreed.

'It was lunchtime and I knew you'd be at Towcester, I always follow your doings. Four winners! It was on the radio just now. Well done.'

'Thanks . . . What happened at the cottage?'

'Nothing, really. I went over when the police came to let them in with my key. They couldn't have been more than five minutes getting there, but there wasn't anyone in the cottage. I felt so foolish, but then one of the policemen said a window was broken, and when they looked around a bit more they said someone had been in there searching. I couldn't see anything missing. Your racing trophies weren't touched. Just the window broken in the cloakroom.'

I sighed. 'Thank you,' I said. 'You are a dear.'

'I got Pedro from down the road to mend the window. I didn't like to leave it. I mean, anyone could get in.'

'I'll take you for a drink in the pub when I get back.'

She chuckled. 'Thank you, dear. That'll be nice.'

The police themselves had nothing to add. I should return, they said, to check my losses.

I got through to my bank manager at his home and listened to him chewing while he spoke. 'Sorry. Piece of toast,' he said. 'A man came into the bank at lunch-time to pay three thousand pounds into your account.'

'What man?'

'I didn't see him, unfortunately. I was out. It was a banker's draft, not a personal cheque.'

'Damn,' I said feelingly.

'Don't worry, it won't appear on your account. I've put a stop on anything being paid into it, as we agreed. The banker's draft is locked in the safe in my office. What do you want me to do with it?'

'Tear it up in front of witnesses,' I said.

'I can't do that,' he protested. 'Someone paid three thousand pounds for it.'

'Where was it issued?'

'At a bank in the City.'

'Can you ask them if they remember who bought it?'

'Yes, I'll try tomorrow. And be a good chap, let me have the no-paying-in instruction in writing pronto.'

'Yes,' I said.

'And well done with the winners. It was on the radio.'

I thanked him and disconnected, and after some thought left the hotel, walked down the street to an Underground station and from a public phone rang Sam Leggatt at the *Flag*.

There was no delay this time. His voice came immediately on the line, brisk and uncompromising.

'Our lawyers say that what you said here yesterday was tantamount to blackmail.'

'What your reporters did at my brother-in-law's house was tantamount to a jail sentence.'

'Our lawyers say if your brother-in-law thinks he has a case for settlement out of court, his lawyers should contact our lawyers.'

'Yeah,' I said. 'And how long would that take?'

'Our lawyers are of the opinion that no compensation should be paid. The information used in the column was essentially true.'

'Are you printing the apology?'

'Not yet. We haven't gone to press yet.'

'Will you print it?'

He paused too long.

'Did you know,' I said, 'that today someone searched

my cottage, someone smashed their way into my car, two men attacked me with knives, and someone tried to bribe me with three thousand pounds, paid directly into my bank account?'

More silence.

'I'll be telling everyone I can think of about the wire-tapping,' I said. 'Starting now.'

'Where are you?' he said.

'At the other end of the telephone line.'

'Wait,' he said. 'Ring me back, will you?'

'How long?'

'Fifteen minutes.'

'All right.'

I put the receiver down and stood looking at it, drumming my fingers and wondering if the *Flag* really did have equipment which could trace where I'd called from, or whether I was being fanciful.

I couldn't afford, I thought, any more punch-ups. I left the Underground station, walked along the street for ten minutes, went into a pub, rang the *Flag*. My call was again expected: the switchboard put me straight through.

When Sam Leggatt said 'Yes' there were voices raised loudly in the backgound.

'Fielding,' I said.

'You're early.' The backgound voices abruptly stopped.

'Your decision,' I said.

'We want to talk to you.'

'You're talking.'

'No. Here, in my office.'

I didn't answer immediately, and he said sharply, 'Are you still there?'

'Yes,' I said. 'What time do you go to press?'

'First edition, six-thirty, to catch the West Country trains. We can hold until seven. That's the limit.'

I looked at my watch. Fourteen minutes after six. Too late, to my mind, for talking.

'Look,' I said. 'Why don't you just print and distribute the apology? It's surely no big deal. It'll cost you nothing but the petrol to Newmarket. I'll come to your office when you assure me that you're doing that.'

'You'd trust my word?'

'Do you trust mine?'

He said grudgingly, 'Yes, I suppose I do expect you to return what you said.'

'I'll do it. I'll act in good faith. But so must you. You seriously did damage Bobby Allardeck, and you must at least try to put it right.'

'Our lawyers say an apology would be an acknowledgment of liability. They say we can't do it.'

'That's it, then,' I said. 'Goodbye.'

'No, Fielding, wait.'

'Your lawyers are fools,' I said, and put down the receiver.

I went out into the street and rubbed a hand over my head, over my hair, feeling depressed and a loser.

Four winners, I thought. It happened so seldom. I

should be knee-deep in champagne, not banging myself against a brick wall that kicked back so viciously.

The cuts on my ribs hurt. I could no longer ignore them.

I walked dispiritedly along to yet another telephone and rang up a long-time surgical ally.

'Oh, hello,' he said cheerfully. 'What is it this time? A little clandestine bone-setting?'

'Sewing,' I said.

'Ah. And when are you racing?'

'Tomorrow.'

'Toddle round, then.'

'Thanks.'

I went in a taxi and got stitched.

'That's not a horseshoe slash,' he observed, dabbing anaesthetic into my right side. 'That's a knife.'

'Yeah.'

'Did you know the bone is showing?'

'I can't see it.'

'Don't tear it open again tomorrow.'

'Then fix it up tight.'

He worked for a while before patting my shoulder. 'It's got absorbable stitches, also clips and gripping tape, but whether it would stand another four winners is anyone's guess.'

I turned my head. I'd said nothing about the winners.

'I heard it on the news,' he said.

He worked less lengthily on the other cut and

said lightly, 'I didn't think getting knifed was your sort of thing.'

'Nor did I.'

'Want to tell me why it happened?'

He was asking, I saw, for reassurance. He would come to my aid on the quiet, but it was important to him that I should be honest.

'Do you mean,' I said, 'have I got myself into trouble with gamblers and race-fixers and such?'

'I suppose so.'

'Then no, I promise you.' I told him briefly of Bobby's problems and felt his reservations fade.

'And the bruises?' he said.

'I fell under some hurdlers the day before yesterday.'

He nodded prosaically. I paid his fee in cash and he showed me to his door.

'Good luck,' he said. 'Come back when you need.'

I thanked him, caught a taxi and rode back to the hotel thinking of the *Flag* thundering off the presses at that moment without carrying the apology. Thinking of Leggatt and the people behind him; lawyers, Nestor Pollgate, Tug Tunny, Owen Watts and Jay Erskine. Thinking of the forces and the furies I had somehow unleashed. You've got to learn there's people you can't push around, one of the knifemen had said.

Well, I was learning.

The rented car booth in the lobby told me I was in luck, they'd got me a Mercedes; here were the keys, it was in the underground car park; the porter would show me when I wanted to go out. I thanked them. We try harder, they said.

Up in my room I ordered some food from room service and telephoned Wykeham to tell him how his winners had won, catching at least an echo of the elation of the afternoon.

'Did they get home all right?' I asked.

'Yes, they all ate up. Dhaulagiri looks as if he had a hard race but Dusty said he won easy.'

'Dhaulagiri ran great,' I said. 'They all did. Kinley's as good as any you've got.'

We talked of Kinley's future and of the runners at Ascot the next day and Saturday. For Wykeham the months of October, November and December were the peak: his horses came annually into their best form then, the present flourish of successes expected and planned for.

Between 30 September and New Year's Day he ran every horse in his charge as often as he could. 'Seize the moment,' he would say. After Christmas, with meetings disrupted by frost and snow, he let his stable more or less hibernate, resting, regrouping, aiming for a second intense flowering in March. My life followed his rhythms to a great extent, as natural to me as to his horses.

'Get some rest, now,' he said jovially. 'You've got six rides tomorrow, another five on Saturday. Get some good sleep.'

'Yes,' I said. 'Goodnight, Wykeham.'

'Goodnight, Paul.'

My food came and I ate bits of it and drank some wine while I got through to the other trainers who'd left messages, and after that I rang Rose Quince.

'Four winners,' she said. 'Laying it on a bit thick, aren't you?'

'These things happen.'

'Oh, sure. Just hold on to your moment of glory, buddy boy, because I've some negative news for you.'

'How negative?'

'A firm and positive thumbs down from the producer of *How's Trade.* There's no way on earth he's going to say who sicked him on to Maynard Allardeck.'

'But someone did?'

'Oh, sure. He just won't say who. I'd guess he got paid to do it as well as paid not to, if you see what I mean.'

'Whoever paid him to do it must be feeling betrayed.'

'Too bad,' she said. 'See you.'

'Listen,' I said hastily, 'what did Jay Erskine go to jail for?'

'I told you. Conspiracy to obstruct the course of justice.'

'But what did he actually do?'

'As far as I remember, he put some frighteners on to a chief prosecution witness who then skipped the country and never gave evidence, so the villain got off. Why?'

'I just wondered. How long did he get?'

'Five years, but he was out in a lot less.'

'Thanks.'

'You're welcome. And by the way, one of the favours you owed me is cancelled. I took your advice. The venom worked a treat and I'm freed, I'm no longer under the jurisdiction of the chauvinist. So thanks, and goodnight.'

'Goodnight.'

If the *Flag* wanted frighteners, Jay Erskine could get them.

I sighed and rubbed my eyes and thought about Holly, who had been hovering in my mind for ages, telling me to ring her up. She would want the money I still wore round my waist and I was going to have to persuade her and Bobby to come to London or Ascot in the morning to fetch it.

I was going to have to tell her that I hadn't after all managed to get the apology printed. That hers and Bobby's lawyers could grind on for ever and get nothing. That reporting the wire-tapping to all and sundry might inconvenience the *Flag*, but would do nothing to change their bank manager's mind. I put the call through to Holly reluctantly.

'Of course we'll come to fetch the money,' she said. 'Will you please stop talking about it and listen.'

'OK.'

'Sam Leggatt telephoned. The editor of the *Flag*.'

'Did he? When?'

'About an hour ago. An hour and a half. About seven o'clock. He said you were in London, somewhere in the Knightsbridge area, and did I know where you would be staying?'

'What did you say?' I asked, alarmed.

'I told him where you stayed last night. I told him to try there. He said that wasn't in Knightsbridge and I said of course not, but hadn't he heard of taxis. Anyway he wanted to get a message to you urgently, he said. He wanted me to write it down. He said to tell you the apology was being printed at that moment and will be delivered.'

'What! Why on earth didn't you say so?'

'But you told me last night it was going to happen. I mean, I thought you knew.'

'Christ Almighty,' I said.

'Also,' Holly said, 'he wants you to go to the *Flag* tonight. He said if you could get there before ten there would be someone there you wanted to meet.'

CHAPTER FOURTEEN

When I pressed the buzzer and walked unannounced through his unlatching door he was sitting alone in his office, shirt-sleeved behind his shiny black desk, reading the *Flag*.

He stood up slowly, his fingers spread on the paper as if to give himself leverage, a short solid man with authority carried easily, as of right.

I was not who he'd expected. A voice behind me was saying, 'Here it is, Sam', and a man came walking close, waving a folder.

'Yes, Dan, just leave it with me, will you?' Leggatt said, stretching out a hand and taking it. 'I'll get back to you.'

'Oh? OK.' The man Dan went away, looking at me curiously, closing the door with a click.

'I got your message,' I said.

He looked down at his copy of the *Flag*, turned a page, reversed the paper and pushed it towards me across the desk.

I read the Intimate Details that would be titillating

a few million Friday breakfasts and saw that at least he'd played fair. The paragraph was in bold black type in a black-outlined box.

It said:

The Daily Flag *acknowledges that the Newmarket racing stable of Robertson (Bobby) Allardeck (32) is a sound business and is not in debt to local traders. The* Daily Flag *apologizes to Mr Allardeck for any inconvenience he may have suffered in consequence of reports to the contrary printed in this column earlier.*

'Well,' he said, when I'd read.

'Thank you.'

'Bobby Allardeck should thank God for his brother-in-law.'

I looked at him in surprise, and I thought of Bobby's schizophrenic untrustable regard for me, and of my sister, for whom I truly acted. That paragraph should at least settle the nerves of the town and the owners and put the stable back into functionable order: given, of course, that its uneasy underlying finances could be equally sorted out.

'What changed your mind?' I asked.

He shrugged. 'You did. The lawyers said you would back down. I said you wouldn't. They think they can intimidate anybody with their threats of long expensive lawsuits.' He smiled twistedly. 'I said you'd be real poisonous trouble if we didn't print, and you would have been, wouldn't you?'

'Yes.'

He nodded. 'I persuaded them we didn't want Jay Erskine and Owen Watts in court, where you would put them.'

'Particularly as Jay Erskine has a criminal record already.'

He was momentarily still. 'Yes,' he said.

It had been that one fact, I thought, that had swayed them.

'Did Jay Erskine write the attacks on Bobby?' I asked.

After a slight hesitation he nodded. 'He wrote everything except the apology. I wrote that myself.'

He pressed a button on an intercom on his desk and said, 'Fielding's here' neutrally to the general air.

'Where are the credit cards, now we've printed?' he asked.

'You'll get them tomorrow, after the newspapers have been delivered, like I said.'

'You never let up, do you? Owen Watts has set off to Newmarket already and the others are in the post.' He looked at me broodingly. 'How did you find out about the bank?'

'I thought you might try to discredit me. I put a stop on all ingoing payments.'

He compressed his mouth. 'They can't see what they're dealing with,' he said.

The buzzer on his door sounded and he pushed the release instantly. I turned and saw a man I didn't know walking in with interest and no caution. Fairly tall, with a receding hairline over a pale forehead, he wore an ordinary dark suit with a brightly striped tie and had a habit of rubbing his fingers together, like a schoolmaster brushing off chalk.

'David Morse, head of our legal department,' said Sam Leggatt briefly.

No one offered to shake hands. David Morse looked me over as an exhibit, up and down, gaze wandering over the unzipped anorak and the blue shirt and tie beneath.

'The jockey,' he said coolly. 'The one making the fuss.'

I gave no reply, as none seemed useful, and through the open door behind him came another man who brought power with him like an aura and walked softly on the outsides of his feet. This one, as tall as the lawyer, had oiled dark hair, olive skin, a rounded chin, a small mouth and eyes like bright dark beads: also heavy shoulders and a flat stomach in smooth navy suiting. He was younger than either Sam Leggatt or Morse and was indefinably their boss.

'I'm Nestor Pollgate,' he announced, giving me a repeat of the Morse inspection and the same absence of greeting. 'I am tired of your antics. You will return my journalists' possessions immediately.'

His voice, like his body, was virile, reverberatingly bass in unaccented basic English.

'Did you ask me here just for that?' I said.

Don't twist their tail, Rose Quince had said. Ah well.

Pollgate's mouth contracted and he moved round to Leggatt's side of the desk, and the lawyer also, so that they were ranged there in a row like a triumvirate of judges with myself before them, as it were, on the carpet.

I had stood before the racing Disciplinary Stewards once or twice in that configuration, and I'd learned to let neither fright nor defiance show. Every bad experience, it seemed, could bring unexpected dividends. I stood without fidgeting and waited.

'Your contention that we mounted a deliberate campaign to ruin your brother-in-law is rubbish,' Pollgate said flatly. 'If you utter that opinion in public we will sue you.'

'You mounted a campaign to ruin Maynard Allardeck's chance of a knighthood,' I said. 'You aimed to destroy his credibility and you didn't give a damn who else you hurt in the process. Your paper was ruthlessly callous. It often is. I will utter that opinion as often as I care to.'

Pollgate perceptibly stiffened. The lawyer's mouth opened a little and Leggatt looked on the verge of inner amusement.

'Tell me why you wanted to wreck Maynard Allardeck,' I said.

'None of your business.' Pollgate answered with the finality of a bank-vault door, and I acknowledged that if I ever found out it wouldn't be by straightforward questions put to anyone in that room.

'You judged,' I said instead, 'that a sideways swipe at Maynard would be most effective, and you decided to get at him through his son. You gave not a thought to the ruin you were bringing on the son. You used him. You should compensate him for that use.'

'No,' Pollgate said.

'We admit nothing,' the lawyer said. A classically lawyer-like phrase. We may be guilty but we'll never say so. He went on, 'If you persist in trying to extort money by menaces, the *Daily Flag* will have you arrested and charged.'

I listened not so much to the words as to the voice, knowing I'd heard it somewhere recently, sorting out the distinctive high pitch and the precision of consonants and the lack of belief in any intelligence I might have.

'Do you live in Hampstead?' I said thoughtfully.

'What's that got to do with anything?' Pollgate said, coldly impatient.

'Three thousand before, ten after.'

'You're talking gibberish,' Pollgate said.

I shook my head. David Morse was looking as if he'd bitten a wasp.

'You were clumsy,' I said to him. 'You don't know the first thing about bribing a jockey.'

'What is the first thing?' Sam Leggatt asked.

I almost smiled. 'The name of the horse.'

'You admit you take bribes, then,' Morse said defensively.

'No I don't, but I've been propositioned now and then, and you didn't sound right. Also you were recording your offer on tape. I heard you start the machine. True would-be corrupters wouldn't do that.'

'I did advise caution,' Sam Leggatt said mildly.

'You've no proof of any of this,' Pollgate said with finality.

'My bank manager's holding a three thousand pound draft issued in the City. He intends on my behalf to ask questions about its origins.'

'He'll get nowhere,' Pollgate said positively.

'Then perhaps he'll do what I asked him first, which is to tear it up.'

There was a short stark silence. If they asked for the draft back they would admit they'd delivered it, and if they didn't, their failed ploy would have cost them the money.

'Or it could be transferred to Bobby Allardeck, as a first small instalment of compensation.'

'I've heard enough,' Pollgate said brusquely. 'Return the property of our journalists immediately. There will be no compensation, do you understand? None. You

265

will come to wish, I promise you, that you had never tried to extort it.'

Under the civilized suiting he hunched his shoulders like a boxer, rotating them as a physical warning of an imminent onslaught, a flexing of literal muscles before an explosion of mental aggression. I saw in his face all the brutality of his newspaper and also the arrogance of absolute power. No one, I thought, could have defied him for too long, and he didn't intend that I should be an exception.

'If you make trouble for us in the courts,' he said grittily, 'I'll smash you. I mean it. I'll see to it that you yourself are accused of some crime that you'll hate, and I'll get you convicted and sent to prison, and you'll go down, I promise you, dishonoured and reviled, with maximum publicity and disgrace.'

The final words were savagely biting, the intention vibratingly real.

Both Leggatt and Morse looked impassive and I wondered what any of them could read on my own face. Show no fright . . . ye gods.

He surely wouldn't do it, I thought wildly. The threat must be only to deter. Surely a man in his position wouldn't risk his own status to frame and jail an adversary who wanted so little, who represented no life-or-death danger to his paper or to himself, who wielded no corporate power.

All the same, it looked horrible. Jockeys were eternally vulnerable to accusations of dishonesty and it took little to disillusion a cynical public. The assumption of guilt would be strong. He could try harder and more subtly to frame me for taking bribes, and certainly for things worse. What his paper had already set their hand to, they could do again and more thoroughly. A crime I would hate.

I could find no immediate words to reply to him, and while I stood there in the lengthening silence the door alarm buzzed fiercely, making Morse jump.

Sam Leggatt flicked a switch. 'Who is it?' he said.

'Erskine.'

Leggatt looked at Pollgate, who nodded. Leggatt pressed the button that unlatched the door, and the man I'd shaken off the ladder came quietly in.

He was of about my height, reddish haired going bald, with a drooping moustache and chillingly unsmiling eyes. He nodded to the triumvirate as if he'd been talking to them earlier and turned to face me directly, chin tucked in, stomach thrust out, a man with a ruined life behind him and a present mind full of malice.

'You'll give me my stuff,' he said. Not a question, not a statement: more a threat.

'Eventually,' I said.

There was a certain quality of stillness, of stiffening, on the far side of Leggatt's desk. I looked at Pollgate's thunderous expression and realized that I had almost without intending it told him with that one word that his threat, his promise, hadn't immediately worked.

'He's yours, Jay,' he said thickly.

I didn't have time to wonder what he meant. Jay Erskine caught hold of my right wrist and twisted my arm behind my back with a strength and speed that spoke of practice. I had done much the same to him in Bobby's garden, pressing his face into the mud, and into my ear with the satisfaction of an account paid he said, 'You tell me where my gear is or I'll break your shoulder so bad you'll ride no more races this side of Doomsday.'

His vigour hurt. I checked the three watching faces. No surprise, not even from the lawyer. Was this, I wondered fleetingly, a normal course of events in the editor's office of the *Daily Flag*?

'Tell me,' Erskine said, shoving.

I took a sharp half-pace backwards, cannoning into him. I went down in a crouch, head nearly to the floor, then straightened my legs with the fiercest possible jerk, pitching Jay Erskine bodily forwards over my shoulders, where he let go of my wrist and sailed sprawlingly into the air. He landed with a crash on a potted palm against the far wall while I completed the rolling somersault and ended upright on my feet. The manoeuvre took a scant second in the execution: the stunned silence afterwards lasted at least twice as long.

Jay Erskine furiously tore a leaf from his mouth and struggled pugnaciously to right himself, almost pawing the carpet like a bull for a second charge.

'That's enough,' I said. 'That's bloody enough.'

I looked directly at Nestor Pollgate. 'Compensation,' I said. 'Another of your banker's drafts. One hundred thousand pounds. Tomorrow. Bobby Allardeck will be coming to Ascot races. You can give it to him there. It could cost you about that much to manufacture a crime I didn't commit and have me convicted. Why not save yourself the trouble.'

Jay Erskine was upright and looking utterly malignant.

I said to him, 'Pray the compensation's paid ... Do you want another dose of the slammer?'

I walked to the door and looked briefly back. Pollgate, Leggatt and Morse had wiped-slate faces: Jay Erskine's was glitteringly cold.

I wondered fearfully for a second if the door's unlatching mechanism also locked and would keep me in; but it seemed not. The handle turned easily, came smoothly towards me, opening the path of escape.

Out of the office, along the passage to the lifts my feet felt alarmingly detached from my legs. If I believed Pollgate's threats I was walking into the bleakest of futures: if I believed Erskine's malevolence it would be violent and soon. Why in God's name, I thought despairingly, hadn't I given in, given them the jackets, let Bobby go bust.

There were running footsteps behind me across the mock-marble hallway outside the lifts, and I turned fast, expecting Erskine and danger, but finding, as once before, Sam Leggatt.

His eyes widened at the speed with which I'd faced him.

'You expected another attack,' he said.

'Mm.'

'I'll come down with you.' He pressed the button for descent and stared at me for a while without speaking while we waited.

'One hundred thousand,' he said finally, 'is too much. I thought you meant less.'

'Yesterday, I did.'

'And today?'

'Today I met Pollgate. He would sneer at a small demand. He doesn't think in peanuts.'

Sam Leggatt went back to staring, blinking his sandy lashes, not showing his unspoken thoughts.

'That threat,' I said slowly, 'about sending me to prison. Has he used that before?'

'What do you mean?'

'On someone else.'

'What makes you think so?'

'You and your lawyer,' I said, 'showed no surprise.'

The lift purred to a halt inside the shaft and the doors opened. Leggatt and I stepped inside.

'Also,' I said, as the doors closed, 'the words he used sounded almost rehearsed. "You'll go down, I promise you, dishonoured and reviled, with maximum publicity and disgrace." Like a play, don't you think?'

He said curiously, 'You remember the exact words?'

'One wouldn't easily forget them.' I paused. 'Did he mean it?'

'Probably.'

'What happened before?'

'He wasn't put to the test.'

'Do you mean, the threat worked?' I asked.

'Twice.'

'Jesus,' I said.

I absent-mindedly rubbed my right shoulder, digging in under the anorak with the left thumb and fingers to massage. 'Does he always get his way by threats?'

Leggatt said evenly, 'The threats vary to suit the circumstances. Does that hurt?'

'What?'

'Your shoulder.'

'Oh. Yes, I suppose so. Not much. No worse than a fall.'

'How did you do that? Fling him off you, like that?'

I half grinned. 'I haven't done it since I was about fifteen, same as the other guy. I wasn't sure it would work with a grown man, but it did, a treat.'

We reached the ground floor and stepped out of the lift.

'Where are you staying?' he asked casually.

'With a friend,' I said.

He came with me halfway across the ornate entrance hall, stopping beside the small fountain.

'Why did Nestor Pollgate want to crunch Maynard Allardeck?' I said.

'I don't know.'

'Then it wasn't your idea or Erskine's? It came from the top?'

'From the top.'

'And beyond,' I said.

'What do you mean?'

I frowned. 'I don't know. Do you?'

'As far as I know, Nestor Pollgate started it.'

I said ruefully, 'Then I didn't exactly smash his face in.'

'Not far off.'

There was no shade of disloyalty in his voice, but I had the impression that he was in some way apologizing: the chief's sworn lieutenant offering comfort to the outcast. The chief's man, I thought. Remember it.

'What do you plan to do next?' he said.

'Ride at Ascot.'

He looked steadily into my eyes and I looked right back. I might have liked him, I thought, if he'd steered any other ship.

'Goodbye,' I said.

He seemed to hesitate a fraction but in the end said merely, 'Goodbye' and turned back to the lifts: and I went out into Fleet Street and breathed great gulps of free air under the stars.

I walked the two miles back to the hotel and sat in my room for a while there contemplating the walls, and then I went down to find the rented Mercedes in the underground park and drove it out to Chiswick.

'You're incredibly early,' Danielle said, faintly alarmed at my arrival. 'I did say two a.m., not half after eleven.'

'I thought I might just sit here and watch you, as no one seemed to mind me being here last time.'

'You'll be bored crazy.'

'No.'

'OK.'

She pointed to a desk and chair close to hers. 'No one's using that tonight. You'll be all right there. Did you get that cut fixed?'

'Yes, it's fine.'

I sat in the chair and listened to the mysteries of newsgathering, American style, for the folks back home. The big six-thirty evening slot, eastern US time, was being aired at that moment, it appeared. The day's major hassle had just ended. From now until two, Danielle said, she would be working on anything new and urgent which might make the eleven o'clock news back home, but would otherwise be on the screens at breakfast.

'Does much news happen here at this time of night?' I asked.

'Right now we've got an out-of-control fire in an oil terminal in Scotland and at midnight Devil-Boy goes on stage at a royal charity gala to unveil a new smash.'

'Who?' I said.

'Never mind. A billion teenagers can't be wrong.'

'And then what?' I said.

'After we get the pictures? Transmit them back here from a mobile van, edit them, and transmit the finished article to the studios in New York. Sometimes at midday here we do live interviews, mostly for the seven-to-nine morning show back home, but nothing live at nights.'

'You do edit the tapes here?'

'Sure. Usually. Want to see?'

'Yes, very much.'

'After I've made these calls.' She gestured to the telephone and I nodded, and subsequently listened to her talking to someone at the fire.

'The talent is on his way back by helicopter from the race riot and should be with you in ten minutes. Get him to call me when he can. How close to the blaze are you? OK, when Cervano gets to you try to go closer, from that distance a volcano would look like a sparkler. OK, tell him to call me when he's reached you. Yeah, OK, get him to call me.'

She put down the receiver, grimacing. 'They're a good mile off. They might as well be in Brooklyn.'

'Who's the talent?' I said.

'Ed Cervano. Oh . . . the talent is any person behind a microphone talking to the camera. News reporter, anchor, anyone.'

She looked along the headings on the board on the

wall behind her chair. 'Slug. That's the story we're working on. Oil fire. Devil-Boy. Embassy. So on.'

'Yes,' I said.

'Locations, obvious. Time, obvious. Crew. That's the camera crew which is allocated to that story, and also the talent. Format, that's how fully we're covering a story. Package means the works, camera crew, talent, interviews, the lot. Voice-over is just a cameraman, with the commentary tagged on later. So on.'

'And it's you who decides who goes where for what?'

She half nodded. 'The bureau chief, and the other coordinators, who work in the daytime, and me, yes.'

'Some job,' I said.

She smiled with her eyes. 'If we do well, the company's ratings go up. If we do badly, we get fired.'

'The news is the news, surely,' I said.

'Oh yes? Which would you prefer, an oil fire from a mile off or to think you feel the flames?'

'Mm.'

Her telephone rang. 'News,' she said, and listened. 'Look,' she said, sounding exasperated, 'if he's late, it's news. If he's sick, it's news. If he doesn't make it on to the stage at a royal gala, it's news. You just stay there, whatever happens is news, OK? Get some shots of royalty leaving, if all else fails.' She put down the receiver. 'Devil-Boy hasn't arrived at the theatre and it takes him a good hour to dress.'

'The joys of the non-event.'

'I don't want to be scooped by one of the other broadcasting companies, now do I?'

'Where do you get the news from in the first place?'

'Oh . . . the press agencies, newspapers, police broadcasts, publicity releases, things like that.'

'I guess I never wondered before how the news arrived on the box.'

'Ten seconds' worth can take all day to gather.'

Her telephone rang again, with the helicoptering Ed Cervano now down to earth at the other end. Danielle asked him in gentle tones to go get himself a first degree burn, and from her smile it seemed he was willing to go up in flames entirely for her sake.

'A sweet-talking guy,' she said, putting down the receiver. 'And he writes like a poet.' Her eyes were shining over the talent's talents, her mouth curving from his honey.

'Writes?' I said.

'Writes what he says on the news. All our news reporters write their own stuff.'

Another message came through from the royal gala: Devil-Boy, horns and all, was reported on his way to the theatre in a bell-ringing ambulance.

'Is he sick?' Danielle asked. 'If it's a stunt, make sure you catch it.' She disconnected, shrugging resignedly. 'The hip-wriggling imp of Satan will get double the oil fire exposure. Real hell stands no chance against the fake. Do you want to see the editing rooms?'

'Yes,' I said, and followed her across the large office and down a passage, admiring the neatness of her walk and wanting to put my hands deep into her cloud of dark hair, wanting to kiss her, wanting quite fiercely to take her to bed.

She said, 'I'll show you the studio first, it's more interesting,' and veered down a secondary passage towards a door warningly marked 'If red light shows, do not enter'. No red light shone. We went in. The room was moderate in size, furnished barely with a couple of armchairs, a coffee table, a television camera, a television set, a teleprompter and a silent coffee machine with paper cups. The only surprise was the window, through which one could see a stretch of the Thames and Hammersmith Bridge, all decked with lights and busily living.

'We do live interviews in here in front of the window,' Danielle said. 'Mostly politicians but also actors, authors, sportsmen, anyone in the news. Red buses go across the bridge in the background. It's impressive.'

'I'm sure,' I said.

She gave me a swift look. 'Am I boring you?'

'Absolutely not.'

She wore pink lipstick and had eyebrows like wings. Dark smiling eyes, creamy skin, long neck to hidden breasts like apples on a slender stem . . . For Christ's sake, Kit, I thought, drag your mind off it and ask some sensible questions.

'How does your stuff get from here to America?' I said.

'From in here.' She walked over to a closed door in one of the walls, and opened it. Beyond it was another room, much smaller, dimly lit, which was warm and hummed faintly with walls of machines.

'This is the transmitter room,' she said. 'Everything goes from in here by satellite, but don't ask me how, we have a man with a haunted expression twiddling the knobs and we leave it to him.'

She closed the transmitter room door and we went through the studio, into the passage and back to the editing rooms, of which there were three.

'OK,' she said, switching a light on and revealing a small area walled on one side by three television screens, several video recorders and racks of tape cassettes, 'this is what we still use, though I'm told there's a load of new technology round the corner. Our guys here like these machines, so I guess we'll have them around for a while yet.'

'How do they work?' I asked.

'You run the unedited tape through on the left-hand screen and pick out the best bits, then you record just those on to the second tape, showing on the second screen. You can switch it all around until it looks good and you get a good feeling. We transmit it like that, but New York often cuts it shorter. Depends how much else they've got to fit in.'

'Can you work these machines yourself?' I asked.

'I'm slow. If you really want to know now, you can watch Joe later when we get the oil fire and Devil-Boy tapes – he's one of the best.'

'Great,' I said.

'I'm surprised you're so interested.'

'Well, I've some tapes I want to edit myself. It would be nice to learn how.'

'Is that why you came here so early?' She sounded as if I might say yes without at all offending her.

I said, 'Partly. Mostly to see you . . . and what you do.'

She was close enough to hug and I had no insight at all into what she was thinking. A brick wall between minds. Disconcerting.

She looked with friendliness but nothing else into my face, and the only thing I was sure of was that she didn't feel as I did about a little uninhibited love-making on the spot.

She asked if I would like to see the library and I said yes please: and the library turned out to be not books but rows and rows of recorded tapes, past years of news stories forgotten but waiting like bombs in the dark, records of things said, undeniable.

'Mostly used for obituaries,' Danielle said. 'Reactivated scandals. Things like that.'

We returned to her news desk, where over the next hour I sat and listened to the progress of events (Devil-Boy had arrived at the stage door, fit, well and fully made-up in a blaze of technicolor lights to the gratified

279

hysterics of a streetful of fans) and met Danielle's working companions, the bureau chief, Joe the editor, the gaunt transmitter expert, two spare cameramen and a bored and unallocated female talent. About sixty people altogether worked for the bureau, Danielle said, but of course never all at one time. The day shift, from ten to six-thirty, was much bigger: in the daytime there were two to do her job.

At one o'clock Ed Cervano telephoned to say they'd gotten a whole load of spectacular shots of the oil fire but the blaze was now under control and the story was as dead as tomorrow's ashes.

'Bring back the tapes anyway,' Danielle said. 'We don't have any oil fire stock shots in the library.'

She put down the receiver resignedly. 'So it goes.'

The crew from the royal gala returned noisily bearing Devil-Boy's capers themselves, and at the same time a delivery man brought a stock of morning newspapers to put on Danielle's desk for her to look through for possible stories. The *Daily Flag*, as it happened, lay on top, and I opened it at Intimate Details to re-read Leggatt's words.

'What are you looking at?' Danielle asked.

I pointed. She read the apology and blinked.

'I didn't think you stood a chance,' she said frankly. 'Did they agree to the compensation also?'

'Not so far.'

'They'll have to,' she said. 'They've practically admitted liability.'

I shook my head. 'British courts don't award huge damages for libel. It's doubtful whether Bobby would actually win if he sued, and even if he won, unless the *Flag* was ordered to pay his costs, which also isn't certain, he simply couldn't afford the lawyers' fees.'

She gazed at me. 'Back home you don't pay the lawyers unless you win. Then the lawyers take their slice of the damages. Forty per cent, sometimes.'

'It's not like that here.'

Here, I thought numbly, one bargained with threats. On the one side: I'll get your wrist slapped by the Press Council, I'll get questions asked in Parliament, I'll see your ex-convict journalist back in the dock. And on the other, I'll slice your tendons, I'll lose you your jockey's licence for taking bribes, I'll put you in prison. Reviled, dishonoured, and with publicity, disgraced.

Catch me first, I thought.

CHAPTER FIFTEEN

I watched Joe the editor, dark-skinned and with rapid fingers, sort his way through a mass of noisy peacock footage, clicking his tongue as a sort of commentary to himself, punctuating the lifted sections he was stringing together to make the most flamboyant impact. Kaleidoscope arrival of Devil-Boy, earlier entrance of royals, wriggling release of new incomprehensible song.

'Thirty seconds,' he said, running through the finished sequence. 'Maybe they'll use it all, maybe they won't.'

'It looks good to me.'

'Thirty seconds is a long news item.' He took the spooled tape from the machine, put it into an already labelled box and handed it to the gaunt transmitter man, who was waiting to take it away. 'Danielle says you want to learn to edit, so what do you want to know?'

'Er . . . what these machines will do, for a start.'

'Quite a lot.' He fluttered his dark fingers over the banks of controls, barely touching them. 'They'll take

282

any size tape, any make, and record on any other. You can bring the sound up, cut it out, transpose it, superimpose any sounds you like. You can put the sound from one tape on to the pictures of another, you can cut two tapes together so that it looks as if the people are talking to each other when they were recorded hours and miles apart, you can tell lies and goddam lies and put a false face on truth.'

'Anything else?'

'That about covers it.'

He showed me how to achieve some of his effects, but his speed confounded me.

'Have you got an actual tape you want to edit?' he asked finally.

'Yes, but I want to add to it first, if I can.'

He looked at me assessingly, a poised black man of perhaps my own age with a touch of humour in the eyes but a rarely smiling mouth. I felt untidy in my anorak beside his neat suit and cream shirt; also battered and sweaty and dim. It had been, I thought ruefully, too long a day.

'Danielle says you're OK,' he said surprisingly. 'I don't see why you can't ask the chief to rent you the use of this room some night we're not busy. You tell me what you want, and I'll edit your tapes for you, if you like.'

*

283

'Joe's a nice guy,' Danielle said, stretching lazily beside me in the rented Mercedes on her way home. 'Sure, if he said he'd edit your tape, he means it. He gets bored. He waited three hours tonight for the Devil-Boy slot. He loves editing. Has a passion for it. He wants to work in movies. He'll enjoy doing your tape.'

The bureau chief, solicited, had proved equally generous. 'If Joe's using the machines, go ahead.' He'd looked over to where Danielle was eyes down marking paragraphs in the morning papers. 'I had New York on the line this evening congratulating me on the upswing of our output recently. That's her doing. She says you're OK, you're OK.'

For her too it had been a long day.

'Towcester,' she said, yawning, 'seems light years back.'

'Mm,' I said. 'What did Princess Casilia say after you went in, when you got back to Eaton Square?'

Danielle looked at me with amusement. 'In the hall she told me that good manners were a sign of strength, and in the drawing room she asked if I thought you would really be fit for Ascot.'

'What did you say?' I asked, faintly alarmed.

'I said yes, you would.'

I relaxed. 'That's all right, then.'

'I did not say,' Danielle said mildly, 'that you were insane, but only that you didn't appear to notice when you'd been injured. Aunt Casilia said she thought this to be fairly typical of steeplechase jockeys.'

'I do notice,' I said.

'But?'

'Well . . . if I don't race, I don't earn. Almost worse, if I miss a race on a horse and it wins, the happy owner may put up that winning jockey the next time, so I can lose not just the one fee but maybe the rides on that horse for ever.'

She looked almost disappointed. 'So it's purely economic, this refusal to look filleted ribs in the face?'

'At least half.'

'And the rest?'

'What you feel for your job. What Joe feels for his. Much the same.'

She nodded, and after a pause said, 'Aunt Casilia wouldn't do that, though. Keep another jockey on, after you were fit again.'

'No, she never has. But your aunt is special.'

'She said,' Danielle said reflectively, 'that I wasn't to think of you as a jockey.'

'But I am.'

'That's what she said this morning on the way to Towcester.'

'Did she explain what she meant?'

'No. I asked her. She said something vague about essences.' She yawned. 'Anyway, this evening she told Uncle Roland all about those horrid men with knives, as she put it, and although he was scandalized and said she shouldn't get involved in such sordid brawls, she seemed quite serene and unaffected. She may look like porcelain, but she's quite tough. The more I get to know her, the more, to be honest, I adore her.'

The road from Chiswick to Eaton Square, clogged by day with stop-go traffic, was at two-fifteen in the morning regrettably empty. Red lights turned green at our approach and even sticking rigidly to the speed limit didn't much seem to lengthen the journey. We slid to a halt outside the princess's house far too soon.

Neither of us made a move to spring at once out of the car: we sat rather for a moment letting the day die in peace.

I said, 'I'll see you then, on Saturday.'

'Yes,' she sighed for no clear reason. 'I guess so.'

'You don't have to,' I said.

'Oh no,' she half laughed. 'I suppose I meant... Saturday's some way off.'

I took her hand. She let it lie in mine, passive, waiting.

'We might have,' I said, 'a lot of Saturdays.'

'Yes, we might.'

I leaned over and kissed her mouth, tasting her pink lipstick, feeling her breath on my cheek, sensing the tremble somewhere in her body. She neither drew back nor clutched forward, but kissed as I'd kissed, as an announcement, as a promise perhaps; as an invitation.

I sat away from her and smiled into her eyes, and then got out of the car and went round to open her door.

We stood briefly together on the pavement.

'Where are you sleeping?' she said. 'It's so late.'

'In a hotel.'

'Near here?'

'Less than a mile.'

'Good . . . you won't have far to drive.'

'No distance.'

'Goodnight, then,' she said.

'Goodnight.'

We kissed again, as before. Then, laughing, she turned away, walked across the pavement and let herself through the princess's porticoed front door with a latchkey: and I drove away thinking that if the princess had disapproved of her jockey making approaches to her niece, she would by now have let both of us know.

I slept like the dead for five hours, then rolled stiffly out of bed, blinked blearily at the heavy cold rain making a mess of the day, and pointed the Mercedes towards Bletchley.

The Golden Lion was warm and alive with the smells of breakfast, and I ate there while the desk processed my bill. Then I telephoned the AA for news of my car (ready Monday) and to Holly to check that the marked *Flag* copies had been delivered as promised (which they had: the feed-merchant had telephoned) and after that I packed all my gear into the car and headed straight back towards the hotel I'd slept in.

No problem, they said helpfully at reception, I could retain my present room for as long as I wanted, and yes, certainly, I could leave items in the strongroom for safe-keeping.

Upstairs I put Jay Erskine's Press Club pass and Owen Watts's credit cards into an envelope and wrote 'URGENT DELIVER TO MR LEGGATT IMMEDIATELY' in large letters on the outside. Then I put the video recordings and all of the journalists' other possessions, except their jackets, into one of the hotel's laundry bags, rolling it into a neat bundle which downstairs was fastened with sticky-tape and labelled before vanishing into the vault.

After that I drove to Fleet Street, parked where I shouldn't, ran through the rain to leave the envelope for Sam Leggatt at the *Flag* front desk, fielded the car from under the nose of a traffic warden, and went lightheartedly to Ascot.

It was a rotten afternoon there in many ways. Sleet fell almost ceaselessly, needle-sharp, ice-cold and slanting, soaking every jockey to the skin before the start and proving a blinding hazard thereafter. Goggles were useless, caked with flying mud; gloves slipped wetly on the reins; racing boots clung clammily to waterlogged feet. A day for gritting one's teeth and getting round safely, for meeting fences exactly right and not slithering along on one's nose on landing. Raw November at its worst.

The crowd was sparse, deterred before it started out by the visible downpour and the drenching forecast, and the few people standing in the open were huddled inside dripping coats looking like mushrooms with their umbrellas.

Holly and Bobby both came but wouldn't stay, arriving after I'd won the first race more by luck than inspiration, and leaving before the second. They took the money out of the money-belt, which I returned to the valet with thanks.

Holly hugged me. 'Three people telephoned, after I'd talked to you, to say they were pleased about the apology,' she said. 'They're offering credit again. It's made all the difference.'

'Take care how you go with running up bills,' I said.

'Of course we will. The bank manager haunts us.'

I said to Bobby, 'I borrowed some of that money. I'll repay it next week.'

'It's all yours, really.' He spoke calmly in friendship, but the life-force was again at a low ebb. No vigour. Too much apathy. Not what was needed.

Holly looked frozen and was shivering. 'Keep the baby warm,' I said. 'Go into the trainers' bar.'

'We're going home.' She kissed me with cold lips. 'We would stay to watch you, but I feel sick. I feel sick most of the time. It's the pits.'

Bobby put his arm round her protectively and took her away under a large umbrella, both of them leaning head down against the icy wind, and I felt depressed for them, and thought also of the risks that lay ahead, before they could be safe.

The princess had invited to her box the friends of hers that I cared for least, a quartet of aristocrats from her old country, and as always when they were there I saw little of her. With two of them she came in red oilskins down to the parade ring before the first of her two runners, smiling cheerfully through the freezing rain and asking what I thought of her chances, and with the other two she repeated the enquiry an hour and a half later.

In each case I said, 'Reasonable.' The first runner finished reasonably fourth, the second runner, second. Neither time did she come down to the unsaddling enclosure, for which one couldn't blame her, and nor did I go up to her box, partly because it was a perfunctory routine when those friends were there, but mostly on account of crashing to the ground on the far side of the course in the last race. By the time I got in and changed, she would be gone.

Oh well, I thought dimly, scraping myself up; six rides, one winner, one second, one fourth, two also-rans, one fall. You can't win four every day, old son. And nothing broken. Even the stitches had survived without leaking. I waited in the blowing sleet for the car to pick me up, and took off my helmet to let the water run through my hair, embracing in a way the wild day, feeling at home. Winter and horses, the old song in the blood.

There was no fruit cake left in the changing room.

'Rotten buggers,' I said.

'But you never eat cake,' my valet said, heaving off my sodden boots.

'Every so often,' I said, 'like on freezing wet Fridays after a fall in the last race.'

'There's some tea still. It's hot.'

I drank the tea, feeling the warmth slide down, heating from inside. There was always tea and fruit cake in the changing rooms; instant energy, instant comfort. Everyone ate cake now and then.

An official put his head through the door: someone to see you, he said.

I pulled on a shirt and shoes and went out to the door from the weighing room to the outside world. No one all day had appeared with a banker's draft from Pollgate, and I suppose I went out with an incredulous flicker of hope. Hope soon extinguished. It was only Dusty, huddled in the weighing room doorway, blue of face, eyes watering with cold.

'Is the horse all right?' I asked. 'I heard you caught him.'

'Yes. Useless bugger. What about you?'

'No damage. I got passed by the doctor. I'll be riding tomorrow.'

'Right, I'll tell the guv'nor. We'll be off, then. So long.'

'So long.'

He scurried away into the leaden early dusk, a small dedicated man who liked to check for himself after I'd fallen that I was in good enough shape to do his charges justice next time out. He had been known to advise Wykeham to stand me down. Wykeham had been known to take the advice. Passing Dusty was sometimes harder than passing the medics.

I showered and dressed and left the racecourse via the cheaper enclosures, walking from there into the darkening town, where I'd left the rented Mercedes in a public parking place in the morning. Maybe it was unlikely that a repeat ambush would be set in the nearly deserted jockeys' car park long after the last race, but I was taking no chances. I climbed unmolested into the Mercedes and drove in safety to London.

There in my comfortable bolthole I again made additions to my astronomical phone bill, arranging first for my obliging neighbour to go into my cottage in the morning and pack one of my suits and some shirts and other things into a suitcase.

'Of course I will, Kit dear, but I thought you'd be back here for sure tonight, after riding at Ascot.'

'Staying with friends,' I said. 'I'll get someone to pick up the suitcase from your place tomorrow morning to take it to Ascot. Would that be all right?'

'Of course, dear.'

I persuaded another jockey who lived in Lambourn to collect the case and bring it with him, and he said sure he would, if he remembered.

I telephoned Wykeham when I judged he'd be indoors after his evening tour of the horses and told him his winner had been steadfast, the princess's two as good as could be hoped for, and one of the also-rans disappointing.

'And Dusty says you made a clear balls-up of the hurdle down by Swinley Bottom in the last.'

'Yeah,' I said. 'If Dusty can see clearly half a mile through driving sleet in poor light he's got better eyesight than I thought.'

'Er . . .' Wykeham said. 'What happened?'

'The one in front fell. Mine went down over him. He wouldn't have won, if that's any consolation. He was beginning to tire already, and he was hating the weather.'

Wykeham grunted assent. 'He's a sun-lover, true-bred. Kit, tomorrow there's Inchcape for the princess in the big race and he's in grand form, jumping out of his skin, improved a mile since you saw him last week.'

'Inchcape,' I said resignedly, 'is dead.'

'What? Did I say Inchcape? No, not Inchcape. What's the princess's horse?'

'Icefall.'

'Icicle's full brother,' he said, not quite making it a question.

'Yes.'

'Of course.' He cleared his throat. 'Icefall. Naturally. He should win, Kit, seriously.'

'Will you be there?' I asked. 'I half expected you today.'

'In that weather?' He sounded surprised. 'No, no, Dusty and you and the princess, you'll do fine.'

'But you've had a whole bunch of winners this week and you haven't seen one of them.'

'I see them here in the yard. I see them on video tapes. You tell Inchcape he's the greatest, and he'll jump Ben Nevis.'

'All right,' I said. Icefall, Inchcape, what did it matter?

'Good. Great. Goodnight, Kit.'

'Goodnight, Wykeham,' I said.

I got through to my answering machine and collected the messages, one of which was from Eric Olderjohn, the civil servant owner of the horse I'd won on for the Lambourn trainer at Towcester.

I called him back without delay at the London number he'd given, and caught him, it seemed, on the point of going out.

'Oh, Kit, yes. Look, I suppose you're in Lambourn?'

'No, actually. In London.'

'Really? That's fine. I've something you might be interested to see, but I can't let it out of my hands.' He paused for thought. 'Would you be free this evening after nine?'

'Yes,' I said.

'Right. Come round to my house, I'll be back by then.' He gave me directions to a street south of Sloane Square, not more than a mile from where I was staying. 'Coffee and brandy, right? Got to run. Bye.'

He disconnected abruptly and I put down my own receiver more slowly saying 'Wow' to myself silently. I hadn't expected much action from Eric Olderjohn, civil servant, and certainly none with such speed.

I sat for a while thinking of the tape of Maynard, and of the list of companies at the end, of those who had suffered from Maynard's philanthropy. Short of finding somewhere to replay the tape, I would have to rely on memory, and the only name I could remember for certain was Purfleet Electronics; chiefly because I'd spent a summer sailing holiday with a schoolfriend there long ago.

Purfleet Electronics, directory enquiries told me, was not listed.

I sucked my teeth a bit and reflected that the only way to find things was to look in the right place. I would go to Purfleet, as to Hitchin, in the morning.

I filled in the evening with eating and more phone calls, and by nine had walked down Sloane Street and found Eric Olderjohn's house. It was narrow, two storeys, one of a long terrace built for low-income early Victorians, now inhabited by the affluent as pieds-à-terre: or so Eric Olderjohn affably told me, opening his dark green front door and waving me in.

From the street one stepped straight into the sitting room, which stretched from side to side of the house; all of four metres. The remarkably small space glowed with pinks and light greens, textured trellised wall-paper, swagged satin curtains, round tables with skirts, china birds, silver photograph frames, fat buttoned arm-chairs, Chinese creamy rugs on the floor. There were softly glowing lamps, and the trellised wallpaper covered the ceiling also, enclosing the crowded contents in an impression of a summer grotto.

My host watched my smile of appreciation as if the reaction were only what he would have expected.

'It's great,' I said.

'My daughter did it.'

'The one you would defend from the *Flag*?'

'My only daughter. Yes. Sit down. Has it stopped raining? You'd like a brandy, I dare say?' He moved the one necessary step to a silver tray of bottles on one of the round tables and poured cognac into two modest balloon glasses. 'I've set some coffee ready. I'll just fetch it. Sit down, do.' He vanished through a rear door camouflaged by trellis and I looked at the photographs in the frames, seeing a well-groomed young woman who might be his daughter, seeing the horse that he owned, with myself on its back.

He returned with another small tray, setting it alongside the first.

'My daughter,' he said, nodding, as he saw I'd been looking. 'She lives here part of the time, part with her mother.' He shrugged. 'One of those things.'

'I'm sorry.'

'Yes. Well, it happens. Coffee?' He poured into two small cups and handed me one. 'Sugar? No, I suppose not. Sit down. Here's the brandy.'

He was neat in movement as in dress, and I found myself thinking 'dapper'; but there was purposefulness

there under the surface, the developed faculty of
getting things done. I sat in one of the armchairs with
coffee and brandy beside me, and he sat also, and
sipped, and looked at me over his cup.

'You were in luck,' he said finally. 'I put out a few
feelers this morning and was told a certain person might
be lunching at his club.' He paused. 'I was sufficiently
interested in your problem to arrange for a friend of
mine to meet and sound out that person, whom he
knows well, and their conversation was, one might say,
fruitful. As a result I myself went to a certain person's
office this afternoon, and the upshot of that meeting
was some information which I'll presently show you.'

His care over the choice of words was typical, I
supposed, of the stratosphere of the civil service: the
wheeler-dealers in subtlety, obliqueness and not saying
quite what one meant. I never discovered the exact
identity of the certain person, on the basis no doubt
that it wasn't something I needed to know, and in view
of what he'd allowed me a sight of, I could scarcely
complain.

'I have some letters,' Eric Olderjohn said. 'More
precisely, photocopies of letters. You can read them,
but I am directly commanded not to let you take
them away. I have to return them on Monday. Is all
that ... er ... quite clear?'

'Yes,' I said.

'Good.'

Without haste he finished his coffee and put down

the cup. Then, raising the skirt of the table which bore the trays, he bent and brought out a brown leather attaché case, which he rested on his knees. He snapped open the locks, raised the lid and paused again.

'They're interesting,' he said, frowning.

I waited.

As if coming to a decision which until that moment he had left open, he drew a single sheet of paper out of the case and passed it across.

The letter had been addressed to the Prime Minister and had been sent in September from a company which made fine china for export. The chairman, who had written the letter, explained that he and the other directors were unanimous in suggesting some signal honour for Mr Maynard Allardeck, in recognition of his great and patriotic services to industry.

Mr Allardeck had come generously to the aid of the historic company, and thanks entirely to his efforts the jobs of two hundred and fifty people had been saved. The skills of many of these people were priceless and included the ability to paint and gild porcelain to the world's highest standards. The company was now exporting more than before and was looking forward to the brightest of futures.

The board would like to propose a knighthood for Mr Allardeck.

I finished reading and looked over at Eric Olderjohn.

'Is this sort of letter normal?' I asked.

'Entirely.' He nodded. 'Most awards are the result

of recommendations to the Prime Minister's office. Anyone can suggest anyone for anything. If the cause seems just, an award is given. The patronage people draw up a list of awards they deem suitable, and the list is passed to the Prime Minister for approval.'

I said, 'So all these people in the honours lists who get medals ... firefighters, music teachers, postmen, people like that, it's because their mates have written in to suggest it?'

'Er, yes. More often their employers, but sometimes their mates.'

He produced a second letter from his briefcase and handed it over. This one also was from an exporting company and stressed Maynard's invaluable contributions to worthwhile industry, chief among them the saving of very many jobs in an area of great local unemployment.

It was impossible to overestimate Mr Allardeck's services to his country in industry, and the firm unreservedly recommended that he should be offered a knighthood.

'Naturally,' I said, 'the patronage people checked that all this was true?'

'Naturally,' Eric Olderjohn said.

'And of course it was?'

'I am assured so. The certain person with whom I talked this afternoon told me that occasionally, if they receive six or seven similar letters all proposing someone unknown to the general public, they may begin to suspect that the person is busily proposing himself by persuading his friends to write in. The writers of the two letters I've shown you were specifically asked, as their recommendations were so similar, if Maynard himself had suggested they write. Each of them emphatically denied any such thing.'

'Mm,' I said. 'Well they would, wouldn't they, if they stood to gain from Maynard for his knighthood.'

'That's a thoroughly scurrilous remark.'

'So it is,' I said cheerfully. 'And your certain person, did he put Maynard down for his Sir?'

He nodded. 'Provisionally. To be considered. Then they received a third letter, emphasizing substantial philanthropy that they already knew about, and the question mark was erased. Maynard Allardeck was definitely in line for his K. The letter inviting him to accept the honour was drafted, and would have been sent out in about ten days from now, at the normal time for the New Year's list.'

'Would have been?' I said.

'Would have been.' He smiled twistedly. 'It is not now considered appropriate, as a result of the stories in the *Daily Flag* and the opinion page in the *Towncrier*.'

'Rose Quince,' I said.

He looked uncomprehending.

'She wrote the piece in the *Towncrier*,' I said.

'Oh . . . yes.'

'Would your, er, certain person,' I asked, 'really take notice of those bits in the newspapers?'

'Oh, definitely. Particularly as in each case the paragraphs were delivered by hand to his office, outlined in red.'

'They weren't!'

Eric Olderjohn raised an eyebrow. 'That means something to you?' he asked.

I explained about the tradespeople and the owners all receiving similarly marked copies.

'There you are, then. A thorough job of demolition. Nothing left to chance.'

'You mentioned a third letter,' I said. 'The clincher.'

He peered carefully into his case and produced it. 'This one may surprise you,' he said.

The third letter was not from a commercial firm but from a charitable organization with a list of patrons that stretched half the way down the left side of the page. The recipients of the charity appeared to be the needy dependants of dead or disabled public servants. Widows, children, the old and the sick.

'How do you define a public servant?' I asked.

'The Civil Service, from the top down.'

Maynard Allardeck, the letter reported, had worked tirelessly over several years to improve the individual lives of those left in dire straits through no fault of their own. He unstintingly poured out his own fortune in aid, besides giving his time and extending a high level of compassionate ongoing care to families in need. The charitable organization said it would itself feel honoured if the reward of a knighthood should be given to one of its most stalwart pillars: to the man they had unanimously chosen to be their next chairman, the appointment to be effective from 1 December of that year.

The letter had been signed by no fewer than four of the charity's officers: the retiring chairman, the head of the board of management, and two of the senior patrons. It was the fourth of these signatures which had me lifting my head in astonishment.

'Well?' Eric Olderjohn asked, watching.

'That's odd,' I said blankly.

'Yes, curious, I agree.'

He held out his hand for the letters, took them from me, snapped them safely back into his case. I sat with thoughts tumbling over themselves and unquestioned assumptions melting like wax.

Was it true, I had wanted to know, if Maynard Allardeck was being considered for a knighthood, and if so, who knew?

The people who had proposed him; they knew.

The letter from the charity, dated 1 October, had been signed by Lord Vaughnley.

CHAPTER SIXTEEN

'Why,' I said, 'did your certain person allow you to show these letters to me?'

'Ah.' Eric Olderjohn joined his fingers together in a steeple and studied them for a while. 'Why do you think?'

'I would suppose,' I said, 'he might think it possible I would stir up a few ponds, get a few muddy answers, without him having to do it himself.'

Eric Olderjohn switched his attention from his hands to my face. 'Something like that,' he said. 'He would like to know for sure Maynard Allardeck isn't just the victim of a hate campaign, for instance. He wants to do him justice. To put him back on the list, perhaps, for a knighthood next time around, in the summer.'

'He wants proof?' I asked.

'Can you supply it?'

'Yes, I think so.'

'What are you planning to do,' he asked with dry humour, 'when you have to give up race-riding?'

'Jump off a cliff, I dare say.'

I stood up, and he also. I thanked him sincerely for the trouble he'd taken. He said he would expect me to win again on his horse next time out. Do my best, I said, and took a last appreciative glance round his bower of a sitting room before making my way back to the hotel.

Lord Vaughnley, I thought.

On 1 October he had recommended Maynard for a knighthood. By the end of that month or the beginning of November there had been a tap on Bobby's telephone.

The tap had been installed by Jay Erskine, who had listened for two weeks and then written the articles in the *Flag*.

Jay Erskine had once worked for Lord Vaughnley, as crime reporter on the *Towncrier*.

But if Lord Vaughnley had got Jay Erskine to attack Maynard Allardeck, why was Nestor Pollgate so aggressive?

Because he didn't want to have to pay compensation, or to admit his paper had done wrong.

Well . . . perhaps.

I went round in circles and came back always to the central and unexpected question: Was it really Lord Vaughnley who had prompted the attacks, and if so, why?

From my hotel room I telephoned Rose Quince's home, catching her again soon after she had come in.

'Bill?' she said. 'Civil Service charity? Oh, sure, he's

a patron of dozens of things. All sorts. Keeps him in touch, he says.'

'Mm,' I said. 'When you wrote that piece about Maynard Allardeck, did he suggest it?'

'Who? Bill? Yes, sure he did. He put the clippings from the *Flag* on my desk and said it looked my sort of thing. I may know him from way back, but he's still the ultimate boss. When he wants something written, it gets written. Martin, our big white chief, always agrees to that.'

'And, er, how did you get on to the *How's Trade* interview? I mean, did you see the programme when it was broadcast?'

'Do me a favour. Of course not.' She paused. 'Bill suggested I try the television company, to ask for a private re-run.'

'Which you did.'

'Yes, of course. Look,' she demanded, 'what's all this about? Bill often suggests subjects to me. There's nothing strange in it.'

'No,' I said. 'Sleep well, Rose.'

'And goodnight to you, too.'

I slept soundly and long, and early in the morning took the video camera and drove to Purfleet along the flat lands just north of the Thames estuary. The rains of the day before had drawn away, leaving the sky washed and pale, and there were seagulls wheeling high over the low-tide mud.

I asked in about twenty places, post office and shops,

before I found anyone who had heard of Purfleet Electronics, but was finally pointed towards someone who had worked there. 'You want George Tarker ... he owned it,' he said.

Following a few further instructions from helpful locals, I eventually pulled up beside a shabby old wooden boatshed optimistically emblazoned with a signboard saying 'George Tarker Repairs All'.

Out of the car and walking across the pot-holed entrance yard to the door one could see that the sign had once had a bottom half, which had split off and was lying propped against the wall, and which read 'Boats and Marine Equipment'.

With a sinking feeling of having come entirely to the wrong place I pushed open the rickety door and stepped straight into the untidiest office in the world, a place where every surface and every shelf was covered with unidentifiable lumps of ships' hardware in advanced age, and where every patch of wall was occupied by ancient calendars, posters, bills and instructions, all attached not by drawing pins but by nails.

In a sagging old chair, oblivious to the mess, sat an elderly grey-bearded man with his feet up on a desk, reading a newspaper and drinking from a cup.

'Mr Tarker?' I said.

'That's me.' He lowered the paper, looking at me critically from over the soles of his shoes. 'What do you want repaired?' He looked towards the bag I was carrying which contained the camera. 'A bit off a boat?'

'I'm afraid I've come to the wrong place,' I said. 'I was looking for Mr George Tarker who used to own Purfleet Electronics.'

He put his cup down carefully on the desk, and his feet on the floor. He was old, I saw, from an inner weariness as much as from age: it lay in the sag of his shoulders and the droop of his eyes and shouted from the disarray of everything around him.

'That George Tarker was my son,' he said.

Was.

'I'm sorry,' I said.

'Do you want anything repaired, or don't you?'

'No,' I said. 'I want to talk about Maynard Allardeck.'

The cheeks fell inwards into shadowed hollows and the eyes seemed to recede darkly into the sockets. He had scattered grey hair, uncombed, and below the short beard, in the thin neck inside the unbuttoned and tieless shirt, the tendons tightened and began to quiver.

'I don't want to distress you,' I said: but I had. 'I'm making a film about the damage Maynard Allardeck has done to many people's lives. I hoped you ... I hoped your son ... might help me.' I gestured vaguely with one hand. 'I know it wouldn't sway you one way or another, but I'm offering a fee.'

He was silent, staring at my face but seeing, I thought, another scene altogether, looking back into memory and finding it almost past bearing. The strain

307

in his face deepened to the point when I did actively regret having come.

'Will it destroy him, your film?' he said huskily.

'In some ways, yes.'

'He deserves hellfire and damnation.'

I took the video camera out of its bag and showed it to him, explaining about talking straight at the lens.

'Will you tell me what happened to your son?' I asked.

'Yes, I will.'

I balanced the camera on a heap of junk and started it running; and with few direct questions from me he repeated in essence the familiar story. Maynard had come smiling to the rescue in a temporary cash crisis caused by a rapid expansion of the business. He had lent at low rates, but at the last and worst moment demanded to be repaid; had taken over the firm and ousted George Tarker, and after a while had stripped the assets, sold the freehold and put the workforce on the dole.

'Charming,' George Tarker said. 'That's what he was. Like a con man, right to the end. Reasonable. Friendly. Then he was gone, and everything with him. My son's business, gone. He started it when he was only eighteen and worked and worked... and after twenty-three years it was growing too fast.'

The gaunt face stared starkly into the lens, and water stood in the corner of each eye.

'My son George ... my only child ... he blamed himself for everything ... for all his workers losing their jobs. He began to drink. He knew such a lot about electricity.' The tears spilled over the lower eyelids and rolled down the lined cheeks to be lost in the beard. 'My son wired himself up ... and hit the switch ...'

The voice stopped as if with the jolt that had stopped his son's heart. I found it unbearable. I wished with an intensity of pity that I hadn't come. I turned off the camera and stood there in silence, not knowing how to apologize for such an intrusion.

He brushed the tears away with the back of his hand. 'Two years ago, just over,' he said. 'He was a good man, you know, my son George. That Allardeck ... just destroyed him.'

I offered him the same amount that I'd given the Perrysides, setting it down in front of him on the desk. He stared at the flat bunch of banknotes for a while, and then pushed it towards me.

'I didn't tell you for money,' he said. 'You take it back. I told you for George.'

I hesitated.

'Go on,' he said. 'I don't want it. Doesn't feel right. Any time you have a boat, you pay me then for repairs.'

'All right,' I said.

He nodded and watched while I picked up the notes.

'You make your film good,' he said. 'Make it for George.'

'Yes,' I said; and he was still sitting there, staring with pain into the past, when I left.

I went to Ascot with the same precautions as before, leaving the Mercedes down in the town and walking into the racecourse from the opposite direction to the jockeys' official car park. No one that I could see took any notice of my arrival, beyond the gatemen with their usual good mornings.

I had rides in the first five of the six races; two for the princess, two others for Wykeham, one for the Lambourn trainer. Dusty reported Wykeham to have a crippling migraine headache which would keep him at home watching on television. Icefall, Dusty said, should zoom in, and all the lads had staked their wages. Dusty's manner to me was as usual a mixture of deference and truculence, a double attitude I had long ago sorted into components: I might do the actual winning for the stable, but the fitness of the horses was the gift of the lads in the yard, and I wasn't to forget it. Dusty and I had worked together for ten years in a truce founded on mutual need, active friendship being neither sought nor necessary. He said the guv'nor wanted me to give the princess and the other owners his regrets about his headache. I'd tell them, I said.

I rode one of Wykeham's horses in the first race with negligible results, and came third in the second race, for the Lambourn trainer. The third race was

Icefall for the princess, and she and Danielle were both waiting in the parade ring, rosily lunched and sparkling-eyed, when I went out there to greet them.

'Wykeham sends his regrets,' I said.

'The poor man.' The princess believed in the migraines as little as I did, but was willing to pretend. 'Will we give him a win to console him?'

'I'm afraid he expects it.'

We watched Icefall walk round, grey and well muscled under his coroneted rug, more compact than his full brother Icicle.

'I schooled him last week,' I said. 'Wykeham says he's come on a ton since then. So there's hope.'

'Hope!' Danielle said. 'He's hot favourite.'

'Odds on,' nodded the princess. 'It never makes one feel better.'

She and I exchanged glances of acknowledgement of the extra pressure that came with too much expectation, and when I went off to mount she said only, 'Get round safely, that's all.'

Icefall at six was at the top of his hurdling form with a string of successes behind him, and his race on that day was a much publicized, much sponsored two-mile event which had cut up, as big-prize races tended occasionally to do, into no more than six runners: Icefall at the top of the handicap, the other five at the bottom, the centre block having decided to duck out for less taxing contests.

Icefall was an easy horse to ride, as willing as his

brother and naturally courageous, and the only foresee-able problem was the amount of weight he carried in relation to the others: twenty pounds and more. Wykeham never liked his horses to be front runners and had tried to dissuade me sometimes from running Icefall in that way; but the horse positively preferred it and let me know it at every start, and even with the weights so much against us, when the tapes went up we were there where he wanted to be, setting the pace.

I'd learned in my teens from an American flat-race jockey how to start a clock in my head, to judge the speed of each section of the race against the clock, and to judge how fast I could go in each section in order to finish at or near the horse's own best time for the distance.

Icefall's best time for two miles at Ascot at almost the same weights on the same sort of wet ground was three minutes forty-eight seconds, and I set out to take him to the finish line in precisely that period, and at a more or less even speed the whole way.

It seemed to the crowd on the stands, I was told afterwards, that I'd set off too fast, that some of the lightweights would definitely catch me; but I'd looked up their times also in the form book, and none of them had ever completed two miles as fast as I aimed to.

All Icefall had to do was jump with perfection, and that he did, informing me of his joy in mid-air at every hurdle. The lightweights never came near us, and we finished ahead, without slackening, by eight lengths, a margin that would do Icefall's handicap no good at all next time out.

Maybe, I thought, pulling up and patting the grey neck hugely, it would have been better for the future not to have won by so far, but the present was what mattered, and with those weights one couldn't take risks.

The princess was flushed and laughing and delighted, and as usual intensified my own pleasure in winning. Victories for glum and grumbling owners were never so sweet.

'My friends say it's sacrilege,' she said, 'for a top-weight to set off so fast and try to make all the running after rain like yesterday's. They were pitying me up in the box, telling me you were mad.'

I smiled at her, unbuckling my saddle. 'When he jumps like today, he can run this course even on wet gound in three minutes forty-eight seconds. That's what we did, more or less.'

Her eyes widened. 'You planned it! You didn't tell me. I didn't expect you to go off so fast, even though he likes it in front.'

'If he'd made a hash of any of the hurdles, I'd have looked a right idiot.' I patted the grey neck over and over. 'He understands racing,' I said. 'He's a great horse to ride. Very generous. He enjoys it.'

'You talk as if horses were people,' Danielle said, standing behind her aunt, listening.

'Yes, they are,' I said. 'Not human, but individuals, all different.'

I took the saddle in and sat on the scales, and changed into other colours and weighed out again for the next race. Then put the princess's colours back on, on top of the others, and went out bareheaded for the sponsors' presentations.

Lord Vaughnley was among the crowd round the sponsors' table of prizes, and he came straight over to me when I went out.

'My dear chap, what a race! I thought you'd gone off your rocker, I'm sorry to say. Now, you are coming to our box, aren't you? Like we agreed?'

He was a puzzle. His grey eyes smiled blandly in the big face, full of friendliness, empty of guile.

'Yes,' I said. 'Thank you. After the fifth race, when I'll have finished for the day, if that's all right?'

Lady Vaughnley appeared at his elbow, reinforcing the invitation. 'Delighted to have you. Do come.'

The princess, overhearing, said, 'Come along to me after,' taking my compliance for granted, not expecting an answer. 'Did you know,' she said with humour, 'the time Icefall took?'

'No, not yet.'

'Three minutes forty-nine seconds.'

'We were one second late.'

'Yes, indeed. Next time, go faster.'

Lady Vaughnley looked at her in astonishment.

'How can you say that?' she protested, and then understood it was merely a joke. 'Oh. For a moment . . .'

The princess patted her arm consolingly, and I watched Danielle, on the far side of the green-baized pot-laden table, talking to the sponsors as to the winning habit born. She turned her head and looked straight at me, and I felt the tingle of that visual connection run right down my spine. She's beautiful, I thought. I want her in bed.

It seemed that she had broken off in the middle of whatever she was saying. The sponsor spoke to her enquiringly. She looked at him blankly, and then with another glance at me seemed to sort out her thoughts and answer whatever he'd asked.

I looked down at the trophies, afraid that my feelings were naked. I had two races and a lot of box-talk to get through before we could be in any real way together, and the memory of her kisses was no help.

The presentations were made, the princess and the others melted away, and I peeled off the princess's colours and went out and rode another winner for Wykeham, scrambling home that time by a neck, all elbows, no elegance, practically throwing the horse ahead of himself, hard on him, squeezing him, making him stretch beyond where he thought he could go.

'Bloody hell,' said his owner, in the winners' unsaddling area. 'Bloody hell, I'd not like you on my back.' He seemed pleased enough all the same, a Sussex farmer, big and forthright, surrounded by chattering friends. 'You're a bloody demon, lad, that's what you are. Hard as bloody nails. He'll know he's had a race, I'll tell you.'

'Yes, well, Mr Davis, he can take it, he's tough, he'd not thank you to be soft. Like his owner, wouldn't you say, Mr Davis?'

He gave a great guffaw and clapped me largely on the shoulder, and I went and weighed in, and changed into the princess's colours again for the fifth race.

The princess's runner, Allegheny, was the second of her only two mares (Bernina being the other), as the princess, perhaps because of her own femininity, had a definite preference for male horses. Not as temperamental as Bernina, Allegheny was a friendly old pudding, running moderately well always but without fire. I'd tried to get Wykeham to persuade the princess to sell her but he wouldn't: Princess Casilia, he said, knew her own mind.

Allegheny's seconds, thirds, fourths, fifths, sixths, also-rans never seemed to disappoint her. It wasn't essential to her, he said, for all her children to be stars.

Allegheny and I set off amicably but as usual my attempts to jolly her into *joie de vivre* got little response. We turned into the straight for the first time lying fourth, going easily, approaching a plain fence, meeting it right, launching into the air, landing, accelerating away ...

In one of her hind legs a suspensory ligament tore apart at the fetlock, and Allegheny went lame in three strides, all rhythm gone; like driving a car on a suddenly flat tyre. I pulled her up and jumped off her back, and walked her a few paces to make sure she hadn't broken a bone.

Just the tendon, I thought in relief. Bad enough, but not a death sentence. Losing a horse to the bolt of a humane killer upset everyone for days. Wykeham had wept sometimes for dead horses, and I also, and the princess. One couldn't help it, sometimes.

The vet sped round in his car, looked her over and pronounced her fit to walk, so I led her back up the course, her head nodding every time she put the injured foot to the ground. The princess and Danielle came down anxiously to the unsaddling area and Dusty assured them the guv'nor would get a vet to Allegheny as soon as possible.

'What do you think?' the princess asked me in depression, as Dusty and the mare's lad led her, nodding, away.

'I don't know.'

'Yes, you do. Tell me.'

The princess's eyes were deep blue. I said, 'She'll be a year off the racecourse, at least.'

She sighed. 'Yes, I suppose so.'

'You could patch her up,' I said, 'and sell her as a brood mare. She's got good blood lines. She could breed in the spring.'

'Oh!' She seemed pleased. 'I'm fond of her, you know.'

'Yes, I know.'

'I do begin to see,' Danielle said, 'what racing is all about.'

My neighbour and the Lambourn fellow jockey having come up trumps in the matter of a suitcase of clothes, I went up to Lord Vaughnley's box in a change for the better. I appeared to have chosen, though, the doldrums of time between events when everyone had gone down to look at the horses or to bet, and not yet returned to watch the race.

There was only one person in there, standing nervously beside the table now laid for tea, shifting from foot to foot: and I was surprised to see it was Hugh Vaughnley, Lord Vaughnley's son.

'Hello,' I said. 'No one's here ... I'll come back.'

'Don't go.'

His voice was urgent. I looked at him curiously, thinking of the family row which had so clearly been in operation on the previous Saturday, seeing only trouble still in the usually cheerful face. Much thinner than his father, more like his mother in build, he had neat features well placed, two disarming dimples, and youth still in the indecision of his mouth. Around nineteen, I thought. Maybe twenty. Not more.

'I ... er ...' he said. 'Do stay. I want someone here, to be honest, when they come back.'

'Do you?'

'Er ...' he said. 'They don't know I'm here. I mean ... Dad might be furious, and he can't be, can he, in front of strangers? That's why I came here, to the races. I mean, I know you're not a stranger, but you know what I mean.'

'Your mother will surely be glad to see you.'

He swallowed. 'I hate quarrelling with them. I can't bear it. To be honest, Dad threw me out almost a month ago. He's making me live with Saul Bradley, and I can't bear it much longer, I want to go home.'

'He threw you out?' I must have sounded as surprised as I felt. 'You always seemed such a solid family. Does he think you should stand on your own two feet? Something like that?'

'Nothing like that. I just wish it was. I did something ... I didn't know he'd be so desperately angry ... not really ...'

I didn't want to hear what it was, with so much else on my mind.

'Drugs?' I said, without sympathy.

'What?'

'Did you take drugs?'

I saw from his face that it hadn't been that. He was simply bewildered by the suggestion.

'I mean,' he said plaintively, 'he thought so much of him. He said so. I mean, I thought he approved of him.'

'Who?' I said.

He looked over my shoulder however and didn't answer, a fresh wave of anxiety blotting out all else.

319

I turned. Lord and Lady Vaughnley had come through the door from the passage and were advancing towards us. I saw their expressions with clarity when they caught sight of their son. Lady Vaughnley's face lifted into a spontaneous uncomplicated smile.

Lord Vaughnley looked from his son to myself, and his reaction wasn't forgiveness, apathy, irritation or even anger.

It was alarm. It was horror.

CHAPTER SEVENTEEN

He recovered fast to some extent. Lady Vaughnley put her arms around Hugh and hugged him, and her husband looked on, stony-faced and displeased. Others of their guests came in good spirits back to the box, and Hugh was proved right to the extent that his father was not ready to fight with him in public.

Lord Vaughnley, in fact, addressed himself solely to me, fussing about cups of tea and making sure I talked no more to his son, seemingly unaware that his instant reaction and his current manner were telling me a good deal more than he probably meant.

'There we are,' he said heartily, getting a waitress to pass me a cup. 'Milk? Sugar? No? Princess Casilia's mare is all right, isn't she? So sad when a horse breaks down in a race. Sandwich?'

I said the mare wouldn't race again, and no thanks to the sandwich.

'Hugh been bothering you with his troubles, has he?' he said.

'Not really.'

'What did he say?'

I glanced at the grey eyes from where the blandness had flown and watchfulness taken over.

'He said he had quarrelled with you and wanted to make it up.'

'Hmph.' An unforgiving noise from a compressed mouth. 'As long as he didn't bother you?'

'No.'

'Good. Good. Then you'll be wanting to talk to Princess Casilia, eh? Let me take your cup. Good of you to come up. Yes. Off you go, then. Can't keep her waiting.'

Short of rudeness I couldn't have stayed, and rudeness at that point, I thought, would accomplish no good that I could think of. I went obediently along to the princess's well-populated box and drank more tea and averted my stomach from another sandwich, and tried not to look too much at Danielle.

'You're abstracted,' the princess said. 'You are not here.'

'I was thinking of Lord Vaughnley ... I just came from his box.'

'Such a nice man.'

'Mm.'

'And for Danielle, this evening, what are your plans?'

I shut out the thoughts of what I would like. If I could read the princess's mind, she could also on occasion read mine.

'I expect we'll talk, and eat, and I'll bring her home.'

She patted my arm. She set me to talk to her guests, most of whom I knew, and I worked my way round to Danielle scattering politeness like confetti.

'Hi,' she said. 'Am I going back with Aunt Casilia, or what?'

'Coming with me from here, if you will.'

'OK.'

We went out on to the balcony with everyone else to watch the sixth race, and afterwards said goodbye correctly to the princess and left.

'Where are we going?' Danielle asked.

'For a walk, for a drink, for dinner. First of all we're walking to Ascot town, where I left the car, so as not to be carved up again in the car park.'

'You're too much,' she said.

I collected my suitcase from the changing room and we walked down through the cheaper enclosures to the furthest gate, and from there again safely to the rented Mercedes.

'I guess I never gave a thought to it happening again,' she said.

'And next time there would be no princess to the rescue.'

'Do you seriously think they'd be lying in wait?'

'I still have what they wanted.' And I'd twisted their tail fiercely, besides. 'I just go where they don't know I'm going, and hope.'

'Yes, but,' she said faintly, 'for how long?'

'Um,' I said, 'I suppose Joe doesn't work on Sundays?'

'No. Not till Monday night, like me. Not weekends. What's that got to do with how long?'

'Tuesday or Wednesday,' I said.

'You're not making much sense.'

'It's because I don't know for sure.' We got into the car and I started the engine. 'I feel like a juggler. Half a dozen clubs in the air and all likely to fall in a heap.'

'With you underneath?'

'Not,' I said, 'if I can help it.'

I drove not very fast to Henley, and stopped near a telephone box to try to reach Rose Quince, who was out. She had an answering machine which invited me to give a number for her to call back. I would try later, I said.

Henley-on-Thames was bright with lights and late Saturday afternoon shopping. Danielle and I left the car in a parking place and walked slowly along in the bustle.

'Where are we going?' she asked.

'To buy you a present.'

'What present?'

'Anything you'd like.'

She stopped walking. 'Are you crazy?'

'No.' We were outside a shop selling sport goods. 'Tennis racket?'

'I don't play tennis.'

I waved at the next shop along. 'Piano?'

'I can't play a piano.'

'Over there,' I pointed at a flower shop. 'Orchids?'

'In their place, but not to pin on me.'

'And over there, an antique chair?'

She laughed, her eyes crinkling. 'Tell me, too, what you like, and what you don't.'

'All right.'

We walked along the shopfronts, looking and telling. She liked blues and pinks but not yellow, she liked things with flowers and birds on, not geometric patterns, she liked baskets and nylon-tipped pens and aquamarines and seedless grapes and books about Leonardo da Vinci. She would choose for me, she said, something simple. If I were giving her a present, I would have to have one as well.

'OK,' I said. 'Twenty minutes. Meet me back at the car. Here's the key, in case you get there first.'

'And not expensive,' she said, 'or I'm not playing.'

'All right.'

When I returned with my parcel she was sitting in the car already, and smiling.

'You've been half an hour,' she said. 'You're disqualified.'

'Too bad.'

I climbed into the car beside her and we sat looking at each other's packages, mine to her in brown paper, hers to me flatter, in a carrier bag.

'Guess,' she said.

I tried to, and nothing came. I said with regret, 'I don't know.'

She eyed the brown-wrapped parcel in my hands. 'Three books? Three pounds of chocolates? A jack-in-a-box?'

'All wrong.'

We exchanged the presents and began to unwrap them. 'More fun than Christmas,' she said. 'Oh. How odd. I'd forgotten it was your name.' She paused very briefly for thought and said it the other way round. 'Christmas is more fun.'

It sounded all right in American. I opened the paper carrier she'd given me and found that our walk along the street had taught her a good deal about me, too. I drew out a soft brown leather zipped-around case which looked as if it would hold a pad of writing paper and a few envelopes: and it had KIT stamped in gold on the top.

'Go on, open it,' she said. 'I couldn't resist it. And you like neat small things, the way I do.'

I unzipped the case, opened it flat, and smiled with pure pleasure. It contained on one side a tool kit and on the other pens, a pocket calculator and a notepad; all in slots, all of top quality, solidly made.

'You do like it,' she said with satisfaction. 'I thought you would. It had your name on it, literally.'

She finished taking off the brown paper and showed me that I had pleased her also, and as much. I'd given her a baby antique chest of drawers which smelled faintly of polish, had little brass handles, and ran smoothly as silk. Neat, small, well-crafted, useful, good-looking, efficient: like the kit.

She looked long at the implications of the presents, and then at my face.

'That,' she said slowly, 'really is amazing, that we should both get it right.'

'Yes, it is.'

'And you broke the rules. That chest's not cheap.'

'So did you. Nor's the kit.'

'God bless credit cards.'

I kissed her, the same way as before, the gifts still on our laps. 'Thank you for mine.'

'Thank you for mine.'

'Well,' I said, reaching over to put my tool kit on the back seat. 'By the time we get there, the pub might be open.'

'What pub?'

'Where we're going.'

'Anyone who wants to know what you're not about to tell them,' she said, 'has a darned sticky time.'

I drove in contentment to the French Horn at Sonning, where the food was legendary and floodlights shone on willow trees drooping over the Thames. We went inside and sat on a sofa, and watched ducks roast on a spit over an open fire, and drank champagne. I stretched and breathed deeply, and felt the tensions of the long week relax: and I'd got to phone Rose Quince.

I went and phoned her. Answering machine again. I

said, 'Rose, Rose, I love you. Rose, I need you. If you come home before eleven, please, I beg you, ring me at the French Horn Hotel, the number is 0734 692204, tell them I'm in the restaurant having dinner.'

I telephoned Wykeham. 'Is the headache better?' I said.

'What?'

'Never mind. How's the mare?'

The mare was sore but eating, Mr Davis's horse was exhausted, Inchcape hardly looked as if he'd had a race.

'Icefall,' I said.

'What? I wish you wouldn't ride him from so far in front.'

'He liked it. And it worked.'

'I was watching on TV. Can you come and school on Tuesday? We have no runners that day, I'm not sending any to Southwell.'

'Yes, all right.'

'Well done, today,' he said with sincerity. 'Very well done.'

'Thanks.'

'Yes. Er. Goodnight then, Paul.'

'Goodnight, Wykeham,' I said.

I went back to Danielle and we spent the whole evening talking and later eating in the restaurant with silver and candlelight gleaming on the tables and a living vine growing over the ceiling; and at the last minute Rose Quince called me back.

'It's after eleven,' she said, 'but I just took a chance.'

'You're a dear.'

'I sure am. So what is so urgent, buddy boy?'

'Um,' I said. 'Does the name Saul Bradfield or Saul Bradley . . . something like that . . . mean anything to you?'

'Saul Bradley? Of course it does. What's so urgent about him?'

'Who is he?'

'He used to be the sports editor of the *Towncrier*. He retired last year . . . everyone's universal father-figure, an old friend of Bill's.'

'Do you know where he lives?'

'Good heavens. Wait while I think. Why do you want him?'

'In the general area of demolishing our business friend of the tapes.'

'Oh. Well, let's see. He moved. He said he was taking his wife to live by the sea. I'd've thought it would drive him mad but no accounting for taste. Worthing, or somewhere. No. Selsey.' Her voice strengthened. 'I remember, Selsey, in Sussex.'

'Terrific,' I said. 'And Lord Vaughnley. Where does he live?'

'Mostly in Regent's Park, in one of the Nash terraces. They've a place in Kent too, near Sevenoaks.'

'Could you tell me exactly?' I said. 'I mean . . . I'd like to write to thank him for my Towncrier trophy, and for all his other help.'

'Sure,' she said easily, and told me both his addresses

329

right down to the postal codes, tacking on the telephone numbers for good measure. 'You might need those. They're not in the directory.'

'I'm back in your debt,' I said, writing it all down.

'Deep, deep, buddy boy.'

I replaced the receiver feeling perfidious but unrepentant, and went to fetch Danielle to drive her home. It was midnight, more or less, when I pulled up in Eaton Square: and it wasn't where I would have preferred to have taken her, but where it was best.

'Thank you,' she said, 'for a great day.'

'What about tomorrow?'

'OK.'

'I don't know what time,' I said. 'I've something to do first.'

'Call me.'

'Yes.'

We sat in the car looking at each other, as if we hadn't been doing that already for hours. I've known her since Tuesday, I thought. In five days she'd grown roots in my life. I kissed her with much more hunger than before, which didn't seem to worry her, and I thought not long, not long . . . but not yet. When it was right, not before.

We said goodnight again on the pavement, and I watched her go into the house, carrying her present and waving as she closed the door. Princess Casilia, I thought, you are severely inhibiting, but I said I'd bring your niece home, and I have; and I don't even know

330

what Danielle wanted, I can't read her mind and she
didn't tell me in words, and tomorrow . . . tomorrow
maybe I'd ask.

Early in the morning I drove to Selsey on the South
Coast and looked up Saul Bradley in the local tele-
phone book, and there he was, address and all, 15 Sea
View Lane.

His house was on two floors and looked more sub-
urban than seaside with mock-Tudor beams in its cream
plastered gables. The mock-Tudor door, when I rang
the bell, was opened by a grey-haired bespectacled
motherly looking person in a flowered overall, and I
could smell bacon frying.

'Hugh?' she said in reply to my question. 'Yes, he's
still here, but he's still in bed. You know what boys
are.'

'I'll wait,' I said.

She looked doubtful.

'I do very much want to see him,' I said.

'You'd better come in,' she said. 'I'll ask my husband.
I think he's shaving, but he'll be down soon.'

She led me across the entrance hall into a smallish
kitchen, all yellow and white tiles, with sunlight
flooding in.

'A friend of Hugh's?' she said.

'Yes . . . I was talking to him yesterday.'

She shook her head worriedly. 'It's all most upsetting.

He shouldn't have gone to the races. He was more miserable than ever when he came back.'

'I'll do my best,' I said, 'to make things better.'

She attended to the breakfast she was frying, pushing the bacon round with a spatula. 'Did you say Fielding, your name was?' She turned from the cooker, the spatula in the air, motion arrested. 'Kit Fielding? The jockey?'

'Yes.'

She didn't know what to make of it, which wasn't surprising. She said uncertainly, 'I'm brewing some tea,' and I said I'd wait until after I'd seen her husband and Hugh.

Her husband came enquiringly into the kitchen, hearing my voice, and he knew me immediately by sight. A sports editor would, I supposed. Bunty Ireland's ex-boss was comfortably large with a bald head and shrewd eyes and a voice grown fruity, as from beer.

My presence nonplussed him, as it had his wife.

'You want to help Hugh? I suppose it's all right. Bill Vaughnley was speaking highly of you a few days ago. I'll go and get Hugh up. He's not good in the mornings. Want some breakfast?'

I hesitated.

'Like that, is it?' He chuckled. 'Starving and daren't put on an ounce.'

He went away into the house and presently returned,

followed shortly by Hugh, tousle-haired, in jeans and a T-shirt, his eyes puffed from sleep.

'Hello,' he said, bewildered. 'How did you find me?'

'You told me where you were staying.'

'Did I? I suppose I did. Er . . . sorry and all that, but what do you want?'

I wanted, I said, to take him out for a drive, to talk things over and see what could be done to help him: and with no more persuasion, he came.

He didn't seem to realize that his father had made sure he didn't speak to me further on the previous day. It had been done too skilfully for him to notice, especially in the anxiety he'd been suffering.

'Your father made you come back here,' I said, as we drove along Sea View Lane. 'Wouldn't let you go home?'

'It's so unfair.' There was self-pity in his voice, and also acceptance. The exile had been earned, I thought, and Hugh knew it.

'Tell me, then,' I said.

'Well, you know him. He's your father-in-law. I mean, no, he's your sister's father-in-law.'

I breathed deeply. 'Maynard Allardeck.'

'Yes. He caused it all. I'd kill him, if I could.'

I glanced at the good-looking immature face, at the dimples. Even the word kill came oddly from that mouth.

'I mean,' he said in an aggrieved voice, 'he's a member of the Jockey Club. Respected. I thought it was all right. I mean, he and Dad are patrons of the same charity. How was I to know? How was I?'

'You weren't,' I said. 'What happened?'

'He introduced me to his bookmaker.'

Whatever I'd imagined he might say, it wasn't that. I rolled the car to a halt in a parking place which at that time on a Sunday November morning was deserted. There was a distant glimpse of shingle banks and scrubby grass and sea glittering in the early sun, and nearby there was little but an acre of tarmac edged by a low brick wall, and a summer ice cream stall firmly shut.

'I've got a video camera,' I said. 'If you'd care to speak into that, I'll show the tape to your father, get him to hear your side of things, see if I can persuade him to let you go home.'

'Would you?' he said, hopefully.

'Yes, I would.'

I stretched behind my seat for the bag with the camera. 'Let's sit on the wall,' I said. 'It might be a bit chilly, but we'd get a better picture than inside the car.'

He made no objection, but came and sat on the wall, where I steadied the camera on one knee bent up, framed his face in the viewfinder and asked him to speak straight at the lens.

'Say that again,' I prompted, 'about the bookmaker.'

'I was at the races with my parents one day and having a bet, and a bookmaker was saying I wasn't old enough and making a fuss, and Maynard Allardeck was there and he said not to worry, he would introduce me to his own bookmaker instead.'

'How do you mean, he was there?'

Hugh's brow furrowed. 'He was just standing there. I mean, I didn't know who he was, but he explained he was a friend of my father.'

'And how old were you, and when did this happen?'

'That's what's so silly. I was twenty. I mean, you can bet on your eighteenth birthday. Do I look seventeen?'

'No,' I said truthfully. 'You look twenty.'

'I was twenty-one, actually, in August. It was right back in April when I met Maynard Allardeck.'

'So you started betting with Maynard Allardeck's bookmaker . . . regularly?'

'Well, yes,' Hugh said unhappily. 'He made it so easy, always so friendly, and he never seemed to worry when I didn't pay his accounts.'

'There isn't a bookmaker born who doesn't insist on his money.'

'This one didn't,' Hugh said defensively. 'I used to apologize. He'd say never mind, one day, I know you'll pay when you can, and he used to joke . . . and let me bet again . . .'

'He let you bet until you were very deeply in debt?'

'Yes. Encouraged me. I mean, I suppose I should have known . . . but he was so friendly, you see. All the summer . . . Flat racing, every day . . . on the telephone.'

'Until all this happened,' I said, 'did you bet much?'

'I've always liked betting. Studying the form. Picking

the good things, following hunches. Never any good, I suppose, but probably any money I ever had went on horses. I'd get someone to put it on for me, on the Tote, when I was ten, and so on. Always. I mean, I won often too, of course. Terrific wins, quite often.'

'Mm.'

'Everyone who goes racing bets,' he said. 'What else do they go for? I mean, there's nothing wrong with a gamble, everyone does it. It's fun.'

'Mm,' I said again. 'But you were betting every day, several bets a day, even though you didn't go.'

'I suppose so, yes.'

'And then one day,' I said, 'it stopped being fun?'

'The Hove Stakes at Brighton,' he said. 'In September.'

'What about it?'

'Three runners. Slateroof couldn't be beaten. Maynard Allardeck told me. Help yourself, he said. Recoup your losses.'

'When did he tell you?'

'Few days before. At the races. Ascot. I went with my parents, and he happened to be there too.'

'And did you go to Brighton?'

'No.' He shook his head. 'Rang up the bookmaker. He said he couldn't give me a good price, Slateroof was a certainty, everyone knew it. Five to one on, he said. If I bet twenty, I could win four.'

'So you bet twenty pounds?'

'No.' Hugh looked surprised. 'Twenty thousand.'

'Twenty ... thousand.' I kept my voice steady, unemotional. 'Was that, er, a big bet, for you, by that time?'

'Biggish. I mean, you can't win much in fivers, can you?'

You couldn't lose much either, I thought. I said, 'What was normal?'

'Anything between one thousand and twenty. I mean, I got there gradually, I suppose. I got used to it. Maynard Allardeck said one had to think big. I never thought of how much they really were. They were just numbers.' He paused, looking unhappy. 'I know it sounds stupid to say it now, but none of it seemed real. I mean, I never had to pay anything out. It was all done on paper. When I won, I felt great. When I lost I didn't really worry. I don't suppose you'll understand. Dad didn't. He couldn't understand how I could have been so stupid. But it just seemed like a game ... and everyone smiled ...'

'So Slateroof got beaten?'

'He didn't even start. He got left flat-footed in the stalls.'

'Oh yes,' I said. 'I remember reading about it. There was an enquiry and the jockey got fined.'

'Yes, but the bets stood, of course.'

'So what happened next?' I said.

'I got this frightful account from the bookmaker. He'd totted up everything, he said, and it seemed to be

337

getting out of hand, and he'd like to be paid. I mean, there were pages of it.'

'Records of all the bets you'd made with him?'

'Yes, that's right. Winners and losers. Many more losers. I mean, there were some losers I couldn't remember backing; though he swore I had, he said he would produce his office records to prove it, if I liked, but he said I was ungenerous to make such a suggestion when he'd been so accommodating and patient.' Hugh swallowed. 'I don't know if he cheated me, I just don't. I mean, I did bet on two horses in the same race quite often, I know that, but I didn't realize I'd done it so much.'

'And you'd kept no record, yourself, of how much you'd bet, and what on?'

'I didn't think of it. I mean, I could remember. I mean, I thought I could.'

'Mm. Well, what next?'

'Maynard Allardeck telephoned me at home and said he'd heard from our mutual bookmaker that I was in difficulties, and could he help, as he felt sort of responsible, having introduced me, so to speak. He said we could meet somewhere and perhaps he could suggest some solutions. So I met him for lunch in a restaurant in London, and talked it all over. He said I should confess to my father and get him to pay my debts but I said I couldn't, he would be so angry, he'd no idea I'd gambled so much, he was always lecturing me about taking care of money. And I didn't want to disappoint him, if you can understand that? I didn't want him to be upset. I mean, I expect it sounds silly, but it wasn't really out of fear, it was, well, sort of love, really, only it's difficult to explain.'

'Yes,' I said, 'go on.'

'Maynard Allardeck said not to worry, he could see why I couldn't tell my father, it reflected well on me, he said, and he would lend me the money himself, and I could pay him back slowly, and he would just charge me a little over, if I thought that was fair. And I did think it was fair, of course. I was so extremely relieved. I thanked him a lot, over and over.'

'So Maynard Allardeck paid your bookmaker?'

'Yes.' Hugh nodded. 'I got a final account from him marked "Paid with thanks", and a note saying it would be best if I laid off betting for a while, but if I needed him in the future, he would accommodate me again. I mean, I thought it very fair and kind, wouldn't you?'

'Mm,' I said dryly. 'And then after a while Maynard Allardeck told you he was short of money himself and would have to call in the debt?'

'Yes,' Hugh said in surprise. 'How did you know? He was so apologetic and embarrassed I almost felt sorry for him, though he was putting me in a terrible hole. Terrible. And then he suggested a way round it, which was so easy ... so simple ... like the sun coming out. I couldn't think why I hadn't thought of it myself.'

'Hugh,' I asked slowly, 'what did you have, that he wanted?'

'My shares in the *Towncrier*,' he said.

CHAPTER EIGHTEEN

He took my breath away. Oh my Christ, I thought. Bloody bingo.

Talk about the sun coming out. So simple, so easy. Why hadn't I thought of it myself.

'Your shares in the *Towncrier* . . .'

'Yes,' Hugh said. 'They were left to me by my grand-father. I mean, I didn't know I had them, until I was twenty-one.'

'In August.'

'Yes. That's right. Anyway, it seemed to solve every-thing. I mean it did solve everything, didn't it? Maynard Allardeck looked up the proper market value and everything, and gave me two or three forms to sign, which I did, and then he said that was fine, we were all square, I had no more debts. I mean, it was so And it wasn't all of my shares. Not even ha

'How much were the shares wort Allard

He hun

After a pause I said, 'Didn't it upset you . . . so much money?'

'Of course not. It was only on paper. And Maynard Allardeck laughed and said if I ever felt like gambling again, well, I had the collateral, and we could always come to the same arrangement again, if it was necessary. I begged him not to tell my father, and he said no, he wouldn't.'

'But your father found out?'

'Yes, it was something to do with voting shares, or preference shares or debentures. I'm really not sure, I didn't know what they were talking about, but they were busy fending off a takeover. They're always fending off takeovers, but this one had them all dead worried, and somewhere in the *Towncrier* they discovered that half of my shares had gone, and Dad made me tell him what I'd done . . . and he was so angry . . . I'd never seen him angry . . . never like that . . .'

His voice faded away, his eyes stark with remembrance.

'He sent me here to Saul Bradley and he said if I ever bet on anything ever again I could never go home . . . I want him . . . I do . . . to forgive me. I want . . . home.'

. . . ed. The intensity of his feelings stared into . . . camera run for a few silent seconds,

to go . . .

He stopp . . .

the lens. I let the . . .

and then turned it o . . .

'I'll show him the film . . . ?'

'Do you think . . . ?'

' I said.

'In time he'll forgive you? Yes, I'd say so.'

'I could go back to just the odd bet in cash on the Tote.' His eyes were speculative, his air much too hopeful. The infection too deep in his system.

'Hugh,' I said, 'would you mind if I gave you some advice?'

'No. Fire away.'

'Take some practical lessons about money. Go away without any, find out it's not just numbers on a page, learn it's the difference between eating and hunger. Bet your dinner, and if you lose, see if it's worth it.'

He said earnestly, 'Yes, I do see what you mean. But I might win.' And I wondered doubtfully whether one could ever reform an irresponsible gambler, be he rich, poor, or the heir to the *Towncrier*.

I drove back to London, added the Hugh Vaughnley tape to the others in the hotel's care, and went upstairs for another session of staring blindly at the walls. Then I telephoned Holly, and got Bobby instead.

'How's things?' I said.

'Not much different. Holly's lying down, do you want to talk to her?'

'You'll do fine.'

'I've had some more cheques from the owners. Almost everyone's paid.'

'That's great.'

'They're a drop in the ocean.' His voice sounded tired. 'Will your valet cash them again?'

'Sure to.'

'Even then,' he said, 'we're right at the end.'

'I suppose,' I said, 'you haven't heard any more from the *Flag*? No letter? No money?'

'Not a thing.'

I sighed internally and said, 'Bobby, I want to talk to your father.'

'It won't do any good. You know what he was like the other day. He's stubborn and mean, and he hates us.'

'He hates me,' I said, 'and Holly. Not you.'

'One wouldn't guess it,' he said bitterly.

'I've no rides on Tuesday,' I said. 'Persuade him to come to your house on Tuesday afternoon. I'm schooling at Wykeham's place in the morning.'

'It's impossible. He wouldn't come here.'

'He might,' I said, 'if you tell him he was right all along, every Fielding is your enemy, and you want his help in getting rid of me, out of your life.'

'Kit!' He was outraged. 'I can't do that. It's the last thing I want.'

'And if you can bring yourself to it, tell him you're getting tired of Holly, as well.'

'No. How can I? I love her so much . . . I couldn't make it sound true.'

'Bobby, nothing less will bring him. Can you think

of anything else? I've been thinking for hours. If you can get him there some other way, we'll do it your way.'

After a pause he said, 'He would come out of hate. Isn't that awful? He's my father . . .'

'Yes. I'm sorry.'

'What do you want to talk to him about?'

'A proposition. Help for you in return for something he'd want. But don't tell him that. Don't tell him I'm coming. Just get him there, if you can.'

He said doubtfully, 'He'll never help us. Never.'

'Well, we'll see. At least give it a try.'

'Yes, all right, but for heaven's sake, Kit . . .'

'What?'

'It's dreadful to say it, but where you're concerned . . . I think he's dangerous.'

'I'll be careful.'

'It goes back so far . . . When I was little he taught me to hit things . . . with my fists, with a stick, anything, and he told me to think I was hitting Kit Fielding.'

I took a breath. 'Like in the garden?'

'God, Kit . . . I've been so sorry.'

'I told you. I mean it. It's all right.'

'I've been thinking about you, and remembering so much. Things I'd forgotten, like him telling me the Fieldings would eat me if I was naughty . . . I must have been three or four. I was scared stiff.'

'When you were four, I was two.'

'It was your father and your grandfather who would eat me. Then when you were growing up he told me

345

to hit Kit Fielding, he taught me how, he said one day it would be you and I, we would have to fight. I'd forgotten all that ... but I remember it now.'

'My grandfather,' I sighed, 'gave me a punchbag and taught me how to hit it. That's Bobby Allardeck, he said. Bash him.'

'Do you mean it?'

'Ask Holly. She knows.'

'Bloody, weren't they.'

'It's finished now,' I said.

We disconnected and I got through to Danielle and said how about lunch and tea and dinner.

'Are you planning to eat all those?' she said.

'All or any.'

'All, then.'

'I'll come straight round.'

She opened the Eaton Square front door as I braked to a halt and came across the pavement with a spring in her step, an evocation of summer in a flower-patterned jacket over cream trousers, the chintz band holding back the fluffy hair.

She climbed into the car beside me and kissed me as if from old habit.

'Aunt Casilia sends her regards and hopes we'll have a nice day.'

'And back by midnight?'

'I would think so, wouldn't you?'

'Does she notice?'

'She sure does. I go past their rooms to get to mine

– she and Uncle Roland sleep separately – and the floors creak. She called me in last night to ask if I'd enjoyed myself. She was sitting in bed, reading, looking a knock-out as usual. I told her what we'd done and showed her the chest of drawers . . . we had quite a long talk.'

I studied her face. She looked seriously back.

'What did she say?' I asked.

'It matters to you, doesn't it, what she thinks?'

'Yes.'

'I guess she'd be glad.'

'Tell me, then.'

'Not yet.' She smiled swiftly, almost secretly. 'What about this lunch?'

We went to a restaurant up a tower and ate looking out over half of London. 'Consommé and strawberries . . . you'll be good for my figure,' she said.

'Have some sugar and cream.'

'Not if you don't.'

'You're thin enough,' I said.

'Don't you get tired of it?'

'Of not eating much? I sure do.'

'But you never let up?'

'A pound overweight in the saddle,' I said wryly, 'can mean a length's difference at the winning post.'

'End of discussion.'

Over coffee I asked if there was anywhere she'd like to go, though I apologized that most of London seemed to shut on Sundays, especially in November.

'I'd like to see where you live,' she said. 'I'd like to see Lambourn.'

'Right,' I said, and drove her there, seventy miles westwards down the M4 motorway, heading back towards Devon, keeping this time law-abidingly within the speed limit, curling off into the large village, small town, where the church stood at the main crossroads and a thousand thoroughbreds lived in boxes.

'It's quiet,' she said.

'It's Sunday.'

'Where's your cottage?'

'We'll drive past there,' I said. 'But we're not going in.'

She was puzzled, and, it seemed, disappointed, looking across at me lengthily. 'Why not?'

I explained about the break in, and the police saying the place had been searched. 'The intruders found nothing they wanted, and they stole nothing. But I'd bet they left something behind.'

'What do you mean?'

'Creepy-crawlies.'

'Bugs?'

'Mm,' I said. 'That's it over there.'

We went past slowly. There was no sign of life. No sign of heavy men lying in the bushes with sharp knives, which they wouldn't be by then, not after three days. Too boring, too cold. Listening somewhere, though, those two, or others.

348

The cottage was brick-built, rather plain, and would perhaps have looked better in June, with the roses.

'It's all right inside,' I said.

'Yuh.' She sounded downcast. 'OK. That's that.'

I drove around and up a hill and took her to the new house instead.

'Whose is this?' she said. 'This is great.'

'This is mine.' I got out of the car, fishing for keys. 'It's empty. Come and look.'

The bright day was fading but there was enough direct sunlight to shine horizontally through the windows and light the big empty rooms, and although the air inside was cold, the central heating, when I switched it on, went into smooth operation with barely a hiccup. There were a few light sockets with bulbs in, but no shades. No curtains. No carpets. Wood-block floor everywhere, swept but not polished. Signs of builders all over the place.

'They're just starting to paint,' I said, opening the double doors from the hall to the sitting room. 'I'll move in alongside, if they don't hurry up.'

There were trestles in the sitting room set up for reaching the ceiling, and an army of tubs of paint, and dustsheets all over the flooring to avoid spatters.

'It's huge,' she said. 'Incredible.'

'It's got a great kitchen. An office. Lots of things.' I explained about the bankrupt builder. 'He designed it for himself.'

We went around and through everywhere and ended

in the big room which led directly off the sitting room, the room where I would sleep. It seemed that the decorators had started with that: it was clean, bare and finished, the bathroom painted and tiled, the woodblocks faintly gleaming with the first layer of polish, the western sun splashing in patches on the white walls.

Danielle stood by the window looking out at the muddy expanse which by summer would be a terrace, with geraniums in pots. The right person . . . in the right place . . . at the right time.

'Will you lie in my bedroom?' I said.

She turned, silhouetted against the sun, her hair like a halo, her face in shadow, hard to read. It seemed that she was listening still to what I'd said, as if to be sure that she had heard right and not misunderstood.

'On the bare floor?' Her voice was steady, uncommitted, friendly and light.

'We could, er, fetch some dustsheets, perhaps.'

She considered it.

'OK,' she said.

We brought a few dustsheets from the sitting room and arranged them in a rough rectangle, with pillows.

'I've seen better marriage beds,' she said.

We took all our clothes off, not hurrying, dropping them in heaps. No real surprises. She was as I had thought, flat and rounded, her skin glowing now in the sun. She stretched out her fingers, touching lightly the stitches, the fading bruises, the known places.

She said, 'When you looked at me at the races yesterday, over those cups, were you thinking of this?'

'Something like this. Was it so obvious?'

'Blinding.'

'I was afraid so.'

We didn't talk a great deal after that. We stood together for a while, and lay down, and on the hard cotton surface learned the ultimate things about each other, pleasing and pleased, with advances and retreats, with murmurs and intensities and breathless primeval energy.

The sunlight faded slowly, the sky lit still with afterglow, gleams reflecting in her eyes and on her teeth, darknesses deepening in hollows and in her hair.

At the end of a long calm afterwards she said prosaically, 'I suppose the water's not hot?'

'Bound to be,' I said lazily. 'It's combined with the heating. Everything's working, lights, plumbing, the lot.'

We got up and went into the bathroom, switching on taps but not lights. It was darker in there and we moved like shadows, more substance than shape.

I turned on the shower, running it warm. Danielle stepped into it with me, and we made love again there in the spray, with tenderness, with passion and in friendship, her arms round my neck, her stomach flat on mine, united as I'd never been before in my life.

I turned off the tap, in the end.

'There aren't any towels,' I said.

'Always the dustsheets.'

We took our bed apart and dried ourselves, and got dressed, and kissed again with temperance, feeling clean. In almost full darkness we dumped the dust sheets in the sitting room, switched off the heating, and went out of the house, locking it behind us.

Danielle looked back before getting into the car. 'I wonder what the house thinks,' she said.

'It thinks holy wow.'

'As a matter of fact, so do I.'

We drove back to London along the old roads, not the motorway, winding through the empty Sunday evening streets of a string of towns, stopping at traffic lights, stretching the journey. I parked the car in central London and we walked for a while, stopping to read menus, and eating eventually in a busy French bistro with red checked tablecloths and an androgynous guitarist; sitting in a corner, holding hands, reading the bill of fare chalked on a blackboard.

'Aunt Casilia,' Danielle said, sometime later over coffee, her eyes shining with amusement, 'said last night, among other things, that while decorum was essential, abstinence was not.'

I laughed in surprise, and kissed her, and in a while and in decorum drove her back to Eaton Square.

I raced at Windsor the next day, parking the car at the railway station and taking a taxi from there right to the jockeys' entrance gate near the weighing room on the racecourse.

The princess had no runners and wasn't expected; I rode two horses each for Wykeham and the Lambourn trainer and got all of them round into the first or second place, which pleased the owners and put grins on the stable lads. Bunty Ireland, beaming, told me I was on the winning streak of all time, and I calculated the odds that I'd come crashing down again by Thursday, and hoped that I wouldn't, and that he was right.

My valet said, sure, he would return me to the station in his van – a not too abnormal service. He was reading aloud from the *Flag* with disfavour. 'Reality is sweaty armpits, sordid sex, junkies dead in public lavatories, it says here.' He threw the paper on to the bench. 'Reality is the gas bill, remembering the wife's birthday, a beer with your mates, that's more like it. Get in the van, Kit, it's right outside the weighing room. I've just about finished here.'

Reality, I thought, going out, was speed over fences, a game of manners, love in a shower: to each his own.

I travelled without incident back to the hotel and telephoned on time to Wykeham.

'Where are you?' he said. 'People keep asking for you.'

'Who?' I said.

'They don't say. Four fellows, at least. All day. Where are you?'

'Staying with friends.'

'Oh.' He didn't ask further. He himself didn't care. We talked about his winner and his second, and discussed the horses I would be schooling in the morning.

'One of those fellows who rang wanted you for some lunch party or other in London,' he said, as if suddenly remembering. 'They invited me, too. The sponsors of Inchcape's race, last Saturday. The princess is going, and they wanted us as well. They said it was a great opportunity as they could see from tomorrow's race programmes that we hadn't any runners.'

'Are you going?'

'No, no. I said I couldn't. But it might be better if you came here early, and do the schooling in good time.'

I agreed, and said goodnight.

'Goodnight, Kit,' he said.

I got through to my answering machine, and there among the messages were the sponsors of Icefall's race, inviting me to lunch the next day. They would be delighted if I could join them and the princess in celebrating our victory in their race, please could I ring back at the given number.

I rang the number and got an answering machine referring me on, reaching finally the head of the sponsors himself.

'Great, great, you can come?' he said. 'Twelve-thirty at the Guineas restaurant in Curzon Street. See you there. That's splendid.'

Sponsors got advertising from racing and in return

pumped in generous cash. There was an unspoken understanding among racing people that sponsors were to be appreciated, and that jockeys should turn up if possible where invited. Part of the job. And I wanted to go, besides, to talk to the princess.

I answered my other messages, none of which were important, and then got through to Holly.

'Bobby spoke to his father,' she said. 'The beast said he would come only if you were there. Bobby didn't like it.'

'Did Bobby say I would be there anyway?'

'No, he waited to know what you wanted him to say. He has to ring back to his father.'

I didn't like it any more than Bobby. 'Why does Maynard want me?' I said. 'I didn't think he would come at all if he knew I'd be there.'

'He said he would help Bobby get rid of you once and for all, but that you had to be there.'

Bang, I thought, goes any advantage of surprise. 'All right,' I said. 'Tell Bobby to tell him I'll be coming. At about four o'clock, I should think. I'm going to a sponsors' lunch in London.'

'Kit . . . whatever you're planning, don't do it.'

'Must.'

'I've a feeling . . .'

'Stifle it. How's the baby?'

'Never have one,' she said. 'It's the pits.'

*

355

I collected all four recorded video tapes from the hotel's vaults and took them with six others, unused, to Chiswick: and kissed Danielle with circumspection at her desk.

'Hi,' she said, smiling deeply in her eyes.

'Hi, yourself.'

'How did it go, today?'

'Two wins, two seconds.'

'And no crunches.'

'No crunches.'

She seemed to relax. 'I'm glad you're OK.'

Joe appeared from the passage to the editing rooms saying he was biting his fingernails with inactivity and had I by any chance brought my tapes. I picked the four recorded tapes off Danielle's desk and he pounced on them, bearing them away.

I followed him with the spare tapes into an editing room and sat beside him while he played the interviews through, one by one, his dark face showing shock.

'Can you stick them together?' I asked, when he'd finished.

'I sure can,' he said sombrely. 'What you need is some voice-over linkage. You got anything else? Shots of scenery, anything like that?'

I shook my head. 'I didn't think of it.'

'It's no good putting a voice-over on a black screen,' he explained. 'You've got to have pictures, to hold interest. We're bound to have something here in the library that we can use.'

Danielle appeared at the doorway, looking enquiring.

'How's it going?' she said.

'I guess you know what's on these tapes,' Joe said.

'No. Kit hasn't told me.'

'Good,' Joe said. 'When I've finished, we'll try it out on you. Get a reaction.'

'OK,' she said. 'It's a quiet night for news, thank goodness.'

She went away and Joe got me to speak into a microphone, explaining who the Perrysides were, giving George Tarker a location, introducing Hugh Vaughnley. I wanted them in that order, I said.

'Right,' he said. 'Now you go away and talk to Danielle and leave it to me, and if you don't like the result, no problem, we can always change it.'

'I brought these unused tapes,' I said, giving them to him. 'Once we've settled on the final version, could we make copies?'

He took one of the new tapes, peeled off the cellophane wrapping and put it into a machine. 'A breeze,' he said.

He spent two or three hours on it, coming out whistling a couple of times to see if the station chief was still happy (which he appeared to be), telling me Spielberg couldn't do better, drinking coffee from a machine, going cheerfully back.

Danielle worked sporadically on a story about a police hunt for a rapist who lurked in bus shelters and had just been arrested, which she said would probably not make it on to network news back home, but kept everyone working, at least. No Devil-Boys, no oil fires that night.

Aunt Casilia, Danielle said, was looking forward to tomorrow's lunch party and hoped I would be there.

'Will you be going?' I asked.

'Nope. Aunt Casilia would have gotten me invited, but I've a college friend passing through London. We're having lunch. Long time date, I can't break it.'

'Pity.'

'You're going? Shall I tell her?'

I nodded. 'I'm schooling some of her horses in the morning, and I'll be coming along after.'

Joe came out finally, stretching his backbone and flexing his fingers.

'Come on, then,' he said. 'Come and see.'

We all went, the station chief as well, sitting in chairs collected from adjoining rooms. Joe started his machine, and there, immediately, was the uncut version of the television interview of Maynard and his tormentor, followed by the list of firms Maynard had acquired. At the end of that the tape returned to repeat the interviewer's outline of Metavane's story, and then came my voice, superimposed on views of horses exercising on Newmarket Health, explaining who Major and Mrs Perryside were, and where they now lived.

The Perrysides appeared in entirety, poignant and

brave; and at the end the tape returned to the television interviewer again repeating the takeover list. This time it stopped after the mention of Purfleet Electronics, and then, over a view of mudflats in the Thames estuary, my voice introduced George Tarker. The whole of that interview was there also, and when he said in tears about his son wiring himself up, Danielle's own eyes filled . . .

Joe left the shot of George Tarker's ravaged face running as long as I'd taped it, and then there was my voice again, this time over a printing press in full production, explaining that the next person to appear would be the son of Lord Vaughnley, who owned the *Daily* and *Sunday Towncrier* newspapers.

All of Hugh's tape was there, ending with his impassioned plea to come home. On the screen after that came a long shot taken from the cut televised version of *How's Trade*, of Maynard smiling and looking noble. The soundtrack of that had been erased, so that one saw him in silence. Then the screen went silently into solid black for about ten seconds before reverting to snow and background crackle.

Even though I'd recorded three of the main segments myself, the total effect was overpowering. Run together they were a punch to the brain, emotional, damning the wicked.

The station chief said, 'Christ', and Danielle blew her nose.

'It runs for one hour, thirteen minutes,' Joe said to me, 'if you're interested.'

'I can't thank you enough.'

'I hope the bastard burns,' he said.

In the morning I went to Wykeham's place south of London and on the Downs there spent two profitable hours teaching his absolute novices how to jump and refreshing the memories of others. We gave the one who had fallen at Ascot a pop to help him get his confidence back after being brought down, and talked about the runners for the rest of that week.

'Thank you for coming,' he said. 'Good of you.'

'A pleasure.'

'Goodbye, P . . . er . . . Kit.'

'Goodbye, Wykeham,' I said.

I went back to London, showered, dressed in grey suit, white shirt, quiet tie, presenting a civilized face to the sponsors.

I put one of the six copies Joe had made of the Allardeck production into a large envelope, sticking it shut, and then zipped a second of them into the big inside pocket of my blue anorak. The other four I took downstairs and lodged in the hotel vault, and carrying both the envelope and the anorak went by taxi to Eric Olderjohn's terrace house behind Sloane Square.

The taxi waited while I rang the bell beside the green door, and not much to my surprise there was no one at home. I wrote on the envelope: 'Mr Olderjohn, Please give this to a Certain Person, for his eyes only. Regards, Kit Fielding' and pushed it through the letter box.

'Right,' I said to the taxi driver. 'The Guineas restaurant, Curzon Street.'

The Guineas, where I'd been several times before, was principally a collection of private dining rooms of various sizes, chiefly used for private parties such as the one I was bound for. Opulent and discreet, it went in for dark green flocked wallpaper, gilded cherubs and waiters in gloves. Every time I had been there, there had been noisettes of lamb.

I left my anorak in the cloakroom downstairs and put the ticket in my pocket, walked up the broad stairs to the next floor, turned right, went down a passage and ended, as directed, at the sponsors' party in the One Thousand Room.

The sponsors greeted me effusively. 'Come in, come in. Have some champagne.' They gave me a glass.

The princess was there, dressed in a cream silk suit with gold and citrines, dark hair piled high, smiling.

'I'm so pleased you've come,' she said, shaking my hand.

'I wouldn't have missed it.'

'How are my horses? How is Icefall? How is my

361

poor Allegheny? Did you know that Lord Vaughnley is here?'

'Is he?'

I looked around. There were about thirty people present, more perhaps than I'd expected. From across the room Lady Vaughnley saw me, and waved.

'The *Towncrier* joined forces with the Icefall people,' the princess said. 'It's a double party, now.'

The Icefall sponsors came to bear her away. 'Do come ... may I present ...'

Lord Vaughnley approached, looking blander than bland.

'Now, everybody,' said one of the sponsors loudly, 'we're all going into another room to see films of our two races, both won by our most honoured guest, Princess Casilia.'

There was a little light applause, and everyone began to move to the door. Lord Vaughnley stood at my elbow. The princess looked back. 'You're coming, Kit?'

'In a minute,' Lord Vaughnley said. 'Just want to ask him something.'

The princess smiled and nodded and went on. Lord Vaughnley shepherded everyone out, and when the room was empty, closed the door and stood with his back to it.

'I wanted to reach you,' I said; but I don't think he heard. He was looking towards a second door, set in a side wall.

The door opened, and two people came through it.

Nestor Pollgate.

Jay Erskine.

Pollgate looked satisfied and Jay Erskine was smirking.

CHAPTER NINETEEN

'Neatly done,' Pollgate said to Lord Vaughnley.

'It worked out well,' he replied, his big head nodding.

He still stood four-square in front of the door. Erskine stood similarly, with folded arms, in front of the other.

There were chairs and tables round the green walls, tables with white cloths bearing bowls of nuts and cigarette-filled ashtrays. Champagne goblets all over the place, some still with bubble contents. There would be waiters, I thought, coming to clear the rubble.

'We won't be disturbed,' Pollgate told Lord Vaughnley. 'The "do not enter" signs are on both doors, and Mario says we have the room for an hour.'

'The lunch will be before that,' Lord Vaughnley said. 'The films take half an hour, no more.'

'He's not going to the lunch,' Pollgate said, meaning me.

'Er, no, perhaps not. But I should be there.'

I thought numbly: catch me first.

It had taken five days ... and the princess.

'You are going to give us,' Pollgate said to me directly, 'the wire-tap and my journalists' belongings. And that will be the end of it.'

The power of the man was such that the words themselves were a threat. What would happen if I didn't comply wasn't mentioned. My compliance was assumed; no discussion.

He walked over to Jay Erskine, producing a flat box from a pocket and taking Jay Erskine's place guarding the door.

Jay Erskine's smirk grew to a twisted smile of anticipation. I disliked intensely the cold eyes, the drooping moustache, his callous pen and his violent nature; and most of all I disliked the message in his sneer.

Pollgate opened the box and held it out to Jay Erskine, who took from it something that looked like the hand-held remote control of a television set. He settled it into his hand and walked in my direction. He came without the wariness one might have expected after I'd thrown him across a room, and he put the remote control thing smoothly between the open fronts of my jacket, on to my shirt.

I felt something like a thud, and the next thing I knew I was lying flat on my back on the floor, wholly disorientated, not sure where I was or what had happened.

Jay Erskine and Lord Vaughnley bent down, took my arms, helped me up, and dropped me on to a chair.

The chair had arms. I held on to them. I felt dazed, and couldn't work out why.

Jay Erskine smiled nastily and put the black object again against my shirt.

The thud had a burn to it that time. And so fast. No time to draw breath.

I would have shot out of the chair if they hadn't held me in it. My wits scattered instantly to the four winds. My muscles didn't work. I wasn't sure who I was or where I was, and nor did I care. Time passed. Time was relative. It was minutes, anyway. Not very quick.

The haze in my brain slowly resolved itself to the point where I knew I was sitting in a chair, and knew the people round me were Nestor Pollgate, Lord Vaughnley and Jay Erskine.

'Right,' Pollgate said. 'Can you hear me?'

I said, after a pause, 'Yes.' It didn't sound like my voice. More a croak.

'You're going to give us the wire-tap,' he said. 'And the other things.'

Some sort of electricity, I thought dimly. Those thuds were electric shocks. Like touching a cold metal door-knob after walking on nylon carpet, but magnified monstrously.

'You understand?' he said.

I didn't answer. I understood, but I didn't know whether I was going to give him the things or not.

'Where are they?' he said.

To hell with it, I thought.

'Where are they?'

Silence.

I didn't even see Jay Erskine put his hand against me the third time. I felt a great burning jolt and went shooting into space, floating for several millennia in a disorientated limbo, ordinary consciousness suspended, living as in dream-state, docile and drifting. I could see them in a way, but I didn't know who they were. I didn't know anything. I existed. I had no form.

Whatever would be done, wherever they might take me, whatever God-awful crime they might plant me in, I couldn't resist.

Thought came back again slowly. There were burns somewhere, stinging. I heard Lord Vaughnley's voice saying something, and Pollgate answering, 'Five thousand volts.'

'He's awake,' Erskine said.

Lord Vaughnley leaned over me, his face close and worried. 'Are you sure he's all right?'

'Yes,' Pollgate said. 'There'll be no permanent harm.'

Thank you, I thought wryly, for that. I felt dizzy and sick. Just as well that with lunch in view I had missed breakfast.

Pollgate was looking at his watch and shaking his head. 'He was dazed for twelve minutes that time. A three-second shock is too much. The two-second is better, but it's taking too long. Twenty minutes already.' He glared down at me. 'I can't waste any more time. You'll give me those things, now, at once.'

It was he who held the electric device now, not Erskine.

I thought I could speak. Tried it. Something came out: the same sort of croak. I said 'It will take ... days.'

It wasn't heroics. I thought vaguely that if they believed it would take days they would give up trying, right there and then. Logic, at that point, was at a low ebb.

Pollgate stepped within touching distance of me and showed me five thousand volts at close range.

'Stun gun,' he said.

It had two short flat metal prongs protruding five centimetres apart from one end of a flat plastic case. He squeezed some switch or other, and between the prongs leapt an electric spark the length of a thumb, bright blue, thick and crackling.

The spark fizzed for a long three seconds of painful promise and disappeared as fast as it had come.

I looked from the stun gun up to Pollgate's face, staring straight at the shiny-bead eyes.

'Weeks,' I said.

It certainly nonplussed him. 'Give us the wire-tap,' he said; and he seemed to be looking, as I was, at a long, tiring battle of wills, much of which I would half sleep through, I supposed.

Lord Vaughnley said to Pollgate uncomfortably, 'You can't go on with this.'

A certain amount of coherence returned to my brain.

The battle of wills, I thought gratefully, shouldn't be necessary.

'He's going to give us those things,' Pollgate said obstinately. 'I'm not letting some clod like this get the better of me.' Pride, loss of face, all the deadly intangibles.

Lord Vaughnley looked down at me anxiously.

'I'll give you,' I said to him, 'something better.'

'What?'

My voice was steadier. Less hoarse, less slow. I moved in the chair, arms and legs coming back into coordination. It seemed to alarm Jay Erskine but I was still a long way from playing judo.

'What will you give us?' Lord Vaughnley said.

I concentrated on making my throat and tongue work properly. 'It's in Newmarket,' I said. 'We'll have to go there for it. Now, this afternoon.'

Pollgate said with impatience. 'That's ridiculous.'

'I'll give you,' I said to Lord Vaughnley, 'Maynard Allardeck.'

A short burst of stun couldn't have had more effect.

'How do you mean?' he said; not with puzzlement, but with hope.

'On a plate,' I said. 'In your power. Where you want him, don't you?'

They both wanted him. I could see it in Pollgate's face just as clearly as in Lord Vaughnley's. I suppose that I had guessed in a way that it would be both.

369

Jay Erskine said aggressively, 'Are our things in Newmarket, then?'

I said with an effort, 'That's where you left them.'

'All right, then.'

He seemed to think that the purpose of their expedition had been achieved, and I didn't tell him differently.

Nestor Pollgate said, 'Jay, fetch the car to the side entrance, will you?' and the obnoxious Erskine went away.

Pollgate and Lord Vaughnley agreed that Mario, whoever he was, should tell Icefall's sponsors not to expect their guests back for lunch, saying I'd had a bilious attack and Lord Vaughnley was helping me. 'But Mario can't tell them until after we've gone,' Lord Vaughnley said, 'or you'll have my wife and I daresay the princess out here in a flash to mother him.'

I sat and listened lethargically, capable of movement but not wanting to move, no longer sick, all right in my head, peaceful, extraordinarily, and totally without energy.

After a while Jay Erskine came back, the exasperating smirk still in place.

'Can you walk?' Pollgate asked me.

I said, 'Yes' and stood up, and we went out of the side door, along a short passage and down some gilded deeply carpeted backstairs, where no doubt many a Guineas visitor made a discreet entrance and exit, avoiding public eyes in the front hall.

I went down the stairs shakily, holding on to the rail.

'Are you all right?' Lord Vaughnley said solicitously, putting his hand supportively under my elbow.

I glanced at him. How he could think I would be all right was beyond me. Perhaps he was remembering that I was used to damage, to falls, to concussion: but bruises and fractures were different from that day's little junket.

'I'm all right,' I said though, because it was true where it counted, and we went safely down to the bottom.

I stopped there. The exit door stood open ahead, a passage stretching away indoors to the right.

'Come along,' Pollgate said, gesturing to the door. 'If we're going, let's go.'

'My anorak,' I said, 'is in the cloakroom.' I produced the ticket from my pocket. 'Anorak,' I said.

'I'll get it,' Lord Vaughnley said, taking the ticket. 'And I'll see Mario. Wait for me in the car.'

It was a large car. Jay Erskine was driving. Nestor Pollgate sat watchfully beside me on the back seat, and Lord Vaughnley, when he returned, sat in the front.

'Your anorak,' he said, holding it out, and I thanked him and put it by my feet, on the floor.

'The films of the races have just ended, Mario says,' he reported to Pollgate. 'He's going straight in to make our apologies. It's all settled. Off we go.'

It took ages to get out of London, partly because of thick traffic, mostly because Jay Erskine was a rotten driver, all impatience and heavy on the brakes. An hour and a half to Newmarket, at that rate: and I would have to be better by then.

No one spoke much. Jay Erskine locked all the doors centrally and Nestor Pollgate put the stun gun in its case in his right-hand jacket pocket, hidden but available; and I sat beside him in ambiguity, half prisoner, half ringmaster, going willingly but under threat, waiting for energy to return, physical, mental and psychic.

Stun guns, I thought. I'd heard of them, never seen one before. Used originally by American police to subdue dangerous violent criminals without shooting them. Instantaneous. Effective. You don't say.

I remembered from long-ago physics lessons that if you squeezed piezoelectric crystals you got sparks, as in the flickering lighters used for gas cookers. Maybe stun guns were like that, multiplied. Maybe not. Maybe I would ask someone. Maybe not. Five thousand volts . . .

I looked with speculation at the back of Lord Vaughnley's head, wondering what he was thinking. He was eager, that was for sure. They had agreed to the journey like thirsty men in a drought. They were going without knowing for sure why, without demanding to be told. Anything that could do Maynard Allardeck harm must be worth doing, in their eyes: that had to be why, at the beginning, Lord Vaughnley had been happy enough to introduce me to Rose Quince, to let me loose on the files. The destruction of Maynard's credibility could only be helped along, he might have thought, by pin pricks from myself.

I dozed, woke with a start, found Pollgate's face turned my way, his eyes watching. He was looking, if anything, puzzled.

In my rag-doll state I could think of nothing useful to say, so I didn't, and presently he turned his head away and looked out of the window, and I still felt very conscious of his force, his ruthlessness, and of the ruin he could make of my life if I got the next few hours wrong.

I thought of how they had set their trap in the Guineas.

Icefall's sponsors, on my answering machine, inviting me to lunch. The sponsors hadn't said where, but they'd said tomorrow, Tuesday: today. The message would have been overheard and despatched to Pollgate, and sent from him to Lord Vaughnley, who would have said, Nothing simpler, my dear fellow, I'll join forces with those sponsors, which they can hardly refuse, and Kit Fielding will definitely come, he'd do anything to please the princess . . .

Pollgate had known the Guineas. Known Mario. Known he could get an isolated room for an hour. The sort of place he would know, for sure.

Maybe Lord Vaughnley had suggested the Guineas to Icefall's sponsors. Maybe he hadn't had to. There were often racing celebration parties at the Guineas.

The sponsors would very likely have chosen it themselves, knowing they could show the films there.

Unprofitable thoughts. However it had been planned, it had worked.

I thought also about the alliance between Lord Vaughnley and Nestor Pollgate, owners of snapping rival newspapers, always at each other's throats in print, and acting in private accord.

Allies, not friends. They didn't move comfortably around each other, as friends did.

On 1 October Lord Vaughnley had signed the charity letter recommending Maynard for a knighthood: signed it casually perhaps, not knowing him well.

Then later in October his son Hugh had confessed to his dealings with Maynard, and Lord Vaughnley, outraged, had sought to unzip Maynard's accolade by getting Pollgate and his *Flag* to do the demolition; because it was the *Flag*'s sort of thing . . . and Jay Erskine, who had worked for Lord Vaughnley once, was in place there in the *Flag*, and was known not to be averse to an illegal sortie, now and then.

I didn't know why Lord Vaughnley should have gone to Pollgate, should have expected him to help. Somewhere between them there was a reason. I didn't suppose I would get an answer, if I asked.

Lord Vaughnley, I thought, could have been expected to tell the charity he wanted to recant his approval of Maynard Allardeck's knighthood: but they might have said too bad, your son was a fool, but

Allardeck definitely helped him. Lord Vaughnley might as a newspaperman have seen a few destructive paragraphs as more certain, and more revengefully satisfying, besides.

Before that, though, I guessed it had been he who had gone to the producers of *How's Trade*, who said dig up what you can about Allardeck, discredit him, I'll pay you: and had been defeated by the producer himself, who according to Rose Quince was known for taking more money in return for helping his victims off the hook.

The *How's Trade* programme on Maynard had gone out loaded in Maynard's favour, which hadn't been the plan at all. And it was after that, I thought, that Lord Vaughnley had gone to Pollgate.

I shut my eyes and drifted. The car hummed. They had the heater on. I thought about horses; more honest than men. Tomorrow I was due to ride at Haydock. Thank God the racecourse doctor hadn't been at the Guineas.

Takeovers, I thought inconsequentially. Always fending off takeovers.

Pollgate would bury me if I didn't get it right.

Towards the end of the journey both mental and physical power came seeping slowly back, like a tide rising, and it was an extraordinary feeling: I hadn't known how much power I did have until I'd both lost it and felt its return. Like not realizing how ill one had been, until one was well.

I stretched thankfully with the renewed strength in my muscles and breathed deeply from the surge in my mind, and Pollgate, for whom the consciousness of power must have been normal, sensed in some way the vital recharging in me and sat up more tensely himself.

Erskine drove into Bobby's stableyard at five minutes past three, and in the middle of what should have been a quiet snooze in the life of the horses, it seemed that there were people and movement all over the place. Erskine stopped the car with his accustomed jerk, and, Pollgate having told him to unlock the doors, we climbed out.

Holly was looking distractedly in our direction, and there were besides three or four cars, a horse trailer with the ramp down and grooms wandering about with head-collars.

There was also, to my disbelief, Jermyn Graves.

Holly came running across to me and said, 'Do something, he's a madman, and Bobby's indoors with Maynard, he came early and they've been shouting at each other and I don't want to go in, and thank God you're here, it's a farce.'

Jermyn Graves, seeing me, followed Holly. His gaze swept over Pollgate, Jay Erskine and Lord Vaughnley and he said belligerently, 'Who the hell are these people? Now see here, Fielding, I've had enough of your smart-arse behaviour, I've come for my horses.'

I put my arm around Holly. 'Did his cheque go through?' I asked her.

'Yes, it bloody well did,' Graves said furiously.

Holly nodded. 'The feed-merchant told us. The cheque was cleared yesterday. He has his money.'

'Just what is all this?' Pollgate said heavily.

'You keep out of it,' Graves said rudely. 'It's you, Fielding, I want. You give me my bloody horses or I'll fetch the police to you.'

'Calm down, Mr Graves,' I said. 'You shall have your horses.'

'They're not in their boxes.' He glared with all his old fury; and it occurred to me that his total disregard of Pollgate was sublime. Perhaps one had to know one should be afraid of someone before one was.

'Mr Graves,' I said conversationally to the two proprietors and one journalist, 'is removing his horses because of what he read in Intimate Details. You see here in action the power of the Press.'

'Shut your trap and give me my horses,' Graves said.

'Yes, all right. Your grooms are going in the wrong direction.'

'Jasper,' Graves yelled. 'Come here.'

The luckless nephew approached, eyeing me warily.

'Come on,' I jerked my head. 'Round the back.'

Jay Erskine would have prevented my going, but Pollgate intervened. I took Jasper round to the other yard and pointed out the boxes that contained Graves's horses. 'Awfully sorry,' Jasper said.

'You're welcome,' I said, and I thought that but for him and his uncle we wouldn't have rigged the bell, and but for the bell we wouldn't have caught Jay Erskine up the ladder, and I felt quite grateful to the Graveses, on the whole.

I went back with Jasper walking behind me leading the first of the horses, and found them all standing there in much the same places, Jermyn Graves blustering on about not having faith when the trainer couldn't meet his bills.

'Bobby's better off without you, Mr Graves,' I said. 'Load your horses up and hop it.'

Apoplexy hovered. He opened and shut his mouth a couple of times and finally walked over to his trailer to let out his spleen on the luckless Jasper.

'Thank God for that,' Holly said. 'I can't stand him. I'm so glad you're here. Did you have a good time at your lunch?'

'Stunning,' I said.

They all heard and looked at me sharply.

Lord Vaughnley said, mystified, 'How can you laugh . . .?'

'What the hell,' I said. 'I'm here. I'm alive.'

Holly looked from one to the other of us, sensing something strongly, not knowing what. 'Something happened?' she said, searching my face.

I nodded a fraction. 'I'm OK.'

She said to Lord Vaughnley, 'He risks his life most days of the week. You can't frighten him much.'

They looked at her speechlessly, to my amusement.

I said to her, 'Do you know who you're talking to?'

and she shook her head slightly, half remembering but not sure.

'This is Lord Vaughnley who owns the *Towncrier*. This is Nestor Pollgate who owns the *Flag*. This is Jay Erskine who wrote the paragraphs in Intimate Details and put the tap on your telephone.' I paused, and to them I said, 'My sister, Bobby's wife.'

She moved closer beside me, her eyes shocked.

'Why are they here? Did you bring them?'

'We sort of brought each other,' I said. 'Where are Maynard and Bobby?'

'In the drawing room, I think.'

Jasper was crunching across the yard with the second horse, Jermyn shouting at him unabated. The other groom who had come with them was scurrying in and out of the trailer, attempting invisibility.

Nestor Pollgate said brusquely, 'We're not standing here watching all this.'

'I'm not leaving Holly alone to put up with that man,' I said. 'He's a menace. It's because of you that he's here, so we'll wait.'

Pollgate stirred restlessly, but there was nowhere particular for him to go. We waited in varying intensities of impatience while Jasper and the groom raised the ramp and clipped it shut, and while Jermyn Graves walked back several steps in our direction and shook his fist at me with the index finger sticking out, jabbing, and said no one messed with him and got away with it, and he'd see I'd be sorry. I'd pay for what I'd done.

'Kit,' Holly said, distressed.

I put my arm round her shoulders and didn't answer Graves, and after a while he turned abruptly on his heel, went over to his car, climbed in, slammed the door, and overburdened his engine, starting with a jerk that must have rocked his horses off their feet in the trailer.

'He's a pig,' Holly said. 'What will he do?'

'He's more threat than action.'

'I,' Pollgate said, 'am not.'

I looked at him, meeting his eyes.

'I do know that,' I said.

The time, I thought, had inescapably come.

Power when I needed it. Give me power, I thought.

I let go of Holly and leaned into the car we had come in, picking up my anorak off the floor.

I said to Holly, 'Will you take these three visitors into the sitting room? I'll get Bobby . . . and his father.'

She said with wide apprehensive eyes, 'Kit, do be careful.'

'I promise.'

She gave me a look of lingering doubt, but set off with me towards the house. We went in by long habit through the kitchen: I don't think it occurred to either of us to use the formal front door.

Pollgate, Lord Vaughnley and Jay Erskine followed, and in the hall Holly peeled them off into the sitting room, where in the evenings she and Bobby watched television sometimes. The larger drawing room lay ahead, and there were voices in there, or one voice, Maynard's, continuously talking.

I screwed up every inner resource to walk through that door, and it was a great and appalling mistake. Bobby told me afterwards that he saw me in the same way as in the stable and in the garden, the hooded, the enemy, the old foe of antiquity, of immense and dark threat.

Maynard was saying monotonously as if he had already said it over and over, ' . . . And if you want to get rid of him you'll do it, and you'll do it today . . .'

Maynard was holding a gun, a hand gun, small and black.

He stopped talking the moment I went in there. His eyes widened. He saw, I supposed, what Bobby saw: Fielding, satanic.

He gave Bobby the pistol, pressing it into his hand.

'Do it,' he said fiercely. 'Do it now.'

His son's eyes were glazed, as in the garden.

He wouldn't do it. He couldn't . . .

'Bobby,' I said explosively, beseechingly: and he raised the gun and pointed it straight at my chest.

CHAPTER TWENTY

I turned my back on him.

I didn't want to see him do it; tear our lives apart, mine and his, and Holly's and the baby's. If he was going to do it, I wasn't going to watch.

Time passed, stretched out, uncountable. Danielle, I thought.

I heard his voice, close behind my shoulder.

'Kit . . .'

I stood rigidly still. You can't frighten him much, Holly had said. Bobby with a gun frightened me into immobility and despair.

He came round in front of me, as white as I felt. He looked into my face. He was holding the gun flat, not aiming, and put it into my hand.

'Forgive me,' he said.

I couldn't speak. He turned away blindly and made for the door. Holly appeared there, questioning, and he enfolded her and hugged her as if he had survived an earthquake, which he had.

I heard a faint noise behind me and turned, and

found Maynard advancing, his face sweating, his teeth showing, the charming image long gone. I turned holding the gun, and he saw it in my hand and went back a pace, and then another and another, looking fearful, looking sick.

'You incited,' I said bitterly, 'your own son to murder. Brainwashed him.'

'It would have been an accident,' he said.

'An Allardeck killing a Fielding would not have been believed as an accident.'

'I would have sworn it,' he said.

I loathed him. I said, 'Go into the sitting room,' and I stood back to let him pass, keeping the gun pointing his way all the while.

He hadn't had the courage to shoot me himself. Making Bobby do it . . . that crime was worse.

It hadn't been a good idea to draw him there with the express purpose of getting rid of me once and for all. He'd too nearly succeeded. My own stupid fault.

We went down the hall and into the sitting room. Pollgate and Erskine and Lord Vaughnley were all there, standing in the centre, with Bobby and Holly, still entwined, to one side. I went in there feeling I was walking into a cageful of tigers, and Holly said later that with the gun in my hand I looked so dangerous she hardly recognized me as her brother.

'Sit down,' I said. 'You,' I pointed to Maynard, 'over there in that chair at the end.' It was a deep chair, enveloping, no good for springing out of suddenly. 'You next, beside him,' I said to Erskine. 'Then Lord Vaughnley, on the sofa.'

Pollgate looked at the spare place beside Lord Vaughnley and took it in silence.

'Take out the stunner,' I said to him. 'Put it on the floor. Kick it this way.'

I could feel the refusal in him, see it in his eyes. Then he shrugged, and took out the flat black box, and did as I'd said.

'Right,' I said, 'you're all going to watch a video.' I glanced down at the pistol. 'I'm not a good shot. I don't know what I'd hit. So stay sitting down.' I held out the anorak in Bobby's direction. 'The tape's zipped into one of the pockets.'

'Put it on now?' he said, finding it and bringing it out. His hands were shaking, his voice unsteady. Damn Maynard, I thought.

'Yes, now,' I said. 'Holly, close the curtains and put on a lamp, it'll be dark before we're finished.'

No one spoke while she shut out the chilly day, while Bobby switched on the video machine and the television, and fed the tape into the slot. Pollgate looked moodily at the anorak which Bobby had laid on a chair and Lord Vaughnley glanced at the gun, and at my face, and away again.

'Ready,' Bobby said.

'Start it off,' I said, 'and you and Holly sit down and watch.'

I shut the door and leaned against it as Lord

Vaughnley had done in the Guineas, and Maynard's face came up bright and clear and smiling on the television screen.

He started to struggle up from his deep chair.

'Sit down,' I said flatly.

He must have guessed that what was coming was the tape he thought he'd suppressed. He looked at the gun in my hand and judged the distance he would have to cover to reach me, and he subsided into the cushions as if suddenly weak.

The interview progressed and went from smooth politeness into direct attack, and Lord Vaughnley's mouth slowly opened.

'You've not seen this before?' I said to him.

He said, 'No, no' with his gaze uninterruptedly on the screen, and I supposed that Rose wouldn't have seen any need to go running to the proprietor with her purloined tape, the two days she had had it in the *Towncrier* building.

I looked at all their faces as they watched. Maynard sick, Erskine blank, Lord Vaughnley riveted, Pollgate awakening to acute interest, Bobby and Holly horrified. Bobby, I thought ruefully, was in for some frightful shocks: it couldn't be much fun to find one's father had done so much cruel damage.

The interview finished, to be replaced by the Perrysides telling how they'd lost Metavane, with George Tarker and his son's suicide after, and Hugh Vaughnley, begging to go home; and finally Maynard again, smugly smiling.

The impact of it all on me was still great, and in the others produced something like suspended animation. Their expressions at the end of the hour and thirteen minutes were identical, of total absorption and stretched eyes, and I thought Joe would have been satisfied with the effect of his cutting, and of his hammer blow of final silence.

The trial was over: the accused, condemned. The sentence alone remained to be delivered.

The screen ran from black into snow, and no one moved.

I peeled myself off the door and walked across and switched off the set.

'Right,' I said, 'now listen.'

The eyes of all of them were looking my way with unadulterated concentration, Maynard's dark with humiliation, his body slack and deep in the chair.

'You,' I said to Lord Vaughnley, 'and you,' I said to Nestor Pollgate. 'You or your newspapers will each pay to Bobby the sum of fifty thousand pounds in compensation. You'll write promissory notes, here and now, in this room, in front of witnesses, to pay the money within three days, and those notes will be legal and binding.'

Lord Vaughnley and Nestor Pollgate simply stared.

'And in return,' I said, 'you shall have the wire-tap and the other evidence of Jay Erskine's criminal activity. You shall have complete silence from me about your various assaults on me and my property. You shall have back the draft for three thousand pounds now lodged in my bank manager's safe. And you shall have the tape you've just watched.'

Maynard said, 'No' in anguished protest, and no one took any notice.

'You,' I said to Maynard, 'will write a promissory note promising to pay to Bobby within three days the sum of two hundred and fifty thousand pounds, which will wipe out the overdrafts and the loans and mortgages on this house and stables, which you and your father made Bobby pay for, and which should rightfully be his by inheritance.'

Maynard's mouth opened, but no sound came out.

'You will also,' I said, 'give to Major and Mrs Perryside the one share you still own in Metavane.'

He began to shake his head weakly.

'And in return,' I said, 'you will have my assurance that many copies of this tape will not turn up simultaneously in droves of sensitive places, such as with the Senior Steward of the Jockey Club, or among the patrons of the civil service charity of which you are the new chairman, or in a dozen places in the City.' I paused. 'When Bobby has the money safe in the bank, you will be safe from me also. But that safety will always be conditional on your doing no harm either to Bobby and Holly or to me in future. The tapes will always exist.'

Maynard found his voice, hoarse and shaken.

'That's extortion,' he said aridly. 'It's blackmail.'

'It's justice,' I said.

There was silence. Maynard shrank as if deflated into the chair, and neither Pollgate nor Lord Vaughnley said anything at all.

'Bobby,' I said, 'take the tape out of the machine and out of this room and put it somewhere safe, and bring back some writing paper for the notes.'

Bobby stood up slowly, looking numb.

'You said we could have the tape,' Pollgate said, demurring.

'So you can, when Bobby's been paid. If the money's all safely in the bank by Friday, you shall have it then, along with Erskine's escape from going to jail.'

Bobby took the tape away, and I contemplated Pollgate's and Lord Vaughnley's expressionless faces and thought they were being a good deal too quiet. Maynard, staring at me blackly from his chair, was simple by comparison, his reactions expected. Erskine looked his usual chilling self, but without the smirk, which was an improvement.

Bobby came back with some large sheets of the headed writing paper he used for the bills for the owners, and gave a sheet each to Nestor Pollgate and Lord Vaughnley, and with stiff legs and an arm outstretched as far as it would go, gave the third to his father with his head turned away, not wanting to look at his face.

I surveyed the three of them sitting there stonily holding the blank sheets, and into my head floated various disjointed words and phrases.

'Wait,' I said. 'Don't write yet.'

The words were 'invalid', and 'obtained by menaces', and 'invalid by reason of having been extorted at gunpoint'.

I wondered if the thought had come on its own or been generated somewhere else in that room, and I looked at their faces carefully, one by one, searching their eyes.

Not Maynard. Not Erskine. Not Lord Vaughnley.

Nestor Pollgate's eyelids flickered.

'Bobby,' I said, 'pick that black box up off the floor and drop it out of the window, into the garden.'

He looked bewildered, but did as I asked, the November air blowing in a great gust through the curtains into the room.

'Now the gun,' I said, and gave it to him.

He took it gingerly and threw it out, and shut the window again.

'Right,' I said, putting my hands with deliberation into my pockets, 'you've all heard the propositions. If you accept them, please write the notes.'

For a long moment no one moved. Then Lord Vaughnley stretched out an arm to the coffee table in front of him and picked up a magazine. He put the sheet of writing paper on the magazine for support. With a slightly pursed mouth but in continued quiet he lifted a pen from a pocket inside his jacket, pressed the top of it with a click, and wrote a short sentence, signing his name and adding the date.

He held it out towards Bobby, who stepped forward hesitantly and took it.

'Read it aloud,' I said.

Bobby's voice said shakily, 'I promise to pay Robertson Allardeck fifty thousand pounds within three days of this date.' He looked up at me. 'It is signed William Vaughnley, and the date is today's.'

I looked at Lord Vaughnley.

'Thank you,' I said neutrally.

He gave the supporting magazine to Nestor Pollgate, and offered his own pen. Nestor Pollgate took both with a completely unmoved face and wrote in his turn.

Bobby took the paper from him, glanced at me, and read aloud, 'I promise to pay Robertson Allardeck fifty thousand pounds within three days of this date. It's signed Nestor Pollgate. It's dated today.'

'Thank you,' I said to Pollgate.

Bobby looked slightly dazedly at the two documents he held. They would clear the debt for the unsold yearlings, I thought. When he sold them, anything he got would be profit.

Lord Vaughnley and Jay Erskine, as if in some ritual, passed the magazine and the pen along to Maynard.

With fury he wrote, the pen jabbing hard on the paper. I took the completed page from him myself and read it aloud, 'I promise to pay my son Robertson two hundred and fifty thousand pounds within three days. Maynard Allardeck. Today's date.'

I looked up at him. 'Thank you,' I said.

'Don't thank me. Your thanks are an insult.'

I was careful, in fact, to show no triumph, though in his case I did feel it: and I had to admit to myself ruefully that in that triumph there was a definite element of the old feud. A Fielding had got the better of an Allardeck, and I dared say my ancestors were gloating.

I gave Maynard's note to Bobby. It would clear all his debts and put him on a sure footing to earn a fair living as a trainer, and he held the paper unbelievingly, as if it would evaporate before his eyes.

'Well, gentlemen,' I said cheerfully, 'bankers' drafts by Friday, and you shall have the notes back, properly receipted.'

Maynard stood up, his greying fair hair still smooth, his face grimly composed, his expensive suit falling into uncreased shape; the outer shell intact, the man inside in shreds.

He looked at nobody, avoiding eyes. He walked to the door, opened it, went out, didn't look back. A silence lengthened behind his exit like the silence at the end of the tape; the enormity of Maynard struck one dumb.

Nestor Pollgate rose to his feet, tall, frowning, still with his power intact. He looked at me judiciously, gave me a brief single nod of the head, and said to Holly, 'Which way do I go out?'

'I'll show you,' she said, sounding subdued, and led the way into the hall.

Erskine followed, his face pinched, the drooping reddish moustache in some way announcing his continuing inflexible hatred of those he had damaged.

Bobby went after him, carrying his three notes carefully as if they were brittle, and Lord Vaughnley, last of all, stood up to go. He shook his head, shrugged his shoulders, spread his hands in a sort of embarrassment.

'What can I say?' he said. 'What am I to say when I see you on racecourses?'

'Good morning, Kit,' I said.

The grey eyes almost smiled before awkwardness returned. 'Yes, but,' he said, 'after what we did to you in the Guineas . . .'

I shrugged. 'Fortunes of war,' I said. 'I don't resent it, if that's what you mean. I took the war to the *Flag*. Seek the battle, don't complain of the wounds.'

He said curiously, 'Is that how you view race-riding? How you view life?'

'I hadn't thought of it, but yes, perhaps.'

'I'm sorry all the same,' he said. 'I had no idea what it would be like. Jay Erskine got the stun gun . . . he said two short shocks and you'd be putty. I don't think Nestor realized himself how bad it would be . . .'

'Yeah,' I said dryly, 'but he agreed to it.'

'That was because,' Lord Vaughnley explained with

a touch of earnestness, wanting me to understand, perhaps to absolve, 'because you ignored all his threats.'

'About prison?' I said.

He nodded. 'Sam Leggatt warned him you were intelligent . . . he said an attempt to frame you could blow up in their faces, that you would get the *Flag* and Nestor himself into deep serious gritty trouble . . . David Morse, their lawyer, was of the same opinion, so he agreed not to try. Sam Leggatt told me. But you have to understand Nestor. He doesn't like to be crossed. He said he wasn't going to be beaten by some . . . er . . . jockey.'

Expletives deleted, I thought, amused.

'You were elusive,' he said. 'Nestor was getting impatient . . .'

'And he had a tap on my telephone?'

'Er, yes.'

'Mm,' I said. 'Is it Maynard Allardeck who is trying to take over the *Towncrier*?'

He blinked, and said 'Er – ' and recovered. 'You guessed?'

'It seemed likely, Maynard got half of Hugh's shares by a trick. I thought it just might be him who was after the whole thing.'

Lord Vaughnley nodded. 'A company . . . Allardeck is behind it. When Hugh confessed, I got people digging up Allardeck's contacts. Just digging for dirt. I'd no idea until then that he owned the company . . . his name hadn't surfaced. All I knew was that it was the same company that nearly acquired the *Flag* a year ago. Very aggressive. It cost Nestor a fortune to cap their bid, far more than he would have had to pay otherwise.'

Holy wow, I thought.

'So when you found out that Maynard was the ultimate enemy,' I said, 'and knew also that he'd recently been proposed for a knighthood, you thought at least you could put paid to that, and casually asked Pollgate to do it in the *Flag*?'

'Not all that casually. Nestor said he'd be pleased to, if it was Allardeck who had cost him so much.'

'Didn't you even consider what hell you were manufacturing for Bobby?'

'Erskine found he couldn't get at Allardeck's phone system . . . they decided on his son.'

'Callous,' I said.

'Er . . . yes.'

'And appallingly spiteful to deliver all those copies to Bobby's suppliers.'

He said without much apology, 'Nestor thought the story would make more of a splash that way. Which it did.'

We began to walk from the sitting room into the hall. He'd told me what I hadn't asked: where the alliance began. In common enmity to Maynard, who had cost them both dear.

'Will you use the tape,' I asked, 'to stop Maynard now in his tracks?'

He glanced at me. 'That would be blackmail,' he said mildly.

'Absolutely.'

'Fifty thousand pounds,' he said. 'That tape's cheap at the price.'

We went into the kitchen and paused again.

'The *Towncrier* is the third newspaper,' he said, 'that has had trouble with Allardeck's company. One paper after another . . . he won't give up till he's got one.'

'He's obsessive,' I said. 'And besides, he's wanted all his life to have power over others . . . to be kowtowed to. To be a lord.'

Lord Vaughnley's mouth opened. I told him about my grandfather, and Maynard at nine. 'He hasn't changed,' I said. 'He still wants those things. Sir first, Lord after. And don't worry, he won't get them. I sent a copy of the tape to where you sent your charity letter.'

He was dumbstruck. He said weakly, 'How did you know about that letter?'

'I saw it,' I said. 'I was shown it. I wanted to know who knew Maynard might be up for a knighthood, and there it was, with your name.'

He shook his head: at life in general, it seemed.

We went on through the kitchen and out into the cold air. All the lights were on round the yard and some of the box doors were open, the lads working there in the routine of evening stables.

'Why did you try to stop me talking to Hugh?' I asked.

'I was wrong, I see that now. But at the time . . . by then you were pressing Nestor for large compensation. He wanted us simply to get back the wire-tap and shut you up.' He spread his hands. 'No one imagined, you see, that you would do all that you've done. I mean, when it was just a matter of disgracing Allardeck in the public eye, no one could have foreseen . . . no one even thought of your existence, let alone considered you a factor. No one knew you would defend your brother-in-law, or be . . . as you are.'

We walked across the yard to the car where Pollgate and Erskine were waiting, shadowy figures behind glass.

'If I were you,' I said, 'I'd find out if Maynard owns the bookmakers that Hugh bet with. If he does, you can threaten him with fraud, and get Hugh's shares back, I should think.'

We stopped a few feet from the car.

'You're generous,' he said.

We stood there, face to face, not knowing whether or not to shake hands.

'Hugh had no chance against Maynard,' I said.

'No.' He paused. 'I'll let him come home.'

He looked at me lengthily, the mind behind the grey eyes perhaps totting up, as I was, where we stood.

Even if he hadn't intended it, he had set in motion the attacks on Bobby; yet because of them Bobby would be much better off. From the dirt, gold.

If he offered his hand, I thought, I would take it.

Tentatively, unsure, that's what he did. I shook it briefly; an acknowledgement, a truce.

'See you at the races,' I said.

When they had gone I went and found the pistol and the stun gun outside the sitting-room window, and with them in my pockets returned to the kitchen, where Holly and Bobby were looking more dazed than happy.

'Tea?' I said hopefully.

They didn't seem to hear. I put the kettle on and got out some cups.

'Kit . . .' Holly said. 'Bobby told me . . .'

'Yeah . . . well . . . have you a lemon?' I said.

She dumbly fetched me one from the refrigerator, and sliced it.

Bobby said, 'I nearly killed you.'

His distress, I saw, was still blotting out any full realization – or celebration – of the change in his fortunes. He still looked pale, still gaunt round the eyes.

'But you didn't,' I said.

'No . . . when you turned your back on me, I thought, I can't shoot him in the back . . . not in the back . . . and I woke up. Like waking from a nightmare. I couldn't . . . how could I . . . I stood there with that gun, sweating at how near I'd come . . .'

'You frightened me silly,' I said. 'Let's forget it.'

'How can we?'

'Easily.' I punched his arm lightly. 'Concentrate, my old chum, on being a daddy.'

The kettle boiled and Holly made the tea; and we heard a car driving into the yard.

'They've come back,' Holly said in dismay.

We went out to see, all of us fearful.

The car was large and bewilderingly familiar. Two of its doors opened and from one came Thomas, the princess's chauffeur, in his best uniform, and from the other, scrambling and running, Danielle.

'Kit . . .' She ran headlong into my arms, her face screwed up with worry. 'Are you . . . are you really OK?'

'Yes, I am. You can see.'

She put her head on my shoulder and I held her close, and felt her trembling, and kissed her hair.

Thomas opened a third door of the car and helped out the princess, holding the sable coat for her to put on over the silk suit against the cold.

'I am glad, Kit,' she said calmly, snuggling into the fur, 'to see you are alive and well.' She looked from me to Bobby and Holly. 'You are Bobby, you are Holly, is that right?' She held out her hand to them, which they blankly shook.

'We are here,' she said, 'because my niece Danielle insisted that we come.' She was explaining, half apologizing for her presence. 'When I went home after the Icefall luncheon,' she said to me, 'Danielle was waiting on the pavement. She said you were in very great danger, and that you were at your sister's house in Newmarket. She didn't know how she knew, but she was certain. She said that we must come at once.'

Bobby and Holly looked astounded.

'As I know that with you, Kit, telepathy definitely exists,' the princess said, 'and as you had disappeared from the lunch and were reported to be ill, and as Danielle was distraught ... we came. And I see she was right in part at least. You are here, at your sister's house.'

'She was right about the rest,' Holly said soberly. 'He was in that danger ... a split second from dying.' She looked at my face. 'Did you think of her then?'

I swallowed. 'Yes, I did.'

'Holy wow,' Holly said.

'Kit says that too,' Danielle said, lifting her head from my neck and beginning to recover. 'It's awesome.'

'We always did,' Holly said. She looked at Danielle with growing interest and understanding, and slowly smiled with pleasure.

'She's like us, isn't she?' she said.

'I don't know,' I said. 'I've never known what she was thinking.'

'You might, after this'; and to Danielle, with friendship, she said, 'Think of something. See if he can tell what it is.'

'OK.'

There was a silence. The only thought in my head

was that telepathy was unpredictable and only sometimes worked to order.

I looked at the princess, and at Bobby and Holly, and saw in their faces the same hope, the same expectation, the same realization that this moment might matter in all our futures.

I smiled into Danielle's eyes. I knew, for a certainty.

'Dustsheets,' I said.

BOLT

CHAPTER ONE

Bitter February, within and without. Mood to match the weather; raw and overcast, near to freezing. I walked from the weighing room to the parade ring at Newbury races trying not to search for the face that wouldn't be there, the intimately known face of Danielle de Brescou, to whom I was formally engaged, diamond ring and all.

Winning the lady, back in November, had been unexpected, an awakening, deeply exciting . . . happy. Keeping her, in the frosts before spring, was proving the merry devil. My much loved dark haired young woman seemed frighteningly to be switching her gaze from a steeplechase jockey (myself) to an older richer sophisticate of superior lineage (he was a prince) who hadn't even the decency to be bad looking.

Unmoved as I might try to appear on the surface, I was finding the frustration erupting instead in the races themselves, sending me hurtling over the fences without prudence, recklessly embracing peril like a drug to blot out rejection. It might not be sensible to do a risky job with a mind two hundred miles from one's fingertips, but tranquillisers could come in many forms.

Princess Casilia, unaccompanied by Danielle, her husband's niece, was waiting as usual in the parade ring, watching her runner, Cascade, walk round. I went across to her, shook the offered hand, made the small bow, acknowledging her rank.

'A cold day,' she said in greeting, the consonants faintly thick, vowels pure and clear, the accent only distantly reminiscent of her European homeland.

'Yes. Cold,' I said.

Danielle hadn't come. Of course she hadn't. Stupid of me to hope. She'd said cheerfully on the telephone that she wouldn't be coming to stay this weekend, she would be going to a fabulous Florentine gathering in a hotel in the Lake District with the prince and some of his friends, where they would listen to lectures on the Italian Renaissance given by the Keeper of the Italian paintings in the Louvre, and various other things of that sort. It was such a great and unique opportunity, she was sure I'd understand.

It would be the third weekend in a row she'd been sure I would understand.

The princess looked distinguished as always, middle-aged, slender, intensely feminine, warm inside a supple sable coat swinging from narrow shoulders. Normally bareheaded, dark smooth hair piled high, she wore on that day a tall Russian-type fur hat with a huge upturning fur brim, and I thought fleetingly that few could have carried it with more style. I had ridden her string of twenty or so horses for more than ten years and I tended to know her racegoing clothes well. The hat was new.

She noted the direction of my glance and the admiration that went with it, but said merely, 'Too cold for Cascade, do you think?'

'He won't mind it,' I said. 'He'll loosen up going down to the start.'

She wouldn't mention Danielle's absence, if I didn't. Always reticent, sheltering her thoughts behind long eyelashes, the princess clung to civilized manners as if to a shield against the world's worst onslaughts, and I'd been in her company enough not to undervalue her chosen social façades. She could calm tempests with politeness, defuse lightning with steadfast chit-chat and disarm the most pugnacious adversaries by expecting them to behave well. I knew she would prefer me to keep my woes to myself, and would feel awkward if I didn't.

She did, on the other hand, understand my present predicament perfectly well. Not only was Danielle her husband's niece, but Litsi, the prince currently diverting Danielle to a fifteenth-century junket, was her own nephew.

Litsi, her nephew, and Danielle, her husband's niece, were both currently guests under her Eaton Square roof, meeting from breakfast to dinner ... and from dinner to breakfast, for all I really knew.

'What are our chances?' the princess asked neutrally.

'Pretty good,' I said.

She nodded in agreement, full of pleasant hope, the prospect of winning real enough.

Cascade, despite an absence of brains, was a prolific winner of two-mile 'chases who had shown his heels in the past to every opponent in that day's field. Given luck he would do it again; but nothing's certain, ever, in racing ... or in life.

Prince Litsi, whose whole name was about a yard long and to my mind unpronounceable, was cosmopolitan, cultured, impressive and friendly. He spoke perfect idiomatic English with none of his aunt's thickened consonants, which was hardly surprising as he'd been born after his royal grandparents had been chased off their throne, and had spent much of his childhood in England.

He lived now in France, but I'd met him a few times over the years when he'd visited his aunt and escorted her to the races, and I'd liked him in a vague way, never knowing him well. When I'd heard he was coming again for a visit, I hadn't given a thought to the impact he might make on a bright American female who worked for a television news agency and thirsted for Leonardo da Vinci.

'Kit,' the princess said.

I retrieved my attention from the Lake District and focused on the calmness in her face.

'Well,' I said, 'some races are easier than others.'

'Do your best.'

'Yes.'

Our pre-race meetings over the years had developed into short comfortable interludes in which little was said but much understood. Most owners went into parade rings accompanied by their trainers, but Wykeham Harlow, trainer of the princess's horses, had altogether stopped going to the races. Wykeham, growing old, couldn't stand the incessant winter journeys. Wykeham, shaky in the memory and jerky in the knees, nevertheless still generated the empathy with horses that had put him straight into the top rank from the beginning. He continued to send out streams of winners from his eighty-strong stable, and I, most thankfully, rode them.

The princess went indomitably to the races in all weathers, delighting in the prowess of her surrogate children, planning their futures, recalling their pasts, filling her days with an unflagging interest. Over many years, she and I had arrived at a relationship that was both formal and deep, sharing intensities of success and moments of grief, understanding each other in easy accord at race meetings, parting to unconnected lives at the gate.

Unconnected, that is to say, until the previous November when Danielle had arrived from America to take up her London posting and ended in my bed. Since then, although the princess had undoubtedly accepted me as a future member of her family and had invited me often to her house, her manner to me, as mine to her, had remained virtually unchanged, especially on racecourses. The pattern had been too long set, and felt right, it seemed, to us both.

'Good luck,' she said lightly, when the time came for mounting, and Cascade and I went down to the start with him presumably warming up from the canter but as usual sending no telepathic messages about his feelings. With some horses, a two-way mental traffic could be almost as explicit as speech, but dark, thin, nippy Cascade was habitually and unhelpfully silent.

The race turned out to be much harder than expected, as one of the other runners seemed to have found an extra gear since I'd beaten him last. He jumped stride for stride with Cascade down the far side and clung like glue round the bend into the straight. Shaping up to the last four fences and the run-in he was still close by Cascade's side, his jockey keeping him there aggressively although there was the whole wide track to accommodate him. It was a demoralizing tactic which that jockey often used against horses he thought frightenable, but I was in no mood to be over-crowded by him or by anybody, and I was conscious, as too often recently, of ruthlessness and rage inside and of repressed desperation bursting out.

I kicked Cascade hard into the final jumps and drove

him unmercifully along the run-in, and if he hated it, at least he wasn't telling me. He stretched out his neck and his dark head towards the winning post and under relentless pressure persevered to the end.

We won by a matter of inches and Cascade slowed to a walk in a few uneven strides, absolutely exhausted. I felt faintly ashamed of myself and took little joy in the victory, and on the long path back to the unsaddling enclosure felt not a cathartic release from tension but an increasing fear that my mount would drop dead from an over-strained heart.

He walked with trembling legs into the winner's place to applause he certainly deserved, and the princess came to greet him with slightly anxious eyes. The result of the photo-finish had already been announced, confirming Cascade's win, and it appeared that the princess wasn't worried about whether she had won, but how.

'Weren't you hard on him?' she asked doubtfully, as I slid to the ground. 'Too hard, perhaps, Kit?'

I patted Cascade's steaming neck, feeling the sweat under my fingers. A lot of horses would have crumbled under so much pressure, but he hadn't.

'He's brave,' I said. 'He gives all he's got.'

She watched me unbuckle the girths and slide my saddle off onto my arm. Her horse stood without moving, drooping with fatigue, while Dusty, the travelling head-lad, covered the brown dripping body with a sweat-sheet to keep him warm.

7

'You have nothing to prove, Kit,' the princess said clearly. 'Not to me. Not to anyone.'

I paused in looping the girths round the saddle and looked at her in surprise. She almost never said anything of so personal a nature, nor with her meaning so plain. I suppose I looked as disconcerted as I felt.

I more slowly finished looping the girths.

'I'd better go and weigh in,' I said, hesitating.

She nodded.

'Thank you,' I said.

She nodded again and patted my arm, a small familiar gesture which always managed to convey both understanding and dismissal. I turned away to go into the weighing room and saw one of the Stewards hurrying purposefully towards Cascade, peering at him intently. Stewards always tended to look like that when inspecting hard-driven horses for ill-treatment, but in this particular Steward's case there was far more to his present zeal than a simple love of animals.

I paused in mid-stride in dismay, and the princess turned her head to follow my gaze, looking back at once to my face. I met her blue eyes and saw there her flash of comprehension.

'Go on,' she said. 'Weigh in.'

I went on gratefully, and left her to face the man who wanted, possibly more than anything else on earth, to see me lose my jockey's licence.

Or, better still, my life.

*

Maynard Allardeck, acting as a Steward for the Newbury meeting (a fact I had temporarily forgotten) had both bad and good reasons to detest me, Kit Fielding.

The bad reasons were inherited and irrational and therefore the hardest to deal with. They stemmed from a feud between families that had endured for more than three centuries and had sown a violent mutual history thick with malevolent deeds. In the past, Fieldings had murdered Allardecks, and Allardecks, Fieldings. I had myself, along with my twin sister Holly, been taught from birth by our grandfather that all Allardecks were dishonest, cowardly, spiteful and treacherous, and so we would probably have gone on believing all our lives had Holly not, in a Capulet–Montague gesture, fallen in love with and married an Allardeck.

Bobby Allardeck, her husband, was demonstrably not dishonest, cowardly, spiteful and treacherous, but on the contrary a pleasant well-meaning fellow training horses in Newmarket. Bobby and I, through his marriage, had finally in our own generation, in our own selves, laid the ancient feud to rest, but Bobby's father, Maynard Allardeck, was still locked in the past.

Maynard had never forgiven Bobby for what he saw as treason, and far from trying for reconciliation had intensified his indoctrinated belief that all Fieldings, Holly and I above all included, were thieving, conniving, perfidious and cruel. My serene sister Holly was demonstrably none of these things, but Maynard saw all Fieldings through distorted pathways.

Holly had told me that when Bobby informed his father (all of them standing in Bobby and Holly's kitchen) that Holly was pregnant, and that like it or not his grandchild would bear both Allardeck and Fielding blood and genes, she'd thought for an instant that Maynard was actually going to strangle her. Instead, with his hands literally stretching towards her throat, he'd whirled suddenly away and vomited into the sink. She'd been very shaken, telling me, and Bobby had sworn never to let his father into the house again.

Maynard Allardeck was a member of the Jockey Club, racing's ruling body, where he was busy climbing with his monumental public charm into every power position he could reach. Maynard Allardeck, acting as Steward already at several big meetings, was aiming for the triumvirate, the three Stewards of the Jockey Club, from among whom the Senior Steward was triannually elected.

For a Fielding who was a jockey, the prospect of an Allardeck in a position of almost total power over him should have been devastating: and that was where Maynard's good and comprehensible reasons for detesting me began, because I had a hold over him of such strength that he couldn't destroy my career, life or reputation without doing the same to his own. He and I and a few others knew of it, just enough to ensure that in all matters of racing he had to be seen to treat me fairly.

If, however, he could prove I had truly ill-treated Cascade, he would get me a fine and a suspension with alacrity and joy. In the heat of the race, in the upsurge of my own uncontrollable feelings, I hadn't given a thought to him watching on the stands.

I went into the weighing room and sat on the scales, and then returned to just inside the door to see what was going on outside. From the shadows, I watched Maynard talking to the princess who was wearing her blandest and most pleasant expression, both of them circling the quivering Cascade, who was steaming all over in the freezing air as Maynard had commanded Dusty to remove the net-like sweat-sheet.

Maynard as always looked uncreased, opulent and trustworthy, an outer image which served him very well both in business deals, where he had made fortunes at others' expense, and in social circles, where he gave largely to charity and patted himself on the back for good works. Only the comparative few who had seen the mean, rough, ruthless reality inside remained cynically unimpressed.

He had removed his hat in deference to the princess and held it clasped to his chest, his greying fair hair brushed tidily into uncontroversial shape. He was almost squirming with the desire to ingratiate himself with the princess while at the same time denigrating her jockey, and I wasn't certain that he couldn't cajole her into agreeing that yes, perhaps, on this one occasion, Kit Fielding had been too hard on her horse.

Well . . . they would find no weals on Cascade because I'd barely touched him with the whip. The other horse had been so close that when I'd raised my arm I found I couldn't bring my whip down without hitting him instead of Cascade. Maynard no doubt had seen my raised arm, but it was legs, feet, wrists and fury that had done the job. There might be whip marks in Cascade's soul, if he had one, but they wouldn't show on his hide.

Maynard deliberated for a lengthy time with pursed lips, shakes of the head and busy eyes, but in the end he bowed stiffly to the sweetly-smiling princess, replaced his hat carefully and stalked disappointedly away.

Greatly relieved, I watched the princess join a bunch of her friends while Dusty, with visible disapproval, replaced the sweat-sheet and told the lad holding Cascade's bridle to lead him off to the stables. Cascade went tiredly, head low, all stamina spent. Sorry, I thought, sorry, old son. Blame it on Litsi.

The princess, I thought gratefully as I peeled off her colours to change into others for the next race, had withstood Maynard's persuasions and kept her reservations private. She knew how things stood between Maynard and myself because Bobby had told her one day back in November, and although she had never referred to it since, she had clearly not forgotten. I would have to do more than half kill her horse, it seemed, before she would deliver me to my enemy.

I rode the next race acutely conscious of him on the stands: two scampering miles over hurdles, finishing fourth. After that, I changed back into the princess's colours and returned to the parade ring for the day's main event, a three-mile steeplechase regarded as a trial race for the Grand National.

Unusually, the princess wasn't already in the ring waiting, and I stood alone for a while watching her sturdy Cotopaxi being led round by his lad. Like many of her horses, he bore the name of a mountain, and in his case it fitted aptly, as he was big, gaunt and craggy, a liver chestnut with splashes of grey on his quarters like dirty snow. At eight years old, he was coming satisfactorily to full uncompromising strength, and for once I really believed I might at last win the big one in a month's time.

I'd won almost every race in the calendar, except the Grand National. I'd been second, third, and fourth, but never first. Cotopaxi had it in him to change that, given the luck.

Dusty came across to disrupt the pleasant daydream. 'Where's the princess?' he said.

'I don't know.'

'She'd never miss old Paxi.' Small, elderly, weather-beaten and habitually suspicious, he looked at me accusingly, as if I'd heard something I wasn't telling.

Dusty depended on me professionally, as I on him,

but we'd never come to liking. He was apt to remind me that, champion jockey or not, I wouldn't get so many winners if it weren't for the hard work of the stable lads, naturally including himself. His manner to me teetered sometimes on the edge of rudeness, never quite tumbling over, and I put up with it equably because he was in fact good at his job, and right about the lads, and besides that I hadn't much choice. Since Wykeham had stopped coming to the races, the horses' welfare away from home depended entirely upon Dusty, and the welfare of the horses was very basically my concern.

'Cascade,' Dusty said, glowering, 'can hardly put one foot in front of the other.'

'He's not lame,' I said mildly.

'He'll take weeks to get over it.'

I didn't answer. I looked around for the princess, who still hadn't appeared. I'd wanted particularly to hear what Maynard had said to her, but it looked as if I would have to wait. And it was extraordinary that she hadn't come into the ring. Almost all owners liked to be in the parade ring before a race, and for the princess especially it was an unvarying routine. More-over, she was particularly proud and fond of Cotopaxi and had been talking all winter about his chances in the National.

The minutes ticked away, the signal was given for jockeys to mount, and Dusty gave me his usual adroit leg-up into the saddle. I rode out onto the course hoping nothing serious had happened, and had time, cantering down to the start, to look up to where the princess's private box was located, high on the stands, expecting anyway to see her there, watching with her friends.

The balcony was however deserted, and I felt the first twinge of real concern. If she'd had to leave the racecourse suddenly, I was sure she would have sent me a message, and I hadn't been exactly hard to find, standing there in the paddock. Messages, though, could go astray, and as messages went, 'tell Kit Fielding that Princess Casilia is going home' wouldn't have rated as emergency material.

I went on down to the start thinking that no doubt I would find out in time, and hoping that there hadn't been sudden bad news about the frail old chairbound husband she travelled home to every evening.

Cotopaxi, unlike Cascade, was positively bombarding me with information, mostly to the effect that he was feeling good, he didn't mind the cold weather, and he was glad to be back on a racecourse for the first time since Christmas. January had been snowy and the first part of February freezing, and keen racers like Cotopaxi got easily bored by long spells in the stables.

Wykeham, unlike most of the daily press, didn't expect Cotopaxi to win at Newbury.

'He's not fully fit,' he'd said on the telephone the previous evening. 'He won't be wound up tight until

Grand National day. Look after him, now, Kit, won't you?'

I'd said I would, and after Cascade, I'd doubly meant it. Look after Cotopaxi, look out for Maynard Allardeck, bury Prince Litsi under the turf. Cotopaxi and I went round circumspectly, collectedly, setting ourselves right at every fence, jumping them all cleanly, enjoying the precision and wasting no time. I did enough stick-waving to give an impression of riding a flat-out finish, and we finished in undisgraced third place, close enough to the winner to be encouraging. A good work-out for Cotopaxi, a reassurance for Wykeham and a tremor of promise for the princess.

She hadn't been on her balcony during the race and she didn't appear in the unsaddling enclosure. Dusty muttered obscurely about her absence and I asked around in the weighing room for any message from her, with no results. I changed again to ride in the fifth race, and after that, in street clothes, decided to go up to her box anyway, as I did at the end of every racing afternoon, to see if the waitress who served there might know what had happened.

The princess rented a private box at several race-courses and had had them all decorated alike with colours of cream, coffee and peach. In each was a dining table with chairs for lunch, with, beyond, glass doors to the viewing balcony. She entertained groups of friends regularly, but on that day even the friends had vanished.

I knocked briefly on the box door and, without waiting for any answer, turned the handle and walked in.

The table as usual had been pushed back against a wall after lunch to allow more space, and was familiarly set with the paraphernalia of tea: small sandwiches, small cakes, cups and saucers, alcohol to hand, boxes of cigars. That day, they were all untouched, and there was no waitress pouring, offering me tea with lemon and a smile.

I had expected the box to be otherwise empty, but it wasn't.

The princess was in there, sitting down.

Near her, silent, stood a man I didn't know. Not one of her usual friends. A man of not much more than my own age, slender, dark haired, with a strong nose and jaw.

'Princess . . .' I said, taking a step into the room.

She turned her head. She was still wearing the sable coat and the Russian hat, although she usually removed outdoor clothes in her box. Her eyes looked at me without expression, glazed and vacant, wide, blue and unfocused.

Shock, I thought.

'Princess,' I said again, concerned for her.

The man spoke. His voice matched his nose and jaw, positive, noticeable, full of strength.

'Go away,' he said.

CHAPTER TWO

I went.

I certainly didn't want to intrude uninvited into any private troubles in the princess's life, and it was that feeling that remained with me to ground level. I had been too long accustomed to our arm's length relationship to think her affairs any of my business, except to the extent that she was Danielle's uncle's wife.

By the time I was walking out to my car, I wished I hadn't left as precipitously without at least asking if I could help. There had been an urgent warning quality in the stranger's peremptory voice which had seemed to me at first to be merely protective of the princess, but in retrospect I wasn't so sure.

Nothing would be lost, I thought, if I waited for her to come down to return home, which she must surely do in the end, and made sure she was all right. If the stranger was still with her, if he was as dismissive as before, if she was looking to him for support, then at least I would let her know I would have assisted if she'd needed it.

I went through the paddock gate to the car park where her chauffeur, Thomas, was routinely waiting for her in her Rolls Royce.

Thomas and I said hello to each other most days in car parks, he, a phlegmatic Londoner, placidly reading books and paying no attention to the sport going on around him. Large and dependable, he had been driving the princess for years, and knew her life and movements as well as anyone in her family.

He saw me coming and gave me a small wave. Normally, after I'd left her box, she would follow fairly soon, my appearance acting as a signal to Thomas to start the engine and warm the car.

I walked across to him, and he lowered a window to talk.

'Is she ready?' he asked.

I shook my head. 'There's a man with her...' I paused. 'Do you know a fairly young man, dark haired, thin, prominent nose and chin?'

He pondered and said no one sprang to mind, and why was it worrying me.

'She didn't watch one of her horses race.'

Thomas sat up straighter. 'She'd never not watch.'

'No. Well, she didn't.'

'That's bad.'

'Yes, I'd think so.'

I told Thomas I would go back to make sure she was OK and left him looking as concerned as I felt myself.

The last race was over, the crowds leaving fast. I stood near the gate where I couldn't miss the princess when she came, and scanned faces. Many I knew, many knew me. I said goodnight fifty times and watched in vain for the fur hat.

The crowd died to a trickle and the trickle to twos and threes. I began to wander slowly back towards the stands, thinking in indecision that perhaps I would go up again to her box.

I'd almost reached the doorway to the private stand when she came out. Even from twenty feet I could see the glaze in her eyes, and she was walking as if she couldn't feel the ground, her feet rising too high and going down hard at each step.

She was alone, and in no state to be.

'Princess,' I said, going fast to her side. 'Let me help.'

She looked at me unseeingly, swaying. I put an arm firmly round her waist, which I would never have done in ordinary circumstances, and felt her stiffen, as if to deny her need for support.

'I'm perfectly all right,' she said, shakily.

'Yes . . . well, hold my arm.' I let go of her waist and offered my arm for her to hold on to, which, after a flicker of hesitation, she accepted.

Her face was pale under the fur hat and there were trembles in her body. I walked with her slowly towards the gate, and through it, and across to where Thomas waited. He was out of the car, looking anxious, opening a rear door at our approach.

'Thank you,' the princess said faintly, climbing in. 'Thank you, Kit.'

She sank into the rear seat, dislodging her hat on the way and apathetically watching it roll to the floor.

She peeled off her gloves and put one hand to her head, covering her eyes. 'I think I . . .' She swallowed, pausing. 'Do we have any water, Thomas?'

'Yes, madam,' he said with alacrity, and went round to the boot to fetch the small refreshment box he habitually took along. Sloe gin, champagne, and sparkling mineral water, the princess's favourites, were always to hand.

I stood by the car's open door, unsure how much help she would consider receiving. I knew all about her pride, her self-control, and her self-expectations. She wouldn't want anyone to think her weak.

Thomas gave her some mineral water in a cut-glass tumbler with ice tinkling, no mean feat. She took two or three small sips and sat staring vaguely into space.

'Princess,' I said diffidently, 'would it perhaps be of any use if I travelled with you to London?'

She turned her eyes my way and a sort of shudder shook her, rattling the ice.

'Yes,' she said with clear relief. 'I need someone to . . .' She stopped, not finding the words.

Someone to prevent her breaking down, I guessed. Not a shoulder to cry on but a reason for not crying.

Thomas, approving the arrangement, said to me prosaically, 'What about your car?'

'It's in the jockeys' car park. I'll put it back by the racecourse stables. It'll be all right there.'

He nodded, and we made a brief stop on our way out of the racecourse for me to move the Mercedes to a safe spot and tell the stable manager I'd be back for it later. The princess seemed not to notice any of these arrangements but continued staring vaguely at thoughts I couldn't imagine, and it wasn't until we were well on the way to London in the early dusk that she finally stirred and absent-mindedly handed me the glass with the remains of bubbles and melted ice as a kind of preliminary to talking.

'I'm so sorry,' she said, 'to have given you trouble.'

'But you haven't.'

'I have had,' she went on carefully, 'a bad shock. And I cannot explain ...' She stopped and shook her head, making hopeless gestures with her hands. It seemed to me all the same that she had come to a point where assistance of some sort might be welcomed.

'Is there anything I can do?' I said neutrally.

'I'm not sure how much I can ask.'

'A great deal,' I said bluntly.

The first signs of a smile crept back into her eyes, but faded again rapidly. 'I've been thinking ...' she said. 'When we reach London, will you come into the house and wait while I talk to my husband?'

'Yes, of course.'

'You can spare the time? Perhaps ... a few hours?'

'Any amount,' I assured her wryly. Danielle had gone to Leonardo and time was a drag without her. I stifled in myself the acute lurch of unhappiness and wondered just what sort of shock the princess had suffered. Nothing, it seemed now, to do with Monsieur de Brescou's health. Something perhaps worse.

While it grew totally dark outside, we travelled another long way in silence, with the princess staring again into space and sighing, and me wondering what to do about the tumbler.

As if reading my thoughts, Thomas suddenly said, 'There's a glass-holder, Mr Fielding, located in the door below the ashtray,' and I realized he'd noticed my dilemma via the rear-view mirror.

'Thank you, Thomas,' I said to the mirror, and met his amused eyes. 'Very thoughtful.'

I hooked out what proved to be a chrome ring like a toothmug holder, and let it embrace the glass. The princess, oblivious, went on staring at uncomfortable visions.

'Thomas,' she said at length, 'please will you see if Mrs Jenkins is still in the house? If she is, would you ask her to see if Mr Gerald Greening would be free to come round this evening?'

'Yes, madam,' Thomas said, and pressed buttons on the car's telephone, glancing down in fractions while he drove.

Mrs Jenkins worked for the princess and M. de Brescou as secretary and all-round personal assistant and was young, newly married and palely waiflike. She worked only weekdays and left promptly at five o'clock, which a glance at my watch put at only a few minutes ahead. Thomas caught her apparently on the doorstep and passed on the message, to the princess's satisfaction. She didn't say who Gerald Greening was, but went quietly back to her grim thoughts.

By the time we reached Eaton Square, she had physically recovered completely, and mentally to a great extent. She still looked pale and strained, though, and took Thomas's strong hand to help her from the car. I followed her onto the pavement, and she stood for a moment looking at Thomas and myself, as we stood there lit by the street-lamps.

'Well,' she said thoughtfully, 'thank you both.'

Thomas looked as always as if he would willingly die for her besides driving her carefully to and from the races, but more mundanely at that moment walked across the pavement and, with his bunch of keys, opened the princess's front door.

She and I went in, leaving Thomas to drive away, and together walked up the wide staircase to the first floor. The ground floor of the big old house consisted of offices, a guest suite, a library and a breakfast room. It was upstairs that the princess and her husband chiefly lived, with drawing room, sitting room and dining room on the first floor and bedrooms on three floors above. Staff lived in the semi-basement, and there was an efficient lift from top to bottom, installed in modern times to accommodate M. de Brescou's wheelchair.

'Will you wait in the sitting room?' she said. 'Help yourself to a drink. If you'd like tea, ring down to Dawson . . .' The social phrases came out automatically, but her eyes were vague, and she was looking very tired.

'I'll be fine,' I said.

'I'm afraid I may be a long time.'

'I'll be here.'

She nodded and went up the next broad flight of stairs to the floor above, where she and her husband each had a private suite of rooms, and where Roland de Brescou spent most of his time. I had never been up there, but Danielle had described his rooms as a mini-hospital, with besides his bedroom and sitting room, a physiotherapy room and a room for a male nurse.

'What's wrong with him?' I'd asked.

'Some frightful virus. I don't know exactly what, but not polio. His legs just stopped working, years ago. They don't say much about it, and you know what they're like, it feels intrusive to ask.'

I went into the sitting room, which had become familiar territory, and phoned down to Dawson, the rather august butler, asking for tea.

'Certainly, sir,' he said austerely. 'Is Princess Casilia with you?'

'She's upstairs with Monsieur de Brescou.'

He said, 'Ah,' and the line clicked off. He appeared in a short time, bearing a small silver tray with tea and lemon but no milk, no sugar and no biscuits.

'Did we have a successful afternoon, sir?' he asked, setting down his burden.

'A win and a third.'

He gave me a small smile, a man nearing sixty, unextended and happy in his work. 'Very gratifying, sir.'

'Yes.'

He nodded and went away, and I poured out and drank the tea and tried not to think of buttered toast. During the February freeze, I had somehow gained three pounds and was in consequence having a worse than usual battle against weight.

The sitting room was comfortable with flowered fabrics, rugs and pools of warm lamplight, altogether friendlier than the satins and gilt of the very French drawing room next door. I switched on the television to watch the news, and switched it off after, and wandered around looking for something to read. I also wondered fleetingly why the princess had wanted me to wait, and exactly what help it was that she might find too much to ask.

Reading materials seemed to be a straight choice between a glossy magazine about architecture in French and a worldwide airline timetable, and I was opting for the second when on a side table I came across a folded leaflet which announced 'Master Classes in a Distinguished Setting', and found myself face to face with Danielle's weekend.

I sat in an armchair and read the booklet from front to back. The hotel, with illustrating photographs, was described as a country house refurbished in the grand manner, with soul-shaking views over fells and lakes and blazing log fires to warm the heart indoors.

The entertainments would begin with a reception on the Friday evening at six o'clock (which meant it was in progress as I read), followed by dinner, followed by Chopin sonatas performed in the gold drawing room.

On Saturday would come the lectures on 'The Masters of the Italian Renaissance', given by the illustrious Keeper of Italian paintings in the Louvre. In the morning, 'Botticelli, Leonardo da Vinci, Raphael: Masterworks in the Louvre', and in the afternoon, 'Giorgione's Concert Champêtre and Titian's Laura Dianti: The Cinquecento in Venice', all to be accompanied by slides illuminating points of brushwork and technique. These lectures, the leaflet said, represented a rare privilege seldom granted outside France by probably the world's greatest expert in Italian Renaissance art.

On Saturday evening there would be a grand Florentine banquet especially created by a master chef from Rome, and on Sunday visits would be arranged to the Lakeland houses of Wordsworth, Ruskin and (if desired) Beatrix Potter. Finally, afternoon tea would be served round the fire in the Great Hall, and everyone would disperse.

I seldom felt unsure either of myself or of my chosen way of life, but I put down the leaflet feeling helplessly inadequate.

I knew practically nothing of the Italian Renaissance and I couldn't reliably have dated da Vinci within a hundred years. I knew he painted the Mona Lisa and drew helicopters and submarines, and that was about all. Of Botticelli, Giorgione and Raphael I knew just as little. If Danielle's interests deeply lay with the Arts, would she ever come back to a man whose work was physical, philistine and insecure? To a man who'd liked biology and chemistry in his teens and not wanted to go to college. To someone who would positively have avoided going where she had gone with excitement.

I shivered. I couldn't bear to lose her, not to long-dead painters, nor to a live prince.

Time passed. I read the worldwide air timetables and found there were many places I'd never heard of, with people busily flying in and out of them every day. There were far too many things I didn't know.

Eventually, shortly after eight, the unruffled Dawson reappeared and invited me upstairs, and I followed him to the unfamiliar door of M. de Brescou's private sitting room.

'Mr Fielding, sir,' Dawson said, announcing me, and I walked in to a room with gold swagged curtains, dark green walls and dark red leather armchairs.

Roland de Brescou sat as usual in his wheelchair, and it was clear at once that he was suffering from the same severe shock that had affected the princess. Always weak-looking, he seemed more than ever to be on the point of expiring, his pale yellow-grey skin stretched over his cheekbones and the eyes gaunt and staring. He had been, I supposed, a good looking man long ago, and he still retained a noble head of white hair and a naturally aristocratic manner. He wore, as ever, a dark suit and tie, making no concessions to illness. Old and frail he might be, but still his own master, unimpaired in his brain. Since my engagement to Danielle, I had met him a few times, but although unfailingly courteous he was reclusive always, and as reticent as the princess herself.

'Come in,' he said to me, his voice, always surprisingly strong, sounding newly hoarse. 'Good evening, Kit.' The French echo in his English was as elusive as the princess's own.

'Good evening, monsieur,' I said, making a small bow to him also, as he disliked shaking hands: his own were so thin that the squeezing of strangers hurt him.

The princess, sitting in one of the armchairs, raised tired fingers in a small greeting, and with Dawson withdrawing and closing the door behind me, she said apologetically, 'We've kept you waiting so long . . .'

'You did warn me.'

She nodded. 'We want you to meet Mr Greening.'

Mr Greening, I presumed, was the person standing

to one side of the room, leaning against a green wall, hands in pockets, rocking on his heels. Mr Greening, in dinner jacket and black tie, was bald, round-bellied and somewhere on the far side of fifty. He was regarding me with bright knowing eyes, assessing my age (thirty-one), height (five foot ten), clothes (grey suit, unremarkable) and possibly my income. He had the look of one used to making quick judgments and not believing what he was told.

'The jockey,' he said in a voice that had been to Eton. 'Strong and brave.'

He was ironic, which I didn't mind. I smiled faintly, went through the obvious categories and came up with a possibility.

'The lawyer?' I suggested. 'Astute?'

He laughed and peeled himself off the paintwork. 'Gerald Greening,' he said, nodding. 'Solicitor. Would you be kind enough to witness some signatures to documents?'

I agreed, of course, reflecting that I wouldn't have expected the princess to ask me to wait so long just for that, but not protesting. Gerald Greening picked up a clipboard which had been lying on a coffee table, peeled a sheet of paper back over the clip and offered a pen to Roland de Brescou for him to sign the second page.

With a shaky flourish, the old man wrote his name beside a round red seal.

'Now you, Mr Fielding.' The pen and the clipboard

came my way, and I signed where he asked, resting the board on my left forearm for support.

The whole two-page document, I noticed, was not typed, but handwritten in neat black script. Roland de Brescou's name and mine were both in the same black ink. Gerald Greening's address and occupation, when he added them at the bottom after his own signature, matched the handwriting of the text.

A rush job, I thought. Tomorrow could be too late.

'There isn't any necessity for you to know what's in the document you signed,' Greening said to me easily, 'but Princess Casilia insists that I tell you.'

'Sit down, Kit,' the princess said, 'it'll take time.'

I sat in one of the leather armchairs and glanced at Roland de Brescou who was looking dubious, as if he thought telling me would be unproductive. He was no doubt right, I thought, but I was undeniably curious.

'Put simply,' Greening said, still on his feet, 'the document states that notwithstanding any former arrangements to the contrary, Monsieur de Brescou may not make any business decisions without the knowledge, assent, and properly witnessed signatures of Princess Casilia, Prince Litsi' – he gave him at least half his full name – 'and Miss Danielle de Brescou.'

I listened in puzzlement. If there was nothing wrong with Roland de Brescou's competence, why the haste for him to sign away his authority?

'This is an interim measure,' Gerald Greening went on. 'A sandbag affair, one might say, to keep back the waters while we build the sea-wall.' He looked pleased with the simile, and I had an impression he'd used it before.

'And, er,' I said, 'does the tidal wave consist of anything in particular?' But it had to, of course, to have upset the princess so much.

Gerald Greening took a turn around the room, hands, complete with clipboard, clasped behind his back. A restless mind in a restless body, I thought, and listened to details about the de Brescous that neither the princess nor her husband would ever have told me themselves.

'You must understand,' Greening said, impressing it upon me, 'that Monsieur de Brescou is of the ancient regime, from before the revolution. His is a patrician family, even though he himself bears no title. It's essential to understand that for him personal and family honour is of supreme importance.'

'Yes,' I said, 'I understand that.'

'Kit's own family,' the princess said mildly, 'stretches back through centuries of tradition.'

Gerald Greening looked slightly startled, and I thought in amusement that the Fielding tradition of pride and hate wasn't exactly what he had in mind. He adjusted my status in his eyes to include ancestors, however, and went on with the story.

'In the mid-nineteenth century,' he said, 'Monsieur de Brescou's great-grandfather was offered an opportunity to contribute to the building of bridges and canals and, in consequence, without quite meaning to, he founded one of France's great construction companies. He never worked in it himself – he was a landowner – but the business prospered hugely and with unusual resilience changed to fit the times. At the beginning of the twentieth century, Monsieur de Brescou's grandfather agreed to merge the family business with another construction company whose chief interest was roads, not canals. The great canal building era was ending, and cars, just appearing, needed better roads. Monsieur de Brescou's grandfather retained fifty per cent of the new company, an arrangement which gave neither partner outright control.'

Gerald Greening's eyes gleamed with disapproval as he paced slowly round behind the chairs.

'Monsieur de Brescou's father was killed in the Second World War without inheriting the business. Monsieur de Brescou himself inherited it when his grandfather died, aged ninety, after the Second World War. Are you with me so far?'

'Yes,' I said.

'Good.' He went on pacing, setting out his story lucidly, almost as if laying facts before a fairly dim jury. 'The firm which had merged with that of Monsieur de Brescou's grandfather was headed by a man called Henri Nanterre, who was also of aristocratic descent and high morals. The two men liked and trusted each other and agreed that their joint business should adhere to the highest principles. They installed managers of good reputation and sat back and ... er ... increased their fortunes.'

'Mm,' I said.

'Before and during the Second World War, the firm went into recession, shrinking to a quarter of its former size, but it was still healthy enough to revive well in the nineteen fifties, despite the deaths of the original managing friends. Monsieur de Brescou remained on good terms with the inheriting Nanterre – Louis – and the tradition of employing top managers went on. And that brings us to three years ago, when Louis Nanterre died and left his fifty per cent share to his only son, Henri. Henri Nanterre is thirty-seven, an able entrepreneur, full of vigour, good at business. The profits of the company are annually increasing.'

Both the princess and her husband listened gloomily to this long recital, which seemed to me to have been a success story of major proportions.

'Henri Nanterre,' Greening explained carefully, 'is of the modern world. That is to say, the old values mean little to him.'

'He has no honour,' Roland de Brescou said with distaste. 'He disgraces his name.'

I said slowly, to the princess, 'What does he look like?'

'You saw him,' she said simply. 'In my box.'

CHAPTER THREE

There was a brief silence, then the princess said to Greening, 'Please go on, Gerald. Tell Kit what that ... that wretched man wants, and what he said to me.'

Roland de Brescou interrupted before he could speak and, turning his wheelchair to face me directly, said, 'I will tell him. I will tell you. I didn't think you should be involved in our affairs, but my wife wishes it ...' He made a faint gesture with a thin hand, acknowledging his affection for her. '... and as you are to marry Danielle, well then, perhaps ... But I will tell you myself.' His voice was slow but stronger, the shock receding in him too, with perhaps anger taking its place.

'As you know,' he said, 'I have been for a long time ...' He gestured down his body, not spelling it out. 'We have lived also a long time in London. Far away from the business, you understand?'

I nodded.

'Louis Nanterre, he used to go there quite often to consult the managers. We would talk often on the telephone and he would tell me everything that was happening ... We would decide together if it looked sensible to go in new directions. He and I, for instance, developed a factory to make things out of plastic, not metal, nor concrete. Things like heavy drain pipes which would not crack under roads, nor corrode. You understand? We developed new plastics, very tough.'

He paused, more it seemed through lack of breath than of things to say. The princess, Greening and I waited until he was ready to go on.

'Louis,' he said eventually, 'used to come to London to this house twice a year, with auditors and lawyers – Gerald would be here – and we would discuss what had been done, and read the reports and suggestions from the boards of managers, and make plans.' He sighed heavily. 'Then Louis died, and I asked Henri to come over for the meetings, and he refused.'

'Refused?' I repeated.

'Absolutely. Then suddenly I don't know any longer what is happening, and I sent Gerald over, and wrote to the auditors ...'

'Henri had sacked the auditors,' Gerald Greening said succinctly into the pause, 'and engaged others of his own choice. He had sacked half the managers and was taking charge directly himself, and had branched out into directions which Monsieur de Brescou knew nothing about.'

'It's intolerable,' Roland de Brescou said.

'And today?' I asked him tentatively. 'What did he say at Newbury today?'

'To go to my wife!' He was quivering with fury. 'To threaten her. It's . . . disgraceful.' There weren't words, it seemed, strong enough for his feelings.

'He told Princess Casilia,' Gerald Greening said with precision, 'that he needed her husband's signature on a document, that Monsieur de Brescou did not want to sign, and that she was to make sure that he did.'

'What document?' I asked flatly.

None of them, it seemed, was in a hurry to say, and it was Gerald Greening, finally, who shrugged heavily and said, 'A French government form for a preliminary application for a licence to manufacture and export guns.'

'Guns?' I said, surprised. 'What sort of guns?'

'Firearms for killing people. Small arms made of plastic.'

'He told me,' the princess said, looking hollow-eyed, 'that it would be simple to use the strong plastics for guns. Many modern pistols and machine-guns can be made of plastic, he said. It is cheaper and lighter, he said. Production would be easy and profitable, once he had the licence. And he said he would definitely be granted a licence, he had done all the groundwork. He had had little difficulty because the de Brescou et Nanterre company is so reputable and respected, and all he needed was my husband's agreement.'

She stopped in a distress that was echoed by her husband.

'Guns,' he said. 'I will never sign. It is dishonourable,

do you understand, to trade nowadays in weapons of war. It is unthinkable. In Europe these days, it is not a business of good repute. Especially guns made of plastic, which were invented so they could be carried through airports without being found. Of course, I know our plastics would be suitable, but never, never shall it happen that my name is used to sell guns that may find their way to terrorists. It is absolutely inconceivable.'

I saw indeed that it was.

'One of our older managers telephoned me a month ago to ask if I truly meant to make guns,' he said, outraged. 'I had heard nothing of it. Nothing. Then Henri Nanterre sent a lawyer's letter, formally asking my assent. I replied that I would never give it, and I expected the matter to end there. There is no question of the company manufacturing guns without my consent. But to threaten my wife!'

'What sort of threats?' I asked.

'Henri Nanterre said to me,' the princess said faintly, 'that he was sure I would persuade my husband to sign, because I wouldn't want any accidents to happen to anyone I liked . . . or employed.'

No wonder she had been devastated, I thought. Guns, threats of violence, a vista of dishonour; all a long way from her sheltered, secure and respected existence. Henri Nanterre, with his strong face and domineering voice, must have been battering at her for at least an hour before I arrived in her box.

'What happened to your friends at Newbury?' I asked her. 'The ones in your box.'

'He told them to go,' she said tiredly. 'He said he needed to talk urgently, and they were not to come back.'

'And they went.'

'Yes.'

Well . . . I'd gone myself.

'I didn't know who he was,' the princess said. 'I was bewildered by him. He came bursting in and turned them out, and drowned my questions and protestations. I have not . . .' she shuddered, 'I have never had to face anyone like that.'

Henri Nanterre sounded pretty much a terrorist himself, I thought. Terrorist behaviour, anyway: loud voice, hustle, threats.

'What did you say to him?' I asked, because if anyone could have tamed a terrorist with words, surely she could.

'I don't know. He didn't listen. He just talked over the top of anything I tried to say, until in the end I wasn't saying anything. It was useless. When I tried to stand up, he pushed me down. When I talked, he talked louder. He went on and on saying the same things over again . . . When you came into the box I was completely dazed.'

'I should have stayed.'

'No . . . much better that you didn't.'

She looked at me calmly. Perhaps I would have had

literally to fight him, I thought, and perhaps I would have lost, and certainly that would have been no help to anyone. All the same, I should have stayed.

Gerald Greening cleared his throat, put the clipboard down on a side table and went back to rocking on his heels against the wall behind my left shoulder.

'Princess Casilia tells me,' he said, jingling coins in his pockets, 'that last November her jockey got the better of two villainous press barons, one villainous asset stripper and various villainous thugs.'

I turned my head and briefly met his glance, which was brightly empty of belief. A jokey man, I thought. Not what I would have chosen in a lawyer.

'Things sort of fell into place,' I said neutrally.

'And are they all still after your blood?' There was a teasing note in his voice, as if no one could take the princess's story seriously.

'Only the asset stripper, as far as I know,' I said.

'Maynard Allardeck?'

'You've heard of him?'

'I've met him,' Greening said with minor triumph. 'A sound and charming man, I would have said. Not a villain at all.'

I made no comment. I avoided talking about Maynard whenever possible, not least because any slanderous thing I might say might drift back to his litigious ears.

'Anyway,' Greening said, rocking on the edge of my vision, and with irony plain in his voice, 'Princess

Casilia would now like you to gallop to the rescue and try to rid Monsieur de Brescou of the obnoxious Nanterre.'

'No, no,' the princess protested, sitting straighter. 'Gerald, I said no such thing.'

I stood slowly up and turned to face Greening directly, and I don't know exactly what he saw, but he stopped rocking and took his hands out of his pockets and said with an abrupt change of tone, 'That's not what she said, but that's undoubtedly what she wants. And I'll admit that until this very moment I thought it all a bit of a joke.' He looked at me uneasily. 'Look, my dear chap, perhaps I got things wrong.'

'Kit,' the princess said behind me, 'please sit down. I most certainly didn't ask that. I wondered only . . . Oh, *do* sit down.'

I sat, leaning forward towards her and looking at her troubled eyes. 'It is,' I said with acceptance, 'what you want. It has to be. I'll do anything I can to help. But I'm still . . . a jockey.'

'You're a Fielding,' she said unexpectedly. 'That's what Gerald has just seen. That something . . . Bobby told me you didn't realize . . .' She broke off in some confusion. She never in normal circumstances spoke to me in that way. 'I wanted to ask you,' she said, with a visible return to composure, 'to do what you could to prevent any "accidents". To think of what might happen, to warn us, advise us. We need someone like you, who can imagine . . .'

41

She stopped. I knew exactly what she meant, but I said, 'Have you thought of enlisting the police?'

She nodded silently, and from behind me Gerald Greening said, 'I telephoned them immediately Princess Casilia described to me what had happened. They said they had noted what I'd told them.'

'No actual action?' I suggested.

'They say they are stretched with crimes that have actually happened, but they would put this house on their surveillance list.'

'And you went pretty high up, of course?'

'As high as I could get this evening.'

There was no possible way, I reflected, to guard anyone perpetually against assassination, but I doubted if Henri Nanterre meant to go that far, if only because he wouldn't necessarily gain from it. Much more likely that he thought he could put the frighteners quite easily on a paralysed old man and an unworldly woman, and was currently underestimating both the princess's courage and her husband's inflexible honour. To a man with few scruples, the moral opposition he expected might have seemed a temporary dislodgeable obstinacy, not an immovably embedded barrier.

I doubted if he were actually at that moment planning accidents: he would be expecting the threats to be enough. How soon, I wondered, would he find out that they weren't?

I said to the princess, 'Did Nanterre give you any

time scale? Did he say when and where he expected Monsieur to sign the form?'

'I shall not sign it,' Roland de Brescou murmured.

'No, Monsieur, but Henri Nanterre doesn't know that yet.'

'He said,' the princess answered weakly, 'that a notary would have to witness my husband signing. He said he would arrange it, and he would tell us when.'

'A notary? A French lawyer?'

'I don't know. He was speaking in English to my friends, but when they'd gone he started in French, and I told him to speak English. I do speak French, of course, but I prefer English, which is second nature to me, as you know.'

I nodded. Danielle had told me that as neither the princess nor her husband preferred to chat in the other's native tongue, they both looked upon English as their chief language, and chose to live in England for that reason.

'What do you suppose Nanterre will do,' I asked Greening, 'when he discovers four people have to sign the application form now, not just Monsieur?'

He stared at me with shiny eyes. Contact lenses, I thought inconsequentially. 'Consequences,' he said, 'are your particular field, as I understand it.'

'It depends then,' I said, 'on how rich he is, how greedy, how power-hungry, how determined and how criminal.'

43

'Oh dear,' the princess said faintly, 'how very horrid this all is.'

I agreed with her. At least as much as she, I would have preferred to be out on a windy racetrack where the rogues had four legs and merely bit.

'There's a simple way,' I said to him, 'to keep all your family safe and to preserve your good name.'

'Go on,' he said. 'How?'

'Change the name of the company and sell your share.'

He blinked. The princess put a hand to her mouth, and I couldn't see Greening's reaction, as he was behind me.

'Unfortunately,' Roland de Brescou said eventually, 'I cannot do either without Henri Nanterre's agreement. The original partnership was set up in that way.' He paused. 'It is, of course, possible that he would agree to such changes if he could set up a consortium to acquire the whole, with himself to be at its head with a majority vote. He could then, if he wished, manufacture guns.'

'It does seem a positive solution,' Gerald Greening said judiciously from the rear. 'You would be free of trouble, Monsieur. You would have capitalized. Yes . . . certainly a proposal to be considered.'

Roland de Brescou studied my face. 'Tell me,' he said, 'would you personally follow that course?'

Would I, I thought. Would I, if I were old and paralysed? Would I if I knew the result would be a load of

44

new guns in a world already awash with them? If I knew I was backing away from my principles? If I cared for my family's safety?

'I don't know, Monsieur,' I said.

He smiled faintly and turned his head towards the princess. 'And you, my dear? Would you?'

Whatever answer she would have given him was interrupted by the buzz of the house's intercom system, a recent installation that saved everyone a lot of walking. The princess picked up the handset, pressed a button, and said 'Yes?' She listened. 'Just a minute.' She looked at her husband, saying, 'Are you expecting visitors? Dawson says two men have called, saying they have an appointment. He's shown them into the library.'

Roland de Brescou was shaking his head doubtfully when there was an audible squawk from the handset. 'What?' asked the princess, returning it to her ear. 'What did you say, Dawson?' She listened but seemed to hear nothing. 'He's gone,' she said, puzzled. 'What do you suppose has happened?'

'I'll go and see, if you like,' I said.

'Yes, Kit, please do.'

I rose and went as far as the door, but before I could touch it, it opened abruptly to reveal two men walking purposefully in. One unmistakably was Henri Nanterre: the other, a pace behind, a pale sharp-faced young man in a narrow black suit, carrying a briefcase.

Dawson, out of breath, appeared with a rush behind

them, mouth open in horror at the unceremonious breaking of his defences.

'Madam,' he was saying helplessly, 'they simply ran past me . . .'

Henri Nanterre rudely shut the door on his explanations and turned to face the roomful of people. He seemed disconcerted to find Gerald Greening there, and he took a second sharp look at me, remembering where he'd seen me before and not particularly liking that, either. I guessed that he had come expecting only the princess and her husband, reckoning he had softened them both up enough for his purpose.

His beaky nose looked somewhat diminished against the darker walls, nor did his aggression seem as concentrated as it had been in the smaller box, but he was still forceful, both in his loud voice and in the total rejection of the good manners he should have inherited.

He clicked his fingers to his companion, who removed a single beige-coloured sheet of paper from the briefcase and handed it to him, and then he said something long and clearly objectionable to Roland de Brescou in French. His target leaned backwards in his wheelchair as if to retreat from unpleasantness, and into the first available pause said testily, 'Speak English.'

Henri Nanterre waved the paper and poured out another lengthy burst of French, drowning de Brescou's attempts to interrupt him. The princess made a helpless gesture with her hand to me, indicating that that was exactly what had happened to her also.

'Nanterre!' Gerald Greening said peremptorily, and got a glance but no pause in the tirade. I went back to the armchair I'd occupied before and sat down there, crossing my legs and swinging my foot. The motion irritated Nanterre into breaking off and saying something to me which might have been '*Et qui êtes vous?*', though I couldn't be sure. My sketchy French had mostly been learned on the racecourses of Auteuil and Cagnes-sur-Mer, and chiefly consisted of words like *courants* (runners), *haies* (fences) and *piste* (track).

I stared mildly at Nanterre and went on swinging my foot.

Greening took the opportunity of the brief silence to say rather pompously, 'Monsieur de Brescou has no power to sign any paper whatsoever.'

'Don't be ridiculous,' Nanterre said, at last speaking English, which, like many French businessmen, he proved to know fluently. 'He has too much power. He is out of touch with the modern world, and his obstructive attitude must cease. I require him to make a decision that will bring new impetus and prosperity to a company that is ageing and suffering from out-of-date methods. The period of road building is over. We must look to new markets. I have found such a market which is uniquely suited to the plastic materials we are accustomed to make use of, and no stupidly old-fashioned ideas shall stand in the way.'

'Monsieur de Brescou has relinquished his power to make solo decisions,' Greening said. 'Four people besides yourself must now put their names to any change of company policy.'

'That is absolutely untrue,' Nanterre said loudly. 'De Brescou has total command.'

'No longer. He has signed it away.'

Nanterre looked flummoxed, and I began to think that Greening's sandbags might actually hold against the flood when he made the stupid error of glancing smugly in the direction of the downturned clipboard. How could he be so damned silly, I thought, and had no sympathy for him when Nanterre followed the direction of his eyes and moved like lightning to the side table, reaching it first.

'Put that down,' Greening said furiously, but Nanterre was skimming the page and handing it briskly to his pale acolyte.

'Is that legal?' he demanded.

Gerald Greening was advancing to retrieve his property, the unintroduced Frenchman backing away while he read and holding the clipboard out of reach. '*Oui*,' he said finally. 'Yes. Legal.'

'In that case . . .' Nanterre snatched the clipboard out of his grasp, tore the handwritten pages off it and ripped them across and across. 'The document no longer exists.'

'Of course it exists,' I said. 'Even in pieces, it exists. It was signed and it was witnessed. Its intention remains a fact, and it can be written again.'

Nanterre's gaze sharpened in my direction. 'Who are you?' he demanded.

'A friend.'

'Stop swinging that foot.'

I went on swinging it. 'Why don't you just face the fact that Monsieur de Brescou will never let his company sell arms?' I said. 'Why, if that's what you want to do, don't you agree to dissolve the existing company, and with your proceeds set up again on your own?'

He narrowed his eyes at me, everyone in the room waiting for an answer. When it came, it was grudging, but clearly the truth. Bad news, also for Roland de Brescou.

'I was told,' Nanterre said with cold anger, 'that only if de Brescou applied personally would I be granted the facility. I was told it was essential to have the backing of his name.'

It struck me that perhaps someone in the French background didn't want Nanterre to make guns, and was taking subtle steps to prevent it while avoiding making a flat and perhaps politically embarrassing refusal. To insist on a condition that wouldn't be fulfilled would be to lay the failure of Nanterre's plans solely and neatly at de Brescou's feet.

'Therefore,' Nanterre went on ominously, 'de Brescou will sign. With or without trouble.' He looked at the torn pages he was still grasping and held them out to his assistant. 'Go and find a bathroom,' he said. 'Get rid of these pieces. Then return.'

The pale young man nodded and went away. Gerald Greening made several protestations which had no effect on Nanterre. He was looking as though various thoughts were occurring to him which gave him no pleasure, and he interrupted Greening, saying loudly 'Where are the people whose names were on the agreement?'

Greening, showing the first piece of lawyerly sense for a long time, said he had no idea.

'Where are they?' Nanterre demanded of Roland de Brescou. For answer, a gallic shrug.

He shouted the question at the princess, who gave a silent shake of the head, and at me, with the same result. 'Where are they?'

They would be listening to the sweet chords of Chopin, I supposed, and wondered if they even knew of the agreement's existence.

'What are their names?' Nanterre said.

No one answered. He went to the door and shouted loudly down the hallway. 'Valery. Come here at once. Valery! Come here.'

The man Valery hurried back empty-handed. 'The agreement is finished,' he said reassuringly. 'All gone down the drain.'

'You read the names on it, didn't you?' Nanterre demanded. 'You remember those names?'

Valery swallowed. 'I didn't er ...' he stuttered. 'I didn't study the names. Er ... the first one was Princess Casilia ...'

'And the others?'

Valery shook his head, eyes wide. He as well as Nanterre saw too late that they had thrown away knowledge they might have used. Pressure couldn't be applied to people one couldn't identify. Bribes and blandishments could go nowhere.

Nanterre transmitted his frustration into an increase of aggression, thrusting the application form again towards Roland de Brescou and demanding he sign it.

Monsieur de Brescou didn't even bother to shake his head. Nanterre was losing it, I thought, and would soon retire: I was wrong.

He handed the form to Valery, put his right hand inside his jacket, and from a hidden holster produced a black and businesslike pistol. With a gliding step, he reached the princess and pressed the end of the barrel against her temple, standing behind her and holding her head firmly with his left hand under the chin.

'Now,' he said gratingly to de Brescou, 'sign the form.'

CHAPTER FOUR

Into an electrified atmosphere, I said plainly, 'Don't be ridiculous.'

'Stop swinging that foot,' Nanterre said furiously.

I stopped swinging it. There was a time for everything.

'If you shoot Princess Casilia,' I said calmly, 'Monsieur de Brescou will not sign the form.'

The princess had her eyes shut and Roland de Brescou looked frail to fainting. Valery's wide eyes risked popping out altogether and Gerald Greening, somewhere behind me, was saying, 'Oh my God,' incredulously under his breath.

I said, my mouth drier than I liked, 'If you shoot Princess Casilia, we are all witnesses. You would have to kill us all, including Valery.'

Valery moaned.

'Monsieur de Brescou would not have signed the form,' I said. 'You would end up in jail for life. What would be the point?'

He stared at me with hot dark eyes, the princess's head firm in his grip.

After a pause which lasted a couple of millennia, he gave the princess's head a shake and let her go.

'There are no bullets,' he said. He shoved the gun back into its holster, holding his jacket open for the purpose. He gave me a bitter glance as if he would impress my face on his memory for ever and without another word walked out of the room.

Valery closed his eyes, opened them a slit, ducked his head and scuttled away in his master's wake, looking as if he wished he were anywhere else.

The princess with a small sound of great distress slid out of her chair onto her knees beside the wheelchair and put her arms round her husband, her face turned to his neck, her shining dark hair against his cheek. He raised a thin hand to stroke her head, and looked at me with sombre eyes.

'I would have signed,' he said.

'Yes, Monsieur.'

I felt sick myself and could hardly imagine their turmoil. The princess was shaking visibly, crying, I thought.

I stood up. 'I'll wait downstairs,' I said.

He gave the briefest of nods, and I followed where Nanterre had gone, looking back for Gerald Greening. Numbly he came after me, closing the door, and we went down to the sitting room where I'd waited before.

'You didn't know,' he said croakily, 'that the gun was empty, did you?'

'No.'

'You took a terrible risk.' He made straight for the tray of bottles and glasses, pouring brandy with a shaking hand. 'Do you want some?'

I nodded and sat rather weakly on one of the chintz sofas. He gave me a glass and collapsed in much the same fashion.

'I've never liked guns,' he said hollowly.

'I wonder if he meant to produce it?' I said. 'He didn't mean to use it or he'd have brought it loaded.'

'Then why carry it at all?'

'A prototype, wouldn't you say?' I suggested. 'His plastic equalizer, demonstration model. I wonder how he got it into England. Through airports undetected, would you say? In pieces?'

Greening made inroads into his brandy and said, 'When I met him in France, I thought him bombastic but shrewd. But these threats ... tonight's behaviour ...'

'Not shrewd but crude,' I said.

He gave me a glance. 'Do you think he'll give up?'

'Nanterre? No, I'm afraid he won't. He must have seen he came near tonight to getting what he wanted. I'd say he'll try again. Another way, perhaps.'

'When you aren't there.' He said it as a statement, all the former doubts missing. If he wasn't careful, I thought, he'd persuade himself too far the other way.

He looked at his watch, sighing deeply. 'I told my wife I'd be slightly delayed. Slightly! I'm supposed to be meeting her at a dinner.' He paused. 'If I go in a short while, will you make my apologies?'

'OK,' I said, a shade surprised. 'Aren't you going . . . er . . . to reinstate the sandbags?'

It took him a moment to see what I meant, and then he said he would have to ask M. de Brescou what he wanted.

'It might safeguard him as you intended, don't you think?' I said. 'Especially as Nanterre doesn't know who else to put pressure on.' I glanced at the Master Classes leaflet which still lay on the coffee table. 'Did Danielle and Prince Litsi know their names had been used?'

He shook his head. 'Princess Casilia couldn't remember the name of the hotel. It didn't affect the legality of the document. Their assent at that stage wasn't necessary.'

A few steps down the road, though, after Nanterre's show of force, I reckoned it was no longer fair to embroil them without their consent, and I was on the point of saying so when the door quietly opened and Princess Casilia came in.

We stood up. If she had been crying, there was no sign of it, although she did have the empty-eyed look and the pallor of people stretched into unreality.

'Gerald, we both want to thank you for coming,' she

said, her voice higher in pitch than usual. 'We are so sorry about your dinner.'

'Princess,' he protested, 'my time is yours.'

'My husband asks if you could return tomorrow morning.'

Greening gave a small squirm as if jettisoning his Saturday golf and asked if ten o'clock would suit, and with evident relief took his departure.

'Kit . . .' The princess turned to me. 'Will you stay here in the house, tonight? In case . . . just in case . . .'

'Yes,' I said.

She closed her eyes and opened them again. 'It has been such a dreadful day.' She paused. 'Nothing seems real.'

'Can I pour you a drink?'

'No. Ask Dawson to bring you some food. Tell him you'll sleep in the bamboo room.' She looked at me without intensity, too tired for emotion. 'My husband wants to see you in the morning.'

'Fairly early,' I suggested. 'I have to be at Newbury for the first race.'

'Goodness! I'd forgotten.' Some of the faraway look left her eyes. 'I didn't even ask how Cotopaxi ran.'

'He was third. Ran well.' It seemed a long time ago. 'You'll see it on the video.'

Like many owners, she bought video tapes of most of her horses' races, to watch and re-enjoy their performances over and over.

'Yes, that'll be nice.'

56

She said goodnight much as if she hadn't had a gun aimed closely against her head half an hour earlier, and with upright carriage went gently away upstairs.

A remarkable woman, I thought, not for the first time, and descended to the basement in search of Dawson who was sitting, jacket off, in front of the television drinking beer. The butler, slightly abashed by having let the uninvited guests outrush him, made no demur at checking with me through the house's defences. Window locks, front door, rear door, basement door, all secure.

John Grundy, the male nurse, he said, would arrive at ten, assist Monsieur to bed, sleep in the room next to him, and in the morning help him bathe, shave and dress. He would do Monsieur's laundry and be gone by eleven.

Only Dawson and his wife (the princess's personal maid) slept in the basement, he said: all the rest of the staff came in by day. Prince Litsi, who was occupying the guest suite on the ground floor, and Miss de Brescou, whose room was beyond the princess's suite, were away, as I knew.

His eyebrows shot up at the mention of the bamboo room, and when he took me by lift to the floor above the princess and her husband, I could see why. Palatial, pale blue, gold and cream, it looked fit for the noblest of visitors, the bamboo of its name found in the pattern of the curtains and the pale Chinese-Chippendale furniture. There was a vast double bed, a dressing room, a bathroom, and an array of various drinks and a good television set hidden behind discreet louvred doors.

Dawson left me there, and I took the opportunity to make my regular evening telephone call to Wykeham, to tell him how his horses had run. He was pleased, he said, about Cotopaxi, but did I realize what I'd done to Cascade? Dusty, he said, had told him angrily all about the race, including Maynard Allardeck's inspection afterwards.

'How is Cascade?' I asked.

'We weighed him. He's lost thirty pounds. He can hardly hold his head up. You don't often send horses back in that state.'

'I'm sorry,' I said.

'There's winning and winning,' he said testily. 'You've ruined him for Cheltenham.'

'I'm sorry,' I said again, contritely. Cheltenham, two and a half weeks ahead, was of course the top meeting of the jumping year, its races loaded with prestige and prizes. Wykeham liked above all to have successes there, as indeed did I and every jump jockey riding. Missing a winner there would serve me right, I supposed, for letting unhappiness get the better of me, but I was genuinely sorry for Wykeham's sake.

'Don't do anything like that tomorrow with Kalgoorlie,' he said severely.

I sighed. Kalgoorlie had been dead for years. Wykeham's memory was apt to slip cogs to the point that sometimes I couldn't work out what horse he was referring to.

'Do you mean Kinley?' I suggested.

'What? Yes, of course, that's what I said. You give him a nice ride, now, Kit.'

At least, I thought, he knew who he was talking to: he still on the telephone called me often by the name of the jockey who'd had my job ten years earlier.

I assured him I would give Kinley a nice ride.

'And win, of course,' he said.

'All right.' A nice ride and a win couldn't always be achieved together, as Cascade very well knew. Kinley however was a white hot hope for Cheltenham, and if he didn't win comfortably at Newbury, the expectations could cool to pink.

'Dusty says the princess didn't come into the ring before Cotopaxi's race, or see him afterwards. He says it was because she was angry about Cascade.' Wykeham's old voice was full of displeasure. 'We can't afford to anger the princess.'

'Dusty's wrong,' I said. 'She wasn't angry. She had some trouble with . . . er . . . a visitor in her box. She explained to me after . . . and invited me to Eaton Square, which is where I am now.'

'Oh,' he said, mollified. 'All right, then. Kinley's race is televised tomorrow,' he said, 'so I'll be watching.'

'Great.'

'Well then . . . Goodnight, Paul.'

'Goodnight, Wykeham,' I said.

Wryly I telephoned to the answering machine in my own house, but there was nothing much in the way of messages, and presently Dawson returned with a supper of chicken soup, cold ham and a banana (my choice).

Later together, we made another tour of the house, meeting John Grundy, a sixty-year-old widower, on his way to his own room. Both men said they would be undisturbed to see me wandering around now and then in the small hours, but although I did prowl up and down once or twice, the big house was silent all night, its clocks ticking in whispers. I slept on and off between linen sheets under a silk coverlet in pyjamas thoughtfully supplied by Dawson, and in the morning was ushered in to see Roland de Brescou.

He was alone in his sitting room, freshly dressed in a city suit with a white shirt and foulard tie. Black shoes, brilliantly polished. White hair, neatly brushed. No concessions to his condition, no concession to weekends.

His wheelchair was unusual in having a high back – and I'd often wondered why more weren't designed that way – so that he could rest his head if he felt like dozing. That morning, although he was awake, he was resting his head anyway.

'Please sit down,' he said civilly, and watched me take the same place as the evening before, in the dark red leather armchair. He looked if possible even frailer, with grey shadows in his skin, and the long hands which lay quiet on the padded armrests had a quality of transparency, the flesh thin as paper over the bones.

I felt almost indecently strong and healthy in contrast, and asked if there were anything I could fetch and carry for him.

He said no with a twitch of eye muscle that might have been interpreted as an understanding smile, as if he were accustomed to such guilt reactions in visitors.

'I wish to thank you,' he said, 'for coming to our defence. For helping Princess Casilia.'

He had never in my presence called her 'my wife', nor would I ever have referred to her in that way to him. His formal patterns of speech were curiously catching.

'Also,' he said, as I opened my mouth to demur, 'for giving me time to consider what to do about Henri Nanterre.' He moistened his dry lips with the tip of an apparently desiccated tongue. 'I have been unable to sleep... I cannot risk harm to Princess Casilia or anyone around us. It is time for me to relinquish control. To find a successor... but I have no children, and there are few de Brescous left. It isn't going to be easy to find any family member to take my place.'

Even the thought of the discussions and decisions such a course would lead to seemed to exhaust him.

'I miss Louis,' he said unexpectedly. 'I cannot continue without him. It is time for me to retire. I should have seen... when Louis died... it was time.' He seemed to be talking to himself as much as me, clarifying his thoughts, his eyes wandering.

I made a nondescript noise of nothing much more than interest. I would have agreed that the time to retire was long past, though, and it almost seemed he caught something of that thought, because he said calmly, 'My grandfather was in total command at ninety. I expected to die also at the head of the company, as I am the Chairman.'

'Yes, I see.'

His gaze steadied on my face. 'Princess Casilia will go to the races today. She hopes you will go with her in her car.' He paused. 'May I ask you ... to defend her from harm?'

'Yes,' I said matter-of-factly, 'with my life.'

It didn't even sound melodramatic after the past evening's events, and he seemed to take it as a normal remark. He merely nodded a fraction and I thought that, in retrospect, I would be hotly embarrassed at myself. But then, I probably meant it, and the truth pops out.

It seemed anyway what he wanted to hear. He nodded again a couple of times slowly as if to seal the pact, and I stood up to take my leave. There was a briefcase, I saw, lying half under one of the chairs between me and the door, and I picked it up to ask him where he would like it put.

'It isn't mine,' he said, without much interest. 'It must be Gerald Greening's. He's returning this morning.'

I had a sudden picture, however, of the pathetic Valery producing the handgun application form from that case, and of scuttling away empty-handed at the end. When I explained to Roland de Brescou, he suggested I took the case downstairs to the hall, so that when its owner called back to collect it, he wouldn't need to come up.

I took the case away with me but, lacking de Brescou's incurious honesty, went up to the bamboo room, not down.

The case, black leather, serviceable, unostentatious, proved to be unlocked and unexciting, containing merely what looked like a duplicate of the form which Roland de Brescou hadn't signed.

On undistinguished buff paper, mostly in small badly printed italics, and of course in French, it hardly looked worth the upheaval it was causing. As far as I could make out, it wasn't specifically to do with armaments, but had many dotted-line spaces needing to be filled in. No one had filled in anything on the duplicate, although presumably the one Valery had taken away with him had been ready for signing.

I put the form in a drawer of a bedside table and took the briefcase downstairs, meeting Gerald Greening as he arrived. We said good mornings with the memory of last night's violence hovering, and he said he had not only rewritten the sandbags but had had the document properly typed and provided with seals. Would I be so good as to repeat my services as witness?

We returned to Roland de Brescou and wrote our names, and I mentioned again about telling Danielle and Prince Litsi. I couldn't help thinking of them. They would be starting about now on 'The Masterworks of Leonardo . . .' dammit, dammit.

'Yes, yes,' Greening was saying, 'I understand they return tomorrow evening. Perhaps you could inform them yourself.'

'Perhaps.'

'And now,' Greening said, 'to update the police.'

He busied himself on the telephone, reaching yesterday's man and higher, obtaining the promise of a CID officer's attentions, admitting he didn't know where Nanterre could be found. 'Immediately he surfaces again, we will inform you,' he was saying, and I wondered how immediately would be immediately, should Nanterre turn up with bullets.

Roland de Brescou however showed approval, not dismay, and I left them beginning to discuss how best to find a de Brescou successor. I made various preparations for the day, and I was waiting in the hall when the princess came down to go to the races, with Dawson hovering and Thomas, alerted by telephone, drawing smoothly to a halt outside. She was wearing a cream-coloured coat, not the sables, with heavy gold earrings and no hat, and although she seemed perfectly calm she couldn't disguise apprehensive glances up and down the street as she was seen across the pavement by her three assorted minders.

'It is important,' she said conversationally as soon as she was settled and Thomas had centrally locked all the doors, 'not to let peril deter one from one's pleasures.'

'Mm,' I said noncommittally.

She smiled sweetly. 'You, Kit, do not.'

'Those pleasures earn me my living.'

'Peril should not, then, deter one from one's duty.' She sighed. 'So stuffy, don't you think, put that way? Duty and pleasure so often coincide, deep down, don't you think?'

I did think, and I thought she was probably right. She was no mean psychologist, in her way.

'Tell me about Cotopaxi,' she commanded, and listened contentedly, asking questions when I paused. After that, we discussed Kinley, her brilliant young hurdler, and after that her other runner for the day, Hillsborough, and it wasn't until we were nearing Newbury that I asked if she would mind if Thomas accompanied her into the meeting and stayed at her side all afternoon.

'Thomas?' she said, surprised. 'But he doesn't like racing. It bores him, doesn't it, Thomas?'

'Ordinarily, madam,' he said.

'Thomas is large and capable,' I said, pointing out facts, 'and Monsieur de Brescou asked that you should enjoy the races unmolested.'

'Oh,' she said, disconcerted. 'How much . . . did you tell Thomas?'

'To look out for a frog with a hawk's nose and keep him from annoying you, madam,' Thomas said.

She was relieved, amused and, it seemed to me, grateful.

Back at the ranch, whether she knew it or not, John Grundy was sacrificing his Saturday afternoon to remain close to Roland de Brescou, with the number of the local police station imprinted on his mind.

'They already know there might be trouble,' I'd told him. 'If you call them, they'll come at once.'

John Grundy, tough for his years, had commented merely that he'd dealt with fighting drunks often enough, and to leave it to him. Dawson, whose wife was going out with her sister, swore he would let no strangers in. It seemed unlikely, to my mind, that Nanterre would actually attempt another head-on attack, but it would be foolish to risk being proved wrong with everything wide open.

Thomas, looking all six foot three a bodyguard, walked a pace behind the princess all afternoon, the princess behaving most of the time as if unaware of her shadow. She hadn't wanted to cancel her afternoon party because of the five friends she'd invited to lunch, and she requested them, at my suggestion, to stay with her whatever happened and not to leave her alone unless she herself asked it.

Two of them came into the parade ring before the

first of her two races, Thomas looming behind, all of them forming a shield when she walked back towards the stands. She was a far more likely target than de Brescou himself, I thought uneasily, watching her go as I rode Hillsborough out onto the course: her husband would never sign away his honour to save his own life, but to free an abducted wife . . . very likely.

He could repudiate a signature obtained under threat. He could retract, kick up a fuss, could say, 'I couldn't help it.' The guns might not then be made, but his health would deteriorate and his name could be rubble. Better to prevent than to rescue, I thought, and wondered what I'd overlooked.

Hillsborough felt dull in my hands and I knew going down to the start that he wouldn't do much good. There were none of the signals that horses feeling well and ready to race give, and although I tried to jolly him along once we'd started, he was as sluggish as a cold engine.

He met most of the fences right but lost ground on landing through not setting off again fast, and when I tried to make him quicken after the last he either couldn't or wouldn't, and lost two places to faster finishers, trailing in eighth of the twelve runners.

It couldn't be helped: one can't win them all. I was irritated, though, when an official came to the changing room afterwards and said the Stewards wanted to see me immediately, and I followed him to the Stewards' Room with more seethe than resignation, and there, as expected, was Maynard Allardeck, sitting at a table with two others, looking as impartial and reasonable as a saint. The Stewards said they wanted to know why my well-backed mount had run so badly. They said they were of the opinion that I hadn't ridden the horse out fully or attempted to win, and would I please give them an explanation.

Maynard was almost certainly the instigator, but not the spokesman. One of the others, a man I respected, had said for openers, 'Mr Fielding, explain the poor showing of Hillsborough.'

He had himself ridden as an amateur in days gone by, and I told him straightforwardly that my horse had seemed not to be feeling well and hadn't been enjoying himself. He had been flat-footed even going down to the start and during the race I'd thought once or twice of pulling him up altogether.

The Steward glanced at Allardeck, and said to me, 'Why didn't you use your whip after the last fence?'

The phrase 'flogging a dead horse' drifted almost irresistibly into my mind but I said only, 'I gave him a lot of signals to quicken, but he couldn't. Beating him wouldn't have made any difference.'

'You appeared to be giving him an easy ride,' he said, but without the aggression of conviction. 'What's your explanation?'

Giving a horse an easy ride was a euphemism for 'not trying to win', or, even worse, for 'trying not to win', a loss-of-licence matter. I said with some force,

'Princess Casilia's horses, Mr Harlow's horses, are always doing their best. Hillsborough was doing his best, but he was having an off day.'

There was a shade of amusement in the Steward's eyes. He knew, as everyone in racing knew, how things stood between Allardecks and Fieldings; Stewards' enquiries had for half a century sorted out the fiery accusations flung at Maynard's father by my grandfather, and at my grandfather by Maynard's father, both of them training Flat racers in Newmarket. The only new twist to the old battle was the recent Allardeck presence on the power side of the table, no doubt highly funny to all but myself.

'We note your explanation,' the Steward said dryly, and told me I could go.

I went without looking directly at Maynard. Twice in two days I'd wriggled off his hooks, and I didn't want him to think I was gloating. I went back fast to the changing room to exchange the princess's colours for those of another owner and to weigh out, but even so I was late into the parade ring for the next race (and one could be fined for that also).

I walked in hurriedly to join the one hopeful little group without a jockey, and saw, thirty feet away, Henri Nanterre.

CHAPTER FIVE

He was standing in another group of owners, trainer and jockey, and was looking my way as if he'd been watching my arrival.

Unwelcome as he was, however, I had to postpone thoughts of him on account of the excited questions of the tubby enthusiastic couple whose dreams I was supposed to make come true within the next ten minutes; and anyway, the princess, I hoped, was safely surrounded upstairs.

The Dream, so named, had been a winner on the Flat and was having his first run over hurdles. He proved to be fast, all right, but he hadn't learned the knack of jumping: he rattled the first three flights ominously and put his feet straight through the fourth, and that was as far as we went. The Dream galloped away loose in fright, I picked myself up undamaged from the grass and waited resignedly for wheels to roll along to pick me up. One had to expect a fall every ten or eleven rides, and mostly they were easy, like that, producing a bruise at worst. The bad ones turned up perhaps twice a year, always unexpected.

I checked in with the doctor, as one had to after every fall, and while changing for the next race made time to talk to the jockey from the group with Nanterre: Jamie Fingall, long a colleague, one of the crowd.

'French guy with the beaky nose? Yeah, well, the guvnor introduced him but I didn't pay much attention. He owns horses in France, something like that.'

'Um ... Was he with your guvnor, or with the owners?'

'With the owners, but it sounded to me like the guvnor was trying to sweet talk the Frenchie into sending him a horse over here.'

'Thanks, then.'

'Be my guest.'

Jamie Fingall's guvnor, Basil Clutter, trained in Lambourn about a mile down the road from my house, but there wasn't time to seek him out before the next race, the three mile 'chase, and after that I had to change again and go out to meet the princess in the parade ring, where Kinley was already stalking round.

As before, she was well guarded and seemed almost to be enjoying it, and I didn't know whether or not to alarm her with news of Nanterre. In the end, I said only to Thomas, 'The frog is here. Stay close to her,' and he gave a sketchy thumbs-up, and looked determined. Thomas looking determined, I thought, would deter Attila the Hun.

Kinley made up for an otherwise disgusting afternoon, sending my spirits soaring from depths to dizzy heights.

The rapport between us, established almost instantly during his first hurdle race the previous November, had deepened in three succeeding outings so that by February he seemed to know in advance what I wanted him to do, as I knew what he wanted to do before he did it. The result was racing at its sublime best, an unexplainable synthesis at a primitive level and undoubtedly a shared joy.

Kinley jumped hurdles with a surge that had almost left me behind the first time I felt it, and even though every time since I'd know what was going to happen, I hadn't outgrown the surprise. The first hurdle left me gasping as usual, and by the end I reckoned we'd stolen twenty clean lengths in the air. He won jauntily and at a canter and I hoped Wykeham, watching on the box, would think it 'a nice ride' and forgive me Cascade. Maynard Allardeck, I grimly thought, walking Kinley back along the path to the unsaddling enclosure, could find no vestige of an excuse that time to carp or cavil, and I realized that he and Kinley and Nanterre between them had at least stopped me brooding over Botticelli, Giorgione, Titian and Raphael.

The princess had her best stars to her blue eyes, looking as if guns weren't invented. I slid to the ground and we smiled in shared triumph, and I refrained with an effort from hugging her.

'He's ready for Cheltenham,' she said, sticking out a glove to pat the dark hide lightly. 'He's as good as Sir Ken.'

Sir Ken had been an all-time star in the nineteen fifties, winning three Champion Hurdles and numerous other top hurdling events. Owning a horse like Sir Ken was the ultimate for many who'd seen him, and the princess, who had, had referred to him often.

'He has a long way to go,' I said, unbuckling the girths. 'He's still so young.'

'Oh yes,' she said happily. 'But . . .' She stopped abruptly, with a gasp. I looked at her and saw her eyes widen as she looked with horror above my right shoulder, and I whipped round fast to see what was there.

Henri Nanterre was there, staring at her.

I stood between them. Thomas and the friends were behind her, more occupied with avoiding Kinley's light-hearted hooves than guarding their charge in the safest and most public of places.

Henri Nanterre momentarily transferred his gaze to my face and then, with shock, stared at me with his mouth opening.

I'd thought in the parade ring that since he'd been watching me, he'd found out who I was, but realized in that second that he'd thought of me then simply as the princess's jockey. He was confounded, it seemed, to identify me from the evening before.

'You're . . .' he said, for once at a loss for loud words. 'You . . .'

'That's right,' I said. 'What do you want?'

He recovered with a snap from his surprise, narrowed his eyes at the princess, and said distinctly, 'Jockeys can have accidents.'

'So can people who carry guns,' I said. 'Is that what you came to say?'

It appeared, actually, that it more or less was.

'Go away,' I said, much as he'd said it to me a day earlier up in the box, and to my complete astonishment, he went.

'Hey,' Thomas said agitatedly, 'that was . . . that was . . . wasn't it?'

'Yes, it was,' I said, looping the girths round my saddle. 'Now you know what he looks like.'

'Madam!' Thomas said penitently. 'Where did he come from?'

'I didn't see,' she said, slightly breathless. 'He was just in there.'

'Fella moves like an eel,' one of her friends said; and certainly there had been a sort of gliding speed to his departure.

'Well, my dears,' the princess said to her friends, laughing a trifle shakily, 'let's go up and celebrate this lovely win. And Kit, come up soon.'

'Yes, Princess.'

I weighed in and, as it was my last ride of the day, changed into street clothes. After that, I made a detour over to the saddling boxes because Basil Clutter, as Jamie had told me, would be there, saddling up his runner for the last race.

Trainers in those places never had time to talk, but he did manage an answer or two, grudgingly, while he settled weight cloth, number cloth and saddle onto his restless charge's back.

'Frenchman? Nanterre, yes. Owns horses in France, trained by Villon. Industrialist of some sort. Where's he staying? How should I know? Ask the Roquevilles, he was with them. Roquevilles? Look, stop asking questions, ring me tonight, right?'

'Right,' I said, sighing, and left him sponging out his horse's mouth so he should look clean and well-groomed before the public. Basil Clutter was hard-working and always bustling, saving money by doing Dusty's job, being his own travelling head lad.

I went up to the princess's box, drank tea with lemon, and re-lived for her and the friends the glories of Kinley's jumping. When it was time to go she said, 'You will come back with me, won't you?' as if it were natural for me to do so, and I said, 'Yes, certainly,' as if I thought so too.

I picked up from my still parked car the overnight bag I habitually carried with me for contingencies, and we travelled without much trouble back to Eaton Square where I telephoned to Wykeham from the bamboo room. He was pleased, he said, about Kinley, but annoyed about Hillsborough. Dusty had told him

I'd made no show and been hauled in by the Stewards for it, and what did I think I was doing, getting into trouble two days in a row?

I could strangle Dusty, I thought, and told Wykeham what I'd told the Stewards. 'They accepted the explanation,' I said. 'Maynard Allardeck was one of them, and he's after me whatever I do.'

'Yes, I suppose he is.' He cheered up a good deal and even chuckled, 'Bookmakers are taking bets on when – not whether – he'll get you suspended.'

'Very funny,' I said, not amused. 'I'm still at Eaton Square, if you want me.'

'Are you?' he said. 'All right then. Goodnight, Kit.'

'Goodnight, Wykeham.'

I got through next to Basil Clutter, who told me the Roquevilles' number, and I caught the Roquevilles on their return from Newbury.

No, Bernard Roqueville said, he didn't know where Henri Nanterre was staying. Yes, he knew him, but not well. He'd met him in Paris at the races, at Longchamp, and Nanterre had renewed the acquaintanceship by inviting him and his wife for a drink at Newbury. Why was I interested, he asked.

I said I was hoping to locate Nanterre while he was in England. Bernard Roqueville regretted he couldn't help, and that was that.

A short lead going nowhere, I thought resignedly, putting down the receiver. Maybe the police would have better luck, although I feared that finding someone to give him a finger-wagging for waving an empty gun at a foreign princess wouldn't exactly bring them out steaming in a full-scale manhunt.

I went downstairs to the sitting room and discussed Hillsborough's fall from grace over a drink with the princess, and later in the evening she, Roland de Brescou and I ate dinner together in the dining room, served by Dawson; and I thought only about twenty times of the Florentine Banquet up north.

It wasn't until after ten, saying goodnight, that she spoke about Nanterre.

'He said, didn't he, that jockeys have accidents.'

'That's what he said. And so they do, pretty often.'

'That wasn't what he meant.'

'Perhaps not.'

'I couldn't forgive myself if because of us you came to harm.'

'That's what he's counting on. But I'll take my chance, and so will Thomas.' And privately I thought that if her husband hadn't cracked instantly with a gun to his wife's head, he was unlikely to bend because of a whole barrage pointed at ours.

She said, remembering with a shiver, 'Accidents would happen to those I liked . . . and employed.'

'It's only noise. He won't do anything,' I said encouragingly, and she said quietly that she hoped not, and went to bed.

I wandered again round the big house, checking its defences, and wondered again what I'd overlooked.

In the morning, I found out.

I was already awake at seven when the intercom buzzed, and when I answered, a sleepy-voiced Dawson asked me to pick up the ordinary telephone as there was an in-coming call for me. I picked up the receiver and found it was Wykeham on the line.

Racing stables wake early on Sundays, as on other days, and I was used to Wykeham's dawn thoughts, as he woke always by five. His voice that day, however, was as incoherently agitated as I'd ever heard it, and at first I wondered wildly what sins I might have committed in my sleep.

'D . . . did you hear what what I s . . . said?' he stuttered. 'Two of them! T . . . two of the p . . . princess's horses are d . . . dead.'

'Two?' I said, sitting bolt upright in bed and feeling cold. 'How? I mean . . . which two?'

'They're dead in their boxes. Stiff. They've been dead for hours . . .'

'Which two?' I said again, fearfully.

There was a silence at the other end. He had difficulty remembering their names at the best of times, and I could imagine that at that moment a whole roll-call of long-gone heroes was fumbling on his tongue.

'The two,' he said in the end, 'that ran on Friday.'

I felt numb.

'Are you there?' he demanded.

'Yes... Do you mean... Cascade... and Cotopaxi?'

He *couldn't* mean it, I thought. It couldn't be true. Not Cotopaxi... not before the Grand National.

'Cascade,' he said. 'Cotopaxi.'

Oh no... 'How?' I said.

'I've got the vet coming,' he said. 'Got him out of bed. I don't know how. That's his job. But two! One might die, I've known it happen, but not two... Tell the princess, Kit.'

'That's your job,' I protested.

'No, no, you're there... Break it to her. Better than on the phone. They're like children to her.'

People she liked... Jesus Christ.

'What about Kinley?' I asked urgently.

'What?'

'Kinley... yesterday's hurdle winner.'

'Oh, yes, him. He's all right. We checked all the others when we found these two. Their boxes were next to each other, I expect you remember... Tell the princess soon, Kit, won't you? We'll have to move these horses out. She'll have to say what she wants done with the carcasses. Though if they're poisoned...'

'Do you think they're poisoned?' I said.

'Don't know. Tell her now, Kit.' He put his receiver down with a crash, and I replaced mine feeling I would burst with ineffectual anger.

To kill her horses! If Henri Nanterre had been there at that moment, I would have stuffed his plastic gun down his loud-voiced throat. Cascade and Cotopaxi . . . people I knew, had known for years. I grieved for them as for friends.

Dawson agreed that his wife would wake the princess and tell her I had some sad news of one of her horses, and would wait for her in the sitting room. I dressed and went down there, and presently she came, without make-up and with anxious eyes.

'What is it?' she asked. 'Which one?'

When I told her it was two, and which two, I watched her horror turn to horrified speculation.

'Oh no, he couldn't,' she exclaimed. 'You don't think, do you . . .'

'If he has,' I said, 'he'll wish he hadn't.'

She decided that we should go down to Wykeham's stable immediately, and wouldn't be deterred when I tried to persuade her not to.

'Of course, I must go. Poor Wykeham, he'll need comforting. I should feel wrong if I didn't go.'

Wykeham needed comforting less than she did, but by eight-thirty we were on the road, the princess in lipstick and Thomas placidly uncomplaining about the loss of his free day. My offer of driving the Rolls instead of him had been turned down like an improper suggestion.

Wykeham's establishment, an hour's drive south of London, was outside a small village on a slope of the Sussex Downs. Sprawling and complex, it had been enlarged haphazardly at intervals over a century, and

was attractive to owners because of its maze of unexpected little courtyards, with eight or ten boxes in each,
and holly bushes in red-painted tubs. To the stable staff,
the picturesque convolution meant a lot of fetching and
carrying, a lot of time wasted.

The princess's horses were spread through five of
the courtyards, not filling any of them. Wykeham, like
many trainers, preferred to scatter an owner's horses
about rather than to clump them all together, and
Cascade and Cotopaxi, as it happened, had been the
only two belonging to the princess to be housed in
the courtyard nearest the entrance drive.

One had to park in a central area and walk through
archways into the courtyards, and when he heard us
arrive, Wykeham came out of the first courtyard to
meet us.

He looked older by the week, I thought uneasily,
watching him roguishly kiss the princess's hand. He
always half-flirted with her, with twinkling eyes and the
remnants of a powerful old charm, but that morning
he simply looked distracted, his white hair blowing
when he removed his hat, his thin old hands shaking.

'My dear Wykeham,' the princess said, alarmed.
'You look so cold.'

'Come into the house,' he said, moving that way.
'That's best.'

The princess hesitated. 'Are my poor horses still
here?'

He nodded miserably. 'The vet's with them.'

'Then I think I'll see them,' she said simply, and walked firmly into the courtyard, Wykeham and I following, not trying to dissuade her.

The doors of two of the boxes stood open, the interiors beyond lit palely with electric light, although there was full daylight outside. All the other boxes were firmly closed, and Wykeham was saying, 'We've just left the other horses here in their boxes. They don't seem to be disturbed, because there's no blood . . . that's what would upset them, you know . . .'

The princess, only half listening, walked more slowly across to where her horses lay on the dark brown peat on the floor of their boxes, their bodies silent humps, all flashing speed gone.

They had died with their night rugs on, but either the vet or Wykeham or the lads had unbuckled those and rolled them back against the walls. We looked in silence at the dark revealed sheen of Cascade, and the snow-splashed chestnut of Cotopaxi.

Robin Curtiss, the tall and gangling boyish vet, had met the princess occasionally on other mornings, and me more often. Dressed in green protective overalls, he nodded to us both and excused himself from shaking hands, saying he would need to wash first.

The princess, acknowledging his greeting, asked at once and with composure, 'Please tell me . . . how did they die?'

Robin Curtiss glanced at Wykeham and me, but

neither of us would have tried to stop him answering, so he looked back to the princess and told her straight.

'Ma'am, they were shot. They knew nothing about it. They were shot with a humane killer. With a bolt.'

CHAPTER SIX

Cascade was lying slantwise across the box, his head in shadow but not far from the door. Robin Curtiss stepped onto the peat and bent down, picking up the black forelock of hair which fell naturally forward from between the horse's ears.

'You can't clearly see, ma'am, as he's so dark, but there's the spot, right under his forelock, where the bolt went in.' He straightened up, dusting his fingers on a handkerchief. 'Easy to miss,' he said. 'You can't see what happened unless you're looking for it.'

The princess turned away from her dead horse with a glitter of tears but a calm face. She stopped for a minute at the door of the next box, where Cotopaxi's rump was nearest, his head virtually out of sight near the manger.

'He's the same,' Robin Curtiss said. 'Under the forelock, almost invisible. It was expert, ma'am. They didn't suffer.'

She nodded, swallowing, then, unable to speak, put one hand on Wykeham's arm and with the other waved towards the arch of the courtyard and Wykeham's house beyond. Robin Curtiss and I watched them go and he sighed in sympathy.

'Poor lady. It always takes them hard.'

'They were murdered,' I said. 'That makes it harder.'

'Yeah, they sure were murdered. Wykeham's called the police, though I told him it wasn't strictly necessary. The law's very vague about killing animals. But with them belonging to Princess Casilia, I suppose he thought it best. And he's in a tizzy about moving the bodies as soon as possible, but we don't know where he stands with the insurance company . . . whether in a case like this, they have to be told first . . . and it's Sunday . . .' He stopped rambling and said more coherently, 'You don't often see wounds like these, nowadays.'

'What do you mean?' I asked.

'Captive bullets are old hat. Almost no one uses them now.'

'Captive bullets?'

'The bolt. Called captive because the killing agent doesn't fly free of the gun, but is retracted back into it. Surely you know that?'

'Yes. I mean, I know the bolt retracts. I saw one, close to, years ago. I didn't know they were old hat. What do you use now, then?'

'You must have seen a horse put down,' he said, astonished. 'All those times, out on the course, when your mount breaks a leg . . .'

'It's only happened to me twice,' I said. 'And both times I took my saddle off and walked away.'

I found myself thinking about it, trying to explain. 'One moment you're in partnership with that big creature, and maybe you like him, and the next moment he's going to die ... So I've not wanted to stay to watch. It may be odd to you, especially as I was brought up in a racing stable, but I never have seen the gun actually put to the head, and I've always vaguely imagined it was shot from the side, like through a human temple.'

'Well,' he said, still surprised and mildly amused, 'you'd better get educated. You of all people. Look,' he said, 'look at Cotopaxi's head.' He picked his way over the stiff chestnut legs until he could show me what he wanted. Cotopaxi's eyes were half open and milky, and although Robin Curtiss was totally unmoved, to me it was still no everyday matter.

'A horse's brain is only the size of a bunched fist,' he said. 'I suppose you know that?'

'Yes, I know it's small.'

He nodded. 'Most of a horse's head is empty space, all sinuses. The brain is up between the ears, at the top of the neck. The bone in that area is pretty solid. There's only the one place where you can be sure a bolt will do the job.' He picked up Cotopaxi's forelock and pointed to a small disturbance of the pale hairs. 'You take a line from the right ear to the left eye,' he said, 'and a line from the left ear to the right eye. Where the lines cross, that's the best ... more or less the only . . . place to aim. And see? The bolt went into Cotopaxi at that exact spot. It wasn't any old haphazard job. Whoever did this knew exactly what to do.'

'Well,' I said thoughtfully, 'now you've told me, I'd know what to do.'

'Yes, but don't forget, you have to get the angle right as well as the place. You have to aim straight at the spot where the spinal cord and the brain meet. Then the result's instantaneous and, as you can see, there's no blood.'

'And meanwhile,' I suggested ironically, 'the horse is simply standing still letting all this happen?'

'Funnily enough, most of them do. Even so, I'm told that for short people it's difficult to get the hand up to the right angle at the right height.'

'Yes, I'm sure,' I said. I looked down at the waste of the great racing spirit. I'd sat on that back, shared that mind, felt the fluid majesty of those muscles, enjoyed his triumphs, schooled him as a young horse, thrilled to his growing strengths. I would still walk away, I thought, if another time came.

I made my way back to the outside air and Robin Curtiss followed me out, still matter-of-factly continuing my education.

'Apart from the difficulty of hitting the right spot, the bolt has another disadvantage, which is that although it retracts at once, the horse begins to fall just as quick, and the hard skull bones tend to bend the bolt after a lot of use, and the gun no longer works.'

'So now you use something else?'

'Yes,' he nodded. 'A free bullet. I'll show you, if you like. I've a pistol in my car.'

We walked unhurriedly out of the courtyard to where his car was parked not far from the princess's Rolls. He unlocked the boot, and in there unlocked an attaché case, and from it produced a brown cloth which he unwrapped.

Inside lay an automatic Luger-type pistol, which looked ordinary except for its barrel. Instead of the straight narrow barrel one would expect, there was a wide bulbous affair with a slanted oval opening at the end.

'This barrel sends the bullet out spinning in a spiral,' he explained.

'Any old bullet?'

'It has to be the right calibre, but yes, any old bullet, and any old gun. That's one big advantage, you can weld a barrel like this onto any pistol you like. Well . . . the bullet leaves the gun with a lot of short-range energy, but because it's going in a spiral, almost any obstruction will stop it. So if you shoot a horse, the bullet will stop in its head. Mostly, that is.' He smiled cheerfully. 'Anyway, you don't have to be so accurate, as with a bolt, because the wobbling bullet does a lot more damage.'

I looked at him thoughtfully. 'How can you be so sure those two were killed with a bolt?'

'Oh . . . with the free bullet you get powder burns at

the entry, and also blood coming down the nose, and probably also from the mouth. Not much, sometimes, but it's there, because of the widespread damage done inside, you see.'

'Yes,' I said, sighing, 'I see.' I watched him wrap up his gun again and said, 'I suppose you have to have a licence for that.'

'Sure. And for the captive bullet also.'

There must be thousands of humane killers about, I reflected. Every vet would have one. Every knackers' yard. A great many sheep and cattle farmers. The huntsman of every pack of hounds. People dealing with police horses . . . the probabilities seemed endless.

'So I suppose there are hundreds of the old bolt-types lying around, out of date and unused.'

'Well,' he said, 'under lock and key.'

'Not last night.'

'No.'

'What time last night, would you say?'

He completed the stowing and locking away of his own pistol.

'Early,' he said positively. 'Not much after midnight. I know it was a cold night, but both horses were stone cold this morning. No internal temperature. That takes hours . . . and they were found at half six.' He grinned. 'The knackermen don't like fetching horses that have been dead that long. They have difficulty moving them when they're stiff, and getting them out of the boxes is a right problem.' He peeled off his overalls and put them in the boot. 'There'll have to be post-mortems. The insurance people insist on it.' He closed the car boot and locked it. 'We may as well go into the house.'

'And leave them there?' I gestured back towards the courtyard.

'They're not going anywhere,' he said, but he went back and shut the boxes' doors, in case, he said, any owners turned up for a nice Sunday look-round and had their sensibilities affronted. Robin's own sensibilities had been sensibly dumped during week one of his veterinary training, I guessed, but he didn't need a bedside manner to be a highly efficient minister to Wykeham's jumpers.

We went into Wykeham's house, ancient and rambling to match the yard, and found him and the princess consoling themselves with tea and memories, she at her most sustaining, he looking warmer and more in command, but puzzled.

He rose to his feet at our appearance and bustled me out of his sitting room making some flimsy remark about showing me where to make hot drinks, which I'd known for ten years.

'I don't understand,' he said, leading the way into the kitchen. 'Why doesn't she ask who killed them? It's the first thing I'd want to know. She hasn't mentioned it once. Just talks about the races in that way she has, and asking about the others. Why doesn't she want to know who killed them?'

'Mm,' I said. 'She suspects she knows.'

'What? For God's sake then, Kit . . . who?'

I hesitated. He looked thin and shaky, with lines cut deep in the wrinkled old face, the dark freckles of age standing out starkly. 'She'd have to tell you herself,' I said, 'but it's something to do with her husband's business. For what it's worth, I don't think you need worry about a traitor in your own camp. If she hasn't told you who she thinks it is, she won't tell anyone until she's discussed it with her husband, and they might decide to say nothing even then, they hate publicity so much.'

'There's going to be publicity anyway,' he said worriedly. 'The ante-post co-favourite for the Grand National shot in his box . . . Even if we try, we can't keep that out of the papers.'

I rattled about making fresh tea for Robin and myself, not relishing any more than he did the fuss lying ahead.

'All the same,' I said, 'your main worry isn't who. Your main worry is keeping all the others safe.'

'Kit!' He was totally appalled. 'B . . . bloody hell, K . . . Kit.' He was back to stuttering. 'It w . . . won't happen again.'

'Well,' I said temperately, but there was no way to soften it, 'I'd say they're all at risk. The whole lot of her horses. Not immediately, not today. But if the princess and her husband decide on one particular course of action, which they may do, then they'll all be at risk,

Kinley, perhaps, above all. So the thing to do is to apply our minds to defensive action.'

'But Kit . . .'

'Dog patrols,' I said.

'They're expensive . . .'

'The princess,' I remarked, 'is rich. Ask her. If she doesn't like the expense, I'll pay for them myself.' Wykeham's mouth opened and closed again when I pointed out, 'I've already lost the best chance I ever had of winning the Grand National. Her horses mean almost as much to me as they do to her and to you, and I'm damned well not going to let anyone pick them off two by two. So you get the security people here by tonight, and make sure there's someone about in the stable the whole time from now on, patrolling all the courtyards night and day.'

'All right,' he said slowly. 'I'll fix it . . . If I knew who'd killed them, I'd kill him myself.'

It sounded extraordinary, said that way, without anger, more as an unexpected self-discovery. What I'd wished I could do in fury, he proposed as a sane course of action; but people say these things, not meaning them, and he wouldn't have a mouse's chance physically, I thought regretfully, against the hawk-like Nanterre.

Wykeham had been a Hercules in his youth, he'd told me, a power-house on legs with the joy of life pumping through his veins. 'Joy of life,' he'd said to me several times, 'that's what I have. That's what you have.

No one gets anywhere without it. Relish the struggle, that's the way.'

He'd been an amateur jockey of note, and he'd dazzled and married the daughter of a mediumly successful trainer whose horses had started winning from the day Wykeham stepped into the yard. Now, fifty years on, with his strength gone, his wife dead and his own daughters grandmothers, he retained only the priceless ability to put the joy of life into his horses. He thought of little besides his horses, cared for little else, walked round at evening stables talking to each as a person, playing with some, admonishing others, coaxing a few, ignoring none.

I'd ridden for him from when I was nineteen, a fact he was apt to relate with complacency. 'Spot 'em young,' he'd told sundry owners. 'That's the thing. I'm good at that.' And he'd steadfastly given me, I sometimes reflected, exactly what he gave his charges: opportunity, trust and job-satisfaction.

He had trained a winner of the Grand National twice when I'd been at school, and in my time had come close, but it was only recently I'd realized how deeply he longed for a third slice of glory. The dead horse outside was for all of us a sickening, dragging, deflating disappointment.

'Cotopaxi,' he said intensely, for once getting the name right, 'was the one I would have saved first in a fire.'

*

The princess and I travelled back to London without waiting for the police, the insurers or the slaughterer's men. ('So horrid, all of that.')

I'd expected her to talk as usual chiefly about her horses, but it was of Wykeham, it seemed, that she was thinking.

'Thirty-five years ago, before you were born,' she said, 'when I first went racing, Wykeham strode the scene like a Colossus. He was almost everything he says he was, a Hercules indeed. Powerful, successful, enormously attractive . . . Half the women swooning over him with their husbands spluttering . . .' She smiled at this memory. 'I suppose it's hard for you to picture, Kit, knowing him only now, when he's old, but he was a splendid man . . . he still is, of course. I felt privileged, long ago, when he agreed to train my horses.'

I glanced in fascination at her serene face. In the past, I'd seen her often with Wykeham at the races, always deferring to him, tapping him playfully on the arm. I hadn't realized how much she must miss him now he stayed at home, how much she must regret the waning of such a titan.

A contemporary of my grandfather (and of Maynard Allardeck's father), Wykeham had been already a legend to me when he'd offered me the job. I'd accepted, almost dazed, and I'd grown up fast, mature at twenty from the demands and responsibility he'd thrust on me. Hundreds of thousands of pounds worth of horseflesh in my hands all the time, the success of the stable on my shoulders. He'd given me no allowances for youth, told me in no uncertain terms from the beginning that the whole enterprise rested finally on its jockey's skill, cool head and commonsense, and told me if I didn't measure up to what was needed, too bad, but bye bye.

Shaken to my soul, I'd wholeheartedly embraced what he offered, knowing there weren't two such chances in any life: and it had worked out fine, on the whole.

The princess's thoughts were following my own. 'When Paul Peck had that dreadful fall and decided to retire,' she said, 'there we were at the height of the season with no stable jockey and all the other top jockeys signed up elsewhere. Wykeham told me and the other owners that there was this young Fielding boy in Newmarket who had been riding as an amateur since he'd left school a year earlier . . .' She smiled. 'We were very doubtful. Wykeham said to trust him, he was never wrong. You know how modest he is!' She paused, considering. 'How long ago was that?'

'Ten years last October.'

She sighed. 'Time goes so fast.'

The older the faster . . . and for me also. Time no longer stretched out to infinity. My years in the saddle would end, maybe in four years, maybe five, whenever my body stopped mending fast from the falls, and I was far from ready to face the inexorability of the march of days. I loved my job intensely and dreaded its ending: anything after, I thought, would be unutterably dreary.

The princess was silent for a while, her thoughts reverting to Cascade and Cotopaxi.

'That bolt,' she said tentatively, 'I didn't like to ask Robin . . . I don't really know what a humane killer looks like.'

'Robin says the bolt type isn't much used nowadays,' I said, 'but I saw one once. My grandfather's vet showed me. It looked like an extra heavy pistol with a very thick barrel. The bolt itself is a metal rod which slides inside the barrel. When the trigger is pulled, the metal rod shoots out, but because it's fixed inside to a spring, it retracts immediately into the barrel again.' I reflected. 'The rod . . . the bolt . . . is a bit thicker than a pencil, and about four inches of it shoots out into . . . er . . . whatever it's aimed at.'

She was surprised. 'So small? I'd thought, somehow, you know, that it would be much bigger. And I didn't know until today that it was . . . from in front.'

She stopped talking abruptly and spent a fair time concentrating on the scenery. She had agreed without reserve to the dog patrols and had told Wykeham not to economize, the vulnerability of her other horses all too clearly understood.

'I had so been looking forward to the Grand National,' she said eventually. 'So very much.'

'Yes, I know. So had I.'

'You'll ride something else. For someone else.'

'It won't be the same.'

She patted my hand rather blindly. 'It's such a waste,' she said passionately. 'So stupid. My husband would never trade in guns to save my horses. *Never.* And I wouldn't ask it. My dear, dear horses.'

She struggled against tears and with a few sniffs and swallows won the battle, and when we reached Eaton Square she said we would go into the sitting room for a drink 'to cheer ourselves up'.

This good plan was revised, however, because the sitting room wasn't empty. Two people, sitting separately in armchairs, stood up as the princess walked in; and they were Prince Litsi and Danielle.

'My dear aunt,' the prince said, bowing to her, kissing her hand, kissing her also on both cheeks. 'Good morning.'

'Good morning,' she said faintly, and kissed Danielle. 'I thought you were returning late this evening.'

'The weather was frightful.' The prince shook my hand. 'Rain. Mist. Freezing. We decided yesterday we'd had enough and left early today, before breakfast.'

I kissed Danielle's smooth cheek, wanting much more. She looked briefly into my eyes and said Dawson had told them I was staying in the house. I hadn't seen her for three weeks and I didn't want to hear about Dawson. Around the princess, however, one kept raw emotions under wraps, and I heard myself asking if she'd enjoyed the lectures, as if I hoped she had.

'They were great.'

The princess decided that Prince Litsi, Danielle and myself should have the drinks, while she went upstairs to see her husband.

'You pour them,' she said to her nephew. 'And you, Kit, tell them everything that's been happening, will you? My dears . . . such horrid troubles.' She waved a hand vaguely and went away, her back straight and slender, a statement in itself.

'Kit,' the prince said, transferring his attention.

'Sir.'

We stood as if assessing each other, he taller, ten years older, a man of a wider world. A big man, Prince Litsi, with heavy shoulders, a large head, full mouth, positive nose and pale intelligent eyes. Light brown hair had begun to recede with distinction from his forehead, and a strong neck rose from a cream open-necked shirt. He looked as impressive as I'd remembered. It had been a year or more since we'd last met.

From his point of view, I suppose he saw brown curly hair, light brown eyes and a leanness imposed by the weights allocated to racehorses. Perhaps he saw also the man whose fiancée he had lured away to esoteric delights, but to do him justice there was nothing in his face of triumph or amusement.

'I'd like a drink,' Danielle said abruptly. She sat down, waiting. 'Litsi . . .'

His gaze lingered my way for another moment, then he turned to busy himself with the bottles. We had talked only on racecourses, I reflected, politely skimming the surface with post-race chit-chat. I knew him really as little as he knew me.

Without enquiring, he poured white wine for Danielle and Scotch for himself and me.

'OK?' he said, proffering the glass.

'Yes, sir.'

'Call me Litsi,' he said easily. 'All this protocol . . . I drop it in private. It's different for Aunt Casilia, but I never knew the old days. There's no throne any more . . . I'll never be king. I live in the modern world . . . so will you let me?'

'Yes,' I said. 'If you like.'

He nodded and sipped his drink. 'You call Aunt Casilia "Princess", anyway,' he pointed out.

'She asked me to.'

'There you are, then.' He waved a large hand, the subject closed. 'Tell us what has been disturbing the household.'

I looked at Danielle, dressed that day in black trousers, white shirt, blue sweater. She wore the usual pink lipstick, her cloudy dark hair held back in a blue band, everything known and loved and familiar. I wanted fiercely to hold her and feel her warmth against me, but she was sitting very firmly in an armchair built for one, and she would only meet my eyes for a flicker or two between concentrations on her drink.

I'm losing her, I thought, and couldn't bear it.

'Kit,' the prince said, sitting down.

I took a slow breath, returned my gaze to his face,

sat down also, and began the long recital, starting chronologically with Henri Nanterre's bullying invasion on Friday afternoon and ending with the dead horses in Wykeham's stable that morning.

Litsi listened with increasing dismay, Danielle with simpler indignation.

'That's horrible,' she said. 'Poor Aunt Casilia.' She frowned. 'I guess it's not right to knuckle under to threats, but why is Uncle Roland so against guns? They're made all over the place, aren't they?'

'In France,' Litisi said, 'for a man of Roland's background to deal in guns would be considered despicable.'

'But he doesn't live in France,' Danielle said.

'He lives in himself.' Litsi glanced my way. 'You understand, don't you, why he can't?'

'Yes,' I said.

He nodded. Danielle looked from one of us to the other and sighed. 'The European mind, I guess. Trading in arms in America isn't any big deal.'

I thought it was probably more of a big deal than she realized, and from his expression Litsi thought so too.

'Would the old four hundred families trade in arms?' he asked, but if he expected a negative, he didn't get it.

'Yes, sure, I guess so,' Danielle said. 'I mean, why would it worry them?'

'Nevertheless,' Litsi said, 'for Roland it is impossible.'

A voice on the stairs interrupted the discussion: a loud female voice coming nearer.

'Where is everyone? In there?' She swept into view in the sitting room doorway. 'Dawson says the bamboo room is occupied. That's ridiculous. I always have the bamboo room. I've told Dawson to remove the things of whoever is in there.'

Dawson gave me a bland look from over her shoulder and continued on his way to the floor above, carrying a suitcase.

'Now then,' said the vision in the doorway. 'Someone fix me a "bloody". The damn plane was two hours late.'

'Good grief,' Danielle said faintly, as all three of us rose to our feet, 'Aunt Beatrice.'

CHAPTER SEVEN

Aunt Beatrice, Roland de Brescou's sister, spoke with a slight French accent heavily overlaid with American. She had a mass of cloudy hair, not dark and long like Danielle's, but white going on pale orange. This framed and rose above a round face with round eyes and an expression of habitual determination.

'Danielle!' Beatrice said, thin eyebrows rising. 'What are you doing here?'

'I work in England.' Danielle went to her aunt to give her a dutiful peck. 'Since last fall.'

'Nobody tells me anything.'

She was wearing a silk jersey suit – her outdoor mink having gone upstairs over Dawson's arm – with a heavy seal on a gold chain shining in front. Her fistful of rings looked like ounce-heavy nuggets, and a crocodile had passed on for her handbag. Beatrice, in short, enjoyed her cash.

She was clearly about to ask who Litsi and I were when the princess entered, having come downstairs, I reckoned, at record speed.

'Beatrice,' she said, advancing with both hands out-stretched and a sugar-substitute smile, 'what a delightful surprise.' She grasped Beatrice's arms and gave her two welcoming kisses, and I saw that her eyes were cold with dismay.

'Surprise?' Beatrice said, as they disengaged. 'I called on Friday and spoke to your secretary. I told her to be sure to give you the message, and she said she would leave a note.'

'Oh.' A look of comprehension crossed the princess's face. 'Then I expect it's down in the office, and I've missed it. We've been . . . rather busy.'

'Casilia, about the bamboo room . . .' Beatrice began purposefully, and the princess with dexterity inter-rupted her.

'Do you know my nephew, Litsi?' she said, making sociable introductions. 'Litsi, this is Roland's sister, Beatrice de Brescou Bunt. Did you leave Palm Beach last evening, Beatrice? Such a long flight from Miami.'

'Casilia . . .' Beatrice shook hands with Litsi. 'The bam—'

'And this is Danielle's fiancé, Christmas Fielding.' The princess went on, obliviously. 'I don't think you've met him either. And now, my dear Beatrice, some tomato juice and vodka?'

'Casilia!' Beatrice said, sticking her toes in. 'I always have the bamboo room.'

I opened my mouth to say obligingly that I didn't mind moving, and received a rapid look of pure steel from the princess. I shut my mouth, amazed and amused, and held my facial muscles in limbo.

'Mrs Dawson is unpacking your things in the rose room, Beatrice,' the princess said firmly. 'You'll be very comfortable there.'

Beatrice, furious but outmanoeuvred, allowed a genial Litsi to concoct her a bloody Mary, she issuing sharp instructions about shaking the tomato juice, about how much Worcestershire sauce, how much lemon, how much ice. The princess watched with a wiped-clean expression of vague benevolence and Danielle was stifling her laughter.

'And now,' Beatrice said, the drink finally fixed to her satisfaction, 'what's all this rubbish about Roland refusing to expand the business?'

After a frosty second of immobility, the princess sat collectedly in an armchair, crossing her wrists and ankles in artificial composure.

Beatrice repeated her question insistently. She was never, I discovered, one to give up. Litsi busied himself with offering her a chair, smoothly settling her into it, discussing cushions and comfort and giving the princess time for mental remustering.

Litsi sat in a third armchair, leaning forward to Beatrice with smothering civility, and Danielle and I took places on a sofa, although with half an acre of flowered chintz between us.

'Roland is being obstructionist and I've come to tell him I object. He must change his mind at once. It is ridiculous not to move with the times and it's time to look for new markets.'

The princess looked at me, and I nodded. We had heard much the same thing, even some of the identical phrases, from Henri Nanterre on Friday evening.

'How do you know of any business proposals?' the princess asked.

'That dynamic young son of Louis Nanterre told me, of course. He made a special journey to see me, and explained the whole thing. He asked me to persuade Roland to drag himself into the twentieth century, let alone the twenty-first, and I decided I would come over here myself and insist on it.'

'You do know,' I said, 'that he's proposing to make and export guns?'

'Of course,' she said, 'but only plastic parts of guns. Roland is old fashioned. I've a good friend in Palm Beach whose husband's corporation makes missiles for the Defense Department. Where's the difference?' She paused. 'And what business is it of yours?' Her gaze travelled to Danielle, and she remembered. 'I suppose if you're engaged to Danielle,' she said grudgingly, 'then it's marginally your business. I didn't know Danielle was engaged. Nobody tells me anything.'

Henri Nanterre, I thought, had told her a great deal too much.

'Beatrice,' the princess said, 'I'm sure you'll want to wash after your journey. Dawson is arranging a late lunch for us, although as we didn't know there would be so many . . .'

'I want to talk to Roland,' Beatrice said obstinately.

'Yes, later. He's resting just now.' The princess stood, and we also, waiting for Danielle's aunt to be impelled upstairs by the sheer unanimity of our expectant good manners; and it was interesting, I thought, that she gave in, put down her unfinished drink and went, albeit grumbling as she departed that she expected to be reinstated in the bamboo room by the following day at the latest.

'She's relentless,' Danielle said as her voice faded away. 'She always gets what she wants. And anyway, the bamboo room's empty, isn't it? How odd of Aunt Casilia to refuse it.'

'I've slept in there the last two nights,' I said.

'Have you indeed!' Litsi's voice answered. 'In accommodation above princes.'

'That's not fair,' Danielle said. 'You said you preferred those rooms on the ground floor because you could go in and out without disturbing anyone.'

Litsi looked at her fondly. 'So I do. I only meant that Aunt Casilia must esteem your fiancé highly.'

'Yes,' Danielle said, giving me an embarrassed glance. 'She does.'

We all sat down again, though Danielle came no nearer to me on the sofa.

Litsi said, 'Why did Henri Nanterre recruit your

Aunt Beatrice so diligently? She won't change Roland's mind.'

'She lives on de Brescou money,' Danielle said unexpectedly. 'My parents do now as well, now that my black sheep of a father has been accepted back into the fold. Uncle Roland set up generous trusts for everybody out of the revenues from his land, but for as long as I've known my aunt, she's complained he could afford more.'

'For as long as you've known her?' Litsi echoed. 'Haven't you always known her?'

She shook her head. 'She disapproved of Dad. He left home originally under the heaviest of clouds, though what exactly he did, he's never told me; he just laughs if I ask, but it must have been pretty bad. It was a choice, Mom says, between exile or jail, and he chose California. She and I came on the scene a lot later. Anyway, about eight years ago, Aunt Beatrice suddenly swooped down on us to see what had become of her disgraced little brother, and I've seen her several times since then. She married an American businessman way way back, and it was after he died she set out to track Dad down. It took her two years – the United States is a big country – but she looks on persistence as a prime virtue. She lives in a marvellous Spanish-style house in Palm Beach – I stayed there for a few days one Spring Break – and she makes trips to New York, and every summer she travels in Europe and spends some time in "our château", as she calls it.'

Litsi was nodding. 'Aunt Casilia has been known to visit me in Paris when her sister-in-law stays too long. Aunt Casilia and Roland,' he explained, unnecessarily, 'go to the château for six weeks or so around July and August, to seek some country air and play their part as landowners. Did you know?'

'They mention it sometimes,' I said.

'Yes, of course.'

'What's the château like?' Danielle asked.

'Not a Disney castle,' Litsi answered, smiling. 'More like a large Georgian country house, built of light-coloured stone, with shutters on all the windows. Château de Brescou . . . The local town is built on land south of Bordeaux mostly owned by Roland, and he takes moral and civil pride in its well being. Even without the construction company, he could fund a mini-Olympics on the income he receives in rents, and his estates are run as the company used to be, with good managers and scrupulous fairness.'

'He *cannot*,' I commented, 'deal in arms.'

Danielle sighed. 'I do see,' she admitted, 'that with all that old aristocratic honour, he simply couldn't face it.'

'But I'm really surprised,' I said, 'that Beatrice could face it quite easily. I would have thought she would have shared her brother's feelings.'

'I'll bet,' Danielle said, 'that Henri Nanterre promised her a million dollar hand-out if she got Uncle Roland to change his mind.'

'In that case,' I suggested mildly, 'your uncle could offer her double to go back to Palm Beach and stay there.'

Danielle looked shocked. 'That wouldn't be right.'

'Morally indefensible,' I agreed, 'but pragmatically an effective solution.'

Litsi's gaze was thoughtful on my face. 'Do you think she's such a threat?'

'I think she could be like water dripping on a stone, wearing it away. Like water dripping on a man's fore-head, driving him mad.'

'The water torture,' Litsi said. 'I'm told it feels like a red hot poker after a while, drilling a hole into the skull.'

'She's just like that,' Danielle said.

There was a short silence while we contemplated the boring capacities of Beatrice de Brescou Bunt, and then Litsi said consideringly, 'It might be a good idea to tell her about the document you witnessed. Tell her the bad news that all four of us would have to agree to the guns, and assure her that even if she drives Roland to collapse, she'll still have to deal with me.'

'Don't tell her,' Danielle begged. 'She'll give none of us any peace.'

Neither of them had objected to the use made of them in their absence; on the contrary, they had been pleased. 'It makes us a family,' Danielle had said, and it was I, the witness, who had felt excluded.

'Upstairs,' I said, reflecting, 'I've got what I think is

a duplicate of the form Henri Nanterre wanted Monsieur de Brescou to sign. It is in French. Would you like to see it?'

'Very much,' Litsi said.

'Right.'

I went upstairs to fetch it and found Beatrice Bunt in my bedroom.

'What are you doing here?' she demanded.

'I came to fetch something,' I said.

She was holding the bright blue running shorts I usually slept in, which I had stored that morning in the bedside table drawer on top of Nanterre's form. The drawer was open, the paper presumably inside.

'These are yours?' she said in disbelief. '*You* are using this room?'

'That's right.' I walked over to her, took the shorts from her hand and returned them to the drawer. The form, I was relieved to see, lay there undisturbed.

'In that case,' she said with triumph, 'there's no problem. I shall have this room, and you can have the other. I always have the bamboo suite, it's the accepted thing. I see some of your things are in the bathroom. It won't take long to switch them over.'

I'd left the door open when I went in and, perhaps hearing her voice, the princess came enquiringly to see what was going on.

'I've told this young man to move, Casilia,' Beatrice said, 'because of course this is my room, naturally.'

'Danielle's fiancé,' the princess said calmly, 'stays in

110

this room as long as he stays in this house. Now come along, Beatrice, do, the rose room is extremely comfortable, you'll find.'

'It's half the size of this one, and there's no dressing room.'

The princess gave her a bland look, admirably concealing irritation. 'When Kit leaves, you shall have the bamboo room, of course.'

'I thought you said his name was Christmas.'

'So it is,' the princess agreed. 'He was born on Christmas day. Come along, Beatrice, let's go down for this very delayed lunch . . .' She positively shepherded her sister-in-law out into the passage, and returned a second later for one brief and remarkable sentence, half instruction, half entreaty.

'Stay in this house,' she said, 'until she is gone.'

After lunch, Litsi, Danielle and I went up to the disputed territory to look at the form, Litsi observing that his money was on Beatrice to winkle me out of all this splendour before tomorrow night.

'Did you see the dagger looks you were getting across the half-defrosted mousseline?'

'Couldn't miss them.'

'And those pointed remarks about good manners, unselfishness, and the proper precedence of rank?'

The princess had behaved as if she hadn't heard, sweetly making enquiries about Beatrice's health, her dogs, and the weather in Florida in February. Roland de Brescou, as very often, had remained upstairs for lunch, his door barricaded, I had no doubt. The princess with soft words would defend him.

'Well,' I said, 'here's this form.'

I retrieved it from under my blue shorts and gave it to Litsi, who wandered with it over to a group of comfortable chairs near the window. He read it attentively, sitting down absentmindedly, a big man with natural presence and unextended power. I liked him and because of Danielle feared him, a contradictory jumble of emotion, but I also trusted his overall air of amiable competence.

I moved across the room to join him, and Danielle also, and after a while he raised his head and frowned.

'For a start,' he said, 'this is not an application form for a licence to make or export arms. Are you sure that's what Nanterre said it was?'

I thought back. 'As far as I remember, it was the lawyer Gerald Greening who said it was a government form for preliminary application for a licence. I understood that that was what Henri Nanterre had told the princess in her box at Newbury.'

'Well, it isn't a government form at all. It isn't an application for any sort of licence. What it is is a very vague and general form which would be used by simple people to draw up a contract.' He paused. 'In England, I believe one can buy from stationers' shops a printed form for making a will. The legal words are all there to ensure that the will is properly executed. One simply inserts in the spaces what one wants done, like leaving the car to one's grandson. It's what's written into the spaces that really counts. Well, this form is rather like that. The legal form of words is correct, so that this would be a binding document, if properly signed and properly witnessed.' He glanced down at the paper. 'It's impossible to tell of course how Henri Nanterre had filled in all the spaces, but I would guess that overall it would say merely that the parties named in the contract had agreed on the course of action outlined by the accompanying documents. I would think that this form would be attached to, and act as page one, of a bulk of papers which would include all sorts of things like factory capacity, overseas sales forces, preliminary orders from customers and the specifications of the guns proposed to be manufactured. All sorts of things. But this simple form with Roland's signature on it would validate the whole presentation. It would be taken very seriously indeed as a full statement of intent. With this in his hands, Henri Nanterre could apply for his licence immediately.'

'And get it,' I said. 'He was sure of it.'

'Yes.'

'But Uncle Roland could say he was forced into signing,' Danielle said. 'He could repudiate it, couldn't he?'

'He might have been able to nullify an application form quite easily, but with a contract it's much more difficult. He could plead threats and harassment, but the legal position might be that it was too late to change his mind, once he'd surrendered.'

'And if he did get the contract overthrown,' I said reflectively, 'Henri Nanterre could start his harassment over again. There could be no end to it, until the contract was re-signed.'

'But all four of us have to sign now,' Danielle said. 'What if we all say we won't?'

'I think,' I said, 'if your uncle decided to sign, you would all follow his lead.'

Litsi nodded. 'The four-signature agreement is a delaying tactic, not a solution.'

'And what,' Danielle said flatly, 'is a solution?'

Litsi looked my way. 'Put Kit to work on it.' He smiled. 'Danielle told me you tied all sorts of strong men into knots last November. Can't you do it again?'

'This is a bit different,' I said.

'What happened last time?' he asked. 'Danielle told me no details.'

'A newspaper was giving my sister Holly and her husband a lot of unearned bad publicity – he's a race-horse trainer and they said he was going broke – and basically I got them to apologize and pay Bobby some compensation.'

'And Bobby's appalling father,' Danielle said, 'tell Litsi about him.'

She could look at me, as now, as if everything were the same. I tried with probably little success to keep my general anxiety about her from showing too much, and told the story to Litsi.

'The real reason for the attacks on Bobby was to get at his father, who'd been trying to take over the newspaper. Bobby's father, Maynard Allardeck, was in line for a knighthood, and the newspaper's idea was to discredit him so that he shouldn't get one. Maynard was a real pain, a ruthless burden on Bobby's back. So I . . . er . . . got him off.'

'How?' Litsi asked curiously.

'Maynard,' I said, 'makes fortunes by lending money to dicky businesses. He puts them straight and then calls in the loan. The businesses can't repay him, so he takes over the businesses, and shortly after sells off their assets, closing them down. The smiling shark comes along and gobbles up the grateful minnows, who don't discover their mistake until they're half digested.'

'So what did you do?' Litsi said.

'Well . . . I went around filming interviews with some of the people he had damaged. They were pretty emotional stuff. An old couple he'd cheated out of a star racehorse, a man whose son committed suicide when he lost his business, and a foolish boy who'd been led into gambling away half his inheritance.'

'I saw the film,' Danielle said. 'It hit like hammers . . . it made me cry. Kit threatened to send video tape copies to all sorts of people if Maynard did any more harm to Bobby. And you've forgotten to say,' she said to me, 'that Maynard tried to get Bobby to kill you.'

Litsi blinked. 'To kill . . .'

'Mm,' I said. 'He's paranoid about Bobby marrying my sister. He's been programmed from birth to hate all Fieldings. He told Bobby when he was a little boy that if he was ever naughty, the Fieldings would eat him.'

I explained about the depth and bitterness of the old Fielding–Allardeck feud.

'Bobby and I,' I said, 'have made it up and are friends, but his father can't stand that.'

'Bobby thinks,' Danielle said to me, 'that Maynard also can't stand you being successful. He wouldn't feel so murderous if you'd been a lousy jockey.'

'Maynard,' I told Litsi, smiling, 'is a member of the Jockey Club and also now turns up quite often as a Steward at various racecourses. He would dearly like to see me lose my licence.'

'Which he can't manage unfairly,' Litsi said thoughtfully, 'because of the existence of the film.'

'It's a stand-off,' I agreed equably.

'OK,' Litsi said, 'then how about a stand-off for Henri Nanterre?'

'I don't know enough about him. I'd known Maynard all my life. I don't know anything about arms or anyone who deals in them.'

Litsi pursed his lips. 'I think I could arrange that,' he said.

CHAPTER EIGHT

I telephoned to Wykeham later that Sunday afternoon and listened to the weariness in his voice. His day had been a procession of frustrations and difficulties which were not yet over. The dog-patrol man, complete with dog, was sitting in his kitchen drinking tea and complaining that the weather was freezing. Wykeham was afraid most of the patrolling would be done all night indoors.

'Is it freezing really?' I asked. Freezing was always bad news because racing would be abandoned, frosty ground being hard, slippery and dangerous.

'Two degrees off it.'

Wykeham kept thermometers above the outdoor water taps so he could switch on low-powered battery heaters in a heavy freeze and keep the water flowing. His whole stable was rich with gadgets he'd adopted over the years, like infra-red lights in the boxes to keep the horses warm and healthy.

'A policeman came,' Wykeham said. 'A detective constable. He said it was probably some boys' prank. I ask you! I told him it was no prank to shoot two horses expertly, but he said it was amazing what boys got up to. He said he'd seen worse things. He'd seen ponies in fields with their eyes gouged out. It was c . . . c . . . crazy. I said Cotopaxi was no pony, he was co-favourite for the Grand National, and he said it was b . . . bad luck on the owner.'

'Did he promise any action?'

'He said he would come back tomorrow and take statements from the lads, but I don't think they know anything. Pete, who looked after Cotopaxi, has been in tears and the others are all indignant. It's worse for them than having one killed accidentally.'

'For us all,' I said.

'Yes.' He sighed. 'It didn't help that the slaughterers had so much trouble getting the bodies out. I didn't watch. I couldn't. I loved both those horses.'

To the slaughterers, of course, dead horses were just so much dogmeat, and although it was perhaps a properly unsentimental way of looking at it, it wasn't always possible for someone like Wykeham, who had cared for them, talked to them, planned for them and lived through their lives. Trainers of steeplechasers usually knew their charges for a longer span than Flat-race trainers, ten years or more sometimes as opposed to three or four. When Wykeham said he loved a horse, he meant it.

He wouldn't yet have the same feeling for Kinley, I

thought. Kinley, the bright star, young and fizzing.
Kinley was excitement, not an old buddy.

'Look after Kinley,' I said.

'Yes, I've moved him. He's in the corner box.'

The corner box, always the last to be used, couldn't
be reached directly from any courtyard but only
through another box. Its position was a nuisance for
lads, but it was also the most secret and safe place in
the stable.

'That's great,' I said with relief, 'and now, what about
tomorrow?'

'Tomorrow?'

'Plumpton races.'

There was a slight silence while he reorganized his
thoughts. He always sent a bunch of horses to go-ahead
Plumpton because it was one of his nearest courses,
and as far as I knew I was riding six of them.

'Dusty has a list,' he said eventually.

'OK.'

'Just ride them as you think best.'

'All right.'

'Goodnight, then, Kit.'

'Goodnight, Wykeham.'

At least he'd got my name right, I thought, disconnecting. Perhaps all the right horses would arrive at
Plumpton.

I went down there on the train the next morning,

feeling glad, as the miles rolled by, to be away from the Eaton Square house. Even diluted by the princess, Litsi and Danielle, an evening spent with Beatrice de Brescou Bunt had opened vistas of social punishment I would as soon have remained closed. I had excused myself early, to openly reproachful looks from the others, but even in sleep I seemed to hear that insistent complaining voice.

When I'd left in the morning, Litsi had said he would himself spend most of the day with Roland after John Grundy had left. The princess and Danielle would occupy Beatrice. Danielle, working evening shifts in her television news company, would have to leave it all to the princess from soon after five-thirty. I had promised to return from Plumpton as soon as possible, but truthfully I was happy to be presented with a very good reason not to, in the shape of a message awaiting me in the changing room. Relayed from the stable manager at Newbury racecourse, the note requested me to remove my car from where I'd left it, as the space was urgently required for something else.

I telephoned to Eaton Square, and as it happened Danielle answered.

I explained about the car. 'I'll get a lift from Plumpton to Newbury. I think I'd better sleep at home in Lambourn, though, as I've got to go to Devon to race tomorrow. Will you apologize to the princess? Tell her I'll come back tomorrow night, after racing, if she'd like.'

'Deserter,' Danielle said. 'You sound suspiciously pleased.'

'It does make sense in terms of miles,' I said.

'Tell it to the marines.'

'Look after yourself,' I said.

She said, 'Yes,' on a sigh after a pause, and put the phone down. Sometimes it seemed that everything was the same between us, and then, on a sigh, it wasn't. Without much enthusiasm, I went in search of Dusty who had arrived with the right horses, the right colours for me to wear and a poor opinion of the detective constable for trying to question the lads while they were working. No one knew anything, anyway, Dusty said, and the lads were in a mood for the lynching of any prowling stranger. The head lad (not Dusty, who was the travelling head lad) had looked round the courtyards as usual at about eleven on Saturday night, when all had appeared quiet. He hadn't looked into all the eighty boxes, only one or two whose inmates weren't well, and he hadn't looked at either Cascade or Cotopaxi. He'd looked in on Kinley and Hillsborough to make sure they'd eaten their food after racing, and he'd gone home to bed. What more could anyone do, Dusty demanded.

'No one's blaming anybody,' I said.

He said, 'Not so far,' darkly, and took my saddle away to put it on the right horse for the first race.

We stage-managed the afternoon between us, as so often, he producing and saddling the horses, I riding them, both of us doing a public relations job on the various owners, congratulating, commiserating, explaining and excusing. We ended with a typical day on two winners, a second, two also rans and a faller, the latter giving me a soft landing and no problems.

'Thanks, Dusty,' I said at the end. 'Thanks for everything.'

'What do you mean?' he said suspiciously.

'I just meant, six races is a busy day for you, and it all went well.'

'It would have gone better if you hadn't fallen off in the fifth,' he said sourly.

I hadn't fallen off. The horse had gone right down under me, leaving grass stains on its number cloth. Dusty knew it perfectly well.

'Well,' I said, 'thanks, anyway.'

He gave me an unsmiling nod and hurried off: and in essential discord we would no doubt act as a team at Newton Abbot the next day and at Ascot the next, effective but cold.

Two other jockeys who lived in Lambourn gave me a lift back with them to Newbury, and I collected my car from its extended parking there and drove home to my house on the hill.

I lit the log fire to cheer things up a bit, ate some grilled chicken and telephoned to Wykeham.

He'd had another wearing day. The insurers had been questioning his security, the detectives had annoyed all the lads, and the dog-patrol man had been found asleep in the hay barn by the head lad when he arrived at six in the morning. Wykeham had informed Weatherbys, the Jockey Club secretariat, of the horses' deaths (a routine obligation) and all afternoon his telephone had been driving him mad as one newspaper after another had called up to ask if it were true that they had been murdered.

Finally, he said, the princess had rung to say she'd cancelled her visit to her friends at Newton Abbot and wouldn't be there to watch her horses, and please would Wykeham tell Kit that yes, she did very definitely want him to return to Eaton Square as soon as he could.

'What's going on there?' Wykeham asked, without pressing interest. 'She sounds unlike herself.'

'Her sister-in-law arrived unexpectedly.'

'Oh?' He didn't pursue it. 'Well done, today, with the winners.'

'Thanks.' I waited, expecting to hear that Dusty had said I'd fallen off, but I'd misjudged the old crosspatch. 'Dusty says Torquil went down flat in the fifth. Were you all right?'

'Not a scratch,' I said, much surprised.

'Good. About tomorrow, then . . .'

We discussed the next day's runners and eventually said goodnight, and he called me Kit, which made it twice in a row. I would know things were returning to normal, I thought, when he went back to Paul.

I played back all the messages on my answering machine and found most of them echoes of Wykeham's:

a whole column of pressmen wanted to know my feelings on the loss of Cotopaxi. Just as well, I thought, that I hadn't been at home to express them.

There was an enquiry from a Devon trainer as to whether I could ride two for him at Newton Abbot, his own jockey having been hurt: I looked up the horses in the form book, telephoned to accept, and peacefully went to bed.

The telephone woke me at approximately two-thirty.

'Hello,' I said sleepily, squinting at the unwelcome news on my watch. 'Who is it?'

'Kit . . .'

I came wide awake in a split second. It was Danielle's voice, very distressed.

'Where are you?' I said.

'I . . . oh . . . I need . . . I'm in a shop.'

'Did you say shock or shop?' I said.

'Oh . . .' she gulped audibly. 'Both, I suppose.'

'What's happened? Take a deep breath. Tell me slowly.'

'I left the studio . . . ten after two . . . started to drive home.' She stopped. She always finished at two, when the studio closed and all the American news-gatherers left for the night, and drove her own small Ford car back to the garage behind Eaton Square where Thomas kept the Rolls.

'Go on,' I said.

'A car seemed to be following me. Then I had a flat tyre. I had to stop. I . . .' she swallowed again. 'I found . . . I had two tyres almost flat. And the other car stopped and a man got out . . . He was wearing . . . a hood.'

Jesus Christ, I thought.

'I ran,' Danielle said, audibly trying to stifle near-hysteria. 'He started after me . . . I ran and ran . . . I saw this shop . . . it's open all night . . . and I ran in here. But the man here doesn't like it. He let me use his telephone . . . but I've no money, I left my purse and my coat in the car . . . and I don't know . . . what to do . . .'

'What you do,' I said, 'is stay there until I reach you.'

'Yes, but . . . the man here doesn't want me to . . . and somewhere outside . . . I can't . . . I simply can't go outside. I feel so stupid . . . but I'm frightened.'

'Yes, you've good reason to be. I'll come at once. You let me talk to the man in the shop . . . and don't worry, I'll be there in under an hour.'

She said, 'All right,' faintly, and in a few seconds an Asian-sounding voice said, 'Hello?'

'My young lady,' I said, 'needs your help. You keep her warm, give her a hot drink, make her comfortable until I arrive, and I'll pay you.'

'Cash,' he said economically.

'Yes, cash.'

'Fifty pounds,' he said.

125

'For that,' I said, 'you look after her very well indeed. And now tell me your address. How do I find you?'

He gave me directions and told me earnestly he would look after the lady, I wasn't to hurry, I would be sure to bring the cash, wouldn't I, and I assured him again that yes, I would.

I dressed, swept some spare clothes into a bag, locked the house and broke the speed limit to London. After a couple of wrong turns and an enquiry from an unwilling night-walker I found the street and the row of dark shops, with one brightly lit near the end next to the Underground station. I stopped with a jerk on double yellow lines and went inside.

The place was a narrow mini-supermarket with a take-away hot-food glass cabinet near the door, the whole of the rest of the space packed to the ceiling with provisions smelling subtly of spices. Two customers were choosing hot food, a third further down the shop looking at tins, but there was no sign of Danielle.

The Asian man serving, smoothly round of face, plump of body and drugged as to eye, gave me a brief glance as I hurried in, and went back methodically to picking out the customers' chosen chapatis and samosas with tongs.

'The young lady,' I said.

He behaved as if he hadn't heard, wrapping the purchases, adding up the cost.

'Where is she?' I insisted, and might as well as not have spoken. The Asian talked to his customers in a language I'd never heard; took their money, gave them change, waited until they had left.

'Where is she?' I said forcefully, growing anxious.

'Give me the money.' His eyes spoke eloquently of his need for cash. 'She is safe.'

'Where?'

'At the back of the shop, behind the door. Give me the money.'

I gave him what he'd asked, left him counting it, and fairly sprinted where he'd pointed. I reached a back wall stocked from floor to ceiling like the rest, and began to feel acutely angry before I saw that the door, too, was covered with racks.

In a small space surrounded by packets of coffee I spotted the door knob; grasped it, turned it, pushed the door inwards. It led into a room piled with more stock in brown cardboard boxes, leaving only a small space for a desk, a chair and a single bar electric fire.

Danielle was sitting on the chair, huddled into a big dark masculine overcoat, trying to keep warm by the inadequate heater and staring blindly into space.

'Hi,' I said.

The look of unplumbable relief on her face was as good, I supposed, as a passionate kiss, which actually I didn't get. She stood though, and slid into my arms as if coming home, and I held her tight, not feeling her much through the thick coat, smelling the musky eastern fragrance of the dark material, smoothing Danielle's hair and breathing deeply with content.

She slowly disengaged herself after a while, though I could have stood there for hours.

'You must think I'm stupid,' she said shakily, sniffing and wiping her eyes on her knuckles. 'A real fool.'

'Far from it.'

'I'm so glad to see you.' It was heartfelt: true.

'Come on, then,' I said, much comforted. 'We'd best be going.'

She slid out of the oversize overcoat and laid it on the chair, shivering a little in her shirt, sweater and trousers. The chill of shock, I thought, because neither the shop nor store-room was actively cold.

'There's a rug in my car,' I said. 'And then we'll go and fetch your coat.'

She nodded, and we went up through the shop towards the street door.

'Thank you,' I said to the Asian.

'Did you switch the fire off?' he demanded.

I shook my head. He looked displeased.

'Goodnight,' I said, and Danielle said, 'Thank you.'

He looked at us with the drugged eyes and didn't answer, and after a few seconds we left him and crossed the pavement to the car.

'He wasn't bad, really,' Danielle said, as I draped the rug round her shoulders. 'He gave me some coffee from that hot counter, and offered me some food, but I couldn't eat it.'

I closed her into the passenger seat, went round and slid behind the wheel, beside her.

'Where's your car?' I said.

She had difficulty in remembering, which wasn't surprising considering the panic of her flight.

'I'd gone only two miles, I guess, when I realized I had a flat. I pulled in off the highway. If we go back towards the studio . . . but I can't remember . . .'

'We'll find it,' I said. 'You can't have run far.' And we found it in fact quite easily, its rear pointing towards us down a seedy side-turning as we coasted along.

I left her in my car while I took a look. Her coat and handbag had vanished, also the windscreen wipers and the radio. Remarkable, I thought, that the car itself was still there, despite the two flat tyres, as the keys were still in the ignition. I took them out, locked the doors and went back to Danielle with the bad news and the good.

'You still have a car,' I said, 'but it could be stripped or gone by morning if we don't get it towed.'

She nodded numbly and stayed in the car again when I found an all-night garage with a tow-truck, and negotiated with the incumbents. Sure, they said lazily, accepting the car's keys, registration number and whereabouts. Leave it to them, they would fetch it at once, fix the tyres, replace the windscreen wipers, and it would be ready for collection in the morning.

It wasn't until we were again on our way towards Eaton Square that Danielle said any more about her would-be attacker, and then it was unwillingly.

'Do you think he was a rapist?' she said tautly.

'It seems ... well ... likely, I'm afraid.' I tried to picture him. 'What sort of clothes was he wearing? What sort of hood?'

'I didn't notice,' she began, and then realized that she remembered more than she'd thought. 'A suit. An ordinary man's suit. And polished leather shoes. The light shone on them, and I could hear them tapping on the ground ... how odd. The hood was ... a woollen hat, dark, pulled down, with holes for eyes and mouth.'

'Horrible,' I said with sympathy.

'I think he was waiting for me to leave the studio.' She shuddered. 'Do you think he fixed my tyres?'

'Two flat at once is no coincidence.'

'What do you think I should do?'

'Tell the police?' I suggested.

'No, certainly not. They think any young woman driving alone in the middle of the night is asking for trouble.'

'All the same ...'

'Do you know,' she said, 'that a friend of a friend of mine – an American – was driving along in part of London, like I was, doing absolutely nothing wrong, when she was stopped by the police and taken to the police station? They stripped her! Can you believe it? They said they were looking for drugs or bombs ... there was a terrorist scare on, and they thought she had a suspicious accent. It took her ages to get people to wake up and say she was truly going home after working late. She's been a wreck ever since, and gave up her job.'

'It does seem unbelievable,' I agreed.

'It happened,' she said.

'They're not all like that,' I said mildly.

She decided nevertheless to tell only her colleagues in the studio, saying they should step up security round the parked cars.

'I'm sorry I made you come so far,' she said, not particularly sounding it. 'But I didn't want the police, and otherwise it meant waking Dawson and getting someone there to come for me. I felt shattered . . . I knew you would come.'

'Mm.'

She sighed, some of the tension at last leaving her voice. 'There wasn't much in my purse, that's one good thing. Just lipstick and a hairbrush, not much money. No credit cards. I never take much with me to work.'

I nodded. 'What about keys?'

'Oh . . .'

'The front door key of Eaton Square?'

'Yes,' she said, dismayed. 'And the key to the back door of the studios, where the staff go in. I'll have to tell them in the morning, when the day shift gets there.'

'Did you have anything with you that had the Eaton Square address on it?'

'No,' she said positively. 'I cleaned the whole car out this afternoon . . . I did it really to evade Aunt

Beatrice . . . and I changed purses. I had no letters or anything like that with me.'

'That's something,' I said.

'You're so practical.'

'I would tell the police,' I said neutrally.

'No. You don't understand, you're not female.'

There seemed to be no reply to that, so I pressed her no further. I drove back to Eaton Square as I'd done so many times before, driving her home from work, and it wasn't until we were nearly there that I wondered whether the hooded man could possibly have been not a rapist at all, but Henri Nanterre.

On the face of it, it didn't seem possible, but coming at that particular time it had to be considered. If it in fact were part of the campaign of harassment and accidents, then we would hear about it, as about the horses also: no act of terrorism was complete without the boasting afterwards.

Danielle had never seen Henri Nanterre and wouldn't have known his general shape, weight, and way of moving. Conversely, nor would he have turned up in Chiswick when he had no reason to know she was in England, even if he knew of her actual existence.

'You're very quiet all of a sudden,' Danielle said, sounding no longer frightened but consequently sleepy. 'What are you thinking?'

I glanced at her softening face, seeing the taut lines of strain smoothing out. Three or four times we'd known what the other was thinking, in the sort of telepathic jump that sometimes occurred between people who knew each other well, but not on a regular basis, and not lately. I was glad at that moment that she couldn't read my thoughts, not knowing if she would be more or less worried if she did.

'Tomorrow evening,' I said, 'get Thomas to drive you to work. He's not going to Devon now . . . and I'll fetch you.'

'But if you're riding in Devon . . .'

'I'll go down and back on the train,' I said. 'I should be back in Eaton Square by nine.'

'All right, I guess . . . thanks.'

I parked my car where hers stood usually, and took my bag from the boot, and with Danielle swathed in the rug like an oversized shawl, we walked round to the front door in Eaton Square.

'I hope you have a key?' she said, yawning. 'We'll look like gypsies if you don't.'

'Dawson lent me one.'

'Good . . . I'm asleep on my feet.'

We went indoors and quietly up the stairs. When we reached her floor, I put my arms round her, rug and all, again holding her close, but there was no clinging relief-driven response this time, and when I bent to kiss her, it was her cheek she offered, not her mouth.

'Goodnight,' I said. 'Will you be all right?'

'Yes.' She would hardly meet my eyes. 'I truly thank you.'

'You owe me nothing,' I said.

'Oh . . .' She looked at me briefly, as if confused. Then she dropped the rug which she had been holding close round her like a defensive stockade, put her arms round my neck and gave me a quick kiss at least reminiscent of better times, even if it landed somewhere on my chin.

'Goodnight,' she said lightly, and walked away along the passage to her room without looking back, and I picked up my bag and the rug and went on upstairs feeling a good deal better than the day before. I opened the door of the bamboo room half expecting to find Beatrice snoring blissfully between my sheets, but the linen was smooth and vacant, and I plummeted there into dreamland for a good two hours.

CHAPTER NINE

Around seven-fifteen in the morning, I knocked on
Litsi's ground floor door until a sleepy voice said, 'Who
is it?'

'Kit.'

A short silence, then, 'Come in, then.'

The room was dark, Litsi leaning up on one elbow
and stretching to switch on a bedside lamp. The light
revealed a large oak-panelled room with a four-poster
bed, brocade curtaining and ancestral paintings: very
suitable, I thought, for Litsi.

'I thought you weren't here,' he said, rubbing his
eyes with his fingers. 'What day is it?'

'Tuesday. I came back here before five this morning,
and that's what I've come to tell you about.'

He went from leaning to sitting up straight while he
listened.

'Do you think it really was Nanterre?' he said when
I'd finished.

'If it was, perhaps he wanted only to catch her and
frighten her . . . tell her what could happen if her uncle

135

didn't give in. She must have surprised whoever it was by running so fast. She wears trainers to work... running shoes, really... and she's always pretty fit. Maybe he simply couldn't catch her.'

'If he meant a warning he couldn't deliver, we'll hear from him.'

'Yes. And about the horses, too.'

'He's unhinged,' Litsi said, 'if it was him.'

'Anyway,' I said, 'I thought I'd better warn you.'

I told him about Danielle's handbag being missing. 'If it was an ordinary thief, it would be all right because there would be no connecting address, but if Nanterre took it, he now has a front door key to this house. Do you think you could explain to the princess, and get the lock changed? I'm off to Devon to ride a few races, and I'll be here again this evening. I'm picking Danielle up when she finishes work, but if I miss the train back, will you make sure she gets home safely? If you need a car, you can borrow mine.'

'Just don't miss the train.'

'No.'

His eyebrows rose and fell. 'Give me the keys, then,' he said.

I gave them to him. 'See if you can find out,' I said, 'if Danielle told her Aunt Beatrice where she works and at what time she leaves.'

He blinked.

'Henri Nanterre,' I reminded him, 'has a spy right in this house.'

'Go and break your neck.'

I smiled and went away, and caught the train to Devon. I might be a fool, I thought, entrusting Danielle to Litsi, but she needed to be safe, and one short ride in my Mercedes, Litsi driving, was unlikely to decide things one way or another.

For all the speed and risks of the job, jump jockeys were seldom killed: it was more dangerous, for instance, to clean windows for a living. All the same, there were occasional days when one ended in hospital, always at frustrating and inconvenient moments. I wouldn't say that I rode exactly carefully that day at Newton Abbot, but it was certainly without the reckless fury of the past two weeks.

Maybe she would finally come back to me, maybe she wouldn't: I had a better chance right under her eyes than two hundred miles away in traction.

The chief topic of conversation all afternoon on the racecourse as far as I was concerned was the killing of Cascade and Cotopaxi. I read accounts in the sports pages of two papers on the train and saw two others in the changing room, all more speculation and bold headlines than hard fact. I was besieged by curious and sympathetic questions from anyone I talked to, but could add little except that yes, I had seen them in their boxes, and yes, of course the princess was upset, and yes, I would be looking for another ride in the Grand National.

Dusty, from his thunderstorm expression, was

putting up with much the same barrage. He was slightly mollified when one of the princess's runners won, greeted by applause and cheers that spoke of her public popularity. The Clerk of the Course and the Chairman of the Board of Directors called me into the directors' room, not to complain of my riding but to commiserate, asking me to pass on their regrets to the princess and to Wykeham. They clapped me gruffly on the shoulder and gave me champagne, and it was all a long way from Maynard Allardeck.

I caught the return train on schedule, dined on a railway sandwich, and was back at Eaton Square before nine. I had to get Dawson to let me in because the lock had indeed been changed, and I went up to the sitting room, opening the door there on the princess, Litsi, and Beatrice Bunt, all sitting immobile in private separate silences, as if they were covered by vacuum bell jars and couldn't hear each other speak.

'Good evening,' I said, my voice sounding loud.

Beatrice Bunt jumped because I'd spoken behind her. The princess's expression changed from blank to welcoming, and Litsi came alive as if one had waved a wand over a waxwork.

'You're back!' he said. 'Thank God for that at least.'

'What's happened?' I asked.

None of them was quite ready to say.

'Is Danielle all right?' I said.

The princess looked surprised. 'Yes, of course. Thomas drove her to work.' She was sitting on a sofa, her back straight, her head high, every muscle on the defensive and no ease anywhere. 'Come over here,' she patted the cushions beside her, 'and tell me how my horses ran.'

It was her refuge, I knew, from unpleasant reality: she'd talked of her runners in the direst of moments in the past, clinging to a rock in a tilting world.

I sat beside her, willingly playing the game.

'Bernina was on the top of her form, and won her hurdle race. She seems to like it in Devon, that's the third time she's won down there.'

'Tell me about her race,' the princess said, looking both pleased and in some inner way still disorientated, and I told her about the race without anything in her expression changing. I glanced at Litsi and saw that he was listening in the same detached way, and at Beatrice, who appeared not to be listening at all.

I passed on the messages of sympathy from the directors, and said how pleased the crowd had been that she'd had a winner.

'How kind,' she murmured.

'What's happened?' I said again.

It was Litsi who eventually answered. 'Henri Nanterre telephoned here about an hour ago. He wanted to speak to Roland, but Roland refused, so he asked for me by name.'

My eyebrows rose.

'He said he knew my name as one of the three others who had to sign business directives with Roland. He said Danielle and the princess were the others: his notary had remembered.'

I frowned. 'I suppose he might have remembered if someone had told him the names ... he might have recognized them.'

Litsi nodded. 'Henri Nanterre said that his notary had left his briefcase in Roland's sitting room. In the briefcase could be found a form of contract with spaces at the bottom for signatures and witnesses. He says all four of us are to sign this form in the presence of his notary, in a place that he will designate. He said he would telephone each morning until everyone was ready to agree.'

'Or else?' I said.

'He mentioned,' Litsi said evenly, 'that it would be a shame for the princess to lose more of her horses needlessly, and that young women out alone at night were always at risk.' He paused, one eyebrow lifting ironically. 'He said that princes weren't immune from accidents, and that a certain jockey, if he wished to stay healthy, should remove himself from the household and mind his own business.'

'His exact words?' I asked interestedly.

Litsi shook his head. 'He spoke in French.'

'We have asked Beatrice,' the princess said with brittle veneer politeness, 'if she has spoken with Henri Nanterre since her arrival in this house on Sunday, but she tells us she doesn't know where he is.'

I looked at Beatrice, who stared implacably back. It

wasn't necessary to know where someone actually was if he had a telephone number, but there seemed to be no point in making her upgrade the evasion into a straightforward lie, which the boldness in her eyes assured me we would get.

The princess said that her husband had asked to talk to me on my return, and suggested that I might go at this point. I went, sensing the three of them stiffening back into their bell jars, and upstairs knocked on Roland de Brescou's door.

He bade me come in and sit down, and asked with nicely feigned interest about my day's fortunes. I said Bernina had won and he said 'Good' absentmindedly, while he arranged in his thoughts what to say next. He was looking, I thought, not so physically frail as on Friday and Saturday, but not as determined either.

'It is going to take time to arrange my retirement,' he said, 'and as soon as I make any positive moves, Henri Nanterre will find out. Gerald Greening thinks that when he does find out, he will demand I withdraw my intention, under pain of more and more threats and vicious actions.' He paused. 'Has Litsi told you about Nanterre's telephone call?'

'Yes, Monsieur.'

'The horses ... Danielle ... my wife ... Litsi ... yourself ... I cannot leave you all open to harm. Gerald Greening advises now that I sign the contract, and then as soon as Nanterre gets his firearms approval, I can sell all my interest in the business. Nanterre will have to agree. I shall make it a condition before signing. Everyone will guess I have sold because of the guns ... some at least of my reputation may be salvaged.' A spasm of distress twisted his mouth. 'It is of the greatest conceivable personal disgrace that I sign this contract, but I see no other way.'

He fell silent but with an implied question, as if inviting my comment; and after a short pause I gave it.

'Don't sign, Monsieur,' I said.

He looked at me consideringly, with the first vestige of a smile.

'Litsi said you would say that,' he said.

'Did he? And what did Litsi himself say?'

'What would you think?'

'Don't sign,' I said.

'You and Litsi.' Again the fugitive smile. 'So different. So alike. He described you as – and these are his words, not mine – "a tough devil with brains", and he said I should give you and him time to think of a way of deterring Nanterre permanently. He said that only if both of you failed and admitted failure should I think of signing.'

'And ... did you agree?'

'If you yourself wish it, I will agree.'

A commitment of positive action, I thought, was a lot different from raising defences; but I thought of the horses, and the princess, and Danielle, and really there was no question.

'I wish it,' I said.

'Very well . . . but I do hope nothing appalling will happen.'

I said we would try our best to prevent it, and asked if he would mind having a guard in the house every day during John Grundy's off-duty hours.

'A guard?' he frowned.

'Not in your rooms, Monsieur. Moving about. You would hardly notice him, but we'd give you a walkie-talkie so you could call him if you needed. And may we also install a telephone which records what's said?'

He lifted a thin hand an inch and let it fall back on the arm of the wheelchair.

'Do what you think best,' he said, and then, with an almost mischievous smile, the only glimpse I'd ever had of the lighter side within, he asked, 'Has Beatrice got you out of the bamboo room yet?'

'No, Monsieur,' I said cheerfully.

'She was up here this morning demanding I move you,' he said, the smile lingering. 'She insists also that I allow Nanterre to run the business as he thinks best, but truly I don't know which of her purposes obsesses her most. She switched from one to the other within the same sentence.' He paused. 'If you can defeat my sister,' he said, 'Nanterre should be easy.'

By the following mid-morning, I'd been out to buy a recording telephone, and the guard had been installed, in the unconventional form of a springy twenty-year-old who had learned karate in the cradle.

Beatrice predictably disapproved, both of his looks and his presence, particularly as he nearly knocked her over on one of the landings, by proving he could run from the basement to the attic faster than the lift could travel the same distance.

He told me his name was Sammy (this week), and he was deeply impressed by the princess, whom he called 'Your Regal Highness', to her discreet and friendly amusement.

'Are you sure . . .?' she said to me tentatively, when he wasn't listening.

'He comes with the very highest references,' I assured her. 'His employer promised he could kick a pistol out of anyone's hand before it was fired.'

Sammy's slightly poltergeist spirits seemed to cheer her greatly, and with firmness she announced that all of us, of course including Beatrice, should go to Ascot races. Lunch was already ordered there, and Sammy would guard her husband: she behaved with the gaiety sometimes induced by risk-taking, which to Litsi and Danielle at least proved infectious.

Beatrice, glowering, complained she didn't like horse racing. Her opinion of me had dropped as low as the Marianas Trench since she'd discovered I was a professional jockey. 'He's the *help*,' I overheard her saying in outrage to the princess. 'Surely there are some rooms in the attic.'

The 'attic', as it happened, was an unused nursery suite, cold and draped in dust sheets, as I'd discovered on my night prowls. The room I could realistically have expected to have been given lay beside the rose room, sharing the rose room's bathroom, but it, too, was palely shrouded.

'I didn't know you were coming, Beatrice, dear,' the princess reminded her. 'And he's Danielle's fiancé.'

'But *really* . . .'

She did go to the races, though, albeit with ill grace, presumably on the premise that even if she gained access again to her brother, and even if she wore him to exhaustion, she couldn't make him sign the contract, because first, he didn't have it (it was now in Litsi's room in case she took the bamboo room by force) and second, his three co-signers couldn't be similarly coerced. Litsi had carefully told her, after Nanterre's telephone call and before my return from Devon, that the contract form was missing.

'Where is it?' she had demanded.

'My dear Beatrice,' Litsi had said blandly, 'I have no idea. The notary's briefcase is still in the hall awaiting collection, but there is no paper of any sort in it.'

And it was after he'd told me of this exchange, before we'd gone to bed on the previous evening, that I'd taken the paper downstairs for his safe-keeping.

Beatrice went to Ascot with the princess in the Rolls; Danielle and Litsi came with me.

Danielle, subdued, sat in the back. She had been

quiet when I'd fetched her during the night, shivering now and again from her thoughts, even though the car had been warm. I told her about Nanterre's telephone call and also about her uncle's agreement with Litsi and me, and although her eyes looked huge with worry, all she'd said was, 'Please be careful. Both of you . . . be careful.'

At Ascot, it was with unmixed feelings of jealousy that I watched Litsi take her away in the direction of the princess's lunch while I peeled off, as one might say, to the office.

I had four races to ride; one for the princess, two others for Wykeham, one for a Lambourn trainer. Dusty was in a bad mood, Maynard Allardeck had again turned up as a Steward, and the tree of my favourite lightweight saddle, my valet told me, had disintegrated. Apart from that it was bitterly cold, and apart from that I had somehow gained another pound, probably via the railway sandwich.

Wykeham's first runner was a four-year-old ex-Flat racer out for his first experience over hurdles, and although I'd schooled him a few times over practice jumps on Wykeham's gallops, I hadn't been able to teach him courage. He went round the whole way letting me know he hated it, and I had difficulty thinking of anything encouraging to say to his owners afterwards. A horse that didn't like racing was a waste of time, a waste of money and a waste of emotion: better to sell him quick and try again. I put it as tactfully as possible, but the owners shook their heads doubtfully and said they would ask Wykeham.

The second of Wykeham's runners finished nowhere also, not from unwillingness, as he was kind-hearted and sure-footed, but from being nowhere near fast enough against the opposition.

I went out for the princess's race with a low *joie de vivre* rating, a feeling not cured by seeing Danielle walk into the parade ring holding onto Litsi's arm and laughing.

The princess, who had been in the ring first, after seeing her horse saddled, followed my gaze and gently tapped my arm.

'She's in a muddle,' she said distinctly. 'Give her time.'

I looked at the princess's blue eyes, half hidden as usual behind reticent lashes. She must have felt very strongly that I needed advice, or she wouldn't have given it.

I said, 'All right,' with an unloosened jaw, and she briefly nodded, turning to greet the others.

'Where's Beatrice?' she asked, looking in vain behind them. 'Didn't she come down?'

'She said it was too cold. She stayed up in the box,' Litsi said: and to me, he added, 'Do we put our money on?'

Col, the princess's runner, was stalking round in his navy blue gold-crested rug, looking bored. He was a horse of limited enthusiasm, difficult to ride because if he reached the front too soon he would lose interest and stop, and if one left the final run too late and got beaten, one looked and felt a fool.

'Don't back him,' I said. It was that sort of day.

'Yes, back him,' the princess said simultaneously.

'Frightfully helpful,' Litsi commented, amused.

Col was a bright chestnut with a white blaze down his nose and three white socks. As with most of the horses Wykeham was particularly hoping to win with at Cheltenham, Col probably wouldn't reach his absolute pinnacle of fitness until the National Hunt Festival in another two weeks, but he should be ready enough for Ascot, a slightly less testing track.

At Cheltenham, he was entered for the Gold Cup, the top event of the meeting, and although not a hot fancy, as Cotopaxi had been for the Grand National, he had a realistic chance of being placed.

'Do your best,' the princess said, as she often did, and as usual I said yes, I would. Dusty gave me a leg-up and I cantered Col down to the start trying to wind up a bit of life-force for us both. A gloomy jockey on a bored horse might as well go straight back to the stable.

By the time we started, I was telling him we were out there to do a job of work, and to take a little pride in it, talking to myself as much as him; and by the third of the twenty-two fences, there were some faint stirrings in both of us of the ebb turning to flood.

Most of the art of jump racing lay in presenting a

horse at a fence so that he could cross it without slowing. Col was one of the comparatively rare sort that could judge distances on his own, leaving his jockey free to worry about tactics, but he would never quicken unless one insisted, and had no personal competitive drive.

I'd ridden and won on him often and understood his needs, and knew that by the end I'd have to dredge up the one wild burst of all-out urging which might wake up his phlegmatic soul.

I dare say that from the stands nothing looked wrong. Even though to me Col seemed to be plodding, his plod was respectably fast. We travelled most of the three miles in fourth or fifth place and came up into third on the last bend when two of the early leaders tired.

There were three fences still to go, with the two hundred and forty yard run-in after. One of the horses ahead was still chock-full of running: it was his speed Col would have to exceed. The jockey on the other already had his whip up and was no doubt feeling the first ominous warning that the steam was running out of the boiler. I gave Col the smallest of pulls to steady him in third place for the first of the three fences in the straight. This he jumped cleanly and was going equally well within himself as we crossed the next, passing that jockey with his whip up before we reached the last.

Too much daylight, I thought. He liked ideally to

jump the last with two or three others still close ahead. He jumped the last with a tremendous leap, though, and it was no problem after all to stoke up the will-win spirit and tell him that now ... now ... was the time.

Col put his leading foot to the ground and it bent and buckled under him. His nose went down to the grass. The reins slid through my fingers to their full extent and I leaned back and gripped fiercely with my legs, trying not to be thrown off. By some agile miracle, his other foreleg struck the ground solidly, and with all his half-ton weight on that slender fetlock, Col pushed himself upright and kept on going.

I gathered the reins. The race had to be lost, but the fire, so long arriving, couldn't easily be put out. Come on, now, you great brute, I was saying to him: now's the time, there is one to beat, get on with it, now show me, show everyone you can do it, you still can do it.

As if he understood every word he put his head forward and accelerated in the brief astonishing last-minute spurt that had snatched last-second victories before from seeming impossibilities.

We nearly made it that time, very nearly. Col ate up the lengths he'd lost and I rode him almost as hard as Cascade but without the fury, and we were up with the other horse's rump, up with the saddle, up with the neck ... and the winning post flashed back three strides too soon.

The princess had said she wouldn't come down to

the unsaddling enclosure unless we won, as it was a long way from her box.

Maynard was there, however, balefully staring at me as I slid to the ground, his eyes dark and his face tight with hate. Why he came near me I couldn't understand. If I'd hated anyone that much, I would have avoided the sight of them as much as possible: and I did loathe Maynard for what he'd tried to do to Bobby, to brainwash his own son into killing.

Dusty put the sheet over Col's heaving chestnut sides with a studied lack of comment on the race's result, and I went and weighed in with much of the afternoon's dissatisfaction drifting around like a cloud.

I rode the next race for the Lambourn trainer and finished third, a good way back, and with a feeling of having accomplished nothing, changed into street clothes, done for the day.

On my way out of the weighing room, en route to the princess's box, a voice said, 'Hey, Kit,' behind me, and I turned to find Basil Clutter walking quickly in my wake.

'Are you still looking for Henri Nanterre?' he said, catching me up.

'Yes, I am.' I stopped and he stopped also, although almost jogging from foot to foot, as he could never easily stand still.

'The Roquevilles are here today; they had a runner in the first race. They've someone with them who knows

Henri Nanterre quite well. They said if you were still interested perhaps you'd like to meet her.'

'Yes, I would.'

He looked at his watch. 'I'm supposed to be joining them in the owners' and trainers' bar for a drink now, so you'd better come along.'

'Thank you,' I said, 'very much.'

I followed him to the bar and, armed with Perrier to their port, met the Roquevilles' friend, who was revealed as small and French-looking, with a gamine chic that had outlasted her youth. The elfin face bore wrinkles, the club-cut black hair showed greyish roots, and she wore high-heeled black boots and a smooth black leather trouser-suit with a silk scarf knotted at the back of her neck, cowboy fashion.

Her speech, surprisingly, was straightforward earthy racecourse English, and she was introduced to me as Madame Madeleine Darcy, English wife of a French racehorse trainer.

'Henri Nanterre?' she said with distaste. 'Of course I know the bastard. We used to train his horses until he whisked them away overnight and sent them to Villon.'

CHAPTER TEN

She talked with the freedom of pique and the pleasure of entertaining an attentive audience.

'He's a cock,' she said, 'with a very loud crow. He struts like a rooster. We have known him since he was young, when the horses belonged to his father Louis, who was a very nice man, a gentleman.'

'So Henri inherited the horses?' I said.

'But yes, along with everything else. Louis was soft-headed. He thought his son could do no wrong. So stupid. Henri is a greedy bully. Villon is welcome to him.'

'In what way is he a greedy bully?' I asked.

Her plucked eyebrows rose. 'We bought a yearling filly with nice blood lines that we were going to race ourselves and breed from later. Henri saw her in the yard – he was always poking round the stables – and said he would buy her. When we said we didn't want to sell, he said that unless we did, he would take all his horses away. He had eight . . . we didn't want to lose them. We were furious. He made us sell him the filly at the price we'd paid for her ... and we'd kept her for months. Then a few weeks later, he telephoned one evening and said horse-boxes would be arriving in the morning to collect his horses. And pouf, they were gone.'

'What happened to the filly?' I said.

Her mouth curved with pleasure. 'She contracted navicular and had to be put down, poor little bitch. And do you know what that bastard Nanterre did?'

She paused for effect. About four voices, mine included, said 'What?'

'Villon told us. He was disgusted. Nanterre said he didn't trust the knackers not to patch up the filly, pump her full of painkillers and sell her, making a profit at his expense, so he insisted on being there. The filly was put down on Villon's land with Nanterre watching.'

Mrs Roqueville looked both sick and disappointed. 'He seemed a pleasant enough man when we met him at Longchamp, and again at Newbury.'

'I expect the Marquis de Sade was perfectly charming on the racecourse,' Madeleine said sweetly. 'It is where anyone can pretend to be a gentleman.'

After a respectful pause, I said, 'Do you know anything of his business affairs?'

'Business!' She wrinkled her nose. 'He is the de Brescou et Nanterre construction company. I don't know anything about his business, only about his horses. I wouldn't trust him in business. As a man deals with his racehorse trainer, so will he deal in business.

The honourable will be honourable. The greedy bully will run true to form.'

'And . . . do you know where I could find him in England?'

'I wouldn't look, if I were you.' She gave me a bright smile. 'He'll bring you nothing but trouble.'

I relayed the conversation to Litsi and Danielle up in the princess's box.

'What's navicular?' Litsi said.

'A disease of the navicular bone in a horse's foot. When it gets bad, the horse can't walk.'

'That Nanterre,' Danielle said disgustedly, 'is gross.'

The princess and Beatrice, a few feet away at the balcony end of the box, were talking to a tall, bulky man with noticeably light grey eyes in a big bland face.

Litsi, following my gaze, said, 'Lord Vaughnley . . . he came to commiserate with Aunt Casilia over Col not winning. Do you know him? He's something in publishing, I think.'

'Mm,' I said neutrally. 'He owns the *Towncrier* newspaper.'

'Does he?' Litsi's agile mind made the jump. 'Not the paper which attacked . . . Bobby?'

'No, that was the *Flag*.'

'Oh.' Litsi seemed disappointed. 'Then he isn't one of the two defeated press barons after all.'

'Yes, he is.' Lord Vaughnley's attention was switching

my way. 'I'll tell you about it, some time,' I said to Litsi, and watched Lord Vaughnley hesitate, as he always did, before offering his hand for me to shake: yet he must have known he would meet me in that place, as my being there at the end of each day's racing was a ritual well known to him.

'Kit,' he said, grasping the nettle, 'a great race . . . such bad luck.'

'The way it goes,' I said.

'Better luck in the Gold Cup, eh?'

'It would be nice.'

'Anything I can do for you, my dear fellow?'

It was a question he asked whenever we met, though I could see Litsi's astonishment out of the side of my eyes. Usually I answered that there wasn't, but on that day thought there was no harm in trying a flier. If one didn't ask, one would never learn.

'Nothing, really,' I said, 'except . . . I suppose you've never come across the name of Henri Nanterre?'

Everyone watched him while he pondered, the princess with rapidly sharpening interest, Litsi and Danielle with simple curiosity, Beatrice with seeming alarm. Lord Vaughnley looked around at the waiting faces, frowned, and finally answered with a question of his own.

'Who is he?' he asked.

'My husband's business partner,' the princess said. 'Dear Lord Vaughnley, do you know of him?'

Lord Vaughnley was puzzled but slowly shook his big head. 'I can't recall ever . . .'

'Could you . . . er . . . see if the *Towncrier* has a file on him?' I asked.

He gave me a resigned little smile, and nodded. 'Write the name down for me,' he said. 'In caps.'

I fished out a pen and small notepad and wrote both the name and that of the construction company, in capital letters as required.

'He's French,' I said. 'Owns horses. He might be on the racing pages, or maybe business. Or even gossip.'

'Anything you want specifically?' he said, still smiling.

'He's over in England just now. Ideally, we'd like to know where he's staying.'

Beatrice's mouth opened and closed again with a snap. She definitely knows, I thought, how to reach him. Perhaps we could make use of that, when we had a plan.

Lord Vaughnley tucked the slip of paper away in an inner pocket, saying he would get the names run through the computer that very evening, if it was important to the princess.

'Indeed it is,' she said with feeling.

'Any little fact,' I said, 'could be helpful.'

'Very well.' He kissed the princess's hand and made general farewells, and to me he said as he was going, 'Have you embarked on another crusade?'

'I guess so.'

'Then God help this Nanterre.'

'What did he mean by that?' Beatrice demanded as Lord Vaughnley departed, and the princess told her soothingly that it was a long story which wasn't to interfere with my telling her all about Col's race. Lord Vaughnley, she added, was a good friend she saw often at the races, and that it was perfectly natural for him to help her in any way.

Beatrice, to do her justice, had been a great deal quieter since Nanterre's telephone call the evening before. She had refused to believe he had killed the horses ('it must have been vandals, as the police said') until he had himself admitted it, and although she was still adamant that Roland should go along with Nanterre in business, we no longer heard praise of him personally.

Her hostility towards me on the other hand seemed to have deepened, and on my account of the race she passed her own opinion.

'Rubbish. You didn't lose the race at the last fence. You were too far back all along. Anyone could see that.' She picked up a small sandwich from the display on the table and bit into it decisively, as if snapping off my head.

No one argued with her pronouncement and, emboldened, she said to Danielle with malice, 'Your fortune-hunter isn't even a good jockey.'

'Beatrice,' the princess immediately said, unruffled,

'Kit has a fortune of his own, and he is heir to his grandfather, who is rich.'

She glanced at me briefly, forbidding me to contradict. Such fortune as I had I'd earned, and although my grandfather owned several chunks of Newmarket, their liquidity was of the consistency of bricks.

'And Aunt Beatrice,' Danielle said, faintly blushing, 'I am poor.'

Beatrice ate her sandwich, letting her round eyes do the talking. Her pale orange hair, I thought inconsequentially, was almost the same colour as the hessian-covered walls.

The sixth and last race was already in progress, the commentary booming outside. Everyone except Beatrice went on the balcony to watch, and I wondered whether a putative million dollars was worth an unquiet mind. 'It's nice to be nice,' our grandmother had said often enough to Holly and me, bringing us up, and 'Hate curdles your brains.' Grandfather, overhearing her heresies, had tried to undo her work with anti-Allardeck slogans, but in the end it was she who'd prevailed. Holly had married Bobby, and apart from the present state of affairs with Danielle and other various past hard knocks, I had grown up, and remained, basically happy. Beatrice, for all her mink-crocodile-Spanish house indulgences in Palm Beach, hadn't been so lucky.

When it came to going home, Beatrice again went with the princess in the Rolls. I had hoped Litsi would

join them, as I was detouring to Chiswick to deliver
Danielle to the studio, but he took Danielle's arm and
steered her and himself, chatting away, in the direction
of the jockeys' car park as if there had never been
any question. Litsi had his aunt's precious knack of
courteously and covertly getting his own way. He would
have made a great king, I thought wryly, given the
chance.

We dropped Danielle off (she waved to both of us
and kissed neither) and I drove the two of us back to
Eaton Square. Beatrice, naturally enough, came into
the conversation.

'You were shocked,' Litsi said, amused, 'when she
called you a fortune-hunter. You hadn't even thought
of Danielle's prospects.'

'She called me a bad jockey,' I said.

'Oh, sure.' He chuckled. 'You're a puritan.'

'Danielle has the money she earns,' I said. 'As I do.'

'Danielle is Roland's niece,' he said as if teaching an
infant. 'Roland and Aunt Casilia are fond of her, and
they have no children.'

'I don't want that complication.'

He grunted beside me and said no more on the
subject, and after a while I said, 'Do you know why
they have no children? Is it choice, or his illness? Or
just that they couldn't?'

'His illness, I've always supposed, but I've never
asked. He was about forty, I think, when they married,
about fifteen years older than her, and he caught the

virus not long after. I can't remember even seeing him walk, though he was a good skier, I believe, in his time.'

'Rotten for them,' I said.

He nodded. 'He was lucky in some respects. Some people who get that virus – and thank God it's rare – lose the use of their arms as well. They never speak of it much, of course.'

'How are we going to save his honour?'

'You invent,' Litsi said lazily, 'and I'll gofer.'

'Gofer a lever,' I said absentmindedly.

'A lever?'

'To move the world.'

He stretched contentedly. 'Do you have any ideas at all?'

'One or two. Rather vague.'

'Which you're not sharing?'

'Not yet. Have to think a bit first.' I told him I'd bought a recording telephone that morning. 'When we get back, we'll rig it and work out a routine.'

'He said he would ring again this evening.'

No need to say who 'he' was.

'Mm,' I said. 'The phone I bought is also a conference phone. It has a loudspeaker, so that everyone in the room can hear what the caller's saying. You don't need the receiver. So when he rings, if it's you that answers, will you get him to speak in English?'

'Perhaps you'd better answer, then he'd have to.'

'All right. And the message we give is . . . no dice?'

'You couldn't just string him along?'

'Yeah, maybe,' I said, 'but to fix him we've got to find him, and he could be anywhere. Beatrice knows where he is, or at least how to reach him. If we get him out in the open . . .' I paused. 'What we ideally need is a tethered goat.'

'And just who,' Litsi enquired ironically, 'are you electing for that dead-end job?'

I smiled. 'A stuffed goat with a mechanical bleat. All real goats must be guarded or careful.'

'Aunt Casilia, Roland and Danielle, guarded.'

'And the horses,' I said.

'OK. And the horses guarded. And you and I . . .'

I nodded. 'Careful.'

Neither of us mentioned that Nanterre had specific-ally threatened each of us as his next targets: there was no point. I didn't think he would actually try to kill either of us, but the damage would have to be more than a pin-prick to expect a result.

'What's he like?' Litsi said. 'You've met him. I've never seen him. Know your enemy . . . first rule for combat.'

'Well, I think he got into all this without thinking it out first,' I said. 'Last Friday, I think he believed he had only to browbeat the princess heavily enough, and Roland would collapse. That's also very nearly what happened.'

'As I understand it, it didn't happen because you were there.'

'I don't know. Anyway, on Friday night when he

pulled the gun out which had no bullets in ... I think
that may be typical of him. He acts on impulse, without
thinking things through. He's used to getting his own
way easily because of his hectoring manner. He's used
to being obeyed. Since his father died – and his father
had customarily indulged him – he has run the construction company pretty well as he likes. I'd say he's quite
likely reached the stage where he literally can't believe
he can be defied, and especially not by an old, ill man
long out of touch with the world. When Roland rejected
him by post, I'd guess he came over thinking, "I'll soon
change all that." I think in some ways he's childish,
which doesn't make him less destructive: more so,
probably.'

I paused, but Litsi made no comment.

'Attacking Danielle,' I said. 'He thought again that
he would have it all his own way. I'll bet it never once
occurred to him that she could run faster than he could.
He turned up there in a city suit and polished leather
shoes. It was a sort of arrogance, an assumption that
he would naturally be faster, stronger, dominant. If
he'd had any doubts at all, he'd have worn a jogging
suit, something like that, and faster shoes.'

'And the horses?' Litsi said.

I hated to think of the horses: 'They were vulnerable,' I said. 'And he knew how to kill them. I don't
know where he would get a humane killer, but he
does deal in guns. He carries one. They attract him,
otherwise he wouldn't be wanting to make them.

163

People mostly do what their natures urge, don't they? He may have a real urge to see things die . . . wanting to make sure the slaughterers didn't cheat him could be just the only acceptable reason he could give for a darker desire. People always think up reasonable reasons for doing what they want.'

'Do you?' he asked curiously.

'Oh sure. I say I race for the money.'

'And you don't?'

'I'd do it for nothing, but being paid is better.'

He nodded, having no difficulty in understanding. 'So what do you expect next from Nanterre?' he asked.

'Another half-baked attack on one of us. He won't have planned properly for contingencies, but we might find ourselves in nasty spots nevertheless.'

'Charming,' he said.

'Don't go down dark alleys to meet strangers.'

'I never do.'

I asked him rather tentatively what he did do, back in Paris, where he lived.

'Frightfully little, I'm afraid,' he said. 'I have an interest in an art gallery. I spend a good deal of my life looking at paintings. The Louvre expert Danielle and I went to listen to is a very old acquaintance. I was sure she would enjoy . . .' He paused. 'She did enjoy it.'

'Yes.'

I could feel him shift in the passenger seat until he could see me better.

'There was a group of us,' he said. 'We weren't alone.'

'Yes, I know.'

He didn't pursue it. He said unexpectedly instead, 'I have been married, but we are separated. Technically I am still married. If either of us wished to remarry, there would be a divorce. But she has lovers, and I also . . .' he shrugged. 'It's common enough, in France.'

I said 'Thank you,' after a pause, and he nodded; and we didn't speak of it again.

'I would like to have been an artist,' he said after a while. 'I studied for years . . . I can see the genius in great paintings, but for myself . . . I can put paint on canvas, but I haven't the great gift. And you, my friend Kit, are damn bloody lucky to have been endowed with the skill to match your desire.'

I was silent; silenced. I'd had the skill from birth, and one couldn't say where it came from; and I hadn't much thought what it would be like to be without it. I looked at life suddenly from Litsi's point of view, and knew that I was in truth damn bloody lucky, that it was the root of my basic happiness, and that I should be humbly grateful.

When we got to Eaton Square, I suggested dropping him at the front door while I went to park the car, but he wouldn't hear of it. Dark alleys, he reminded me, and being careful.

'There's some light in the mews,' I said.

'All the same, we'll park the car together and walk back together, and take our own advice.'

'OK,' I said, and reflected that at one-thirty, when I

went to fetch Danielle, I would be going alone into the self-same dark alley, and it would be then that I'd better be careful.

Litsi and I let ourselves in, Dawson meeting us in the hall saying the princess and Beatrice had vanished to their rooms to change and rest.

'Where is Sammy?' I said.

Sammy, Dawson said with faint disapproval, was walking about, and was never in any place longer than a minute. I went upstairs to fetch the new telephone and found Sammy coming down the stairs from the top floor.

'Did you know there's another kitchen up there?' he said.

'Yes, I looked.'

'And there's a skylight or two. I rigged a nice little pair of booby traps under those. If you hear a lot of old brass firearms crashing around up there, you get the force here pronto.'

I assured him I would, and took him downstairs with me to show him, as well as Dawson and Litsi, how the recording telephone worked.

The normal telephone arrangements in that house were both simple and complicated: there was only one line, but about a dozen scattered instruments.

Incoming calls rang in only three of those: the one in the sitting room, one in the office where Mrs Jenkins worked by day, and one in the basement. Whoever was near one of those instruments when a call came in would answer, and if it were for someone else, reach that person via the intercom, as Dawson had reached me when Wykeham rang the previous Sunday. This arrangement was to save six or more people answering whenever the telephone rang.

From each guest bedroom outgoing calls could be directly made, as from the princess's rooms, and her husband's. The house was rarely as full as at present, Dawson said, and the telephone was seldom busy. The system normally worked smoothly.

I explained that to work the new telephone, one had simply to unplug the ordinary instrument and plug in the new one.

'If you press that button,' I said, pointing, 'the whole conversation will be recorded. If you press that one, everyone in the room can hear what's being said.'

I plugged the simple box of tricks into the sitting room socket. 'It had better be in here while we are all around. During the day, if everyone's out, like today, it can go to Mrs Jenkins' office, and at night, if Dawson wouldn't mind, in the basement. It doesn't matter how many calls are unnecessarily recorded, we can scrub them out, but every time . . . if one could develop the habit?'

They all nodded.

'Such an uncouth man,' Dawson commented. 'I would know that loud voice anywhere.'

'It's a pity,' Litsi said, when Dawson and Sammy had

gone, 'that we can't somehow tap Beatrice's phone and record what she says.'

'Anytime she's upstairs, like now, we can just lift the receiver and listen.'

We lifted the receiver, but no one in the house was talking. We could wait and listen for hours, but meanwhile no outside calls could come in. Regretfully Litsi put the receiver back again, saying we might be lucky, he would try every few minutes; but by the time Beatrice reappeared for dinner the intermittent vigil had produced no results.

I had meanwhile talked to Wykeham and collected the messages off my answering machine, neither a lengthy event, and if anyone had inadvertently broken in on the calls, I'd heard no clicks on the line.

Beatrice came down demanding her 'bloody' in a flattering white dress covered in sunflowers, Litsi fussing over her with amiable solicitude, and refusing to be disconcerted by ungraciousness.

'I know you don't want me here,' she said bluntly, 'but until Roland signs on the dotted line, I'm staying.'

The princess came down to dinner, but not Roland, and on our return to the sitting room afterwards Litsi, without seeming to, manoeuvred everyone around so that it was I who ended up sitting by the telephone. He smiled over his coffee cup, and everyone waited.

When the bell finally rang, Beatrice jumped.

I picked up the receiver, pressing both the recorder

and conference buttons; and a voice spoke French loudly into our expectations.

CHAPTER ELEVEN

Litsi rose immediately to his feet, came over to me and made gestures for me to give him the phone.

'It isn't Nanterre,' he said.

He took the receiver, disengaged the conference button and spoke privately in French. *'Oui ... non ... certainement ... ce soir ... oui ... merci.'*

He put down the receiver and almost immediately the bell rang again. Litsi picked up the receiver again, briefly listened, grimaced, pressed the record and conference buttons again, and passed the buck to me.

'It's him,' he said succinctly, and indeed everyone could hear the familiar domineering voice saying words that meant nothing to me at all.

'Speak English, please,' I said.

'I said,' Nanterre said in English, 'I wish to speak to Prince Litsi and he is to be brought to the telephone immediately.'

'He isn't available,' I said. 'I can give him a message.'

'Who are you?' he said. 'I know who you are. You are the jockey.'

'Yes.'

'I left instructions for you to leave the house.'

'I don't obey your instructions.'

'You'll regret it.'

'In what way?' I asked, but he wouldn't be drawn into a specific threat; quite likely, I supposed, because he hadn't yet thought up a particular mayhem.

'My notary will arrive at the house tomorrow morning at ten o'clock,' he said. 'He will be shown to the library, as before. He will wait there. Roland de Brescou and Princess Casilia will go down there when he arrives. Also Prince Litsi and Danielle de Brescou will go down. All will sign the form which is in the notary's briefcase. The notary will witness each signature, and carry the document away in his briefcase. Is this understood?'

'It is understood,' I said calmly, 'but it's not going to happen.'

'It must happen.'

'There's no document in the briefcase.'

It stopped him barely a second. 'My notary will bring a paper bearing the same form of words. Everyone will sign the notary's document.'

'No, they aren't ready to,' I said.

'I have warned what will happen if the document is not signed.'

'What will happen?' I asked. 'You can't make people behave against their consciences.'

'Every conscience has its price,' he said furiously,

171

and instantly disconnected. The telephone clicked a few times and came forth with the dialling tone, and I put the receiver back in its cradle to shut it off.

Litsi shook his head regretfully. 'He's being cautious. Nothing he said can be presented to the police as a threat requiring action on their part.'

'You should all sign his document,' Beatrice said aggrievedly, 'and be done with all this obstruction to expanding his business.'

No one bothered to argue with her: the ground had already been covered too often. Litsi then asked the princess if she would mind if he and I went out for a little while. Sammy was still in the house to look after things until John Grundy came, and I would be back in good time to fetch Danielle.

The princess acquiesced with this arrangement while looking anything but ecstatic over further time alone with Beatrice, and it was with twinges of guilt that I happily followed Litsi out of the room.

'We'll go in a taxi,' he said, 'to the Marylebone Plaza hotel.'

'That's not your sort of place,' I observed mildly.

'We're going to meet someone. It's his sort of place.'

'Who?'

'Someone to tell you about the arms trade.'

'Really?' I said, interested. 'Who is he?'

'I don't precisely know. We are to go to room eleven twelve and talk to a Mr Mohammed. That isn't his real name, which he would prefer we didn't know. He will be helpful, I'm told.'

'How did you find him?' I asked.

Litsi smiled. 'I didn't exactly. But I asked someone in France who would know . . . who could tell me what's going on in the handguns world. Mr Mohammed is the result. Be satisfied with that.'

'OK.'

'Your name is Mr Smith,' he said. 'Mine is Mr Jones.'

'Such stunning originality.'

The Marylebone Plaza hotel was about three miles distant from Eaton Square geographically and in a different world economically. The Marylebone Plaza was frankly a bare-bones overnight stopping place for impecunious travellers, huge, impersonal, a shelter for the anonymous. I'd passed it fairly often but never been through its doors before, and nor, it was clear, had Litsi. We made our way however across an expanse of hard grey mottled flooring, and took a lift to the eleventh floor.

Upstairs the passages were narrow, though carpeted; the lighting economical. We peered at door numbers, found eleven twelve, and knocked.

The door was opened to us by a swarthy-skinned man in a good suit with a white shirt, gold cufflinks, and an impassive expression.

'Mr Jones and Mr Smith,' Litsi said.

The man opened the door further and gestured to us to go in, and inside we found another man similarly dressed, except that he wore also a heavy gold ring inset with four diamonds arranged in a square.

'Mohammed,' he said, extending the hand with the ring to be shaken. He nodded over our shoulders to his friend, who silently went out of the door, closing it behind him.

Mohammed, somewhere between Litsi's age and mine, I judged, had dark hair, dark eyes, olive skin and a heavy dark moustache. The opulence of the ring was echoed in the leather suitcase lying on the bed and in his wristwatch, which looked like gold nuggets strung together round his wrist.

He was in good humour, and apologized for meeting us 'where no one would know any of us'.

'I am legitimately in the arms trade,' he assured us. 'I will tell you anything you want to know, as long as you do not say who told you.'

He apologized again for the fact that the room was furnished with a single chair, and offered it to Litsi. I perched against a table, Mohammed sat on the bed. There were reddish curtains across the window, a brown patterned carpet on the floor, a striped cotton bed-spread; all clean looking and in good repair.

'I will leave in an hour,' Mohammed said, consulting the nuggets. 'You wish to ask about plastic guns. Please go ahead.'

'Er . . .' Litsi said.

'Who makes them?' I asked.

Mohammed switched his dark gaze my way. 'The

best known,' he said straightforwardly, 'are made by Glock of Austria. The Glock 17.' He reached unhurriedly towards the suitcase and unclipped the locks. 'I brought one to show you.'

Beneath his educated English there was an accent I couldn't place. Arab, in some way, I thought. Definitely Mediterranean, not Italian, perhaps French.

'The Glock 17,' he was saying, 'is mostly plastic but has metal parts. Future guns of this sort can be made entirely from plastic. It's a matter of a suitable formula for the material.'

From the suitcase he produced a neat square black box.

'This handgun is legitimately in my possession,' he said. 'Despite the manner of our meeting, I am a reputable dealer.'

We assured him that we hadn't thought otherwise.

He nodded in satisfaction and took the lid off the box. Inside, packed in a moulded tray, like a toy, lay a black pistol, an ammunition clip, and eighteen golden bullets, flat caps uppermost, points invisible, arranged neatly in three horizontal rows of six.

Mohammed lifted the weapon out of the box.

'This pistol,' he said, 'has many advantages. It is light, it is cheaper and easier to make than all-metal guns, and also it is more accurate.'

He let the information sink into our brains in true salesman fashion.

'It pulls apart.' He showed us, snapping off the entire

top of the pistol, revealing a metal rod lying within. 'This is the metal barrel.' He picked it out, 'There is also a metal spring. The bullets also are metal. The butt and the ammunition clip are plastic. The pieces pop back together again very easily.' He reassembled the pistol fast, closing its top into place with a snap. 'Extremely easy, as you see. The clip holds nine bullets at a time. People who use this weapon, including some police forces, consider it a great advance, the fore-runner of a whole new concept of handguns.'

'Aren't they trying to ban it in America?' Litsi said.

'Yes.' Mohammed shrugged. 'Amendment 4194 to Title 18, forbidding the import, manufacture and sales of any such gun made after January 1, 1986. It is because the plastic is undetectable by X-ray scanners. They fear the guns will be carried through airports and into government buildings by terrorists.'

'And won't they?' I said.

'Perhaps.' He shrugged. 'Approximately two million private citizens in America own handguns,' he said. 'They believe in the right to carry arms. This Glock pistol is the beginning of the future. It may result in the widespread development of plastic-detectors . . . and perhaps in the banning of all hand-luggage on aeroplanes except ladies' handbags and flat briefcases that can be searched by hand.' He looked from me to Litsi. 'Is terrorism your concern?'

'No,' Litsi said. 'Not directly.'

Mohammed seemed relieved. 'This gun wasn't

invented as a terrorist weapon,' he said. 'It is seriously a good pistol, better all round.'

'We understand that,' I said. 'How profitable is it?'

'To whom?'

'To the manufacturer.'

'Ah.' He cleared his throat. 'It depends.' He considered. 'It costs less to make and is consequently cheaper in price than metal guns. The profit margin may not be so very different overall, but the gross profit of course depends on the number of items sold.' He smiled cheerfully. 'It's calculated that most of the two million people already owning guns in America, for instance, will want to up-grade to the new product. The new is better and more prestigious, and so on. Also their police forces would like to have them. Apart from there, the world is thirsty for guns for use – private Americans, you understand, own them mostly for historical reasons, for sport, for fantasy, for the feeling of personal power, not because they intend to kill people – but in many many places, killing is the purpose. Killing, security and defence. The market is wide open for really cheap good reliable new pistols. For a while at least, until the demand is filled, manufacturers could make big honest money fast.'

Litsi and I listened to him with respect.

'What about dishonest money?' I asked.

He paused only momentarily. 'It depends who we're talking about.'

'We're still talking about the manufacturer,' I said.

'Ah. A corporation?'

'A private company with one man in charge.'

He produced a smile packed with worldly disillusion.

'Such a man can print his own millions.'

'How, exactly?' I asked.

'The easiest way,' he said, 'is to ship the product in two parts.' He pulled the plastic gun again into components. 'Say you packed all the pieces into a box, like this, omitting only the barrel. A barrel, say, made of special plastic that won't melt or buckle from the heat caused by the friction of the bullet passing through.'

He looked at us to see if we appreciated such simple matters, and seemingly reassured, went on. 'The manufacturer exports the barrels separately. This, he says, ensures that if either shipment is diverted – which is a euphemism for stolen – in passage, the goods will be useless. Only when both shipments have reached their destination safely can the pistols be assembled. Right?'

'Right,' we both said.

'The manufacturer does all the correct paperwork. Each shipment is exported accompanied by customs dockets, such shipment is what it purports to be, everything is legal. The next step depends on how badly the customer wants the guns.'

'How do you mean?' Litsi said.

'Suppose,' Mohammed answered, enjoying himself, 'the customer's need is great and pressing. The manufacturer sends the guns without the barrels. The customer pays. The manufacturer sends the barrels. Good?'

We nodded.

'The manufacturer tells the customer he must pay the price on the invoices to the manufacturing company, but he must also pay a sum into a different bank account – number and country supplied – and when *that* payment is safely in the manufacturer's secret possession, then he will despatch the barrels.'

'Simple,' I said.

'Of course. A widespread practice. The sort of thing which goes on the whole world over. Money up front, above board settlement, offshore funds sub rosa.'

'Kick backs,' I said.

'Of course. In many countries, it is the accepted system. Trade cannot continue without it. A little commission, here and there . . .' He shrugged. 'Your manufacturer with an all-plastic reliable cheaply made handgun could pass an adequate profit through his company's books and pocket a fortune for himself out of sight.'

He reassembled the gun dexterously and held it out to me.

'Feel it,' he said. 'An all-plastic gun would be much lighter even than this.'

I took the gun, looking at its matt black surface of purposeful shape, the metal rim of the barrel showing at the business end. It certainly was remarkably light to handle, even with metal parts. All-plastic, it could be a plaything for babies.

With an inward shiver I gave it to Litsi. It was the second time in four days I'd been instructed in the use of handguns, and although I'd handled one before, I wasn't a good shot, nor ever likely to practise. Litsi weighed the gun thoughtfully in his palm and returned it to its owner.

'Are we talking of any manufacturer in particular?' Mohammed asked.

'About one who wants to be granted a licence to manufacture and export plastic guns,' I said, 'but who hasn't been in the arms business before.'

He raised his eyebrows. 'In France?'

'Yes,' Litsi said without surprise, and I realized that Mohammed must have known the enquiry had come to him through French channels, even if it hadn't been he who'd spoken to Litsi on the telephone.

Mohammed pursed his lips under the big moustache. 'To get a licence, your manufacturer would have to be a person of particularly good standing. These licences, you understand, are never thrown about like confetti. He must certainly have the capability, the factory, that is to say, also the prototype, also probably definite orders, but above all he must have the good name.'

'You've been extremely helpful,' Litsi said.

Mohammed radiated bonhomie.

'How would the manufacturer set about selling his guns? Would he advertise?' I said.

'Certainly. In firearms' and trade magazines the world over. He might also engage an agent, such as myself.' He smiled. 'I work on commission. I am well known. People who want guns come to me and say, "What will suit us best? How much is it? How soon can you get it?" ' He spread his palms. 'I'm a middleman. We are indispensable.' He looked at his watch. 'Anything else?'

I said on impulse, 'If someone wanted a humane killer, could you supply it? A captive bolt?'

'Obsolete,' he said promptly. 'In England, made by Accles and Shelvoke in Birmingham. Do you mean those? Point 405 calibre, perhaps? One point two-five grain caps?'

'I dare say,' I said. 'I don't know.'

'I don't deal in humane killers. They're too specialized. It wouldn't be worth your while to pay me to find you one. There are many around, all out of date. I would ask older veterinarians, they might be pleased to sell. You'd need a licence to own one, of course.' He paused. 'To be frank, gentlemen, I find it most profitable to deal with customers to whom personal licences are irrelevant.'

'Is there anyone,' I asked, 'and please don't take this as an insult, because it's not meant that way, but is there anyone to whom you would refuse to sell guns?'

He took no offence. He said, 'Only if I thought they couldn't or wouldn't pay. On moral grounds, no. I don't ask what they want them for. If I cared, I'd be in the wrong trade. I sell the hardware, I don't agonize over its use.'

Both Litsi and I seemed to have run out of questions. Mohammed put the pistol back into its box, where it sat neatly above its prim little rows of bullets. He replaced the lid on the box and returned the whole to the suitcase.

'Never forget,' he said, still smiling, 'that attack and defence are as old as the human race. Once upon a time, I would have been selling nicely sharpened spearhead flints.'

'Mr Mohammed,' I said, 'thank you very much.'

He nodded affably. Litsi stood up and shook hands again with the diamond ring, as did I, and Mohammed said if we saw his friend loitering in the passage not to worry and not to speak to him, he would return to the room when we had gone.

We paid no attention to the friend waiting by the lifts and rode down without incident to the ground floor. It wasn't until we were in a taxi on the way back to Eaton Square that either of us spoke.

'He was justifying himself,' Litsi said.

'Everyone does. It's healthy.'

He turned his head. 'How do you mean?'

'The alternative is guilty despair. Self-justification may be an illusion, but it keeps you from suicide.'

'You could self-justify suicide.'

I smiled at him sideways. 'So you could.'

'Nanterre,' he said, 'has a powerful urge to sharpen flints.'

'Mm. Lighter, cheaper, razor-like flints.'

'Bearing the de Brescou cachet.'

'I had a powerful vision,' I said, 'of Roland shaking hands on a deal with Mohammed.'

Litsi laughed. 'We must save him from the justification.'

'How did you get hold of Mohammed?' I asked.

'One of the useful things about being a prince,' Litsi said, 'is that if one seriously asks, one is seldom refused. Another is that one knows and has met a great many people in useful positions. I simply set a few wheels in motion, much as you did yesterday, incidentally, with Lord Vaughnley.' He paused. 'Why is a man you defeated so anxious to please you?'

'Well . . . in defeating him I also saved him. Maynard Allardeck was out to take over his newspaper by fair means and definitely foul, and I gave him the means of stopping him permanently, which was a copy of that film.'

'I do see,' Litsi said ironically, 'that he owes you a favour or two.'

'Also,' I said, 'the boy who gambled half his inheritance away under Maynard's influence was Hugh Vaughnley, Lord Vaughnley's son. By threatening to publish the film, Lord Vaughnley made Maynard give the inheritance back. The inheritance, actually, was shares in the *Towncrier* newspaper.'

'A spot of poetic blackmail. Your idea?'

'Well . . . sort of.'

He chuckled, 'I suppose I should disapprove. It was surely against the law.'

'The law doesn't always deliver justice. The victim mostly loses. Too often the law can only punish, it can't put things right.'

'And you think righting the victims' wrongs is more important than anything else?'

'Where it's possible, the highest priority.'

'And you'd break the law to do it?'

'It's too late at night for being tied into knots,' I said, 'and we're back at Eaton Square.'

We went upstairs to the sitting room and, the princess and Beatrice having gone to bed, drank a brandy nightcap in relaxation. I liked Litsi more and more as a person, and wished him permanently on the other side of the globe; and looking at him looking at me, I wondered if he were possibly thinking the same thing.

'What are you doing tomorrow?' he said.

'Racing at Bradbury.'

'Where's that?'

'Half way to Devon.'

'I don't know where you get the energy.' He yawned. 'I spent a gentle afternoon walking round Ascot racecourse, and I'm whacked.'

Large and polished, he drank his brandy, and in time we unplugged the recording telephone, carried it down to the basement, and replugged it in the hallway there.

Then we went up to the ground floor and paused for a moment outside Litsi's door.

'Goodnight,' I said.

'Goodnight.' He hesitated, and then held out his hand. I shook it. 'Such a silly habit,' he said with irony, 'but what else can one do?' He gave me a sketchy wave and went into his room, and I continued on up to see if I were still to sleep among the bamboo shoots, which it seemed I was.

I dozed on top of the bedclothes for an hour or so and then went down, out, and round the back to get the car to fetch Danielle.

I thought, as I walked quietly into the dark, deserted alley, that it really was a perfect place for an ambush.

CHAPTER TWELVE

The alley was a cobbled cul-de-sac about twenty feet wide and a hundred yards long, with a wider place at the far end for turning, the backs of tall buildings closing it all in like a canyon. Its sides were lined with garage doors, the wide garages themselves running in under the backs of the buildings, and unlike many other mews where the garages had originally been built as housing for coaches and horses, Falmouth Mews, as it was called, had no residential entrances.

By day, the mews was alive and busy, as a firm of motor mechanics occupied several of the garages, doing repairs for the surrounding neighbourhood. At night, when they'd gone home, the place was a shadowy lane of big closed doors, lit only from the windows of the buildings above.

The garage where Thomas kept the Rolls was further than halfway in. Next, beyond, was a garage belonging to the mechanics, which Thomas had persuaded them to rent temporarily to the princess, to accommodate Danielle's car (now recovered from the menders by

Thomas). My Mercedes, unhoused, was parked along outside Danielle's garage doors, and other cars, here and there along the mews, were similarly placed. In a two-car family, one typically was in the generous sized lock-up, the second lengthways outside.

Around and behind these second cars there were a myriad hiding places.

I ought to have brought a torch, I thought. Tomorrow I would buy one. The mews could shelter a host of monsters . . . and Beatrice knew what time I set off each night to Chiswick.

I walked down the centre of the alley feeling my heart thud, yet I'd gone down there the night before without a tremor. The power of imagination, I thought wryly: and nothing rustled in the undergrowth, nothing pounced, the tiger wasn't around for the goat.

The car looked exactly as I'd left it, but I checked the wiring under the bonnet and under the dashboard before switching on the ignition. I checked there was no oil leaking from under the engine, and that all the tyres were hard, and I tested the brakes with a sudden stop before turning out into the road.

Satisfied, I drove without trouble to Chiswick, collecting Danielle at two o'clock. She was tired from the long day and talked little, telling me only that they'd spent all evening on a story about snow and ice houses which she thought was a waste of time.

'What snow and ice houses?' I asked, more just to talk to her than from wanting to know.

'Sculptures for a competition. Some of the guys had
been out filming them in an exhibition. Like sandcastles,
only made of snow and ice. Some of them were quite
pretty and even had lights inside them. The guys said the
place they were in was like filming in an igloo without a blanket. All good fun, I guess, but not world news.'

She yawned and fell silent, and in a short while we
were back in the mews: it was always a quick journey
at night, with no traffic.

'You can't keep coming to pick me up,' she said, as
we walked round into Eaton Square.

'I like to.'

'Litsi told me that the man in the hood was Henri
Nanterre.' She shivered. 'I don't know if it makes it
better or worse. Anyway, I'm not working Friday nights
right now, or Saturdays or Sundays, of course. You can
sleep, Friday night.'

We let ourselves into the house with the new keys
and said goodnight again on her landing. We never had
slept in the same bed in that house, so there were no
such memories or regrets to deal with, but I fiercely
wished as I walked up one more flight that she would
come up there with me: yet it had been no use suggesting it, because her goodnight kiss had again been
a defence, not a promise, and had landed again any
way but squarely.

Give her time. . . . Time was an aching anxiety with
no certainty ahead.

*

Breakfast, warmth and newspapers were to be found each day down in the morning room, whose door was across the hall from Litsi's. I was in there about nine on that Thursday morning, drinking orange juice and checking on the day's runners at Bradbury, when the intercom buzzed, and Dawson's voice told me there was a call from Mr Harlow.

I picked up the outside receiver fearfully.

'Wykeham?'

'Oh, Kit. Look, I thought I'd better tell you, but don't alarm the princess. We had a prowler last night.'

'Are the horses all right? Kinley?'

'Yes, yes. Nothing much happened. The man with the dog said his dog was restless, as if someone was moving about. He says his dog was very alert and whining softly for a good half hour, and that they patrolled the courtyards twice. They didn't see anyone, though, and after a while the dog relaxed again. So . . . what do you think?'

'I think it's a bloody good job you've got the dog.'

'Yes . . . it's very worrying.'

'What time was all this?'

'About midnight. I'd gone to bed, of course, and the guard didn't wake me, as nothing had happened. There's no sign that anyone was here.'

'Just keep on with the patrols,' I said, 'and make sure you don't get the man that slept in the hay barn.'

'No. I told them not to send him. They've all been very sharp, since that first night.'

We discussed the two horses he was sending to Bradbury, neither of them the princess's. He sometimes sent his slowest horses to Bradbury in the belief that if they didn't win there, they wouldn't win anywhere, but he avoided it most of the time. It was a small country course, with a flat circuit of little more than a mile, easy to ride on if one stuck to the inside.

'Give Mélisande a nice ride, now.'

'Yes, Wykeham,' I said. Mélisande had been before my time. 'Do you mean Pinkeye?'

'Well . . . of course.' He cleared his throat. 'How long are you staying in Eaton Square?'

'I don't know. I'll tell you, though, when I leave.'

We disconnected and I put a slice of wholemeal bread in the toaster and thought about prowlers.

Litsi came in and poured himself some coffee. 'I thought,' he said conversationally, assembling a bowl of muesli and cream, 'that I might go to the races today.'

'To Bradbury?' I was surprised. 'It's not like Ascot. It's the bare bones of the industry. Not much comfort.'

'Are you saying you don't want to take me?'

'No. Just warning you.'

He sat down at the table and watched me eat toast without butter or marmalade.

'Your diet's disgusting.'

'I'm used to it.'

He watched me swallow a pill with black coffee. 'What are those for?' he asked.

190

'Vitamins.'

He shook his head resignedly and dug into his own hopelessly fattening concoction, and Danielle came in looking fresh and clear-eyed in a baggy white sweater.

'Hi!' she said to neither of us in particular. 'I wondered if you'd be here. What are you doing today?'

'Going to the races,' Litsi said.

'Are you?' She looked at him directly, in surprise. 'With Kit?'

'Certainly, with Kit.'

'Oh. Then . . . er . . . can I come?'

She looked from one of us to the other, undoubtedly seeing double pleasure.

'In half an hour,' I said, smiling.

'Easy.'

So all three of us went to Bradbury races, parting in the hall from the princess who had come down to go through some secretarial work with Mrs Jenkins and who looked wistfully at our outdoor clothes, and also from Beatrice, who had come down out of nosiness.

Her sharp round gaze fastened on me. 'Are you coming back?' she demanded.

'Yes, he is,' the princess said smoothly. 'And tomorrow we can all go to see my two runners at Sandown, isn't that nice?'

Beatrice looked not quite sure how the one followed on the other and, in the moment of uncertainty, Litsi, Danielle and I departed.

Bradbury racecourse, we found when we arrived,

was undergoing an ambitious upgrading. There were notices everywhere apologizing for the inconvenience of heaps of builders' materials and machines. A whole new grandstand was going up inside scaffolding in the cheaper ring, and most of the top tier of the members' stand was being turned into a glassed-in viewing room with tables, chairs and refreshments. They had made provision up there also for a backward-facing viewing gallery, from which one could see the horses walk round in the parade ring.

There was a small model on a table outside the weighing room, showing what it would all be like when finished, and the racecourse executive were going around with pleased smiles accepting compliments.

Litsi and Danielle went off in search of a drink and a sandwich in the old unrefurbished bar under the emerging dream, and I, sliding into nylon tights, breeches and boots, tried not to think about that too much. I pulled on a thin vest, and my valet neatly tied the white stock around my neck. After that, I put on the padded back-guard which saved one's spine and kidneys from too much damage, and on top of that the first set of colours for the day. Crash helmet, goggles, whip, number cloth, weight cloth, saddle; I checked them all, weighed out, handed the necessary to Dusty to go and saddle up, put on an anorak because of the cold and went out to ride.

I wouldn't have minded, just once, having a day when I could stand on the stands and go racing with

Danielle like anyone else. Eat a sandwich, have a drink, place a bet. I saw them smiling and waving to me as I rode onto the track, and I waved back, wanting to be right there beside them on the ground.

The horse I was riding won the race, which would surprise and please Wykeham but not make up for Col's losing the day before.

Besides Wykeham's two runners I'd been booked for three others. I rode one of those without results in the second race and put Pinkeye's red and blue striped colours on for the third, walking out in my warming anorak towards the parade ring to talk to the fussiest and most critical of all Wykeham's owners.

I didn't get as far as the parade ring. There was a cry high up, and a voice calling, 'Help,' and along with everyone else I twisted my head round to see what was happening.

There was a man hanging by one hand from the new viewing balcony high on the members' stand. A big man in a dark overcoat.

Litsi.

In absolute horror, I watched him swing round until he had two hands on the top of the balcony wall, but he was too big and heavy to pull himself up, and below him there was a fifty foot drop direct to hard tarmac.

I sprinted over there, tore off my anorak and laid it on the ground directly under where Litsi hung.

'Take off your coat,' I said to the nearest man. 'Lay it on the ground.'

'Someone must go up and help him,' he said. 'Someone will go.'

'Take off your coat.' I turned to a woman. 'Take off your coat. Lay it on the ground. Quick, quick, lay coats on the ground.'

She looked at me blindly. She was wearing a full-length expensive fur. She slid out of her coat and threw it on top of my anorak, and said fiercely to the man next to her, 'Take off your coat, take off your coat.'

I ran from person to person, 'Take off your coat, quick, quick . . . Take off your coat.'

A whole crowd had collected, staring upwards, arrested on their drift back to the stands for the next race.

'Take off your coat,' I could hear people saying. 'Take off your coat.'

Dear God, Litsi, I prayed, just hang on.

There were other people yelling to him, 'Hang on, hang on,' and one or two foolishly screaming, and it seemed to me there was a great deal of noise, although very many were silent.

A little boy with huge eyes unzipped his tiny blue anorak and pulled off his small patterned jersey and flung them onto the growing, spreading pile, and I heard him running about in the crowd, in his bright cotton T-shirt, his high voice calling, 'Quick, quick, take off your coats.'

It was working. The coats came off in dozens and were thrown, were passed through the crowd, were chucked higgledy-piggledy to form a mattress, until the circle on the ground was wide enough to contain him if he fell, but could be thicker, thicker.

No one had reached Litsi from the balcony side: no strong arms clutching to haul him up.

Coats were flying like leaves. The word had spread to everyone in sight. 'Take off your coat, take off your coat, quick . . . quick . . .'

When Litsi fell, he looked like another flying over-coat, except that he came down fast, like a plummet. One second he was hanging there, the next he was down. He fell straight to begin with, then his heavy shoulders tipped his balance backwards and he landed almost flat on his back.

He bounced heavily on the coats and rolled and slid off them and ended with his head on one coat and his body on the tarmac, sprawling on his side, limp as a rag.

I sprang to kneel beside him and saw immediately that although he was dazed, he was truly alive. Hands stretched to help him up, but he wasn't ready for that, and I said, 'Don't move him . . . let him move first . . . you have to be careful.'

Everyone who went racing knew about spinal injuries and not moving jockeys until it was safe, and there I was, in my jockey's colours, to remind them. The hands were ready, but they didn't touch.

I looked up at that crowd, all in shirt-sleeves, all shivering with cold, all saints. Some were in tears, particularly the woman who'd laid her mink on the line.

'Litsi,' I said, looking down and seeing some sort of order return to his eyes. 'Litsi, how are you doing?'

'I . . . Did I fall?' He moved a hand, and then his feet, just a little, and the crowd murmured with relief.

'Yes, you fell,' I said. 'Just stay there for a minute. Everything's fine.'

Somebody above was calling down, 'Is he all right?' and there, up on the balcony, were the two men who'd apparently gone up to save him.

The crowd shouted, 'Yes,' and started clapping, and in almost gala mood began collecting their coats from the pile. There must have been almost two hundred of them, I thought, watching. Anoraks, huskies, tweeds, raincoats, furs, suit jackets, sweaters, even a horse rug. It was taking much longer to disentangle the huge heap than it had to collect it.

The little boy with big eyes picked up his blue anorak and zipped it on over his jersey, staring at me. I hugged him. 'What's your name?' I said.

'Matthew.'

'You're a great guy.'

'That's my daddy's coat,' he said, 'under the man's head.'

'Ask him to leave it there just another minute.'

Someone had run to fetch the first-aid men, who arrived with a stretcher.

'I'm all right,' Litsi said weakly, but he was still winded and disorientated, and made no demur when they made preparations for transporting him.

Danielle was suddenly there beside him, her face white.

'Litsi,' she was saying, 'Oh, God . . .' She looked at me. 'I was waiting for him . . . someone said a man fell . . . is he all right?'

'He's going to be,' I said. 'He'll be fine.'

'Oh . . .'

I put my arms round her. 'It's all right. Really it is. Nothing seems to be hurting him, he's just had his breath knocked out.'

She slowly disengaged herself and walked away beside the stretcher when they lifted it onto a rolling platform, a gurney.

'Are you his wife?' I heard a first-aid man say.

'No . . . a friend.'

The little boy's father picked up his coat and shook my hand. The woman picked up her squashed mink, brushed dust off it and gave me a kiss. A Steward came out and said would I now please get on my horse and go down to the start, as the race would already be off late, and I looked at the racecourse clock and saw in amazement that it was barely fifteen minutes since I'd walked out of the weighing room.

All the horses, all the owners and trainers were still in the parade ring, as if time had stopped, but now the jockeys were mounting; death had been averted, life could thankfully go on.

I picked up my anorak. All the coats had been reclaimed, and it lay there alone on the tarmac, with my whip underneath. I looked up at the balcony, so far above, so deserted and unremarkable. Nothing suddenly seemed real, yet the questions hadn't even begun to be asked. Why had he been up there? How had he come to be clinging to life by his fingertips? In what way had he not been careful?

Litsi lay on a bed in the first-aid room until the races were over, but insisted then that he had entirely recovered and was ready to return to London.

He apologized to the racecourse executive for having been so foolish as to go up to the balcony to look at the new, much-vaunted view, and said that it was entirely his own clumsiness which had caused him to stumble over some builders' materials and lose his balance.

When asked for his name, he'd given a shortened version of his surname without the 'prince' in front, and he hoped there wouldn't be too much public fuss over his stupidity.

He was sitting in the back of the car, telling us all this, Danielle sitting beside him, as we started towards London.

'How did you stumble?' I asked, glancing at him

from time to time in the driving mirror. 'Was there a lot of junk up there?'

'Planks and things.' He sounded puzzled. 'I don't really know how I stumbled. I stood on something that rocked, and I put a hand out to steady myself, and it went out into space, over the wall. It happened so fast . . . I just lost my footing.'

'Did anyone push you?' I asked.

'Kit!' Danielle said, horrified, but it had to be considered, and Litsi, it seemed, had already done so.

'I've been lying there all afternoon,' he said slowly, 'trying to remember exactly how it happened. I didn't see anyone up there at all, I'm certain of that. I stood on something that rocked like a see-saw, and totally lost my balance. I wouldn't say I was pushed.'

'Well,' I said thoughtfully, 'do you mind if we go back there? I should have gone up for a look when I'd finished racing.'

'The racecourse people went up,' Litsi said. 'They came and told me that there was nothing particularly dangerous, but of course I shouldn't have gone.'

'We'll go back,' I said, and although Danielle protested that she'd be late for work, back we went.

Leaving Danielle and Litsi outside in the car, I walked through the gates and up the grandstand. As with most grandstands, it was a long haul to the top, up not too generous stairways, and one could see why, with a stream of people piling up that way to the main tier to watch the race, those going up to rescue Litsi from above had been a fair time on their journey.

The broad viewing steps of the main tier led right down to the ground and were openly accessible, on the side facing the racecourse, but the upper tier could be reached only by the stairways, of which there were two, one at each end.

I went up the stairway at the end nearest the weighing room, the stairway Litsi said he had used to reach the place where he'd overbalanced. Looking up at the back of the grandstand from the ground, that place was near the end of the balcony, on the left.

The stairway led first onto the upper steps of the main tier, and then continued upwards and I climbed to the top landing, where the refreshment room was in process of construction. The whole area had been glassed in, leaving only the balcony open. The balcony ran along the back of the refreshment room which had several glass doors, now closed, to lead eventually to the sandwiches. Inside the glass and without, there were copious piles of builders' materials, planks, drums of paint and ladders.

I went gingerly forward to the cold, open, windy balcony, towards the place where Litsi had overbalanced, and saw what had very likely happened. Planks lay side by side and several deep along all the short passage to the balcony, raising one, as one walked along them, higher than normal in proportion to the chest-high wall. When I was walking on the planks, the wall ahead seemed barely waist-high and Litsi was taller than I by three or four inches.

Whatever had rocked under Litsi's feet was no longer rocking, but several planks by the balcony wall itself were scattered like spillikins, not lying flat as in the passage. I picked my way among them, feeling them move when I pushed, and reached the spot where Litsi had fallen.

With my feet firmly on the floor, I looked over. One could see all the parade ring area beautifully, with magnificent hills beyond. Very attractive, that balcony, and with one's feet on the floor, very safe.

I went along its whole length intending to go down by the stairway at the other end, nearest the car park, but found I couldn't: the stairs themselves were missing, being in the middle of reconstruction. I walked back to the end where I had come up, renegotiated the planks, and descended to ground level.

'Well?' Litsi asked, when I was back in the car. 'What did you think?'

'Those planks looked pretty unsafe.'

'Yes,' he said ruefully, as I started the car and drove out of the racecourse gates. 'I thought, after I'd overbalanced, and managed somehow to catch hold of the wall, that if I just hung on, someone would come and rescue me, but you know ... my fingers just gave way ... I didn't leave go consciously. When I was falling, I thought I would die ... and I would have done ... it's incredible that all those people took off their coats.' He paused, 'I wish I could thank them,' he said.

'I couldn't think where you'd got to,' Danielle reflected. 'I was waiting for you on the stands, where we'd arranged to meet after I'd been to the ladies room. I didn't imagine . . .'

'But,' said Litsi, 'I went up to that balcony because I was supposed to meet you up there, Danielle.'

I stopped the car abruptly.

'Say that again,' I said.

CHAPTER THIRTEEN

Litsi said it again. 'I got this message that Danielle was waiting for me up on the balcony to look at the view.'

'I didn't send any such message,' Danielle said blankly. 'I was waiting where we'd watched the race before, where we'd said we'd meet.'

'Who gave you the message?' I asked Litsi.

'Just a man.'

'What did he look like?'

'Well ... an ordinary man. Not very young. He had a *Sporting Life* in his hands, and a sort of form book, with his finger keeping the place ... and binoculars.'

'What sort of voice?'

'Just ... ordinary.'

I let the brakes off with a sigh and started off towards Chiswick. Litsi had walked straight into a booby trap which had been meant either to frighten him or to kill him, and no one would have set it but Henri Nanterre. I hadn't seen Nanterre at the races, and neither Litsi nor Danielle knew him by sight.

If Nanterre had set the trap, he'd known where Litsi

would be that day, and the only way he could have known was via Beatrice. I couldn't believe that she would have known what use would be made of her little tit-bit, and it occurred to me that I didn't want her to know, either. It was important that Beatrice should keep right on telling.

Litsi and Danielle were quiet in the back of the car, no doubt travelling along much the same mental track. They protested, though, when I asked them not to tell Beatrice about the fake message.

'But she's got to know,' Danielle said vehemently. 'Then she'll see she must *stop* it. She'll see how murderous that man is . . .'

'I don't want her to stop it just yet,' I said. 'Not until Tuesday.'

'Why ever not? Why Tuesday?'

'We'll do what Kit wants,' Litsi said. 'I'll tell Beatrice just what I told the racecourse people, that I went up to look at the view.'

'She's dangerous,' Danielle said.

'I don't see how we can catch Nanterre without her,' I said. 'So be a darling.'

I wasn't sure whether or not it was the actual word which silenced her, but she made no more objections, and we travelled for a while without saying anything significant. Litsi's arms and shoulders were aching from the strain of having hung onto the wall so long, and he shifted uncomfortably from time to time, making small grunts.

I went back to thinking about the man who had delivered the misleading message, and asked Litsi if he was absolutely positive the man had used the word 'Danielle'.

'Positive,' Litsi said without hesitation. 'What he said to me first was, "Do you know someone called Danielle?" When I said I did, he said she wanted me to go up the stairs to the balcony to look at the view. He pointed up there. So I went.'

'OK,' I said. 'Then we'll take a spot of positive action.'

Like almost everyone in the racing world, I had a telephone in my car, and I put a call through to the *Towncrier* and asked for the Sports Desk. I wasn't sure whether their racing correspondent, Bunty Ireland, would be in the office at that time, but it seemed he was. He hadn't been at Bradbury: he went mostly to major meetings and on other days wrote his column in the office.

'I want to pay for an advertisement,' I told him, 'but it has to be on the racing page and in a conspicuous place.'

'Are you touting for rides?' he asked sardonically. 'A Grand National mount? Have saddle, will travel, that sort of thing?'

'Yeah,' I said. 'Very funny.' Bunty had an elephant-ine sense of humour but he was kind at heart. 'Write this down word for word, and persuade the racing page editor to print it in nice big noticeable letters.'

'Fire away, then.'

'Large reward offered to anyone who passed on a message from Danielle at Bradbury races on Thursday afternoon.' I dictated it slowly and added the telephone number of the house in Eaton Square.

Bunty's mystification came clearly across the air waves. 'You want the personal column for that,' he said.

'No. The *racing* page. Did you get it straight?'

He read it over, word for word.

'Hey,' he said, 'if you were riding at Bradbury, perhaps you can confirm this very odd story we've got about a guy falling from a balcony onto a pile of coats. Is someone having us on, or should we print it?'

'It happened,' I said.

'Did you see it?'

'Yes,' I said.

'Was the guy hurt?'

'No, not at all. Look, Bunty, get the story from someone else, will you? I'm in my car, and I want to get that ad in the *Sporting Life* and the *Racing Post*, before they go to press. And could you give me their numbers?'

'Sure, hold on.'

I put the receiver down temporarily and passed my pen and notebook back to Danielle, and when Bunty returned with the numbers, repeated them aloud for her to write down.

'Hey, Kit,' Bunty said, 'give me a quote I can use about your chances on Abseil tomorrow.'

'You know I can't, Bunty, Wykeham Harlow doesn't like it.'

'Yeah, yeah. He's an uncooperative old bugger.'

'Don't forget the ad,' I said.

He promised to see to it, and I made the calls with the same request to the two sporting papers.

'Tomorrow and Saturday,' I said to them. 'In big black type on the front page.'

'It'll cost you,' they said.

'Send me the bill.'

Danielle and Litsi listened to these conversations in silence, and when I'd finished, Litsi said doubtfully, 'Do you expect any results?'

'You never know. You can't get results if you don't try.'

Danielle said, 'Your motto for life.'

'Not a bad one,' Litsi said.

We dropped Danielle at the studio just on time and returned to Eaton Square. Litsi decided to say nothing at all about his narrow escape, and asked for my advice in the matter of strained muscles.

'A sauna and a massage,' I said. 'Failing that, a long hot soak and some aspirins. And John Grundy might give you a massage tomorrow morning.'

He decided on the home cures and, reaching the house, disappeared into his rooms to deal with his woes in private. I continued up to the bamboo room, still uninvaded territory, where, in the evening routine, I telephoned to Wykeham and picked up my messages.

Wykeham said the owners of Pinkeye were irritated that the race had been delayed, and had complained to him that I'd been off-hand with them afterwards.

'But Pinkeye won,' I said. I'd ridden the whole race automatically, like driving a well-known journey with a preoccupied mind and not remembering a yard of it on arrival. When I'd gone past the winning post, I hadn't been able to remember much about the jumps.

'You know what they're like,' Wykeham said. 'Never satisfied, even when they win.'

'Mm,' I said. 'Is the horse all right?'

All the horses were fine, Wykeham said, and Abseil (pronounced Absail) was jumping out of his skin and should trot up on the morrow.

'Great,' I said. 'Well, goodnight Wykeham.'

'Goodnight, Paul.'

Normality, I thought with a smile, disconnecting, was definitely on its way back.

Dinner was a stilted affair of manufactured conversations, with Roland de Brescou sitting at the head of the table in his wheelchair, looking abstracted.

Beatrice spent some time complaining that Harrods was now impossible (*busloads* of tourists, Casilia) and that Fortnums was too crowded, and that her favourite fur shop had closed and vanished. Beatrice's day of shopping had included a visit to the hairdresser, with a consequent intensification of peach tint. Beatrice's pleasures, I saw, were a way of passing time which had no other purpose: a vista of smothering pointlessness, infinitely depressing. No wonder, I thought, that she complained, with all that void pursuing her.

She looked at me, no doubt feeling my gaze, and said with undisguisable sudden venom, 'It's you that's standing in the way of progress. I know it is, don't deny it. Roland admitted it this morning. I'm sure he would have agreed to Henri's plans if it hadn't been for you. He admitted you're against it. You've influenced him. You're evil.'

'Beatrice,' the princess remonstrated, 'he's our guest.'

'I don't care,' she said passionately. 'He shouldn't be. It's he all the time who's standing in my way.'

'In *your* way, Beatrice?' Roland asked.

Beatrice hesitated. 'In my room,' she said finally.

'It's true,' I said without aggression, 'that I'm against Monsieur de Brescou signing anything against his conscience.'

'I'll get rid of you,' she said.

'No, Beatrice, really, that's too much,' the princess exclaimed. 'Kit, please accept my apologies.'

'It's all right,' I assured her truthfully. 'Perfectly all right. I do stand in Mrs Bunt's way. In the matter of Monsieur acting against his conscience, I always will.'

Litsi looked at me speculatively. I had made a very explicit and provocative declaration, and he seemed to be wondering if I was aware of it. I, on the other hand, was glad to have been presented with the opportunity, and I would repeat what I'd said, given the chance.

'You are after Danielle's money,' Beatrice said furiously.

'You know she has none.'

'After her inheritance from Roland.'

The princess and Roland were looking poleaxed. No one, I guessed, had conducted such open warfare before at that polite dinner table.

'On the contrary,' I said civilly. 'If selling guns would make Monsieur richer, and if I were after Danielle's mythical inheritance, then I would be urging him to sign at once.'

She stared at me, temporarily silenced. I kept my face entirely noncommittal, a habit learned from dealing with Maynard Allardeck, and behaved as if we had been having a normal conversation. 'In general,' I said pleasantly, 'I would implacably oppose anyone trying to get their way by threats and harassment. Henri Nanterre has behaved like a thug, and while I'm here I'll try my hardest to ensure he fails in his objective.'

Litsi opened his mouth, thought better of it, and said nothing. The speculation however disappeared from his forehead to be replaced by an unspecified anxiety.

'Well,' Beatrice said. 'Well . . .'

I said mildly, as before, 'It's really as well to make oneself perfectly clear, isn't it? As you have admirably done, Mrs Bunt.'

We were eating dover sole at the time. Beatrice decided there were a good many bones all of a sudden demanding her attention, and Litsi smoothly said that he had been invited to the opening of a new art gallery in Dover Street, on the following Wednesday, and would his Aunt Casilia care to go with him.

'Wednesday?' The princess looked from Litsi to me. 'Where's the racing next Wednesday?'

'Folkestone,' I said.

The princess accepted Litsi's invitation, because she didn't go to Folkestone normally, and he and she batted a few platitudes across the table to flatten out those Bunt–Fielding ripples. When we moved to the sitting room, Litsi again helped make sure I was next to the telephone, but it remained silent all evening. No messages, threats or boasting from Nanterre. It was too much to hope for, I thought, that he had folded his tents and departed.

When Roland, the princess and Beatrice finally went to bed, Litsi, rising to his feet to follow them, said, 'You elected yourself as goat, then?'

'I don't intend to get eaten,' I said, smiling and standing also.

'Don't go up to any balconies.'

'No,' I said. 'Sleep well.'

I did the rounds of the house, but everything seemed safe, and in due time went to the car, to go to fetch Danielle.

The alley seemed just as spooky, and I took even more precautions with the guts of the car, but again everything appeared safe, and I drove to Chiswick without incident.

Danielle looked pale and tired. 'A hectic evening,' she said. Her job as bureau coordinator involved deciding how individual news stories should be covered, and despatching camera crews accordingly. I'd been in the studio with her several times and seen her working, seen the mental energy and drive which went into making her the success she'd proved there. I'd seen her decisiveness and her inspirational sparkle, and knew that afterwards they could die away fast into weary silence.

The silences between us, though, were no longer companionable spaces of deep accord, but almost embarrassments, as between strangers. We had been passionate weekend lovers through November, December and January, and in her the joy had evaporated from one week to the next.

I drove back to Eaton Square thinking how very much I loved her, how much I longed for her to be as she had been, and when I stopped the car in the mews, I said impulsively, before she could get out, 'Danielle, please . . . please . . . tell me what's wrong.'

It was clumsily said and came straight from desperation, and I was disregarding the princess's advice; and as soon as I'd said it, I wished I hadn't because the last thing on earth I wanted to hear her say was that she loved Litsi. I thought I might even be driving her into saying it, and in a panic I said, 'Don't answer. It doesn't matter. Don't answer.'

She turned her head and looked at me, and then looked away.

'It was wonderful, at the beginning, wasn't it?' she said. 'It happened so fast. It was . . . magic.'

I couldn't bear to listen. I opened the car door and started to get out.

'Wait,' she said, 'I must – now I've started.'

'No,' I said. 'Don't.'

'About a month ago,' she said, all the repressed things pouring out in a jumble, 'when you had that dreadful fall at Kempton and I saw you lying on a stretcher unconscious while they unloaded you from the ambulance . . . and it gave me diarrhoea, I was so frightened you would die . . . and I was overwhelmed by how much danger there is in your life . . . and how much pain . . . and I seemed to see myself here in a strange country . . . with a commitment made for my whole life . . . not just enjoying a delicious unexpected romance but trapped for ever into a life far from home, full of fear every day . . . and I didn't know it was so cold and wet here and I was brought up in California . . . and then Litsi came . . . and he knows so much . . . and it seemed so simple being with him going to safe things like exhibitions and not hearing my heart thud . . . I could hear the worry in your voice on the telephone and see it this week in your face, but I couldn't seem to tell you . . .' She paused very briefly. 'I told Aunt Casilia. I asked her what to do.'

I loosened my throat. 'What did she say?' I said.

'She said no one could decide for me. I asked her if she thought I would get used to the idea of living for ever in a foreign country, like she has, and also to facing the possibility you'd be killed or horrifically injured . . . and don't say it doesn't happen, there was a jockey killed last week . . . and I asked her if she thought I was stupid.'

She swallowed. 'She said that nothing would change you, that you are as you are, and I was to see you clearly. She said the question wasn't whether I could face life here with you, but whether I could face life anywhere without you.'

She paused again. 'I told her how calm I felt with Litsi . . . she said Litsi was a nice man . . . she said in time I would see . . . understand . . . what I wanted most . . . She said time has a way of resolving things in one's mind . . . she said you would be patient, and she's right, you are, you are . . . But I can't go on like this for ever, I know it's unfair. I went racing yesterday and today to see if I could go back . . . but I can't. I hardly watch the races. I blank out of my mind what you're doing . . . that you're there. I promised Aunt Casilia I'd go . . . and try . . . but I just talk to Litsi . . .' Her voice faded in silence, tired and unhappy.

'I love you very much,' I said slowly. 'Do you want me to give up my job?'

'Aunt Casilia said if I asked, and you did, and we married, it would be disastrous, we would be divorced within five years. She was very vehement. She said I must not ask it, it was totally unfair, I would be destroying you because I don't have your courage.' She swallowed convulsively, tears filling her eyes.

I looked along the shadowy mews and thought of danger and fear, those old tamed friends. One couldn't teach anyone how to live with them: it had to come from inside. It got easier with practice, like everything else, but also it could vanish overnight. Nerve came and nerve went: there could be an overload of the capacity for endurance.

'Come on,' I said, 'it's getting cold.' I paused. 'Thank you for telling me.'

'What . . . are you going to do?'

'Go indoors and sleep till morning.'

'No . . .' she sobbed on a laugh. 'About what I said.'

'I'm going to wait,' I said, 'like Princess Casilia told me to.'

'Told you!' Danielle exclaimed. 'Did you tell her?'

'No, I didn't. She said it out of the blue in the parade ring at Ascot.'

'Oh,' Danielle said in a small voice. 'It was on Tuesday, while you were in Devon, that I asked her.'

We got out of the car and I locked the doors. What Danielle had said had been bad enough, but not as bad as an irrevocable declaration for Litsi. Until she took off the engagement ring she still wore, I would cling to some sort of hope.

We walked back side by side to the square, and said goodnight again briefly on the landing. I went on upstairs and lay on the bed and suffered a good deal, for which there was no aspirin.

When I went in to breakfast, both Litsi and Danielle were already in the morning room, he sitting at the table reading the *Sporting Life*, she leaning over his shoulder to do the same.

'Is it in?' I said.

'Is what in?' Litsi asked, intently reading.

'The advertisement,' I said, 'for the message-passer.'

'Yes, it's in,' Litsi said. 'There's a picture of you in the paper.'

I fetched some grapefruit juice, unexcited. There were photographs of me in newspapers quite often: result of the job.

'It says here,' Litsi said, 'that Champion jockey Kit Fielding saved the life of a man at Bradbury by persuading the crowd to take off their coats...' He lowered the paper and stared at me. 'You didn't say a word about it being your idea.'

Danielle too was staring. 'Why didn't you tell us?'

'An uprush of modesty,' I said, drinking the juice.

Litsi laughed. 'I won't thank you, then.'

'No, don't.'

Danielle said to me, 'Do you want some toast?'

'Yes ... please,' I said.

She walked over to the sideboard, cut a slice of wholemeal bread and put it in the toaster. I watched her do it, and Litsi, I found, watched me. I met his eyes and couldn't tell what he was thinking, and wondered how much had been visible in my own face.

'How are the muscles?' I asked.

'Stiff.'

I nodded. The toast popped up in the toaster and Danielle put the slice on a plate, brought it over and put it down in front of me.

'Thank you,' I said.

'You're welcome.' It was lightly said, but not a return to November. I ate the toast while it was still hot, and was grateful for small mercies.

'Are you busy again this afternoon?' Litsi asked.

'Five rides,' I said. 'Are you coming?'

'Aunt Casilia said we're all going.'

'So she did.' I reflected a little, remembering the morning conversation in the hall. 'It might be a good idea,' I said to Danielle, 'if you could casually mention in front of Beatrice, but so as to make sure she hears, that you'll only be working on Monday next week.'

She looked astonished. 'But I'm not. I'm working a normal schedule.'

'I want Beatrice to think Monday's your last night for coming home so late.'

'Why?' Danielle asked. 'I don't mean I won't do it, but why?'

Litsi was watching me steadily. 'What else?' he said.

I said conversationally, 'There's no harm in laying

out a line with a few baited hooks. If the fish doesn't take the opportunity, nothing will have been lost.'

'And if he does?'

'Net him.'

'What sort of line and hooks?' Danielle asked.

'A time and place,' I said, 'for removing an immovable object.'

She said to Litsi, 'Do you know what he means?'

'I'm afraid I do,' he said. 'He told Beatrice last night that while he was here to prevent it, Roland would never sign a contract for arms. Kit is also the only one of us that Nanterre hasn't directly attacked in any way, although he has twice promised to do it. Kit's directing him to a time and place which we may be able to turn to our advantage. The time, I gather, is early Tuesday morning, when he leaves this house to fetch you from work.'

'And the place?' Danielle said, her eyes wide.

Litsi glanced at me. 'We all know the perfect place,' he said.

After the briefest of pauses, she said flatly, 'The alley.'

I nodded. 'When Thomas drives the princess and Beatrice to the races today, he'll say he's forgotten something essential which he has to fetch from the garage on the way. He's going to drive the Rolls right down the mews to the turning circle, to give Beatrice a full view of it, and on the way back he'll stop by the garage but behind my Mercedes. He's going to say how deserted and dark the alley is at night . . . he's going to point out that the Mercedes is my car, and he's going to mention that I fetch you in it every night. If Beatrice does her stuff, there's just a chance Nanterre will come. And if he doesn't, as I said, nothing's lost.'

'Will you be there,' Danielle said, 'in the alley?' She didn't wait for an answer. 'Silly question,' she said.

'I'll hire a chauffeur-driven car to go to Chiswick to bring you back,' I said.

'Couldn't Thomas . . .?'

'Thomas,' I said, 'says he wouldn't miss the show for anything. He and Sammy will both be there. I'm not walking into that alley on my own.'

'I won't be able to work,' Danielle said. 'I don't think I'll go.'

'Indeed you must,' Litsi said. 'Everything must look normal.'

'But what if he comes?' she said. 'What if you catch him, what then?'

'I'll make him an offer he can't resist,' I said, and although they both wanted to know what it was, I thought I wouldn't tell them just yet.

CHAPTER FOURTEEN

We all went to Sandown races, except of course for
Roland, still in the care of Sammy.

The recording telephone was in Mrs Jenkins' office,
with instructions to everybody that if anyone telephoned about any messages for Danielle, every word
was to be recorded, and the caller must be asked for a
number or an address for us to get back to him.

'He may ask about a reward,' I said to the wispy-
waif secretary, and also to Dawson and to Sammy. 'If
he does, assure him he'll get one.' And they all nodded
and asked no questions.

Litsi, Danielle and I delayed leaving the house until
after Thomas had driven away with the princess and
Beatrice, who was complaining that she didn't like
going to the races twice in one week. Thomas, closing
her into the back seat, gave me a large wink before
settling himself behind the wheel, and I thought how
trusting all the princess's staff were, doing things whose
purpose they didn't wholly understand, content only to
be told that it was ultimately for the princess's sake.

There was no sign of the Rolls when we walked round to the mews, and I alarmed Litsi and Danielle greatly by checking my car again for traps. I borrowed the sliding mirror-on-wheels which the mechanics used for quick inspections of cars' undersides, but found no explosive sticky strangers, yet all the same I wouldn't let the other two get into the car before I'd started it, driven it a few yards, and braked fiercely to a halt.

'Do you do this every time you go out?' Litsi asked thoughtfully, as they eventually took their seats.

'Every time, just now.'

'Why don't you park somewhere else?' Danielle asked reasonably.

'I did think of it,' I said. 'But it takes less time to check than find parking places.'

'Apart from which,' Litsi said, 'you want Nanterre to know where you keep your car, if he doesn't know already.'

'Mm.'

'I wish this wasn't happening,' Danielle said.

When we reached the racecourse, they again went off to lunch and I to work. Litsi might have been lucky enough to dodge the publicity, but too many papers had spelled my name dead right, and so many strangers shook my hand that I found the whole afternoon embarrassing.

The one who was predictably upset by the general climate of approval was Maynard Allardeck who seemed to be dogging my footsteps, presumably hoping to catch me in some infringement of the rules.

Although not one of the Stewards officially acting at that meeting, he was standing in the parade ring before every race, watching everything I did, and each time I returned I found him on the weighing room steps, his eyes hostile and intent.

He was looking noble as usual, a pillar of society, a gentleman who wouldn't know an asset if it stripped in front of him. When I went out for the third of my rides, on the princess's runner Abseil, she at once remarked on Maynard's presence at a distance of no more than a few yards.

'Mr Allardeck,' she said, when I joined her, Litsi, Danielle and Beatrice in the parade ring, 'is staring at you.'

'Yes, I know.'

'Who is Mr Allardeck?' Beatrice demanded.

'Kit's sister's husband's father,' Danielle answered succinctly, which left her aunt not much better informed.

'It's unnerving,' Litsi said.

I nodded. 'I think it's supposed to be. He's been doing it all afternoon.'

'You don't, however, appear to be unnerved.'

'Not so far.' I turned to the princess. 'I always meant to ask you what he said after Cascade won last week.'

The princess made a small gesture of distress at the thought of her horse's fate, but said, 'He insisted you'd flogged the horse unmercifully. Those were his words. If he'd been able to find a mark on Cascade . . .' she shrugged. 'He wanted me to confirm you'd been excessively cruel.'

'Thank you for not doing it.'

She nodded, knowing I meant it.

'I'll be gentle on Abseil,' I said.

'Not too gentle.' She smiled. 'I do like to win.'

'He's still staring,' Danielle said. 'If looks could kill, you'd be in your grave.'

The princess decided on a frontal approach, and as if spotting Maynard for the first time raised both gloved hands in greeting and said 'Ah, Mr Allardeck, such a splendid day, isn't it?' walking three or four paces towards him to make talking easier.

He removed his hat and bowed to her, and said rather hoarsely for him that yes, it was. The princess said how nice it was to see the sun again after so much cloudy weather, and Maynard agreed. It was cold, of course, the princess said, but one had to expect it at this time of the year. Yes, Maynard said.

The princess glanced across to us all and said to Maynard, 'I do enjoy Sandown, don't you? And my horses all seem to jump well here, always, which is most pleasing.'

This on-the-face-of-it innocent remark produced in Maynard an intenser than ever stare in my direction – a look of black and dangerous poison.

'Why,' Litsi said in my ear, puzzled, 'did that make him so angry?'

'I can't tell you here,' I said.

'Later, then.'

'Perhaps.'

The signal was given for jockeys to mount, and with a sweet smile the princess wished Maynard good fortune for the afternoon and came to say, before I went off to where Abseil waited, 'Come back safely.'

'Yes, Princess,' I said.

Her eyes flicked momentarily in the direction of Danielle, and I suddenly understood her inner thought: come back safe because your young woman will be lost for ever if you don't.

'Do your best,' the princess said quietly, as if negating her first instruction, and I nodded and can- tered Abseil to the start thinking that certainly I could ride round conscious chiefly of safety, and certainly to some extent I'd been doing it all week, but if I intended to do it for ever I might as well retire at once. Caution and winning were incompatible. A too-careful jockey would lose his reputation, his owners, his career . . . and in my case anyway, his self-respect. The stark choice between Danielle and my job, unresolved all night, had sat on my shoulder already that afternoon through two undemanding hurdle races, and I had, in fact, been acutely aware of her being there on the stands in a way I hadn't been when I hadn't known of her turmoil of fears.

Abseil, a grey eight-year-old steeplechaser, was a fluid, agile jumper with reasonable speed and questionable stamina. Together we'd won a few races, but had more often finished second, third or fourth, because he could produce no acceleration in a crisis. His one advantage was his boldness over fences: if I restrained him in that, we could trail in last.

Sandown racecourse, right-handed, undulating, with seven fences close together down the far side, was a track where good jumpers could excel. I particularly liked riding there, and it was a good place for Abseil, except that the uphill finish could find him out. To win there, he had to be flying in the lead coming round the last long bend, and jump the last three fences at his fastest speed. Then, if he faded on the hill, one might just hang on in front as far as the post.

Abseil himself was unmistakably keen to race, sending me signals of vigour and impatience. 'Jumping out of his skin,' Wykeham had said; and this one would be wound up tight because he wouldn't be running at the Cheltenham Festival as he wasn't quite in the top class.

The start of two mile, five furlong 'chases was midway down the far side, with one's back to the water jump. There were eight runners that day, a pleasant sized field, and Abseil was second favourite. We set off in a bunch at no great pace, because no one wanted to make the running, and I had no trouble at all being careful over the first three fences, also round the long bottom bend, over the three fences which would be the last three next time round, and uphill past the stands.

It was when we turned right-handed at the top of the hill to go out on the second circuit that the decision was immediately there, staring me in the face. To go at racing pace over the next fence with its downhill landing, graveyard of many a hope, or to check, rein back, jump it carefully, lose maybe four lengths . . .

Abseil wanted to go. I kicked him. We flew the fence, passing two horses in mid-air, landing on the downhill slope with precision and skimming speed, going round the bend into the back straight in second place.

The seven fences along there were so designed that if one met the first right, one met them all right, like traffic lights. The trick was to judge one's distance a good way back from the first, to make any adjustments early, so that when one's mount reached the fence he was in the right place for jumping without shortening or lengthening his stride. It was a skill learned young by all successful jockeys, becoming second nature. Abseil took a hint, shortened one stride, galloped happily on, and soared over the first of the seven fences with perfection.

The decision had been made almost unconsciously. I couldn't do anything else. What I was, what I could do, lay there in front of me, and even for Danielle I couldn't deny it.

Abseil took the lead from the favourite at the second of the seven fences, and I sent him mental messages –

'Go on there, go for it, pull the stops out, this is the way it is, and you're going to get your chance, I am as I am and I can't help it, this is living . . . get on and fly.'

He flew the open ditch and then the water jump. He sailed over the last three fences on the far side. He was in front by a good thirty yards all the way round the last bend.

Three more fences.

He had his ears pricked, enjoying himself. Caution had long lost the battle, in his mind as in mine. He went over the first of them at full racing pace, and over the second, and over the last of all with me almost lying on his neck to keep up with him, weight forward, head near his head.

He tired very fast on the hill, as I'd feared he would. I had to keep him balanced, but I could feel him begin to flounder and waver and tell me he'd gone far enough.

'Come on, hang on to it, we've almost made it, just keep on, keep going you old bugger, we're not losing it now, we're so near, so get on . . .'

I could hear the crowd yelling, which one usually couldn't. I could hear another horse coming behind me, hooves thudding. I could see him in my peripheral vision, the jockey's arm swinging high in the air as he scented Abseil flagging . . . and the winning post came just in time for me that time, not three strides too late.

Abseil was proud of himself, as he deserved to be. I patted his neck hugely and told him he was OK, he'd done a good job of work, he was a truly great fellow, and he trotted back towards the unsaddling enclosure with his ears still pricked and his fetlocks springy.

The princess was flushed and pleased in the way she always was after close races.

I slid to the ground, smiled at her, and began to unbuckle the girths.

'Is that,' she said, without censure, 'what you call being gentle?'

'I'd call it compulsion,' I said.

Abseil was practically bowing to the crowd, knowing the applause had been his. I patted his neck again, thanking him. He tossed his grey head, turning it to look at me with both eyes, blowing down his nostrils, nodding again.

'They talk to you,' the princess said.

'Some of them.'

I looped the girths round my saddle, and turned to go in to weigh in, and found Maynard Allardeck standing directly in my path, much as Henri Nanterre had done at Newbury. Maynard's hatred came across loud and clear.

I stopped. I never liked speaking to him, because anything I said gave him offence. One of us was going to have to give way, and it was going to be me, because in any sort of confrontation between a Steward and a jockey, the jockey would lose.

'Why, Mr Allardeck,' said the princess, stepping to my side, 'are you congratulating me? Wasn't that a delightful win?'

Maynard took off his hat and manfully said he was delighted she'd been lucky, especially as her jockey had come to the front far too soon and nearly thrown away the race on the run-in.

'Oh, but Mr Allardeck,' I heard her saying sweetly as I side-stepped Maynard politely and headed for the weighing room door, 'if he hadn't opened up such a lead he couldn't have hung on to win.'

She wasn't only a great lady, I thought gratefully, sitting on the scales, she actually understood what had been going on in a race, which many owners didn't.

Maynard troubled me, though, because it had looked very much as if he were trying to force me into jostling him, and I was going to have to be extremely careful pretty well for ever to avoid physical contact. The film I'd made of him would destroy his credibility where it mattered, but it was an ultimate defence, not to be lightly used, as it shielded Bobby and Holly from any destructive consequences of Maynard's obsession, not just myself. If I used it, Maynard's life would be in tatters, but his full fury would be unleashed. He would have nothing more to lose, and we would all be in real peril.

Meanwhile, as always, there were more races to ride. I went twice more from start to finish without caution and, the gods being kind, also without hitting the turf. Maynard continued glaring and I continued being carefully civil, and somehow or other persevered unscathed to tea time.

I changed into street clothes and went up to the princess's box, and found Lord Vaughnley there with her and Litsi and Danielle: no sign of Beatrice.

'My dear chap,' Lord Vaughnley said, his large bland face full of kindness, 'I came to congratulate Princess Casilia. Well done, well done, my dear fellow, a nice tactical race.'

'Thank you,' I said mildly.

'And yesterday, too. That was splendid, absolutely first class.'

'I didn't have any runners yesterday,' the princess said, smiling.

'No, no, not a winner. Saving that fellow's life, don't you know, at Bradbury races.'

'What fellow?' the princess asked.

'Some damn fool who went where he shouldn't and fell off a balcony. Didn't Kit tell you? No,' he considered, 'I suppose he wouldn't. Anyway, everyone has been talking about it all afternoon and it was in most of the papers.'

'I didn't see the papers this morning,' the princess said.

Lord Vaughnley obligingly gave her a full second-hand account of the proceedings which was accurate in essence. Litsi and Danielle looked studiously out of the windows and I wished I could eat the cream cakes, and eventually Lord Vaughnley ran out of superlatives.

'By the way,' he said to me, picking up a large brown envelope which lay on the tea table, 'this is for you.

All we could find. Hope it will be of some help.' He held the envelope towards me.

'Thank you very much,' I said taking it.

'Right,' said Lord Vaughnley, beaming. 'Thank you so much, dear Princess Casilia, for my tea. And again, congratulations.' He went away in clouds of benevolence, leaving the princess wide-eyed.

'You were at Bradbury,' the princess said to Danielle and Litsi. 'Did you see all this?'

'No,' Danielle said, 'we didn't. We read about it this morning in the *Sporting Life*.'

'Why didn't you tell me?'

'Kit didn't want a fuss.'

The princess looked at me. I said, shrugging, 'That's true, I didn't. And I'd be awfully grateful, Princess, if you didn't tell Mrs Bunt.'

She had no chance to ask me why not, as Beatrice reappeared as if on cue, coming into the box with a smug expression which visibly deepened when she saw I was there. Watching me all the time she ate a cream cake with gusto, as if positively enjoying my hunger. I could more easily put up with that, I thought wryly, than with most other tribulations of that day.

The princess told Beatrice it was time to leave, the last race being long over, and shepherded her off to the Rolls. There was no chance of Litsi going with them, even if he wanted to, as Danielle clung firmly to his arm all the way to the car park. She didn't want to be alone with me after her explanations in the night, and I saw, as I suppose I'd known all day, that she couldn't have come at all without his support. Racing was again at Sandown the next day, and I began to think it would be less of a strain for everybody if she stayed away.

When we reached the car, Litsi sat in the front at Danielle's insistence, with herself in the rear, and before starting the car I opened the large brown envelope Lord Vaughnley had brought.

Inside there was a small clipping from a newspaper, a larger piece from a colour magazine, a black and white eight by ten photograph, and a compliments slip from Lord Vaughnley, asking me to return the pieces to the *Towncrier*, which now only had photocopies.

'What is it?' Litsi said.

I passed him the black and white photograph, which was of a prize-giving ceremony after a race, a group of people giving and receiving a trophy. Danielle looked over Litsi's shoulder and asked, 'Who are those people?'

'The man receiving the pot is Henri Nanterre.'

They both exclaimed, peering closer.

'The man at his side is the French racehorse trainer Villon, and at a guess, the racecourse is Longchamp. Look at the back, there might be some information.'

Litsi turned the photograph over. 'It just says, "After the Prix de la Cité, Villon, Nanterre, Duval".'

'Duval is the jockey,' I said.

'So that's what Nanterre looks like,' Litsi said

thoughtfully. 'Once seen, easily remembered.' He passed the photograph back to Danielle. 'What other goodies do you have?'

'This piece is from an English magazine and seems to be a Derby preview from last year. Villon apparently had a runner, and the article says "fresh from his triumph at Longchamp". Nanterre's mentioned as one of his owners.'

The newspaper clipping, also from an English paper, was no more helpful. Prudhomme, owned by French industrialist H. Nanterre, trained by Villon, had come to run at Newmarket and dropped dead of a heart attack on pulling up: end of story.

'Who took the photograph?' I asked, twisting round to see Danielle. 'Does it say?'

'Copyright *Towncrier*,' she said, reading the back.

I shrugged. 'They must have gone over for some big race or other. The Arc, I dare say.'

I took the photograph back and put all the bits into the envelope.

'He has a very strong face,' Danielle said, meaning Nanterre.

'And a very strong voice.'

'And we're no further forward,' Litsi said.

I started the car and drove us to London, where we found that nothing of any interest had happened at all, with the result that Sammy was getting bored.

'Just by being here,' I said, 'you earn your bread.'

'No one knows I'm here, man.'

'They sure do,' I said dryly. 'Everything that happens in this house reaches the ears of the man you're guarding its owner against, so don't go to sleep.'

'I'd never,' he said, aggrieved.

'Good.' I showed him the *Towncrier*'s photograph. 'That man, there,' I said, pointing. 'If ever you see him, that's when you take care. He carries a gun, which may or may not have bullets in it, and he's full of all sorts of tricks.'

He looked at the photograph long and thoughtfully. 'I'll know him,' he said.

I took Lord Vaughnley's offerings up to the bamboo room, telephoned Wykeham, picked up my messages, dealt with them: the usual routine. When I went down to the sitting room for a drink before dinner, Litsi, Danielle and the princess were discussing French impressionist painters exhibiting in Paris around 1880.

Cézanne ... Pissarro ... Renoir ... Degas ... at least I'd heard of them. I went across to the drinks tray and picked up the scotch.

'Berthe Morisot was one of the best,' Litsi said to the room in general. 'Don't you think?'

'What did he paint?' I asked, opening the bottle.

'He was a she,' Litsi said.

I grunted slightly and poured a trickle of whisky. 'She, then, what did she paint?'

'Young women, babies, studies in light.'

I sat in an armchair and drank the scotch, looking at Litsi. At least he didn't patronize me, I thought.

234

'They're not all easy to see,' he said. 'Many are in private collections, some are in Paris, several are in the National Gallery of Art in Washington.'

I was unlikely, he must have known, to chase them up.

'Delightful pictures,' the princess said. 'Luminous.'

'And there was Mary Cassatt,' Danielle said. 'She was brilliant too.' She turned to me. 'She was American, but she was a student of Degas in Paris.'

I would go with her to galleries, I thought, if that would please her. 'One of these days,' I said casually, 'you can educate me.'

She turned her head away almost as if she would cry, which hadn't in the least been my intention; and perhaps it was as well that Beatrice arrived for her 'bloody'.

Beatrice was suffering a severe sense of humour failure over Sammy who had, it appeared, said, 'Sorry, me old darlin', not used to slow traffic,' while again cannoning into her on the stairs.

She saw the laugh on my face, which gravely displeased her, and Litsi smothered his in his drink. The princess, with twitching lips, assured her sister-in-law that she would ask Sammy to be more careful and Beatrice said it was all my fault for having brought him into the house. It entirely lightened and enlivened the evening, which passed more easily than some of the others: but there was still no one telephoning in response to the advertisements, and there was again no sound from Nanterre.

Early next morning, well before seven, Dawson woke me again with the intercom, saying there was a call for me from Wykeham Harlow.

I picked up the receiver, sleep forgotten.

'Wykeham?' I said.

'K . . . K . . . Kit.' He was stuttering dreadfully. 'C . . . C . . . Come down here. C . . . Come at once.'

CHAPTER FIFTEEN

He put the receiver down immediately, without telling me what had happened, and when I instantly rang back there was no reply. With appalling foreboding, I flung on some clothes, sprinted round to the car, did very cursory checks on it, and drove fast through the almost empty streets towards Sussex.

Wykeham had sounded near disintegration, shock and age trembling ominously in his voice. By the time I reached him, they had been joined by anger, which filled and shook him with impotent fire.

He was standing in the parking space with Robin Curtiss, the vet, when I drove in.

'What's happened?' I said, getting out of the car.

Robin made a helpless gesture with his hands and Wykeham said with fury. 'C . . . Come and look.'

I followed him into the courtyard next to the one which had held Cascade and Cotopaxi. Wykeham, shaky on his knees but straight-backed with emotion, went across to one of the closed doors and put his hand flat on it.

'In there,' he said.

The box door was closed but not bolted. Not bolted, because the horse inside wasn't going to escape.

I pulled the doors open, the upper and the lower, and saw the body lying on the peat.

Bright chestnut, three white socks, white blaze.

It was Col.

Speechlessly I turned to Wykeham and Robin, feeling all of Wykeham's rage and a lot of private despair. Nanterre was too quick on his feet, and it wouldn't take much more for Roland de Brescou to crumble.

'It's the same as before,' Robin said. 'The bolt.' He bent down, lifted the chestnut forelock, showed me the mark on the white blaze. 'There's a lot of oil in the wound . . . the gun's been oiled since last time.' He let go of the forelock and straightened. 'The horse is stone cold. It was done early, I should say before midnight.'

Col . . . gallant at Ascot, getting ready for Cheltenham, for the Gold Cup.

'Where was the patrol?' I said, at last finding my voice.

'He was here,' Wykeham said. 'In the stable, I mean, not in the courtyard.'

'He's gone, I suppose.'

'No, I told him to wait for you. He's in the kitchen.'

'Col,' I said, 'is the only one . . . isn't he?'

Robin nodded. 'Something to be thankful for.'

Not much, I thought. Cotopaxi and Col had been two of the princess's three best horses, and it could be no coincidence that they'd been targeted.

'Kinley,' I said to Wykeham. 'You did check Kinley, didn't you?'

'Yes, straight away. He's in the corner box still, in the next courtyard.'

'The insurers aren't going to like this,' Robin said, looking down at the dead horse. 'With the first two, it might have been just bad luck that they were two good ones, but three . . .' he shrugged. 'Not my problem, of course.'

'How did he know where to find them?' I said, as much to myself as to Robin and Wykeham. 'Is this Col's usual box?'

'Yes,' Wykeham said. 'I suppose now I'll have to change them all around, but it does disrupt the stable . . .'

'Abseil,' I said, 'is he all right?'

'Who?'

'Yesterday's winner.'

Wykeham's doubts cleared. 'Oh, yes, he's all right.'

Abseil was as easy to recognize as the others, I thought. Not chestnut, not nearly black like Cascade, but grey, with a black mane and tail.

'Where is he?' I asked.

'In the last courtyard, near the house.'

Although I was down at Wykeham's fairly often, it was always to do the schooling, for which we would drive up to the Downs, where I would ride relays of the horses over jumps, teaching them. I almost never rode the horses in or out of the yard, and although I knew where some of the horses lived, like Cotopaxi, I wasn't sure of them all.

I put a hand down to touch Col's foreleg, and felt its rigidity, its chill. The foreleg that had saved us from disaster at Ascot, that had borne all his weight.

'I'll have to tell the princess,' Wykeham said unhappily. 'Unless you would, Kit?'

'Yes, I'll tell her,' I said. 'At Sandown.'

He nodded vaguely. 'What are we running?' he said.

'Helikon for the princess, and three others.'

'Dusty has the list, of course.'

'Yeah,' I said.

Wykeham took a long look again at the dead splendour on the peat.

'I'd kill the shit who did that,' he said, 'with his own damned bolt.'

Robin sighed and closed the stable doors, saying he would arrange for the carcass to be collected, if Wykeham liked.

Wykeham silently nodded, and we all walked out of the courtyard and made our way to Wykeham's house, where Robin went off to telephone in the office. The dog-handler was still in the kitchen, restive but chastened, with his dog, a black Dobermann, lying on the floor and yawning at his feet.

'Tell Kit Fielding what you told me,' Wykeham said.

The dog-handler, in a navy blue battle-dress uniform, was middle-aged and running to fat. His voice was defensively belligerent and his intelligence middling, and I wished I'd had the speedy Sammy here in his place. I sat at the table across from him and asked how he'd missed the visitor who had shot Col.

'I couldn't help it, could I?' he said. 'Not with those bombs going off.'

'What bombs?' I glanced at Wykeham, who'd clearly heard about the bombs before. 'What bombs, for God's sake?'

The dog-handler had a moustache which he groomed frequently with a thumb and forefinger, working outwards from the nose.

'Well, how was I to know they wasn't proper bombs?' he said. 'They made enough noise.'

'Just start,' I said, 'at the beginning. Start with when you came on duty. And er . . . have you been here any other nights?'

'Yes,' he said. 'Monday to Friday, five nights.'

'Right,' I said. 'Describe last night.'

'I come on duty sevenish, when the head lad's finished the feeding. I make a base here in the kitchen and do a recce every half hour. Standard procedure.'

'How long do the recces take?'

'Fifteen minutes, maybe more. It's bitter cold these nights.'

'And you go into all the courtyards?'

'Never miss a one,' he said piously.

'And where else?'

'Look in the hay barn, tack room, feed shed, round the back where the tractor is, and the harrow, muckheap, the lot.'

'Go on, then,' I said, 'how many recces had you done when the bombs went off?'

He worked it out on his fingers. 'Nine, say. The head lad had been in for a quick look round last thing, like he does, and everything was quiet. So I comes back here for a bit of a warm, and goes out again half eleven, I should say. I start on the rounds, and there's this almighty bang and crashing round the back. So I went off there with Ranger . . .' he looked down at his dog. 'Well, I would, wouldn't I? Stands to reason.'

'Yes,' I said. 'Where exactly, round the back?'

'I couldn't see at first because there isn't much light round there, and there was this strong smell of burning, got right down your throat, and then another one went off not ten feet away. Nearly burst my eardrums.'

'Where were the bombs?' I said again.

'The first one was round the back of the muck-heap. I found what was left of it with my torch, after.'

'But you don't use your torch all the time?'

'You don't need to in the courtyards. Most of them have lights in.'

'Mm. OK. Where was the second one?'

'Under the harrow.'

Wykeham, like many trainers, used the harrow

occasionally for raking his paddocks, keeping them in good shape.

'Did it blow up the harrow?' I said, frowning.

'No, see, they weren't that sort of bomb.'

'What other sort is there?'

'It went off through the harrow with a huge shower of sparks. Golden sparks, all over. Little burning sparks. Some of them fell on me ... They were fireworks. I found the empty boxes. They said "bomb" on them, where they weren't burned.'

'Where are they now,' I asked.

'Where they went off. I didn't touch them, except to kick them over to read what was on the side.'

'So what was your dog doing all this time?'

The dog-handler looked disillusioned. 'I had him on the leash. I always do, of course. He didn't like the bangs or the sparks or the smell. He's supposed to be trained to ignore gun shots, but he didn't like the fireworks. He was barking fit to bust, and trying to run off.'

'He was trying to run in a different direction, but you stopped him?'

'That's right.'

'Maybe he was trying to run after the man who shot the horse.'

The dog-handler's mouth opened and snapped shut. He smoothed his moustache several times and grew noticeably more aggressive. 'Ranger was barking at the bombs,' he said.

I nodded. It was too late for it to matter.

'And I suppose,' I said, 'that you didn't hear any other bangs in the distance ... you didn't hear the shot?'

'No, I didn't. My ears were ringing and Ranger was kicking up a racket.'

'So what did you do next?'

'Nothing,' he said. 'I thought it was some of those lads who work here. Proper little monkeys. So I just went on with the patrols, regular like. There wasn't anything wrong ... it didn't look like it, that's to say.'

I turned to Wykeham, who had been gloomily listening. 'Didn't *you* hear the fireworks?' I asked.

'No, I was asleep.' He hesitated, then added, 'I don't sleep very well ... I can't seem to sleep at all these days without sleeping pills. We'd had four quiet nights and I'd been awake most of those, so ... last night I took a pill.'

I sighed. If Wykeham had been awake, he would anyway have gone towards the commotion and nothing would have been different.

I said to the dog-handler, 'You were here on Wednesday, when you had the prowler?'

'Yes, I was. Ranger was whining but I couldn't find anyone.'

Nanterre, I thought, had come to the stable on Wednesday night, intending to kill, and had been thwarted by the dog's presence: and he'd come back two nights later with his diversions.

He must have been at Ascot, I supposed, and learned what Col looked like, but I hadn't seen him, as I hadn't seen him at Bradbury either: but among large crowds on racecourses, especially while I was busy, that wasn't extraordinary.

I looked down at Ranger, wondering about his responses.

'When people arrive here,' I asked, 'like I did a short while ago, how does Ranger behave?'

'He gets up and goes to the door and whines a bit. He's a quiet dog, mostly. Doesn't bark. That's why I knew it was the bombs he was barking at.'

'Well, er, during your spells in the kitchen, what would you be doing?'

'Making a cuppa. Eating. Relieving myself. Reading. Watching the telly.' He smoothed his moustache, not liking me or my questions. 'I don't doze off, if that's what you mean.'

It was what I meant, and obviously what he'd done, at some point or another. During four long quiet cold nights I supposed it was understandable, if not excusable.

'Over the weekend,' I said to Wykeham, 'we'll have double and treble patrols. Constant.'

He nodded. 'Have to.'

'Have you told the police yet?'

'Not yet. Soon, though.' He looked with disgust at the dog-handler. 'They'll want to hear what you've said.'

The dog-handler however stood up, announced it was an hour after he should have left and if the police wanted him they could reach him through his firm. He, he said, was going to bed.

Wykeham morosely watched him go and said, 'What the hell is going on, Kit? The princess knows who killed them all, and so do you. So tell me.'

It wasn't fair, I thought, for him not to know, so I told him the outline: a man was trying to extract a signature from Roland de Brescou by attacking his family wherever he could.

'But that's . . . terrorism.' Wykeham used the word at arm's length, as if its very existence affronted him.

'In a small way,' I said.

'Small?' he exclaimed. 'Do you call three dead great horses small?'

I didn't. It made me sick and angry to think of them. It was small on a world scale of terrorism, but rooted in the same wicked conviction that the path to attaining one's end lay in slaughtering the innocent.

I stirred. 'Show me where all the princess's horses are,' I suggested to Wykeham, and together we went out again into the cold air and made the rounds of the courtyards.

Cascade's and Cotopaxi's boxes were still empty, and no others of the princess's horses had been in the first courtyard. In the second had been only Col. In the one beyond that, Hillsborough and Berina, with Kinley in the deep corner box there.

About a third of the stable's inmates were out at exercise on the Downs, and while we were leaving Kinley's yard, they came clattering back, filling the whole place with noise and movement, the lads dismounting and leading their horses into the boxes. Wykeham and I sorted our way round as the lads brushed down their charges, tidied the bedding, filled the buckets, brought hay to the racks, propped their saddles outside the boxes, bolted the doors and went off to their breakfasts.

I saw all the old friends in their quarters; among them North Face, Dhaulagiri, Icicle and Icefall, and young Helikon, the four-year-old hurdler going to Sandown that afternoon. Wykeham got half of their names right, waiting for me to prompt him on the others. He unerringly knew their careers, though, and their personalities; they were real to him in a way that needed no name tags. His secretary was adept at sorting out what he intended when he wrote down his lists of entries to races.

In the last courtyard we came to Abseil and opened the top half of his door. Abseil came towards the opening daylight and put his head out enquiringly. I rubbed his grey nose and upper lip with my hand and put my head next to his and breathed out gently like a reversed sniff into his nostril. He rubbed his nose a couple of times against my cheek and then lifted his head away, the greeting done. Wykeham paid no attention. Wykeham talked to horses that way himself, when they were that sort of horse. With some, one would never do it, one could get one's nose bitten off.

Wykeham gave Abseil a carrot from a deep pocket, and closed him back into his twilight.

Wykeham slapped his hand on the next box along. 'That's Kinley's box usually. It's empty now. I don't like keeping him in that corner box, it's dark and boring for him.'

'It won't be for much longer, I hope,' I said, and suggested going round to see the 'bombs'.

Wykeham had seen them earlier, and pointed them out to me, and as expected they were the bottom parts of cardboard containers, each four inches square in shape, the top parts burned away. They were both the same, with gaudy red and yellow pictured flames still visible on the singed surfaces, and the words GOLDEN BOMB in jazzy letters on the one under the harrow.

'We'd better leave them there for the police,' I said.

Wykeham agreed, but he said fireworks would convince the police even more that it was the work of boys.

We went back into the house, where Wykeham telephoned the police and received a promise of attention, and I got through to Dawson, asking him to tell the princess I was down at Wykeham's and would go to Sandown from there.

Wykeham and I had breakfast and drove up to the Downs in his big-wheeled pick-up to see the second lot exercise, and under the wide cold windy sky he surprised me by saying apropos of nothing special that he was thinking of taking another assistant. He'd had assistants in the past, I'd heard, who'd never lasted long, but there hadn't been one there in my time.

'Are you?' I said. 'I thought you couldn't stand assistants.'

'They never knew anything,' he said. 'But I'm getting old . . . It'll have to be someone the princess likes. Someone you get on with, too. So if you think of anyone, let me know. I don't know who's around so much these days.'

'All right,' I said, but with misgivings. Wykeham, for all his odd mental quirks, was irreplaceable. 'You're not going to retire, are you?'

'No, I'm not. Never. I wouldn't mind dying up here, watching my horses.' He laughed suddenly, in his eyes a flash of the vigour that had been there always not so long ago, when he'd been a titan. 'I've had a great life, you know. One of the best.'

'Stick around,' I said.

He nodded. 'Maybe next year,' he said, 'we'll win the Grand National.'

Wykeham's four runners at Sandown were in the first three races and the fifth, and I didn't see the princess until she came down to the parade ring for Helikon's race, which was the third on the card.

Beatrice was with her, and also Litsi, and also

Danielle, who after the faintest of greetings was busy blanking me out, it seemed, by looking carefully at the circling horses. The fact that she was there, that she was still trying, was something, I supposed.

'Good morning,' the princess said, when I bowed to her. 'Dawson said Wykeham telephoned early... again.' There was a shade of apprehension in her face, which abruptly deepened at what she read in my own.

She walked a little away from her family and I followed.

'*Again?*' she said, not wanting to believe it. 'Which ones?'

'One,' I said. 'Col.'

She absorbed the shock with a long blink.

'The same way... as before?' she said.

'Yes. With the bolt.'

'My poor horse.'

'I'm so sorry.'

'I will not tell my husband,' she said. 'Please tell none of them, Kit.'

'It will be in the newspapers tomorrow or on Monday,' I said, 'probably worse than before.'

'Oh...' The prospect affected her almost as much as Col's death. 'I will not add to the pressure on my husband,' she said fiercely. 'He cannot sign this wretched contract. He will die, you know, if he does. He will not survive the disgrace in his own mind. He will wish to die... as all these years, although his condition is such a trial to him, he has wished to live.' She

250

made a small gesture with her gloved hand. 'He is . . . very dear to me, Kit.'

I heard in my memory my grandmother saying, 'I love the old bugger, Kit,' of my pugnacious grandfather, an equal declaration of passion for a man not obviously lovable.

That the princess should have made it was astonishing, but not as impossible as before the advent of Nanterre. A great deal, I saw, had changed between us in the last eight days.

To save his honour, to save his life, to save their life together . . . My God, I thought, what a burden. She needed Superman, not me.

'Don't tell him about Col,' she said again.

'No, I won't.'

Her gaze rested on Beatrice.

'I won't tell other people,' I said. 'But it may not stay a secret on the racecourse. Dusty and the lads who came with Wykeham's horses all know, and they'll tell other lads . . . it'll spread, I'm afraid.'

She nodded slightly, unhappily, and switched her attention from Beatrice to Helikon, who happened to be passing. She watched him for several seconds, turning her head after him as he went.

'What do you think of him?' she asked, her defence mechanism switching on smoothly. 'What shall I expect?'

'He's still a bit hot-headed,' I said, 'but if I can settle him, he should run well.'

'But not another Kinley?' she suggested.

'Not so far.'

'Do your best . . .'

I said as usual that I would, and we rejoined the others as if all we'd been talking about was her hurdler.

'Have you noticed who's still staring?' Danielle said, and I answered that indeed I had, those eyes followed me everywhere.

'Doesn't it get on your nerves?' Danielle asked.

'What nerves?' Litsi said.

'Are you talking about Mr Allardeck?' Beatrice demanded. 'I can't think why you don't like him. He looks perfectly darling.'

The perfectly darling man was projecting his implacable thoughts my way from a distance signalling unmistakable invasion of psychological territory, and I thought uneasily again about the state of mind that was compelling him to do it. The evil eye, I thought: and no shield from it that I could see.

The time came to mount, and hot-headed Helikon and I went out onto the track. He was nervous as well as impetuous; not a joy to ride. I tried to get him to relax on the way to the start, but as usual it was like trying to relax a coil of barbed wire. The princess had bought him as a yearling and had great hopes for him, but although he jumped well enough, neither Wykeham nor I had been able to straighten out his kinks.

There were twenty or more runners, and Helikon and I set off near the front because if he were bumped in the pack he'd be frightened into stopping; yet I also had to keep a tight hold, as he could take charge and decamp.

He went through the routine of head-tossing against the restraint, but I had him anchored and running fairly well, and by the third flight of hurdles I thought the worst was over, we could now settle a little and design a passable race.

It wasn't his day. At the fourth flight the horse nearest ahead put his foot through the obstacle and went down with a crash, slithering along the ground on his side. Helikon fell over him, going down fast, pitching me off: and I didn't actually see the subsequent course of events all that clearly, though it was a pile-up worthy of a fog on a motorway. Five horses, I found afterwards, hit the deck at that jump. One of them seemed to land smack on top of me; not frightfully good for one's health.

CHAPTER SIXTEEN

I lay on the grass, assessing things.

I was conscious and felt like a squashed beetle, but I hadn't broken my legs, which I always feared most.

One of the other jockeys from the mêlée squatted beside me and asked if I was all right, but I couldn't answer him on account of having no breath.

'He's winded,' my colleague said to someone behind me, and I thought, 'Just like Litsi at Bradbury, heigh ho.' My colleague unbuckled my helmet and pushed it off, for which I couldn't thank him.

Breath came back, as it does. By the time the ambulance arrived along with a doctor in a car, I'd come to the welcome conclusion that nothing was broken at all and that it was time to stand up and get on with things. Standing, I felt hammered and sore in several places, but one had to accept that, and I reckoned I'd been lucky to get out of that sort of crash so lightly.

One of the other jockeys hadn't been so fortunate and was flat out, white and silent, with the first-aid men kneeling anxiously beside him. He woke up slightly during the ambulance ride back to the stands and began groaning intermittently which alarmed his attendants but at least showed signs of life.

When we reached the first-aid room and the ambulance's rear doors were opened, I climbed out first, and found the other jockey's wife waiting there, pregnant and pretty, screwed up with anxiety.

'Is Joe all right?' she said to me, and then saw him coming out on the stretcher, very far from all right. I saw the deep shock in her face, the quick pallor, the dry mouth . . . the agony.

That was what had happened to Danielle, I thought. That was much what she'd seen, and that was what she'd felt.

I put my arm round Joe's wife and held her close, and told her Joe would be fine, he would be fine, and neither of us knew if he would.

Joe was carried into the first-aid room, the door closing behind him, but presently the doctor came out with kindness and told Joe's wife they would be sending him to the hospital as soon as an outside ambulance could be brought.

'You can come in and sit with him, if you like,' he said to her, and to me added, 'You'd better come in too, hadn't you?'

I went in and he checked me over, and said, 'What aren't you telling me?'

'Nothing.'

'I know you,' he said. 'And everywhere I touch you, you stifle a wince.'

'Ouch, then,' I said.

'Where is ouch?'

'Ankle, mostly.'

He pulled my boot off and I said 'ouch' quite loudly but, as I'd believed, there were no cracked bits. He said to get some strapping and some rest, and added that I could ride on Monday, if I could walk and if I were mad enough.

He went back to tending Joe, and one of the nurses answered a knock on the door, coming back to tell me that I was wanted outside. I put my boot on again, ran my fingers through my hair and went out, to find Litsi and Danielle there, waiting.

Litsi had his arm round Danielle's shoulders, and Danielle looked as if this were the last place on earth she wanted to be.

I was aware of my dishevelled state, of the limp I couldn't help, of the grass stains and the tear in my breeches down my left thigh.

Litsi took it all in, and I smiled at him slightly.

'The nitty gritty,' I said.

'So I see.' He looked thoughtful. 'Aunt Casilia sent us to see ... how you were.'

It had taken a great deal of courage, I thought, for Danielle to be there, to face what might have happened again as it had happened in January. I said to Litsi, but with my eyes on Danielle, 'Please tell her I'm all right. I'll be riding on Monday.'

'How can you ride?' Danielle said intensely.

'Sit in the saddle, put the feet in the stirrups, pick up the reins.'

'Don't be damn stupid. How can you joke ... and don't answer that. I know both the answers. Easily or with difficulty, whichever is funnier.'

She suddenly couldn't help laughing, but it was partly hysterical, and it was against Litsi's big shoulder she smothered her face.

'I'll come up to the box,' I said to him, and he nodded, but before they could leave, the first-aid room door opened and Joe's wife came out.

'Kit,' she said with relief, seeing me still there. 'I've got to go to the ladies ... my stomach's all churning up ... they say I can go to the hospital with Joe but if they come for him while I'm not here, they may take him without me ... Will you wait here and tell them? Don't let him go without me.'

'I'll see to it,' I said.

She said 'thanks' faintly and half ran in the direction of relief, and Danielle, her eyes stretched wide, said, 'But that's ... just like me. Is her husband ... hurt badly?'

'It's too soon to tell, I think.'

'How can she stand it?'

'I don't know,' I said. 'I really don't know. It's much simpler from Joe's side ... and mine.'

'I'll go and see if she needs help,' Danielle said abruptly, and, leaving Litsi's shelter, set off after Joe's wife.

'Seriously,' Litsi said, watching her go, 'how can you joke?'

'Seriously? Seriously not about Joe, nor about his wife, but about myself, why not?'

'But . . . is it worth it?'

I said, 'If you could paint as you'd like to, would you put up with a bit of discomfort?'

He smiled, his eyebrows rising. 'Yes, I would.'

'Much the same thing,' I said. 'Fulfilment.'

We stood in a backwater of the racecourse, with the stands and bustle out in the mainstream, gradually moving towards the next race. Dusty arrived at a rush, his eyes searching, suspicious.

'I've wrenched my ankle,' I said. 'You'll have to get Jamie for the fifth race, I know he's free. But I'm cleared for Monday. Is Helikon all right?'

He nodded briskly a couple of times and departed, wasting no words.

Litsi said, 'It's a wonder you're not worse. It looked atrocious. Aunt Casilia was watching through binoculars, and she was very concerned until she saw you stand up. She said then that you accepted the risks and one had to expect these things from time to time.'

'She's right,' I said.

He, in the sober suiting of civilization, looked at the marks of the earth on the princess's colours, looked at my torn green-stained breeches, and at the leg I was putting no weight on.

'How do you face it, over and over again?' he said. He saw my lips twitch and added, 'Easily or with difficulty, whichever is funnier.'

I laughed. 'I never expect it, for a start. It's always an unpleasant surprise.'

'And now that it's happened, how do you deal with it?'

'Think about something else,' I said. 'Take a lot of aspirins and concentrate on getting back as soon as possible. I don't like other jockeys loose on my horses, like now. I want to be on them. When I've taught them and know them, they're mine.'

'And you like winning.'

'Yes, I like winning.'

The hospital ambulance arrived only moments before Danielle and Joe's wife returned, and Litsi, Danielle and I stood with Joe's wife while Joe was transferred. He was still half-conscious, still groaning, looking grey. The ambulance men helped his wife into the interior in his wake, and we had a final view of her face, young and frightened, looking back at us, before they closed the doors and drove slowly away.

Litsi and Danielle looked at me, and I looked at them; and there was nothing to say, really.

Litsi put his arm again round Danielle's shoulders, and they turned and walked away; and I hobbled off and showered and changed my clothes after just another fall, in just a day in a working life.

When I went out of the weighing room to go to the princess's box, Maynard Allardeck stepped into my way. He was looking, as always, splendidly tailored, the total English gentleman from Lock's hat to hand-sewn shoes. He wore a silk striped tie and pigskin gloves, and his eyes were as near madness as I'd ever seen them.

I stopped, my spirits sinking.

Outside the weighing room, where we stood, there was a covered verandah with three wide steps leading down to the area used for unsaddling the first four in every race. There was a tarmac path across the grass there, giving access to the rest of the paddock.

The horses from the fifth race had been unsaddled and led away, and there was a scatter of people about, but not a crowd.

Maynard stood between me and the steps, and to avoid him I would have to edge sideways and round him.

'*Fielding*,' he said with intensity; and he wasn't simply addressing me by name, he was using the word as a curse, in the way the Allardecks had used it for vengeful generations. He was cursing my ancestry and my existence, the feudal spite like bile in his mouth, the irrational side of his hatred for me well in command.

He overtopped me by about four inches and out-weighed me by fifty pounds, but he was twenty years older and unfit. Without the complication of a sprained ankle, I could have dodged him easily, but as it was, when I took a step sideways, so did he.

'Mr Allardeck,' I said neutrally, 'Princess Casilia's expecting me.'

He gave no sign of hearing, but when I took another sideways step he didn't move. Nor did he move when I went past him, but two steps further on, at the top of the steps, I received a violent shove between the shoulders.

Unbalanced, I fell stumbling down the three steps, landing in a sprawl on the tarmac path. I rolled, half expecting Maynard to jump down on me, but he was standing on the top step, staring, and as I watched, he turned away, took three paces and attached himself to a small group of similar-looking men.

A trainer I sometimes rode for, who happened to be near, put a hand under my elbow and helped me to my feet.

'He pushed you,' he said incredulously. 'I saw it. I can't believe it. That man stepped right behind you and pushed.'

I stood on one leg and brushed off some of the debris from the path. 'Thanks,' I said.

'But he pushed you! Aren't you going to complain?'
'Who to?'

'But Kit . . .' He slowly took stock of the situation. 'That's Maynard Allardeck.'

'Yeah.'

'But he can't go around attacking you. And you've hurt your leg.'

'He didn't do that,' I said. 'That's from a fall in the third race.'

'That was some mess...' He looked at me doubtfully. 'If you want to complain, I'll say what I saw.'

I thanked him again and said I wouldn't bother, which he still found inexplicable. I glanced briefly at Maynard who by then had his back to me as if unaware of my presence, and with perturbation set off again towards the princess's box.

The push itself had been a relatively small matter, but as Maynard was basically murderous, it had to be taken as a substitute killing, a relief explosion, a jet of steam to stop the top blowing off the volcano.

The film, I thought uneasily, would keep that volcano in check; and I supposed I could put up with the jets of steam if I thought of them as safety valves reducing his boiling pressure. I didn't want him uncontrollably erupting. I'd rather fall down more steps; but I would also be more careful where I walked.

The princess was out on the balcony when I reached her box, huddled into her furs, and alone.

I went out there to join her, and found her gazing blind-eyed over the racecourse, her thoughts obviously unwelcome.

'Princess,' I said.

She turned her head, her eyes focusing on my face.

'Don't give up,' I said.

'No.' She stretched her neck and her backbone as if to disclaim any thought of it. 'Is Helikon all right?' she asked.

'Dusty said so.'

'Good.' She sighed. 'Have you any idea what's running next week? It's all a blank in my mind.'

It was a fair blank in mine also. 'Icefall goes on Thursday at Lingfield.'

'How did Helikon fall?' she asked, and I told her that it wasn't her horse's fault, he'd been brought down.

'He was going well at the time,' I said. 'He's growing up and getting easier to settle. I'll school him next week one morning to get his confidence back.'

She showed a glimmer of pleasure in an otherwise unpleasurable day. She didn't ask directly after my state of health, because she never did: she considered the results of falls to lie within the domain of my personal privacy into which she wouldn't intrude. It was an attitude stemming from her own habit of reticence and, far from minding it, I valued it. It was fussing I couldn't stand.

We went inside for some tea, joining Danielle, Litsi and Beatrice, and presently Lord Vaughnley appeared on one of his more or less regular visits to the princess's box.

His faint air of anxiety vanished when he saw me drinking there, and after a few minutes he managed to cut me off from the pack and steer me into a corner.

I thanked him for his packet of yesterday.

'What? Oh yes, my dear chap, you're welcome. But that's not what I wanted to say to you, not at all. I'm afraid there's been a bit of a leak ... it's all very awkward.'

'What sort of leak?' I asked, puzzled.

'About the film you made of Maynard Allardeck.'

I felt my spine shiver. I desperately needed that film to remain secret.

'I'm afraid,' Lord Vaughnley said, 'that Allardeck knows you sent a copy of it to the Honours people in Downing Street. He knows he will never again be considered for a knighthood, because of your sending it.' He smiled half anxiously but couldn't resist the journalistic summary: 'Never Sir Maynard, never Lord Allardeck, thanks to Kit Fielding.'

'How in hell's teeth did he find out?' I demanded.

'I don't know,' Lord Vaughnley said uncomfortably. 'Not from me, my dear fellow, I assure you. I've never told anyone. But sometimes there are whispers of these things. Someone in the civil service ... don't you know.'

I looked at him in dismay. 'How long has he known?' I said.

'I think since sometime last week.' He shook his head unhappily. 'I heard about it this morning in a committee meeting of the charity of which Allardeck and I are both directors. He's chairman, of course. The civil service charity, you remember.'

I remembered. It was through good works for the

sick and needy dependants of civil servants that Maynard had tried hardest to climb to his knighthood.

'No one in the charity has seen the film, have they?' I asked urgently.

'No, no, my dear fellow. They've simply heard it exists. One of them apparently asked Allardeck if he knew anything about it.'

Oh God, I thought; how leaks could trickle through cracks.

'I thought you'd better know,' Lord Vaughnley said. 'And don't forget I've as strong an interest in that film as you have. If it's shown all over the place, we'll have lost our lever.'

'Maynard will have lost his saintly reputation.'

'He might operate without it.'

'The only copies,' I said, 'are the ones I gave to you and to the Honours people, and the three I have in the bank. Unless you or the Honours people show them . . . I can't believe they will,' I said explosively. 'They were all so hush-hush.'

'I thought I should warn you.'

'I'm glad you did.'

It explained so much, I thought, about Maynard's recent behaviour. Considering how he must be seething with fury, just pushing me down the steps showed amazing restraint.

But then . . . I did still have the film, and so far it hadn't been shown to a wider audience, and Maynard really wouldn't want it shown, however much he had lost through it already.

Lord Vaughnley apologized to the princess for monopolizing her jockey, and asked if I was still interested in more information regarding Nanterre.

'Yes, please,' I said, and he nodded and said it was still flickering through computers, somewhere.

'Trouble?' Litsi asked at my elbow, when Lord Vaughnley had gone.

'Allardeck trouble, not Nanterre.' I smiled lopsidedly. 'The Fieldings have had Allardeck trouble for centuries. Nanterre's much more pressing.'

We watched the last race, on my part without concentration, and in due course returned to the cars, Litsi and Danielle, deserting the Rolls, saying they were coming with me.

On the walk from the box to the car park, I stopped a few times to take the weight off my foot. No one made a remark, but when we arrived at my car, Danielle said positively, 'I'm driving. You can tell me the way.'

'You don't need a left foot with automatic transmission,' I pointed out.

'I'm driving,' she said fiercely. 'I've driven your car before.' She had, on a similar occasion.

I sat in the passenger seat without more demur, and asked her to stop at a chemist's shop a short distance along the road.

'What do you need?' she said brusquely, pulling up. 'I'll get it.'

'Some strapping, and mineral water.'

'Aspirin?'

'There's some here in the glove compartment.'

She went with quick movements into the shop and returned with a paper bag which she dumped on my lap.

'I'll tell you the scenario,' she said to Litsi with a sort of suppressed violence as she restarted the car and set off towards London. 'He'll strap his own ankle and sit with it surrounded by icepacks to reduce the swelling. He'll have hoof-shaped bruises that'll be black by tomorrow, and he'll ache all over. He won't want you to notice he can't put that foot on the ground without pain shooting up his leg. If you ask him how he feels, he'll say "with every nerve ending". He doesn't like sympathy. Injuries embarrass him and he'll do his best to ignore them.'

Litsi said, when she paused, 'You must know him very well.'

It silenced Danielle. She was driving with the same throttled anger, and took a while to relax.

I swallowed some aspirins with the mineral water and thought about what she'd said. And Litsi was right, I reflected: she did truly know me. She unfortunately sounded as if she wished she didn't.

'Kit, you never did tell me,' Litsi said after a while, 'why it annoyed Maynard Allardeck so much when the

267

princess said her horses always jumped well at Sandown. Why on earth should that anger anyone?'

'Modesty forbids me to tell you,' I said, smiling.

'Well, have a try.'

'She was paying me a compliment which Maynard didn't want to hear.'

'Do you mean it's because of your skill that her horses jump well?'

'Experience,' I said. 'Something like that.'

'He's obsessed,' Litsi said.

He was dangerous, I thought: and there was such a thing as contract killing, by persons unknown, which I didn't like the thought of very much. To remove the mind from scary concepts, I asked Danielle if she'd managed to tell Beatrice that Monday was her last evening stint.

Danielle, after a lengthy pause, said that no, she hadn't.

'I wish you would,' I said, alarmed. 'You said you would.'

'I can't tell her . . . What if Nanterre turns up and shoots you?'

'He won't,' I said. 'But if we don't catch him . . .' I paused. 'The princess told me today that if Roland signs the arms contract to save us all, he will literally die of shame. He wouldn't want to go on living. She's extremely worried that he'll give in . . . she loves him . . . she wants him alive. So we've got to stop Nanterre; and stop him soon.'

Danielle didn't answer for two or three miles, and it was Litsi eventually who broke the silence.

'I'll tell Beatrice,' he said firmly.

'No,' Danielle protested.

'Last night,' I said, 'Nanterre killed another of the princess's horses. The princess doesn't want Roland to know . . . or Beatrice, who would tell him.'

They both exclaimed in distress.

'No wonder she's been so sad,' Litsi said. 'It wasn't just Helikon falling.'

'Which horse?' Danielle asked.

'Col,' I said. 'The one I rode at Ascot.'

'That didn't quite win?' Litsi asked.

'Yes,' Danielle said. 'Her Gold Cup horse.' She swallowed. 'If Litsi tells Beatrice Monday's my last day, I won't deny it.'

We spent another slightly claustrophobic evening in the house. Roland came down to dinner, and conversation was a trifle stilted owing to everyone having to remember what was not known and shouldn't be said.

Litsi managed to tell Beatrice positively but naturally that the last time I would be fetching Danielle at night would be Monday, as Danielle would no longer be working in the evenings, a piece of news which surprised the princess greatly.

Beatrice took in the information satisfactorily, with

her eyes sliding my way, and one could almost see the cogs clicking as she added the hour to the place.

I wondered if she understood the nature of what I hoped she was going to arrange. She seemed to have no doubts or compunction about laying an ambush which would remove me from her path; but, of course, she didn't know about the attack on Litsi or about Col's death, which we couldn't tell her because either she would instantly apply breaking-point pressure to her brother by informing him, or she would suffer renewed pangs of remorse and not set up the ambush at all.

Beatrice was a real wild card, I thought, who could win us or lose us the game.

Nanterre again didn't telephone; and there had been no one all day asking about a Bradbury reward.

The advertisements had been prominent in the racing papers for two days, and noticeable in the *Towncrier*, but either the message-bearer hadn't seen them or hadn't thought answering worth while.

Well, I thought in disappointment, going a little painfully to bed, it had seemed a good idea at the time, as Eve no doubt told Adam after the apple.

Dawson buzzed through on the intercom before seven on Sunday morning. Phone call, he said.

Not again, I thought: Christ, not again.

I picked up the receiver with the most fearful foreboding, trying hard not to shake.

'Look here,' a voice said, 'this message from Danielle. I don't want any trouble, but is this reward business straight up?'

CHAPTER SEVENTEEN

'Yes,' I said, dry-mouthed, 'it is.'

'How much then?'

I took a deep breath, hardly believing, my heart thumping.

'Quite a lot,' I said. 'It depends how much you can tell me . . . I'd like to come and see you.'

'Don't know about that,' he said grudgingly.

'The reward would be bigger,' I said. 'And I'd bring it with me.' Breathing was easier. My hands had stopped trembling.

'I don't want any trouble,' he said.

'There won't be any. You tell me where you'll meet me, and I'll come.'

'What's your name?' he demanded.

I hesitated fractionally. 'Christmas,' I said.

'Well, Mr Christmas, I'm not meeting you for less than a hundred quid.' He was belligerent, suspicious and cautious, all in one.

'All right,' I said slowly. 'I agree.'

'Up front, on the table,' he said.

'Yes, all right.'

'And if I tell you what you want to hear, you'll double it.'

'If you tell me the truth, yes.'

'Huh,' he said sourly. 'Right then . . . you're in London, aren't you? That's a London number.'

'Yes.'

'I'll meet you in Bradbury,' he said. 'In the town, not the racecourse. You get to Bradbury by twelve o'clock, I'll meet you in the pub there . . . the King's Head, half way along the High Street.'

'I'll be there,' I said. 'How will I know you?'

He thought, breathing heavily. 'I'll take the *Sporting Life* with your ad in it.'

'And . . . er . . . what's your name?' I asked.

He had the answer to that question all ready. 'John Smith,' he said promptly. 'I'll see you, then, Mr Christmas. OK?'

'OK,' I said.

He disconnected and I lay back on the pillows feeling more apprehensive than delighted. The fish, I thought, hadn't sounded securely on the hook. He'd nibbled at the bait, but was full of reservations. I just hoped to hell he'd turn up where and when he'd said, and that he'd be the right man if he did.

His accent had been country English, not broad, just the normal local speech of Berkshire which I heard every day in Lambourn. He hadn't seemed over-bright

273

or cunning, and the amount he'd asked for, I thought, revealed a good deal about his income and his needs.

Large reward... When I hadn't objected to one hundred, he'd doubled it to two. But to him, two hundred equated large.

He was a gambler: Litsi had described him as having a sporting paper, a form book and binoculars. What was now certain was that he gambled small, a punter to whom a hundred was a substantial win. I supposed I should be glad he didn't think of a hundred as a basic stake: a large reward to someone like that might have been a thousand.

Thankfully I set about the business of getting up, which on the mornings after a crunch was always slow and twingy. The icepacks from bedtime had long melted, but the puffball my ankle had swollen to on the previous afternoon had definitely contracted. I took the strapping off, inspected the blackening bruising, and wrapped it up again snugly; and I could still get my shoe on, which was lucky.

In trousers, shirt and sweater I went down by lift to the basement and nicked more ice cubes from the fridge, fastening them into plastic bags and wedging them down inside my sock. Dawson appeared in his dressing-gown to see what was going on in his kitchen and merely raised his eyebrows much as he had the evening before when I'd pinched every ice cube in the house.

'Did I do right,' he asked, watching, 'putting that phone call through to you?'

'You certainly did.'

'He said it was to do with the advertisement: he said he was in a hurry as he was using a public telephone.'

'Was he?' I pushed the trouser leg down over the loaded sock, feeling the chill strike deep through the strapping.

'Yes,' Dawson said. 'I could hear the pips. Don't you give yourself frostbite, doing that?'

'Never have, yet.'

Breakfast, he said a shade resignedly, would be ready in the morning room in half an hour, and I thanked him and spent the interval waking up Litsi, who said bleary-eyed that he was unaccustomed to life before ten on Sunday mornings.

'We've had a tug on the line,' I explained, and told him about John Smith.

'Are you sure it isn't Nanterre setting a trap?' Litsi said, waking up thoroughly. 'Don't forget, Nanterre could have seen that advertisement too. He could be reeling *you* in, not the other way round ... I suppose you did think of that?'

'Yes, I did. But I think John Smith is genuine. If he'd been a trap, he would've been different, more positive.'

He frowned. 'I'll come with you,' he said.

I shook my head. 'I'd like your company but Sammy has the day off because we're all here, and if we both go ...'

275

'All right,' he said. 'But don't go onto balconies. How's your ankle? Or am I not supposed to ask?'

'Half way to normal,' I said. 'Danielle exaggerates.'

'Not so much.' He rubbed a hand through his hair. 'Have you enough cash for John Smith?'

'Yes, in my house. I'll go there on the way. I'll be back here this afternoon, sometime.'

'All being well,' he said dryly.

I drove to Lambourn after a particularly thorough inspection of the car. It was still possible that John Smith was a trap, though on balance I didn't believe it. Nanterre couldn't have found an actor to convey the subtleties in John Smith's attitudes, nor could he himself possibly have imitated the voice. John Smith might be someone trying to snatch the reward without any goods to deliver; he might be a fraud, I thought, but not a deadly danger.

My house felt cold and empty. I opened all the letters that had accumulated there since Monday, took the ones that mattered, and dumped the junk into the dustbin along with several unread newspapers. I leafed through the present Sunday's papers and found two or three mentions, both as general news stories and as special paragraphs on the sports pages, about Col being shot. All the stories recalled Cascade and Cotopaxi, but raised no great questions of *why*, and said *who* was still a complete mystery. I hadn't seen Beatrice reading any English newspaper since she'd arrived, and just hoped to hell she wouldn't start that morning.

I collected a few things to take with me; clean clothes, the cash, some writing paper, a pocket-sized tape recorder, spare cassettes and a few photographs sorted from a disorganized drawerful.

I also loaded into the car the video-recorder I'd used to make parts of the film indicting Maynard, and some spare tapes and batteries for that, but more on an 'in case' basis than with any clear plans for their use: and I picked up from the kitchen, where I kept it, a small gadget I'd bought in New York that started cars from a distance. It worked by radio, transmitting to a receiver in the car which then switched on the ignition and activated the starter-motor. I liked gadgets, and that one was most useful in freezing weather, since one could start one's car from indoors and warm up the engine before plunging out into snowstorms oneself.

I checked my answering machine for messages and dealt with those, repacked my sock with new ice cubes and finally set off again to Bradbury, arriving in the small country town with ten minutes in hand.

The King's Head, I found, was a square smallish brick building, relatively modern and dedicated to beer. No old world charm, no warming pans, oak beams, red lampshades, pewter mugs: no car park either. The Bradbury Arms, across the road, looked plentifully supplied with everything.

I parked in the street and went into the King's Head

public bar, trying that first, and finding a darts board, several benches, low tables, sisal matting and an under-stocked bar.

No customers.

I tried the saloon bar, genteelly furnished with glass-topped tables and moderately comfortable wooden armchairs, in one of which I sat while I waited.

A man appeared behind the bar there and asked what I'd like.

'Half of mild,' I said.

He pulled it, and I paid.

I laid on the glass-topped table in front of me the large brown envelope which contained Lord Vaughn-ley's file photograph of Nanterre. The envelope currently bulged also with the tape recorder, four more photographs, two bundles of banknotes in small separate envelopes and some plain writing paper. All that I needed for John Smith was ready, but there was no sign of John Smith.

A few local people well known to the innkeeper came into the bar, ordering 'the usual' and eying me, the stranger. None of them carried a newspaper. None of them, I noticed with surprise, was a woman.

I could hear the thud . . . thud . . . thud of someone playing darts in the public bar, so I picked up my envelope and beer and walked back there to look.

There were three customers by that time; two playing darts and one sitting on the edge of a bench glancing at his watch.

Beside him on the bench lay Saturday's *Sporting Life*, the bold-printed advertisement uppermost.

With a great sigh of relief I went over and sat down on the bench, leaving the newspaper between him and me.

'Mr Smith?' I said.

He jumped nervously, even though he'd watched me walk across to join him.

He was perhaps in his fifties, wore a zip-fronted fawn jacket and had an air of habitual defeat. His hair, still black, was brushed in careful lines across a balding scalp, and the tip of his nose pointed straight downwards, as if someone had punched it that way long ago.

'My name's Christmas,' I said.

He looked at me carefully and frowned. 'I know you, don't I?'

'Maybe,' I said. 'I brought your money . . . Would you like a drink?'

'I'll get it,' he said. He stood up with alacrity to go over to the bar, and from that distance studied me doubtfully. I put a hand into the big envelope, switched on the tape recorder, and drew out the first of the packets of money, laying it on the table beside my glass.

He came back at length with a pint and drank a third of it thirstily.

'Why are you limping?' he said, putting the glass down watchfully.

'Twisted my ankle.'

'You're that jockey,' he said. 'Kit Fielding.'

I could feel alarm vibrating in him at the identification and I pushed the money towards him, to anchor him, to prevent flight.

'A hundred,' I said, 'up front.'

'It wasn't my fault,' he said in a rush, half aggressively, on the defensive.

'No, I know that. Take the money.'

He stretched out a big-knuckled hand, picked up the booty, checked it, and slotted it into an internal pocket.

'Tell me what happened,' I said.

He wasn't ready, however. The unease, cause and effect, had to be dealt with first.

'Look, I don't want this going any further,' he said nervously. 'I've been in two minds . . . I saw this advertisement Friday . . . but, look, see, by rights I shouldn't have been at the races. I'm telling you I was there, but I don't want it going no further.'

'Mm,' I said non-committally.

'But, see, I could do with some untaxed dosh, who couldn't? So I thought, maybe if it was worth two hundred to you, I'd tell you.'

'The rest's in here,' I said, pointing to the brown envelope. 'Just . . . tell me what happened.'

'Look, I was supposed to be at work. I made out I'd got flu. I wouldn't get fired if the bosses found out, just a dressing down, but I don't want the wife knowing, see what I mean? She thought I was at work. I went home my regular time. She'd bellyache something chronic if she knew. She's dead set against gambling, see what I mean?'

'And you,' I said, 'like your little flutter.'

'Nothing wrong in that, is there?' he demanded.

'No,' I said.

'The wife doesn't know I'm here,' he said. 'This isn't my local. I told her I had to come into Bradbury for a part for my motor. I'm draining the sump and I need a new filter. I'll have to keep quiet about meeting you, see? I had to ring you up this morning while I was out with the dog. So, see what I mean, I don't want this getting about.'

I thought without guilt of my sharp-eared little recorder, but reflected that Mr Smith's gusher would dry in a micro-second if he found it was there. He seemed, however, not the sort of man who would ever suspect its existence.

'I'm sure it won't get about, Mr Smith,' I said.

He jumped again slightly at the name.

'See, the name's not Smith, I expect you guessed. But well, if you don't know, I'm that much safer, see what I mean?'

'Yes,' I said.

He drank most of the beer and wiped his mouth with a handkerchief; white with brown lines and checks round the edge. The two men playing darts finished their game and went out to the saloon bar, leaving us alone in our spartan surroundings.

'I'd been looking at the horses in the paddock,' he

said, 'and I was going off towards the bookies when this character came up to me and offered me a fiver to deliver a message.'

'A fiver,' I said.

'Yeah ... well, see what I mean, I said, "Ten, and you're on." ' He sniffed. 'He wasn't best pleased. He gave me a right filthy look, but in the end he coughed up. Ten smackers. It meant I'd be betting free on that race, see what I mean?'

'Yes,' I said.

'So he says, this character, that all I'd got to do was walk over to a man he would point out, and tell him that Danielle wanted him to go up to the balcony to see the view.'

'He said that precisely?'

'He made me repeat it twice. Then he gave me two fivers and pointed at a big man in a dark overcoat, very distinguished looking, and when I turned round, he'd gone. Anyway, he paid me to pass on the message, so I did. I didn't think anything of it, see what I mean?' I mean, there didn't seem any harm in it. I knew the balcony wasn't open, but if he wanted to go up there, so what, see what I mean?'

'I can see that,' I said.

'I passed on the message, and the distinguished looking gent thanked me, and I went on out to the bookies and put two fivers on Applejack.'

Mr Smith was a loser, I thought. I'd beaten Applejack into second place, on Pinkeye.

'You're not drinking,' he observed, eying my still full glass.

Beer was fattening . . . 'You can have it,' I said, 'if you like.'

He took the glass without ado and started on the contents.

'Look,' he said. 'You'd better tell me . . . was it the man I gave the message to, who fell off the balcony?' His eyes were worried, almost pleading for any answer but the one he feared.

'I'm afraid so,' I said.

'I thought it would be. I didn't see him fall, I was out front with the bookies, see what I mean? But later on, here and there, I heard people talking about coats and such . . . I didn't know what they were on about, though, until the next day, when it was all in the paper.' He shook his head. 'I couldn't say anything, though, could I, on account of being at the races when I'd said I wasn't.'

'Difficult,' I agreed.

'It wasn't my fault he fell off the balcony,' he said aggrievedly. 'So I thought, what was the point of telling anyone about the message. I'd keep my mouth shut. Maybe this Danielle pushed him, I thought. Maybe he was her husband and her lover got me to send him up there, so she could push him off. See what I mean?'

I stifled a smile and saw what he meant.

'I didn't want to be mixed up with the police, see? I

mean, he wasn't killed, thanks to you, so no harm done, was there?'

'No,' I said. 'And he wasn't pushed. He overbalanced on some loose planks the builders had left there. He told me about it, explaining how he'd fallen.'

'Oh.' Mr Anonymous Smith seemed both relieved and disappointed that he hadn't been involved in an attempted crime of passion. 'I see.'

'But,' I said, 'he was curious about the message. He thought he'd like to know who asked you to give it to him, so we decided to put that advertisement in the paper.'

'Do you know him then?' he said, perplexed.

'I do now,' I said.

'Ah.' He nodded.

'The man who gave you the message,' I said, casually, 'do you remember what he looked like?'

I tried not to hold my breath. Mr Smith, however, sensed that this was a crucial question and looked meaningfully at the envelope, his mind on the second instalment.

'The second hundred's yours,' I said, 'if you can describe him.'

'He wasn't English,' he said, taking the plunge. 'Strong sort of character, hard voice, big nose.'

'Do you remember him clearly?' I asked, relaxing greatly inside. 'Would you know him again?'

'I've been thinking about him since Thursday,' he said simply. 'I reckon I would.'

Without making a big thing of it I pulled the five photographs out of the envelope: all eight by ten black and white glossy pictures of people receiving trophies after races. In four of the groups the winning jockey was Fielding, but I'd had my back to the camera in two of them: the pictures were as fair a test as I'd been able to devise at short notice.

'Would you look at these photographs,' I said, 'and see if he's there?'

He brought out a pair of glasses and sat them on the flattened nose: an ineffectual man, not unhappy.

He took the photographs, and looked at them carefully, one by one. I'd put Nanterre's picture in fourth place of the five; and he glanced at it and passed on. He looked at the fifth and put them all down on the table, and I hoped he wouldn't guess at the extent of my disappointment.

'Well,' he said judiciously, 'yes, he's there.'

I watched him breathlessly and waited. If he could truly recognize Nanterre, I would play any game he had in mind.

'Look,' he said, as if scared by his own boldness. 'You're Kit Fielding, right? You're not short of a bob or two. And that man who fell, he looked pretty well heeled. See what I mean? Make it two fifty, and I'll tell you which one he is.'

I breathed deeply and pretended to be considering it with reluctance.

'All right,' I said eventually. 'Two fifty.'

285

He flicked through the photographs and pointed unerringly to Nanterre.

'Him,' he said.

'You've got your two fifty,' I said. I gave him the second of the small envelopes. 'There's a hundred in there.' I fished out my wallet and sorted out fifty more. 'Thanks,' I said.

He nodded and put the money away carefully, as before.

'Mr Smith,' I said easily. 'What would you do for another hundred?'

He stared at me through the glasses. 'What do you mean?' Hopefully, on the whole.

I said, 'If I write a sentence on a sheet of paper, will you sign your name to it? The name John Smith will do very well.'

'What sentence?' he said, looking worried again.

'I'll write it,' I said. 'Then see if you will sign.'

'For a hundred?'

'That's right.'

I pulled a sheet of plain writing paper from the envelope, unclipped my pen and wrote:

'At Bradbury races (I put the date) I gave a man a message to the effect that Danielle wanted him to go up to the viewing balcony. I identify the man who gave me that message as the man I have indicated in the photograph.'

I handed it to Mr Smith. He read it. He was unsure of the consequences of signing, but he was thinking of a hundred pounds.

'Sign it John Smith?' he said.

'Yes. With a flourish, like a proper signature.'

I handed him my pen. With almost no further hesitation he did as I'd asked.

'Great,' I said, taking the page and slipping it, with the photographs, back into the envelope. I took out my wallet again and gave him another hundred pounds, and saw him looking almost hungrily at the money he could see I still had.

'There's another hundred and fifty in there,' I said, showing him. 'It would round you up to five hundred altogether.'

He liked the game increasingly. He said, 'For that, what would you want?'

'To save me following you home,' I said pleasantly, 'I'd like you to write your real name and address down for me, on a separate sheet of paper.'

I produced a clean sheet from the envelope. 'You still have my pen,' I reminded him. 'Be a good fellow and write.'

He looked as if I'd punched him in the brain.

'I came in on the bus,' he said faintly.

'I can follow buses,' I said.

He looked sick.

'I won't tell your wife you were at the races,' I said.

'Not if you'll write down your name so I won't have to follow you.'

'For a hundred and fifty?' he said weakly.

'Yes.'

He wrote a name and address in capital letters:

A. V. Hodges,
44, Carleton Avenue,
Widderlawn, nr Bradbury.

'What does the A. V. stand for?' I asked.

'Arnold Vincent,' he said without guile.

'OK,' I said. 'Here's the rest of the money.' I counted it out for him. 'Don't lose it all at once.'

He looked startled and then shamefacedly raised a laugh. 'I can't go racing often, see what I mean? My wife knows how much money I've got.'

'She doesn't now,' I said cheerfully. 'Thank you very much, Mr Smith.'

CHAPTER EIGHTEEN

I had plenty of time and thought I might as well make sure. I dawdled invisibly around while John Smith bought his oil filter at a garage and caught his bus, and I followed the bus unobtrusively to Widderlawn.

John Smith descended and walked to Carleton Avenue where at number 44, a well-tended council semi-detached, he let himself in with a latchkey.

Satisfied on all counts, I drove back to London and found Litsi coming out of the library as I entered the hall.

'I saw you coming,' he said lazily. The library windows looked out to the street. 'I'm delighted you're back.' He had been watching for me, I thought.

'It wasn't a trap,' I said.

'So I see.'

I smiled suddenly and he said, 'A purring cat, if ever I saw one.'

I nodded towards the library. 'Let's go in there, and I'll tell you.'

I carried the bag with clothes in and the big envelope

into the long panelled room with its grille-fronted bookshelves, its Persian rugs, its net and red velvet curtains. A nobly proportioned room, it was chiefly used for entertaining callers not intimate enough to be invited upstairs, and to me had the lifeless air of expensive waiting rooms.

Litsi looked down at my feet. 'Are you *squelching*?' he asked disbelievingly.

'Mm.' I put down the bag and the envelope and peeled off my left shoe, into which one of the icepacks had leaked.

To his discriminating horror, I pulled the one intact bag out of my sock and emptied the contents onto a convenient potted plant. The second bag, having emptied itself, followed the first into the waste paper basket. I pulled off my drenched sock, left it folded on top of my bag, and replaced my wet shoe.

'I suppose,' Litsi said, 'all that started out as mobile refrigeration.'

'Quite right.'

'I'd have kept a sprain warm,' he said thoughtfully.

'Cold is quicker.'

I took the envelope over to where a pair of armchairs stood, one on each side of a table with a lamp on it: switched on the lamp, sat in a chair. Litsi, following, took the other armchair. The library itself was perpetually dark, needing lights almost always, the grey afternoon on that day giving up the contest in the folds of cream net at the street end of the room.

'Mr Smith,' I said, 'can speak for himself.'

I put the small recorder on the table, rewound the cassette, and started it going. Litsi, the distinguished looking gent, listened with wry fascination to the way he'd been set up, and towards the end his eyebrows started climbing, a sign with him which meant a degree of not understanding.

I showed him the paper John Smith had signed, and while he watched drew a circle with my pen round the head of Nanterre in the photograph.

'Mr Smith did live where he wrote,' I said. 'I did follow him home, to make sure.'

'But,' Litsi said surprised, 'if you followed him anyway, why did you give him the last hundred and fifty?'

'Oh ... mm ... it saved me having to discover his name from the neighbours.' Litsi looked sceptical. 'Well,' I said, 'he deserved it.'

'What are you going to do with these things?' he asked, waving a hand.

'With a bit of luck,' I said, 'this.' And I told him.

Grateful for the lift, I went up three floors to the bamboo room to stow away my gear, to shower and change, to put on dry strapping and decide on no more ice.

The palatial room was beginning to feel like home, I thought. Beatrice seemed to have given up plans for active invasion, though leaving me in no doubt about the strength of her feelings; and as my affection for the room grew, so did my understanding of her pique.

She wasn't in the sitting room when I went down for the evening; only Danielle and the princess, with Litsi pouring their drinks.

I bowed slightly to the princess, as it was the first time I'd seen her that day, and kissed Danielle on the cheek.

'Where have you been?' she asked neutrally.

'Fishing.'

'Did you catch anything?'

'Sharkbait,' I said.

She looked at me swiftly, laughingly, in the eyes, the old loving Danielle there and gone in a flash. I took the glass into which Litsi had poured a scant ounce of scotch and tried to stifle regret: and Beatrice walked into the room with round dazed eyes and stood vaguely in the centre as if not sure what to do next.

Litsi began to mix her drink the way she liked it: he'd have made a good king but an even better barman, I thought, liking him. Beatrice went across to the sofa where the princess was sitting and took the place beside her as if her knees had given way.

'There we are, Beatrice,' Litsi said with good humour, setting the red drink down on the low table in front of her. 'Dash of Worcestershire, twist of lemon.'

Beatrice looked at the drink unseeingly.

'Casilia,' she said, as if the words were hurting her throat, 'I have been such a fool.'

'My dear Beatrice . . .' the princess said.

Beatrice without warning started to cry, not silently but with 'Ohs' of distress that were close to groans.

The princess looked uncomfortable, and it was Litsi who came to Beatrice's aid with a large white handkerchief and comforting noises.

'Tell us what's troubling you,' he said, 'and surely we can help you.'

Beatrice wailed 'Oh' again with her open mouth twisted into an agonized circle, and pressed Litsi's handkerchief hard to her eyes.

'Do try to pull yourself together, Beatrice, dear,' the princess said with a touch of astringency. 'We can't help you until we know what's the matter.'

Beatrice's faintly theatrical paroxysm abated, leaving a real distress showing. The overbid for sympathy might have misfired, but the need for it existed.

'I can't help it,' she said, drying her eyes and blotting her mascara carefully, laying the folded edge of handkerchief flat over her lower eyelid and blinking her top lashes onto it, leaving tiny black streaks. No one in extremis, I thought, wiped their eyes so methodically.

'I've been such a fool,' she said.

'In what way, dear?' asked the princess, giving the unmistakable impression that she already thought her sister-in-law a fool in most ways most of the time.

'I . . . I've been talking to Henri Nanterre,' Beatrice said.

'When?' Litsi asked swiftly.

'Just now. Upstairs, in my room.'

Both he and I looked at the recording telephone which had remained silent. Neither Litsi nor I had lifted a receiver at the right time after all.

'You telephoned him?' Litsi said.

'Yes, of course.' Beatrice began to recover such wits as she had. 'Well, I mean . . .'

'What did he say,' Litsi asked, not pursuing it, 'that has so upset you?'

'I . . . I . . . He was so charming when he came to see me in Palm Beach, but I've been wrong . . . terribly wrong.'

'What did he say just now?' Litsi asked again.

'He said . . .' she looked at him a shade wildly, 'that he'd thought Roland would crack when you were nearly killed . . . he asked me why he hadn't. But I . . . I didn't know you'd been nearly killed. I said I hadn't heard anything about it, and I was sure Roland and Casilia hadn't, and he was furiously angry, *shouting* . . .' She shook her head. 'I had to hold the telephone away from my ear . . . he was hurting me.'

The princess was looking astounded and distressed.

'Litsi! What happened? You never said . . .'

'Henri boasted,' Beatrice said miserably, 'that he organized an accident for Litsi that would have brilliantly succeeded, except that this . . . this . . .' She didn't know what to call me, and contented herself in pointing. '*He* saved Litsi's life.' Beatrice gulped. 'I never thought . . . never ever . . . that he would do anything so *frightful* . . . that he would really *harm* anyone. And he said . . . he said . . . he thought Roland and Casilia wouldn't have wanted any more horses killed, and how had she reacted about her horse called Col . . . and when I told him I didn't know anything about it, he flew into a *rage* . . . He asked if Roland knew and I said I didn't know . . . he was shouting down the telephone . . . he was totally *furious* . . . he said he'd never thought that they would hold out so long . . . he said it was all taking too long and he would step up the pressure.'

Beatrice's shock was deep.

'He said the jockey was always in his way, blocking him, bringing in guards and recording telephones; so he would get rid of the jockey first. Then after that, Danielle would lose her beauty – and then no one would stop Roland signing. He said,' she added, her eyes round and dry again, 'I was to tell Roland what he'd threatened. I was to say he had telephoned here and I'd happened to answer.'

The princess, aghast but straight backed, said, 'I won't let you tell Roland anything, Beatrice.'

'Henri put the telephone down,' Beatrice said, 'and I sat there thinking he didn't mean it, he couldn't possibly spoil Danielle's face . . . she's my niece as well as Roland's . . . I wouldn't want that, not for all the money in the world ... I tried to make myself believe it was just a threat, but he did chase after her that evening, and he did kill the horses; he boasted of it ... and I didn't want to believe he had tried to kill Litsi ... to kill! ... it wasn't possible ... but he sounded so vicious ... I wouldn't have believed he could be like that.' She turned imploringly to the princess. 'I may have been foolish, but I'm not *wicked*, Casilia.'

I listened to the outpouring with profound disturbance. I didn't want her late-flowering remorse tangling the carefully-laid lines. I would much have preferred her purposefulness to remain strong and intact.

'Did you ring him back?' I asked.

Beatrice didn't like talking to me, and didn't answer until Litsi asked her the same question.

'I did,' she said passionately, asking for absolution, 'but he'd already gone.'

'Already?' Litsi asked.

Beatrice said in a much smaller voice, 'He'd said I couldn't reach him again at that number. He wasn't there half the time in any event. I mean ...'

'How many times have you talked to him?' Litsi asked mildly. 'And at what time of day?'

Beatrice hesitated but answered, 'Today and yesterday, at about six, and Thursday morning, and ...' she tried to remember, 'it must have been Wednesday evening at six, and Monday twice, after I'd found out ...' Her voice trailed away, the admission, half out, suddenly alarming her.

'Found out what?' Litsi asked without censure.

She said unhappily, 'The make and colour of Danielle's car. He wanted to know . . . I had no idea,' she suddenly wailed, 'that he meant to attack her. I couldn't believe it, when he said on the telephone . . . when he told Litsi . . . saying that young women shouldn't drive alone at night. Danielle,' she said beseechingly, turning to her, 'I'd never cause harm to you, ever.'

'But on Thursday you told him Danielle and I were going to Bradbury races,' Litsi commented.

'Yes, but he *asked* me to tell him things like that,' Beatrice said fiercely. 'He wanted to know the least little thing, every time. He asked what was happening . . . he said as it was important to me for him to succeed, I should help him with details, any details, however tiny.'

I said, in Litsi's unprovoking manner, 'To what extent was it important to you, Mrs Bunt?'

She was provoked all the same: glared at me and didn't answer.

Litsi rephrased the question, 'Did Henri promise you . . . perhaps a nice present . . . if he succeeded?'

Beatrice looked uncertainly at the princess, whose gaze was on the hands on her lap, whose face was severe. No blandishments on earth would have induced her to spy comprehensively for her host's, her brother's enemy, and she was trying hard, I imagined, not to show open disgust.

To Litsi, Beatrice said, self-excusingly, 'I have the de

Brescou trust fund, of course, but it's expensive to keep one's *position* in Palm Beach. My soirées, you know, just for fifty dear friends ... nothing large ... and my servants, just a married couple ... are barely *enough*, and Henri said ... Henri promised ...' She paused doubtfully.

'A million dollars?' Litsi suggested.

'No, no,' she protested, 'not so much. He said when the pistols were in production and when he'd made his first good arms deal, which would be in under a year, he thought, he would send a gift of two hundred and fifty thousand ... and a hundred thousand each year afterwards for three years. Not so very much ... but it would have made a useful difference to me, you see.'

A soirée for a hundred, I thought sardonically. A small rise in status among the comfortably rich. More than half a million dollars overall. One could see the difference with clarity.

'I didn't see any wrong in trying to persuade Roland,' she said. 'When I came over here I was certain I could do it and have Henri's lovely money to spend afterwards.'

'Did he give you a written contract?' I asked.

'No, of course not,' she said, forgetting she was speaking to me, 'but he promised. He's a *gentleman*.'

Even she, once she'd said it, could see that although Nanterre was many things from an aristocrat to an entrepreneur, a gentleman he was not.

'He promised,' she reiterated.

Beatrice seemed to be feeling better about things, as if full confession excused the sin.

I was anxious to know how much information she'd passed on before the dawn of realization and the consequent change of heart: a lot of good plans had gone down the drain if she hadn't relayed what we'd wanted.

'Mrs Bunt,' I said diffidently, 'if Henri Nanterre told you he was going to get rid of the jockey, did he say how? Or perhaps when? Or where?'

'No, he didn't,' she said promptly, looking at me with disfavour.

'But did you perhaps tell him where I'd be going, and when, in the way you told him about Danielle and Litsi?'

She simply stared at me. Litsi, understanding what I wanted to know, said, 'Beatrice, if you've told Nanterre where Kit might be vulnerable, you must tell us now, seriously you must.'

She looked at him defensively. 'It's because of him,' she meant me, 'that Roland hasn't agreed to Henri's plans. Roland told me so. So did *he*.' She jerked her head in my direction. 'He said it straight out at dinner . . . you heard him . . . that while he was here, Roland wouldn't sign. He has so much power . . . you all do what he says . . . If he hadn't been here, Henri said, it would all have been settled on the very first day, even before I got here. Everything's *his* fault. It was *he* who drove Henri to do all those awful things. It's because of *him* that I probably won't get my money.

299

So when Henri asked me if I could find out when and where the jockey would be alone ... well ... I said I would ... and I was glad to!'

'Aunt Beatrice!' Danielle exclaimed. 'How could you?'

'He has my room,' Beatrice said explosively. 'My *room*!'

There was a small intense silence. Then I said mildly, 'If you'd tell us what you told Henri Nanterre, then I wouldn't go there ... wherever.'

'You must tell us,' the princess said vehemently. 'If any harm comes to Kit because of you, Beatrice, you will never be received again either in this house or in the château.'

Beatrice looked stunned by this direst of threats.

'Moreover,' Litsi said in a tone loaded with strength, 'you are not my sister, my sister-in-law or my aunt. I have no family feeling for you. You gave information which might have led to my death. If you've done the same regarding Kit, which it appears you have, and Nanterre succeeds in killing him, you'll be guilty of conspiracy to murder, and I shall inform the police to that effect.'

Beatrice crumbled totally inside. It was all far more than she'd meant to involve herself in, and Litsi's threat sounded like the heavy tread of an unthinkable future of penal reckoning.

Beatrice said to Litsi with a touch of sullenness, 'I told Henri where he keeps his car, while he's here. This evening I told Henri that he'll be fetching Danielle for the last time tomorrow . . . that he goes round to his car at one-thirty in the morning . . . Henri said that was excellent . . . but then he talked about you at Bradbury . . . and the horses dying . . . and he started shouting, and I realized . . . how he'd used me.' Her face crumpled as if she would cry again but, perhaps sensing a universal lack of sympathy, she smothered the impulse and looked from one to the other of us, searching for pity.

Litsi was looking quietly triumphant, much as I was feeling myself. The princess however was shocked and wide-eyed.

'That dark mews!' she said, horrified. 'Kit, don't go down there.'

'No,' I assured her. 'I'll park somewhere else.' She relaxed, clearly satisfied by the simple solution, and Danielle looked at me broodingly, knowing I wouldn't.

I winked at her.

She almost laughed. 'How can you?' she said. 'How can you joke? Don't say it, don't say it . . . easily.'

The princess and Beatrice looked mystified but paid not much attention.

'Are you absolutely certain,' I said to Beatrice, 'that you can't get in touch with Nanterre again?'

'Yes, I am,' she said uncertainly, and looked nervously at Litsi. 'But . . . but . . .'

'But what, Beatrice?'

'He's going to telephone here this evening. He

wanted me to tell Roland about your accident and about Col being shot, and then he would find out if Roland was ready to sign ... and if not ...' She squirmed. 'I couldn't let him hurt Danielle. I couldn't!'

Her eyes seemed to focus on her untouched drink. She stretched out a scarlet-nailed much be-ringed hand and gave a good imitation of one fresh from the desert. The princess, hardly able to look at her sister-in-law, headed for the door, motioning with her hand for me to go with her.

I followed. She went into the dining room where dinner was laid and asked me to close the door, which I did.

She said, with intense worry, 'Nothing has changed, has it, because of what Beatrice has told us?'

'No,' I said, with a thankfulness she didn't hear.

'We can't go on and on. We can't risk Danielle's face. You can't risk that.' The dilemma was dreadful, as Nanterre had meant.

'No,' I said, 'I can't risk that. But give me until Tuesday. Don't let Monsieur know of the threats until then. We have a plan. We have a lever, but we need a stronger one. We'll get rid of Nanterre,' I promised, 'if you'll give us that time.'

'You and Litsi?'

'Yes.'

'Litsi was the man who fell from the balcony,' she said, wanting confirmation.

I nodded, and told her of the decoy message but not about finding the messenger.

'Dear heaven. Surely we must tell the police.'

'Wait until Tuesday,' I begged. 'We will then, if we have to.'

She agreed easily enough because police enquiries could lead to publicity; and I hoped for John Smith Arnold Vincent Hodges' sake that we wouldn't have to drop him into hot water with his wife.

I asked the princess if I could have ten minutes' private conversation with her husband that evening, and without more ado she whisked us both up in the lift and arranged it on the spot, saying it was a convenient time as he would not be coming down to dinner.

She saw me in and left us, and I took the red leather armchair as indicated by Roland.

'How can I help you?' he said civilly, his head supported by the high-backed wheelchair. 'More guards? I have met Sammy,' he smiled faintly. 'He's amusing.'

'No, monsieur, not more guards. I wondered if I could go to see your lawyer, Gerald Greening, early tomorrow morning. Would you mind if I made an appointment?'

'Is this to do with Henri Nanterre?'

'Yes, monsieur.'

'Could you say why you want Gerald?'

I explained. He said wearily that he saw no prospect of success, but that I needn't go to Gerald's office, Gerald would come to the house. The world, I saw in amusement, was divided between those who went to lawyers' offices, and those to whom lawyers came.

Roland said that if I would look up Gerald's home number and get through to it, he would speak to Gerald himself, if he were in, and in a short time the appointment was made.

'He will come here on his way to his office,' Roland said, handing me the receiver to replace. 'Eight-thirty. Give him breakfast.'

'Yes, monsieur.'

He nodded a fraction. 'Goodnight, Kit.'

I went down to dinner, which took place in more silence than ever, and later, as he'd threatened, Nanterre telephoned.

When I heard his voice, I pressed the record button, but again not that for conference.

'I'll talk to anyone but you,' he said.

'Then no one.'

He shouted, 'I want to talk to Casilia.'

'No.'

'I will talk to Roland.'

'No.'

'To Beatrice.'

'No.'

'You'll regret it,' he yelled, and crashed down the receiver.

CHAPTER NINETEEN

Litsi and I entertained Gerald Greening in the morning room, where he ate copiously of kippers followed by eggs and bacon, all furnished by Dawson, forewarned.

'Mm, mm,' Greening grunted as we explained what we wanted. 'Mm . . . no problem at all. Would you pass me the butter?'

He was rounded and jovial, patting his stomach. 'Is there any toast?'

From his briefcase, he produced a large pad of white paper upon which he made notes. 'Yes, yes,' he said busily, writing away. 'I get the gist, absolutely. You want your intentions cast into foolproof legal language, is that right?'

We said it was.

'And you want this typed up properly this morning and furnished with seals?'

Yes please, we said. Two copies.

'No problem.' He gave me his coffee cup absent-mindedly to take to the sideboard for a hot refill. 'I can bring them back here by...' he consulted his watch, '... say twelve noon. That all right?'

We said it would do.

He pursed his lips. 'Can't manage it any faster. Have to draft it properly, get it typed without mistakes, all that sort of thing, checked, drive over from the City.'

We understood.

'Marmalade?'

We passed it.

'Anything else?'

'Yes,' Litsi said, fetching from a side table the buff French form which had been in the notary's briefcase, 'some advice on this.'

Gerald Greening said in surprise, 'Surely the Frenchmen took that away with them when Monsieur de Brescou refused to sign?'

'This is a duplicate blank copy, not filled in,' Litsi said. 'We think the one Henri Nanterre wanted signed would have represented the first page of a whole bunch of documents. Kit and I want this unused copy to form page one of our own bunch of documents.' He passed it to Greening. 'As you see, it's a general form of contract, with spaces for details, and in French, of course. It must be binding, or Henri Nanterre wouldn't have used it. I propose to write in French in the spaces provided, so that this and the accompanying document together constitute a binding contract under French law. I'd be grateful,' he said in his most princely tone, 'if you would advise me as to wording.'

'In French?' Greening said apprehensively.

'In English . . . I'll translate.'

They worked on it together until each was satisfied and Greening had embarked on round four of toast. I envied him not his bulk nor his appetite, but his freedom from restraint, and swallowed my character-less vitamins wishing they at least smelled of breakfast.

He left after the fifth slice, bearing away his notes and promising immediate action; and, true to his word, he reappeared in his chauffeur-driven car at ten minutes to twelve. Litsi and I were both by then in the library watching the street, and we opened the front door to the bulky solicitor and took him into the office used by the elfin Mrs Jenkins.

There we stapled to the front page of one of Greening's imposing-looking documents the original French form, and a photocopy of it to the other, each with the new wording typed in neatly, leaving large spaces for signing.

From there we rode up in the lift to Roland de Brescou's private sitting room where he and the princess and Danielle were all waiting.

Gerald Greening with vaguely theatrical flourishes presented the documents to each of them in turn, and to Litsi, asking them each to sign their names four times, once on each of the French forms; once at the end of each document.

Each document was sewn through with pink tape down the left hand margin, as with wills, and each space for a signature at the end was provided with a round red seal.

Greening made everyone say aloud archaic words about signing, sealing and delivering, made them put a finger on each seal and witnessed each signature himself with precision. He required that I also witness each signature, which I did.

'I don't know how much of all this is strictly necessary,' he said happily, 'but Mr Fielding wanted these documents unbreakable by any possible quibble of law, as he put it, so we have two witnesses, seals, declarations, everything. I do hope you all understand exactly what you've been signing as unless you should burn them or otherwise destroy them, these documents are irrevocable.'

Everyone nodded, Roland de Brescou with sadness.

'That's splendid,' Greening said expansively, and began looking around him and at his watch expectantly.

'And now Gerald, some sherry?' the princess suggested with quiet amusement.

'Princess Casilia, what a splendid idea!' he said with imitation surprise. 'A glass would be lovely.'

I excused myself from the party on the grounds that I was riding in the two-thirty at Windsor and should have left fifteen minutes ago.

Litsi picked up the signed documents, returned them to the large envelope Gerald Greening had brought them in, and handed me the completed package.

'Don't forget to telephone,' he said.

'No.'

He hesitated. 'Good luck,' he said.

They all thought he meant with the races, which was perfectly proper.

The princess had no runners as she almost never went to Windsor races, having no box there. Beatrice was spending the day in the beauty parlour, renovating her self-esteem. Litsi was covering for Sammy who was supposed to be resting. I hadn't expected Danielle to come with me on her own, but she followed me onto the landing from Roland's room and said, 'If I come with you, can you get me to work by six-thirty?'

'With an hour to spare.'

'Shall I come?'

'Yes,' I said.

She nodded and went off past the princess's rooms to her own to fetch a coat, and we walked round to the mews in a reasonable replica of the old companionship. She watched me check the car and without comment waited some distance away while I started the engine and stamped on the brakes, and we talked about Gerald Greening on the way to Windsor, and about Beatrice at Palm Beach, and about her news bureau: safe subjects, but I was glad just to have her there at all.

She was wearing the fur-lined swinging green-grey shower proof jacket I'd given her for Christmas, also black trousers, a white high-necked sweater and a wide floral chintz headband holding back her cloud of dark hair. The consensus among other jockeys that she was a 'knock-out' had never found me disagreeing.

I drove fast to Windsor and we hurried from car park to weighing room, finding Dusty hovering about there looking pointedly at the clock.

'What about your ankle?' he said suspiciously. 'You're still limping.'

'Not when I'm riding,' I said.

Dusty gave me a look as good as his name and scurried away, and Danielle said she would go buy a sandwich and coffee.

'Will you be all right by yourself?'

'Of course . . . or I wouldn't have come.'

She'd made friends over the past months with the wife of a Lambourn trainer I often rode for, and with the wives of one or two of the other jockeys, but I knew the afternoons were lonely when she went racing without her aunt.

'I'm not riding in the fourth; we can watch that together,' I said.

'Yes. Go in and change. You're late.'

I'd taken the packet of documents into the racecourse rather than leave them in the car, and in the changing room gave them into the safekeeping of my valet. My valet's safekeeping would have shamed the vaults of the Bank of England and consisted of stowing things (like one's wallet) in the capacious front pocket of a black vinyl apron. The apron, I guessed, had evolved for that purpose: there were no lockers in the changing rooms, and one hung one's clothes on a peg.

It wasn't a demanding day from the riding point of view. I won the first of my races (the second on the card) by twenty lengths, which Dusty said was too far, and lost the next by the same distance, again to his disapproval. The next was the fourth race, which I spent on the stands with Danielle, having seen her also briefly on walks from the weighing room to parade ring. I told her the news of Joe, the jockey injured at Sandown, who was conscious and on the mend, and she said she'd had coffee with Betsy, the Lambourn trainer's wife. Everything was fine, she said, just fine.

It was the third day of March, blustery and cold, and the Cheltenham National Hunt Festival was all of a sudden as near as next week.

'Betsy says it's a shame about the Gold Cup,' Danielle said. 'She says you won't have a ride in it, now Col's dead.'

'Not unless some poor bugger breaks his collar bone.'

'Kit!'

'That's how it goes.'

She looked as if she didn't need to be reminded, and I was sorry I had. I went out to the fifth race wondering if that day was some sort of test: if she were finding out for herself with finality whether or not she could permanently face what life with me entailed. I shivered slightly in the wind and thought the danger of losing her the worst one of all.

I finished third in the race, and when I returned to the unsaddling enclosure, Danielle was standing there waiting, looking strained and pale and visibly trembling.

'What is it?' I said sharply, sliding down from the horse. 'What's the matter?'

'He's here,' she said with shock. 'Henri Nanterre. I'm sure . . . it's him.'

'Look,' I said, 'I've got to weigh in, just sit on the scales. I'll come straight back out. You just stand right outside the weighing room door . . . don't move from there.'

'No.'

She went where I pointed, and I unsaddled the horse and made vaguely hopeful remarks to the mildly pleased owners. I passed the scales, gave my saddle, whip and helmet to my valet and went out to Danielle, who had stopped actually trembling but still looked upset.

'Where did you see him?' I asked.

'On the stands, during the race. He seemed to be edging towards me, coming up from below, coming sideways, saying "excuse me" to people and looking at me now and then as if checking where I was.'

'You're sure it was him?'

'He was just like the photograph. Like you've described him. I didn't realize to begin with . . . then I recognized him. I was . . .' she swallowed, ' . . . terrified. He sort of snaked round people, sliding like an eel.'

'That's him,' I said grimly.

'I slid away from him,' Danielle said. 'It was like . . . panic. I couldn't move fast . . . so many people, all watching the race and annoyed with me . . . when I got off the stands the race was over . . . and I ran . . . What am I going to do? You're riding in the next race.'

'Well, what you're going to do is dead boring, but you'll be safe.' I smiled apologetically. 'Go into the Ladies and stay there. Find a chair there and wait. Tell the attendant you're sick, faint, tired, anything. Stay there until after the race, and I'll come and fetch you. Half an hour, not much more. I'll send someone in with a message . . . and don't come out for any message except mine. We'll need a password . . .'

'Christmas Day,' she said.

'OK. Don't come out without the password, not even if you get a message saying I'm on my way to hospital, or something like that. I'll give my valet the password and tell him to fetch you if I can't . . . but I will,' I said, seeing the extra fright in her expression. 'I'll ride bloody carefully. Try not to let Nanterre see you going in there, but if he does . . .'

'Don't come out,' she said. 'Don't worry, I won't.'

'Danielle . . .'

'Yes?'

'I do love you,' I said.

She blinked, ducked her head, and went away fast,

and I thought Nanterre would have known I would be at Windsor races, he had only to look in the newspaper, and that I and anyone in the princess's family was vulnerable everywhere not just in dark alleys.

I followed Danielle, keeping her in sight until her backview vanished into the one place Nanterre couldn't follow, and then hurried back to change colours and weigh out. I didn't see the Frenchman anywhere, which didn't mean he hadn't seen me. The highly public nature of my work on racecourses, however, I thought, might be acting in our favour: Nanterre couldn't easily attack me at the races because everywhere I went, people were watching. In parade rings, on horses, on the stands . . . wherever a jockey went in breeches and colours, heads turned to look. Anonymity took over at the racecourse exits.

I rode that last race at Windsor with extreme concentration, particularly as it was a steeplechase for novice jumpers, always an unpredictable event. My mount was trained not by Wykeham but by Betsy's husband, the Lambourn trainer, and it would be fair to say he got a good schooling run rather than a flat-out scramble.

Betsy's husband was satisfied with fourth place because the horse had jumped well, and I said, 'Next time, he'll win,' as one does, to please him and the owners.

I weighed in for fourth place, changed fast, collected my valuables from the valet and wrote a short note for Danielle.

'Christmas Day has dawned. Time to go.'

It was Betsy, in the end, who took the note into the Ladies, coming out smiling with Danielle a minute later.

I sighed with relief: Danielle also, it seemed. Betsy shook her head over our childish games, and Danielle and I went out to the rapidly emptying car park.

'Did you see Nanterre?' Danielle asked.

'No. Nowhere.'

'I'm sure it was him.'

'Yes, so am I.'

My car stood almost alone at the end of a line, its neighbours having departed. I stopped well before we reached it and brought the car-starter out of my pocket.

'But that,' Danielle said in surprise, 'is your toy for freezes.'

'Mm,' I said, and pressed its switch.

There was no explosion. The engine started sweetly, purring to life. We went on towards the car and I did the other checks anyway, but finding nothing wrong.

'What if it had blown up?' Danielle said.

'Better the car than us.'

'Do you think he *would*?'

'I really don't know. I don't mind taking precautions that turn out to be unnecessary. It's "if only" that would be embarrassing.'

I drove out onto the motorway and at the first intersection went off it and round and started back in the opposite direction.

'More avoidance of "if only"?' Danielle said with irony.

'Do you want acid squirted in your face?'

'Not especially.'

'Well . . . we don't know what sort of transport Nanterre's got. And one car can sit inconspicuously behind you for hours on a motorway. I'd not like him to jump us in those small streets at Chiswick.'

When we reached the next intersection I reversed the process and Danielle studied the traffic out of the rear window.

'Nothing came all the way round after us,' she said.

'Good.'

'So can we relax?'

'The man who's coming to fetch you tonight is called Swallow,' I said. 'When the car comes for you, get those big men on the studio reception desk to ask him his name. If he doesn't say Swallow, check up with the car-hire firm.' I slid my wallet out. 'Their card's in there, in the front.'

She took the card and passed the wallet back.

'What haven't you thought of?'

'I wish I knew.'

Even with the wrong direction detour, it was a short journey from Windsor to Chiswick, and we arrived in the streets leading to the studio a good hour before six-thirty.

'Do you want to go in early?' I asked.

'No . . . Park the car where we can sit and look at the river.'

I found a spot where we could see brown water sliding slowly upstream, covering the mud-flats as the tide came in. There were seagulls flying against the wind, raucously calling, and a coxed four feathering their oars with curved fanatical backs.

'I have . . . er . . . something to tell you,' Danielle said nervously.

'No,' I said with pain.

'You don't know what it is.'

'Today was a test,' I said.

Danielle said slowly, 'I forget sometimes that you can read minds.'

'I can't. Not often. You know that.'

'You just did.'

'There are better days than today,' I said hopelessly.

'And worse.'

I nodded.

'Don't look so sad,' she said. 'I can't bear it.'

'I'll give it up if you'll marry me,' I said.

'Do you mean that?'

'Yes.'

She didn't seem overjoyed. I'd lost, it seemed, on all counts.

'I . . . er . . .' she said faintly. 'If you don't give it up, I'll marry you.'

I thought I hadn't heard right.

'*What* did you say?' I demanded.

'I said . . .' She stopped. 'Do you want to marry me or don't you?'

'That's a bloody silly question.'

I leaned towards her and she to me, and we kissed like a homecoming.

I suggested transferring to the rear seat, which we did, but not for gymnastic love-making, partly because of daylight and frequent passers-by, partly because of the unsatisfactoriness of the available space. We sat with our arms round each other, which after the past weeks I found unbelievable and boringly said so several times over.

'I didn't mean to do this,' she said. 'When I came back from the Lake District, I was going to find a way of saying it was all over . . . a mistake.'

'What changed your mind?'

'I don't know . . . lots of things. Being with you so much . . . missing you yesterday . . . Odd things . . . seeing how Litsi respects you . . . Betsy saying I was lucky . . . and Joe's wife . . . She threw up, you know. Everything up. Everything down. She was sweating and cold . . . and pregnant . . . I asked her how she managed to live with the fear . . . she said if it was fear and Joe against no fear, no Joe, the choice was easy.'

I held her close. I could feel her heart beating.

'Today I was wandering about, looking at things,' she said. 'Wondering if I wanted a life of racecourses and winter and perpetual anxiety . . . watching you go out on those horses, with you not knowing . . . and not caring . . . if it's going to be your last half-hour ever . . . and doing that five or six hundred times every year. I looked at the other jockeys on their way out to the parade ring, and they're all like you . . . perfectly calm, as if they're going to an office.'

'Much better than an office.'

'Yes, for you.' She kissed me. 'You can thank Aunt Casilia for shaming me into going racing again . . . but most of all, Joe's wife. I thought today clearly of what life would be like without you . . . no fear, no Kit . . . like she said . . . I guess I'll take the fear.'

'And throw up.'

'Everything up, everything down. She said it was like that for all of the wives, sometime or other. And a few husbands, I guess.'

It was odd, I thought, how life could totally change from one minute to the next. The fog of wretchedness of the past month had vanished like ruptured cobwebs. I felt light-heartedly, miraculously happy, more even than in the beginning. Perhaps one truly had to have lost and regained, to know that sort of joy.

'You won't change your mind, will you?' I said.

'No, I won't,' she answered, and spent a fair time doing her best, in the restricted circumstances, to show me she meant it.

I saw her eventually into the studio and drove back towards Eaton Square on euphoric auto-pilot, returning to earth in time to park carefully and methodically in the usual place in the mews.

319

I switched off the engine and sat looking vaguely at my hands, sat there for a while thinking of what might lie ahead. Then with a mental shiver I telephoned to the house, and got Litsi immediately, as if he'd been waiting.

'I'm in the alley,' I said.

CHAPTER TWENTY

We didn't know how he would come, or when, or even *if*.

We'd shown him an opportunity and loaded him with a motive. Given him a time and place when he could remove an immovable obstruction: but whether or not he would accept the circuitous invitation, heaven alone knew.

Henri Nanterre . . . his very name sounded threatening.

I thought about his being at Windsor and making his way through the crowds on the stands, moving upwards and sideways, approaching Danielle. I thought that until that afternoon he might not have reliably known what she looked like. He'd seen her in the dark the previous Monday, when he'd opened her tyre valves and chased her, but it had been her car he had identified her by, not her face.

He'd probably have seen her with Litsi at Bradbury, but maybe not from close to. He'd have known she was the young woman with Litsi because Beatrice had told him they were going together with me.

Nanterre might not have known that Danielle had gone to Windsor at all until he'd seen her with me several times in the paddock and on the stands during the fourth race. He couldn't have gone to Windsor with any advance plans, but what he'd meant to do if he'd reached Danielle was anyone's nightmare.

I was sitting with these thoughts not in my own car but on a foam cushion on the floor inside the garage where Danielle was keeping her little Ford. One of the garage doors was open about a hand's span, enough for me to see the Mercedes and a good deal of the mews, looking up towards the road entrance. A few people were coming home from work, opening their garages, shunting the cars in, closing and locking. A few were reversing the process, going out for the evening. The mechanics had long gone, all their garages silent. Several cars, like the Mercedes, were parked in the open, close to the sides, leaving a scant passage free in the centre.

Dusk had turned to night, and local bustle died into the restless distant roar of London's traffic. I sat quietly with a few pre-positioned necessities to hand, like Perrier, smoked salmon and an apple, and rehearsed in my mind all sorts of eventualities, none of which happened.

Every half hour or so, I rose to my feet, stretched my spine, paced round Danielle's car, and sat down again. Nothing of much interest occurred in the mews, and the hands of my watch travelled like slugs; eight o'clock, nine o'clock, ten.

I thought of Danielle, and of what she'd said when I left her.

'For Aunt Casilia's sake I must hope that the rattlesnake turns up in the mews, but if you get yourself killed, I'll never forgive you.'

'A thought for eternity,' I said.

'You just make sure eternity is spent right here on earth, with me.'

'Yes, ma'am,' I said, and kissed her.

The rattlesnake, I thought, yawning as eleven o'clock passed, was taking his time. I normally went round to the mews at one-thirty so as to be at Chiswick before two, and I thought that if Nanterre was planning a direct physical attack of any sort, he would be there well before that time, seeking a shadow to hide in. He hadn't been there before seven, because I'd searched every cranny before settling in the garage, and there were no entrances other than the way in from the street. If he'd sneaked in somehow since then without my seeing him, we were maybe in trouble.

At eleven-fifteen, I stretched my legs round Danielle's car and sat down again.

At eleven-seventeen, unaware, he came to the lure.

I'd been hoping against hope, longing for him to come, wanting to expect it . . . and yet, when he did, my skin crawled with animal fear as if the tiger were indeed stalking the goat.

He walked openly down the centre of the mews as if he owned a car there, moving with his distinctive eel-like lope, fluid and smooth, not a march.

He was turning his head from side to side, looking at the silent parked cars, and even in the dim light filtering down from the high windows of the surrounding buildings, the shape of nose and jaw were unmistakable.

He came closer and closer; and he wasn't looking for a hiding place, I saw, but for my car.

For one appalling moment he looked straight at the partly opened door of the garage where I sat, but I was immobile in dark clothes in dark shadow, and I started breathing again when he appeared to see nothing to alarm him or frighten him away.

Nanterre was there, I thought exultantly; right there in front of my eyes, and all our planning had come to pass. Whatever should happen, I reckoned that that was a triumph.

Nanterre looked back the way he'd come, but nothing stirred behind him.

He came close to my car. He stopped beside it, about the length of a Rolls Royce away, and he coolly fiddled about and opened the passenger's seat door with some sort of key as if he'd spent a lifetime thieving.

Well bloody well, I thought, and heard him unlatch the bonnet with the release knob inside the car. He raised the bonnet, propped it open with its strut, and leaned over the engine with a lighted torch as if working on a fault: anyone coming into the mews at that point would have paid no attention.

After a while, he switched off the torch and closed the bonnet gently, latching it by direct downward pressure of both palms, not by a more normal brisk slam. Finally he shut the open passenger door quietly; and as he turned away to leave, I saw he was smiling.

I wondered whether what he'd left by my engine was plastic, like his guns.

He'd walked several paces along the mews before I stood, slid out through the door and started after him, not wanting him to hear me too soon.

I waited until he was nearing a particular small white car parked on one side, and then I ran swiftly up behind him, quiet in rubber soles on the cobbles, and shone a torch of my own on the back of his neck.

'Henri Nanterre,' I said.

He was struck for a long moment into slow motion, unable to move from shock. Then he was fumbling, tearing at the front of a bloused gaberdine jacket, trying to free the pistol holstered beneath.

'Sammy,' I yelled, and Sammy shot like a screaming cannonball out of the small white car, my voice and his whooping cries filling the quiet place with nerve-breaking noise.

Nanterre, his face rigid, pulled the pistol free. He

swung it towards me, taking aim ... and Sammy, true to his boast, kicked it straight out of his hand.

Nanterre ran, leaving the gun clattering to the ground.

Sammy and I ran after him, and from another, larger, parked car, both Thomas and Litsi, shouting manfully and shining bright torches, emerged to stand in his way.

Thomas and Litsi stopped him and Sammy and I caught hold of him, Sammy tying Nanterre's left wrist to Thomas's right with nylon cord and an intriguingly nice line in knots.

Not the most elegant of captures, I thought, but effective all the same; and for all the noise we'd made, no one came with curious questions to the fracas, no one in London would be so foolish. Dark alleys were dark alleys, and with noise, even worse.

We made Nanterre walk back towards the Mercedes. Thomas half dragging him, Sammy stepping behind him and kicking him encouragingly on the calves of the legs.

When we reached the pistol, Sammy picked it up, weighed it with surprise in his hand, and briefly whistled.

'Bullets?' I asked.

He slid out the clip and nodded. Seven,' he said. 'Bright little darlin's.'

He slapped the gun together again, looked around him, and dodged off sideways to hide it under a nearby car, knowing I didn't want to use it myself.

Nanterre was beginning to recover his usual brow-beating manner and to bluster that what we were doing was against the law. He didn't specify which law, and nor was he right. Citizens' arrests were perfectly legal.

Not knowing what to expect, we'd had to make the best plans we could to meet anything that might happen. I'd hired the small white car and the larger dark one, both with tinted windows, and Thomas and I had parked them that morning in spaces which we knew from mews-observation weren't going to obstruct anyone else: the larger car in the space nearest to the way in from the road, the white car half way between there and the Mercedes.

Litsi, Thomas and Sammy had entered the cars after I'd searched the whole place and telephoned reassuringly again to Litsi, and they'd been prepared to wait until one-thirty and hope.

No one had known what Nanterre would do if he came to the mews. We'd decided that if he came in past Litsi and Thomas and hid himself before he reached the white car, Litsi and Thomas would set up a racket and shine torches to summon Sammy and me to their aid, and we'd reckoned that if he came in past Sammy, I would see him, and everyone would wait for my cue, which they had.

We'd all acknowledged that Nanterre, if he came to the area, might decide to sit in his car out in the street, waiting for me to walk round from the square, and that if he did that, or if he didn't come at all, we'd spent a long while preparing for a big anti-climax.

There had been the danger that even if he came, we could lose him, that he'd slip through our grasp and escape: and there had been the worse danger that we would panic him into shooting, and that one or more of us could be hurt. Yet when that moment had come, when he'd freed his gun and pointed it my way, the peril, long faced, had gone by so fast that it seemed suddenly nothing, not worth the consideration.

We had meant, if we captured Nanterre, to take him into the garage where I'd waited for him to come, but I did a fast rethink on the way down the alley, and stopped by my car.

The others paused enquiringly.

'Thomas,' I said, 'untie your wrist and attach Mr Nanterre to the rear-view mirror beside the front passenger door.'

Thomas, unquestioning, took a loop of cord off one of his fingers and pulled it, and all the knots round his wrist fell apart: Sammy's talents seemed endless. Thomas tied much more secure knots round the sturdy mirror assembly, and Nanterre told us very loudly and continuously that we were making punishable mistakes.

'Shut up,' I said equally loudly, without much effect.

'Let's gag him,' Thomas said cheerfully. He produced a used handkerchief from his trousers pocket, at the sight of which Nanterre blessedly stopped talking.

'Gag him if someone comes into the mews,' I said, and Thomas nodded.

'Was there enough light,' I asked Litsi, Sammy and Thomas, 'for you to see Mr Nanterre lift up the bonnet of my car?'

They all said that they'd seen.

Nanterre's mouth fell soundlessly open, and for the first time seemed to realize he was in serious trouble.

'Mr Nanterre,' I said conversationally to the others, 'is an amateur who has left his fingerprints all over my paintwork. It might be a good idea at this point to bring in the police.'

The others looked impassive because they knew I didn't want to, but Nanterre suddenly tugged frantically at Sammy's securely tied knots.

'There's an alternative,' I said.

Nanterre, still struggling under Sammy's interested gaze, said, 'What alternative?' furiously.

'Tell us why you came here tonight, and what you put in my car.'

'*Tell you . . .*'

'Yes. Tell us.'

He was a stupid man, essentially. He said violently, 'Beatrice must have warned you. That cow. She got frightened and told you . . .' He glared at me with concentration. 'All that stood between me and my *millions* was de Brescou's signature and you . . . you . . . everywhere, in my way.'

'So you decided on a little bomb, and pouf, no obstructions?'

'You made me,' he shouted. 'You drove me ... If you were dead, he would sign.'

I let a moment go by, then I said, 'We talked to the man who gave your message to Prince Litsi at Bradbury. He picked you out from a photograph. We have his signed statement.'

Nanterre said viciously, 'I saw your advertisement. If Prince Litsi had died, no one would have known of the message.'

'Did you mean him to die?'

'Live, die, I didn't care. To frighten him, yes. To get de Brescou to sign.' He tried ineffectually still to unravel his bonds. 'Let me go.'

I went instead into the garage where I'd waited and came out again with the big envelope of signed documents.

'Stop struggling,' I said to Nanterre, 'and listen carefully.'

He paid little attention.

'Listen,' I said, 'or I fetch the police.'

He said sullenly then that he was listening.

'The price of your freedom,' I said, 'is that you put your signature to these contracts.'

'What are they?' he said furiously, looking at their impressive appearance. 'What contracts?'

'They change the name of the de Brescou et Nanterre construction company to the Gascony construction company, and they constitute an agreement between the two equal owners to turn the private company into a public company, and for each owner to put his entire holding up for public sale.'

He was angrily and bitterly astounded.

'The company is *mine* . . . I manage it . . . I will *never* agree!'

'You'll have to,' I said prosaically.

I produced the small tape recorder from the pocket of my jacket, pressed the rewind button slightly, and started it playing.

Nanterre's voice came out clearly 'Live, die, I didn't care. To frighten him, yes. To get de Brescou to sign.'

I switched off. Nanterre, incredibly, was silent, remembering, perhaps, the other incriminating things he had said.

'We have the evidence of the messenger at Bradbury,' I said. 'We have your voice on this tape. We have your bomb, I suspect, in my car. You'll sign the contract, you know.'

'There's no bomb in your car,' he said furiously.

'Perhaps a firework?' I said.

He looked at me blankly.

'Someone's coming into the mews,' Thomas said urgently, producing the handkerchief. 'What do we do?' A car had driven in, coming home to its garage.

'If you yell,' I said to Nanterre with menace, 'the police will be here in five minutes and you'll regret it . . . They're not kind to people who plant bombs in cars.'

The incoming car drove towards us and stopped just before reaching Sammy's white hiding place. The people got out, opened their garage, drove in, closed the doors, and looked our way dubiously.

'Goodnight,' I called out, full of cheer.

'Goodnight,' they replied, reassured, and walked away to the street.

'Right,' I said, relaxing, 'time to sign.'

'I will not sell the company. I *will not*.'

I said patiently, 'You have no alternative except going to prison for attempting to murder both Prince Litsi and myself.'

He still refused to face facts: and perhaps he felt as outraged at being coerced to sign against his will as Roland had done.

I brought the car-starting gadget out of my pocket and explained what it was.

Nanterre at last began to shake, and Litsi, Sammy and Thomas backed away from the car in freshly awakened genuine alarm, as if really realizing for the first time what was in there, under the bonnet.

'It'll be lonely for you,' I said to Nanterre. 'We'll walk to the end of the mews, leaving you here. Prince Litsi and the other two will go away. When they're safely back in the house in Eaton Square, I'll press the switch that starts my engine.'

Litsi, Sammy and Thomas had already retreated a good way along the mews.

'You'll die by your own bomb,' I said, and put into my voice and manner every shred of force and conviction I could summon. 'Goodbye,' I said.

I turned away. Walked several steps. Wondered if he would be too scared to call my bluff; wondered if anyone would have the nerve to risk it.

'Come back,' he yelled. There was real fear in the rising voice. Real deadly fear.

Without any pity, I stopped and turned.

'Come back . . .'

I went back. There was sweat in great drops on his forehead, running down. He was struggling frantically still with the knots, but also trembling too much to succeed.

'I want to make guns,' he said feverishly. 'I'd make millions . . . I'd have *power* . . . The de Brescous are rich, the Nanterres never were . . . I want to be rich by world standards . . . to have power . . . I'll give you a million pounds . . . more . . . if . . . you get Roland to sign . . . to make guns.'

'No,' I said flatly, and turned away again, showing him the starter.

'All right, all right . . .' He gave in completely, finally almost sobbing. 'Put that thing down . . . put it down . . .'

I called up the mews, 'Litsi.'

The other three stopped and came slowly back.

333

'Mr Nanterre will sign,' I said.

'Put that thing down,' Nanterre said again faintly, all the bullying megatones gone. 'Put it down.'

I put the starter back in my pocket, which still frightened him.

'It can't go off by itself, can it?' Litsi asked, not with nervousness, but out of caution.

I shook my head. 'The switch needs firm pressure.'

I showed Nanterre the contracts more closely and saw the flicker of fury in his eyes when he saw the first page of each was the same sort of form he'd demanded that Roland should sign.

'We need your signature four times,' I said. 'On each front page, and on each attached document. When you sign the attached documents, put your forefinger on the red seal beside your name. The three of us who are not in any way involved in the de Brescou et Nanterre business will sign under your name as witnesses.'

I put my pen into his shaking right hand and rested the first of the documents on top of my car.

Nanterre signed the French form. I turned to the last page of the longer contract and pointed to the space allotted to him. He signed again, and he put his finger on the seal.

With enormous internal relief, I produced the second set for a repeat performance. In silence, with sweat dripping off his cheeks, he signed appropriately again.

I put my name under his in all four places, followed each time by Thomas and Sammy.

'That's fine,' I said, when all were completed. 'Monsieur de Brescou's lawyers will put the contracts into operation at once. One of these two contracts will be sent to you or your lawyers in France.'

I put the documents back into their envelope and handed it to Litsi, who put it inside his coat, hugging it to his chest.

'Let me go,' Nanterre said, almost whispering.

'We'll untie you from the mirror so that you can remove what you put in my car,' I said. 'After that, you can go.'

He shuddered, but it seemed not very difficult for him, in the end, to unfix the tampered-with wiring and remove what looked like, in size and shape, a bag of sugar. It was the detonator sticking out of it that he treated with delicate respect, unclipping and separating, and stowing the pieces away in several pockets. 'Now let me go,' he said, wiping sweat away from his face with the backs of his hands.

I said, 'Remember we'll always have the Bradbury messenger's affidavit and the tape recording of your voice . . . and we all heard what you said. Stay away from the de Brescous, cause no more trouble.'

He gave me a sick, furious and defeated glare. Sammy didn't try to undo his handiwork but cut the nylon cord off Nanterre's wrist with a pair of scissors.

'Start the car,' Litsi said, 'to show him you weren't fooling.'

'Come away from it,' I said.

We walked twenty paces up the mews, Nanterre among us, and I took out the starter and pressed the switch.

The engine fired safely, strong, smooth and powerful.

I looked directly at Nanterre, at the convinced droop of his mouth, at the unwilling acceptance that his campaign was lost. He gave us all a last comprehensive, unashamed, unrepentant stare, and with Thomas and Sammy stepping aside to let him pass, he walked away along the mews, that nose, that jaw, still strong, but the shoulders sagging.

We watched him in silence until he reached the end of the mews and turned into the street, not looking back.

Then Sammy let out a poltergeist 'Youwee' yell of uncomplicated victory, and went with jumping feet to fetch the pistol from where he'd hidden it.

He presented it to me with a flourish, laying it flat onto my hands.

'Spoils of war,' he said, grinning.

CHAPTER TWENTY-ONE

Litsi and I drank brandy in the sitting room to celebrate, having thanked Thomas and Sammy copiously
for their support; and we telephoned to Danielle to tell
her we weren't lying in puddles of blood.

'Thank goodness,' she said. 'I haven't been able to
think what I'm doing.'

'I suppose what we did was thoroughly immoral,'
Litsi commented, after I'd put down the receiver.

'Absolutely,' I agreed equably. 'We did exactly what
Nanterre intended to do; extorted a signature under
threat.'

'We took the law into our own hands, I suppose.'

'Justice,' I said, 'in our own hands.'

'And like you said,' he said, smiling, 'there's a difference.'

'He's free, unpunished and rich,' I said, 'and in a
way that's not justice. But he didn't, and can't, destroy
Roland. It was a fair enough bargain.'

I waited up for Danielle after Litsi had gone yawning

337

downstairs, and went to meet her when I heard her come in. She walked straight into my arms, smiling.

'I didn't think you'd go to bed without me,' she said.

'As seldom as possible for the rest of my life.'

We went quietly up to the bamboo room and, mindful of Beatrice next door, quietly to bed and quietly to love. Intensity, I thought, drowning in sensations, hadn't any direct link to noise and could be exquisite in whispers; and if we were more inhibited than earlier in what we said, the silent rediscovery of each other grew into an increased dimension of passion.

We slept, embracing, and woke again before morning, hungry again after deep satisfaction.

'You love me more,' she said, murmuring in my ear.

'I loved you always.'

'Not like this.'

We slept again, languorously, and before seven she showered in my bathroom, put on yesterday's clothes and went decorously down to her own room. Aunt Casilia, she said with composure, would expect her niece to make a pretence at least of having slept in her own bed.

'Would she mind that you didn't?'

'Pretty much the reverse, I would think.'

Litsi and I were already drinking coffee in the morning room when Danielle reappeared, dressed by then in fresh blues and greens. She fetched juice and cereal and made me some toast, and Litsi watched us both with speculation and finally enlightenment.

'Congratulations,' he said to me dryly.

'The wedding,' Danielle said collectedly, 'will take place.'

'So I gathered,' he said.

He and I, a while later, went up to see Roland de Brescou, to give him and the princess the completed contracts.

'I was sure,' Roland said weakly, 'that Nanterre wouldn't agree to dissolve the company. Without it, he can't possibly make guns . . . can he?'

'If ever he does,' I said, 'your name won't be linked with it.'

Gascony, the name we'd given to the new public company, was the ancient name of the province in France where the Château de Brescou stood. Roland had been both pleased and saddened by the choice.

'How did you persuade him, Kit?' the princess asked, looking disbelievingly at the Nanterre signatures.

'Um . . . tied him in knots.'

She gave me a brief glance. 'Then I'd better not ask.'

'He's unhurt and unmarked.'

'And the police?' Roland asked.

'No police,' I said. 'We had to promise no police to get him to sign.'

'A bargain's a bargain,' Litsi nodded. 'We have to let him go free.'

The princess and her husband understood all about keeping one's word, and when I left Roland's room she followed me down to the sitting room, leaving Litsi behind.

'No thanks are enough . . . How *can* we thank you?' she asked with frustration.

'You don't need to. And . . . um . . . Danielle and I will marry in June.'

'I'm very pleased indeed,' she said with evident pleasure, and kissed me warmly on one cheek and then the other. I thought of the times I'd wanted to hug her; and one day perhaps I would do it, though not on a racecourse.

'I'm so sorry about your horses,' I said.

'Yes . . . When you next talk to Wykeham, ask him to start looking about for replacements. We can't expect another Cotopaxi, but next year, perhaps, a runner anyway in the Grand National . . . And don't forget, next week at Cheltenham, we still have Kinley.'

'The Triumph Hurdle,' I said.

I went to Folkestone races by train later that morning with a light heart but without Danielle, who had an appointment with the dentist.

I rode four races and won two, and felt fit, well, bursting with health and for the first time in weeks, carefree. It was a tremendous feeling, while it lasted.

Bunty Ireland, the *Towncrier*'s racing correspondent, gave me a large envelope from Lord Vaughnley: 'Hot off the computers,' Bunty said. The envelope again felt as if it contained very little, but I thanked him for it, and reflecting that I thankfully didn't need the contents any more, I took it unopened with me back to London.

Dinner that evening was practically festive, although Danielle wasn't there, having driven herself to work in her Ford.

'I thought yesterday was her last night for working,' Beatrice said, unsuspiciously.

'They changed the schedules again,' I explained.

'Oh, how irritating.'

Beatrice had decided to return to Palm Beach the next day. Her darling dogs would be missing her, she said. The princess had apparently told her that Nanterre's case was lost, which had subdued her querulousness amazingly.

I'd grown used to her ways: to her pale orange hair and round eyes, her knuckleduster rings and her Florida clothes. Life would be quite dull without the old bag; and moreover, once she had gone, I would soon have to leave also. How long, I wondered, would Litsi be staying . . .

Roland came down to dinner and offered champagne, raising his half-full glass to Litsi and to me in a toast. Beatrice scowled a little but blossomed like a sunflower when Roland said that perhaps, with all the extra capital generated by the sale of the business, he might consider increasing her trust fund. Too forgiving, I thought, yet without her we would very likely not have prevailed.

Roland, the princess and Beatrice retired fairly early,

leaving Litsi and me passing the time in the sitting room. Quite late, I remembered Lord Vaughnley's envelope which I'd put down on a side table on my return.

Litsi incuriously watched me open it and draw out the contents: one glossy black and white photograph, as before, and one short clipping from a newspaper column. Also a brief compliments slip from the *Towncrier*: 'Regret nothing more re Nanterre.'

The picture showed Nanterre in evening dress surrounded by other people similarly clad, on the deck of a yacht. I handed it to Litsi and read the accompanying clipping.

'Arms dealer Ahmed Fuad's fiftieth birthday bash, held on his yacht *Felissima* in Monte Carlo harbour on Friday evening drew guests from as far as California, Peru and Darwin, Australia. With no expense spared, Fuad fed caviar and foie gras to jet-setting friends from his hobby worlds of backgammon, nightclubs and horseracing.'

Litsi passed back the photograph and I gave him the clipping.

'That's what Nanterre wanted,' I said. 'To be the host on a yacht in the Mediterranean, dressed in a white dinner jacket, dispensing rich goodies, enjoying the adulation and the flattery. That's what he wanted . . . those multi-millions, and that power.'

I turned the photograph over, reading the flimsy

information strip stuck to the back: a list of names, and the date.

'That's odd,' I said blankly.

'What is?'

'That party was held last Friday night.'

'What of it? Nanterre must have jetted out there and back, like the others.'

'On Friday night, Col was shot.'

Litsi stared at me.

'Nanterre couldn't have done it,' I said. 'He was in Monte Carlo.'

'But he said he did. He boasted of it to Beatrice.'

I frowned. 'Yes, he did.'

'He must have got someone else to do it,' Litsi said.

I shook my head. 'He did everything himself. Threatened the princess, chased Danielle, set the trap for you, came to put the bomb in my car. He didn't trust any of that to anyone else. He knows about horses, he wanted to see his own filly shot . . . he would have shot Col . . . but he didn't.'

'He confessed to all the horses,' Litsi insisted.

'Yes, but suppose . . . he read about them in the papers . . . read that their deaths were mysterious and no one knew who had killed them . . . He wanted ways to frighten Roland and the princess. Suppose he *said* he'd killed them, when he hadn't?'

'But in that case,' Litsi said blankly, 'who did? Who would want to kill her best horses, if not Nanterre?'

I rose slowly to my feet, feeling almost faint.

'What's the matter?' Litsi said, alarmed. 'You've gone as white as snow.'

'He killed,' I said with a mouth stickily dry, 'the horse I might have won the Grand National on. The horse on which I might have won the Gold Cup.'

'Kit . . .' Litsi said.

'There's only one person,' I said with difficulty, 'who hates me enough to do that. Who couldn't bear to see me win those races . . . who would take away the prizes I hold dearest, because I took away his prize . . .'

I felt breathless and dizzy.

'Sit down,' Litsi said, alarmed.

'Kinley,' I said.

I went jerkily to the telephone and got through to Wykeham.

'I was just going to bed,' he complained.

'Did you stop the dog-patrols?' I demanded.

'Yes, of course. You told me this morning there was no more need for them.'

'I think I was wrong. I can't risk that I was wrong. I'm coming down to your stables now, tonight, and we'll get the dog-patrols back again, stronger than ever, for tomorrow and every day until Cheltenham, and probably beyond.'

'I don't understand,' he said.

'Have you taken your sleeping pill?' I asked.

'No, not yet.'

'Don't do it until I get down to you, will you? And where's Kinley tonight?'

'Back in his own box, of course. You said the danger was past.'

'We'll move him back into the corner box when I get down to you.'

'Kit, no, not in the middle of the night.'

'You want to keep him safe,' I said; and there was no arguing with that.

We disconnected and Litsi said slowly, 'Do you mean Maynard Allardeck?'

'Yes, I do. He found out, about two weeks ago, that he'll never get a knighthood because I sent the film I made of him to the Honours department. He's wanted that knighthood since he was a child, when he told my grandfather that one day the Fieldings would have to bow down to him, because he'd be a lord. He knows horses better than Nanterre . . . he was brought up in his father's racing stable and was his assistant trainer for years. He saw Cascade and Cotopaxi at Newbury, and they were distinctive horses . . . and Col at Ascot . . . unmistakable.'

I went to the door.

'I'll telephone in the morning,' I said.

'I'll come with you,' he said.

I shook my head. 'You'd be up all night.'

'Get going,' he said. 'You saved my family's honour . . . let me pay some of their debt.'

I was grateful, indeed, for the company. We went round again to the dark mews where Litsi said, if I had the car-starter in my pocket, we might as well be sure:

but Nanterre and his bombs hadn't returned, and the Mercedes fired obligingly from a fifty-yard distance.

I drove towards Sussex, telephoning to Danielle on the way to tell her where and why we were going. She had no trouble believing anything bad of Maynard Allardeck, saying he'd looked perfectly crazy at Ascot and Sandown, glaring at me continuously in the way he had.

'*Curdling* with hate,' she said. 'You could feel it like shock waves.'

'We'll be back for breakfast,' I said, smiling. 'Sleep well.' And I could hear her laughing as she disconnected.

I told Litsi on the way about the firework bombs that had been used to decoy the dog-handler away from Col's courtyard, and said, 'You know, in the alley, when Nanterre said he hadn't put a bomb in my car, I asked him if it was a firework. He looked totally blank . . . I didn't think much of it then, but now I realize he simply didn't know what I was talking about. He didn't know about the fireworks at Wykeham's because they didn't get into the papers.'

Litsi made a 'Huh' sort of noise of appreciation and assent, and we came companionably in time into Wykeham's village.

'What are you going to do here?' Litsi said.

I shrugged. 'Walk round the stables.' I explained about the many little courtyards. 'It's not an easy place to patrol.'

'You do seriously think Allardeck will risk trying to kill another of Aunt Casilia's horses?'

'Yes. Kinley, particularly, her brilliant hurdler. I don't seriously suppose he'll try tonight rather than tomorrow or thereafter, but I'm not taking chances.' I paused. 'However am I going to apologize to Princess Casilia . . . to repay . . .'

'What do you mean?'

'Cascade and Cotopaxi and Col died because of the Fielding and Allardeck feud. Because of me.'

'She won't think of it that way.'

'It's the truth.' I turned into Wykeham's driveway. 'I won't let Kinley die.'

I stopped the car in the parking space, and we stepped out into the silence of midnight under a clear sky sparkling with diamond-like stars. The heights and depths of the universe: enough to humble the sweaty strivings of earth.

I took a deep breath of its peace . . . and heard, in the quiet distance, the dull unmistakable thudding explosion of a bolt.

Dear God, I thought. *We're too late.*

I ran. I knew where. To the last courtyard, the one nearest to Wykeham's house. Ran with the furies at my heels, my heart sick, my mind a jumble of rage and fear and dreadful regrets.

I could have driven faster . . . I could have started sooner . . . I could have opened Lord Vaughnley's envelope hours before ... Kinley was dead, and I'd killed him.

I ran into the courtyard, and for all my speed, events on the other side of it moved faster.

As I watched, as I ran, I saw Wykeham struggle to his feet from where he'd been lying on the path outside the doors of the boxes.

Two of the box doors were open, the boxes in shadow, lit only by the light outside in the courtyard. In one box, I could see a horse lying on its side, its legs still jerking in convulsive death throes. Into the other went Wykeham.

While I was still yards away, I saw him pick up something which had been lying inside the box on the brick windowsill. I saw his back going deeper into the box, his feet silent on the peat.

I ran.

I saw another man in the box, taller, grabbing a horse by its head collar.

I saw Wykeham put the thing he held against the second man's head. I saw the tiny flash, heard the awful bang ...

When I reached the door there was a dead man on the peat, a live horse tossing his head and snorting in fright, a smell of burning powder and Wykeham standing, looking down, with the humane killer in his hands.

The live horse was Kinley ... and I felt no relief.

'Wykeham!' I said.

He turned his head, looked at me vaguely.

'He shot my horses,' he said.

'Yes.'

'I killed him. I said I would . . . and I have.'

I looked down at the dead man, at the beautiful suit and the hand-sewn shoes.

He was lying half on his face, and he had a nylon stocking pulled over his head as a mask, with a hole in it behind his right ear.

Litsi ran into the courtyard calling breathlessly to know what had happened. I turned towards him in the box doorway, obstructing his view of what was inside.

'Litsi,' I said, 'go and telephone the police. Use the telephone in the car. Press O and you'll get the operator . . . ask for the police. Tell them a man has been killed here in an accident.'

'*A man!*' he exclaimed. 'Not a horse?'

'Both . . . but tell them a man.'

'Yes,' he said unhappily. 'Right.'

He went back the way he'd come and I turned towards Wykeham, who was wide-eyed now, and beginning to tremble.

'It wasn't an accident,' he said, with pride somewhere in the carriage of his head, in the tone of his voice. 'I killed him.'

'Wykeham,' I said urgently. 'Listen. Are you listening?'

'Yes.'

'Where do you want to spend your last years, in prison or out on the Downs with your horses?'

He stared.

'Are you listening?'

'Yes.'

'There'll be an inquest,' I said. 'And this was an *accident*. Are you listening?'

He nodded.

'You came out to see if all was well in the yard before you went to bed.'

'Yes, I did.'

'You'd had three horses killed in the last ten days . . . the police haven't been able to discover who did it . . . You knew I was coming down to help patrol the yards tonight, but you were naturally worried.'

'Yes.'

'You came into this courtyard, and you saw and heard someone shoot one of your horses.'

'Yes, I did.'

'Is it Abseil?' I longed for him to say no, but he said, 'Yes.'

Abseil . . . racing at breakneck speed over the last three fences at Sandown, clinging to victory right to the post.

I said, 'You ran across to try to stop the intruder doing any more damage . . . you tried to pull the humane killer out of his hands.'

'Yes.'

'He was younger and stronger and taller than you . . .

he knocked you down with the humane killer . . . you fell on the path, momentarily stunned.'

'How do you know?' Wykeham asked, bewildered.

'The marks of the end of the barrel are all down your cheek. It's been bleeding. Don't touch it,' I said, as he began to raise a hand to feel. 'He knocked you down and went into the second box to kill a second horse.'

'Yes, to kill Kinley.'

'Listen . . . He had the humane killer in his hand.'

Wykeham began to shake his head, and then stopped.

I said, 'The man was going to shoot your horse. You grabbed at the gun to stop him. You were trying to take it away from him . . . he was trying to pull it back from your grasp. He was succeeding with a jerk, but you still had your hands on the gun, and in the struggle, when he jerked the gun towards him, the thick end of the barrel hit his head, and the jerk also caused your grasp somehow to pull the trigger.'

He stared.

'You did *not* mean to kill him; are you listening, Wykeham? You meant to stop him shooting your horse.'

'K . . Kit . . .' he said, finally stuttering.

'What are you going to tell the police?'

'I . . . t . . tried to s . . stop him shooting . . .' He swallowed. 'He j . . . jerked the gun . . . against his head . . . It w . . went off.'

He was still holding the gun by its rough wooden butt.

'Throw it down on the peat,' I said.

He did so, and we both looked at it: a heavy, ugly, clumsy instrument of death.

On the windowsill there were several small bright golden caps full of gunpowder. One cocked the gun, fed in the cap, pulled the trigger . . . the gunpowder exploded and shot out the bolt.

Litsi came back, saying the police would be coming, and it was he who switched the light on, revealing every detail of the scene.

I bent down and took a closer look at Maynard's head. There was oil on the nylon stocking where the bolt had gone through, and I remembered Robin Curtiss saying the bolt had been oiled before Col . . . Robin would remember . . . there would be no doubt that Maynard had killed all four horses.

'Do you know who it is?' I said to Wykeham, straightening up.

He half-knew, half couldn't believe it.

'Allardeck?' he said, unconvinced.

'Allardeck.'

Wykeham bent down to pull off the stocking-mask.

'Don't do that,' I said sharply. 'Don't touch it. Anyone can see he came here trying not to be recognized . . . to kill horses . . . no one out for an evening stroll goes around in a nylon mask carrying a humane killer.'

'Did he kill Kinley?' Litsi asked anxiously.

'No, this is Kinley. He killed Abseil.'

Litsi looked stricken. 'Poor Aunt Casilia . . . She said how brilliantly you'd won on Abseil. Why kill that one, who couldn't possibly win the Grand National?' He looked down at Maynard, understanding. 'Allardeck couldn't bear you being brilliant, not on anything.'

The feud was dead, I thought. Finally over. The long obsession had died with Maynard, and he had been dead before he hit the peat, like Cascade and Cotopaxi, Abseil and Col.

A fitting end, I thought.

Litsi said he had told the police he would meet them in the parking place to show them where to come, and presently he went off there.

Wykeham spent a long while looking at Kinley, who was now standing quietly, no longer disturbed, and then less time looking at Maynard.

'I'm glad I killed him,' he said fiercely.

'Yes, I know.'

'Mind you win the Triumph Hurdle.'

I thought of the schooling sessions I'd done with that horse, teaching him distances up on the Downs with Wykeham watching, shaping the glorious natural talent into accomplished experience.

I would do my best, I said.

He smiled. 'Thank you, Kit,' he said. 'Thank you for everything.'

The police came with Litsi: two of them, highly

official, taking notes, talking of summoning medical officers and photographers.

They took Wykeham through what had happened.

'I came out . . . found the intruder . . . he shot my horse.' Wykeham's voice shook. 'I fought him . . . he knocked me down . . . he was going to shoot this horse also . . . I got to my feet . . .'

He paused.

'Yes, sir?' the policeman said, not unsympathetically.

They saw, standing before them on the peat inside the box, standing beside a dead intruder with the intruder's deadly weapon shining with menace in the light, they saw an old thin man with dishevelled white hair, with the dark freckles of age on his ancient forehead, with the pistol marks of dried blood on his cheek.

They saw, as the coroner would see, and the lawyers, and the press, the shaking deteriorating exterior, not the titan who still lived inside.

Wykeham looked at Kinley; at the future, at the horse that could fly on the Downs, tail streaming, jumping like an angel to his destiny.

He looked at the policemen, and his eyes seemed full of sky.

'It was an accident,' he said.

DICK FRANCIS

Omnibus One

PAN BOOKS £9.99

Dick Francis has been thrilling readers for over thirty years with his stories from the world of racing – all fully charged with action, suspense, greed and secrets. Now in one combined edition, here are three novels set to captivate his many fans and new readers alike:

Longshot – Survival writer John Franklin gets the unlikely job of writing the biography of a racehorse trainer. Suddenly, he finds his own survival tips becoming deadly traps . . .

> 'Exceptionally well plotted with convincing characters . . .
> truly exciting'
> ***Spectator***

Straight – On the death of his brother, injured jockey Derek Franklin, inherits a jewellery business – along with some shadowy business associates . . . things are going from bad to worse.

> 'Still the best bet for a winning read'
> ***Mail On Sunday***

High Stakes – Racing may have its rewards but, as Steven Scott finds out to his own cost when he sacks the trainer of his horses, not all of them are innocent . . . or legal.

> 'An unfailing supply of well-managed twists'
> ***Sunday Times***

DICK FRANCIS

Omnibus Two

PAN BOOKS £9.99

Dick Francis has been thrilling readers for over thirty years with his stories from the world of racing – all fully charged with action, suspense, greed and secrets. Now in one combined edition, here are three novels set to captivate his many fans and new readers alike:

Forfeit – A Fleet Street racing correspondent, James Tyrone, has stumbled upon explosive material which is about to blow the roof off the number one policy of the *Sunday Blaze* . . .

> 'Real classic form . . . on no account miss it'
> **Sunday Times**

Risk – An amateur jockey, Roland Britten, has been kidnapped from a racecourse after winning the Cheltenham Gold Cup . . . why?

> 'Dick Francis holds his form like a top-class chaser'
> **Times Literary Supplement**

Reflex – Phillip Nore has discovered the photographs of a dead racing photographer, uncovering corruption on a scale he had never imagined.

> 'Dick Francis has excelled himself'
> **Daily Telegraph**

DICK FRANCIS

Omnibus Three

PAN BOOKS £8.99

Dick Francis has been thrilling readers for over thirty years with his stories from the world of racing. Now in one combined edition, here are three novels set to captivate his many fans and new readers alike:

Slay Ride – David Cleveland has gone to Norway on a straightforward-looking case. An English jockey has gone missing; and so have the racecourse takings. But a simple case goes awry when a dead body turns up . . .

'Enthralling and finely written'
Sunday Telegraph

Proof – Wine merchant Tony Beach witnesses a tragic accident when a runaway horsebox ploughs into a marquee, under which the racing season is being celebrated. When he's called in to advise on sub-standard alcohol in a local nightclub, connections start to click . . .

'Put together brilliantly . . . gripping'
Times Literary Supplement

Banker –Tim Ekaterin's merchant bank is about to invest in £5 million of prime horseflesh – a stallion called Sandcastle. Top breeders reckon it's the safest bet in racing . . . but is it?

'Astonishing . . . fascinating . . . holds us spellbound'
New York Times Book Review

DICK FRANCIS

Omnibus Four

PAN BOOKS £8.99

Dick Francis has been thrilling readers for over thirty years with his stories from the world of racing. Now in one combined edition, here are three novels set to captivate his many fans and new readers alike:

Rat Race – Matt Shore, an experienced pilot, is expecting the quiet life ferrying high-class punters around England's race courses. But then his plane explodes . . .

'A thriller that really thrills'
Daily Mail

Smokescreen – Film action man Edward Lincoln has been asked by a dying friend to find out why her South African racing stable no longer produces winning horses. Now he's being forced to play the resourceful hero for real – or die in one take.

'Wonderfully vivid and sinister'
Sunday Times

Enquiry – No jockey likes being labelled a cheat and Kelly Hughes's career seems doomed. He knows he's been framed, but finding out why could prove fatal . . .

'Highly ingenious'
Times Literary Supplement

OTHER BOOKS

AVAILABLE FROM PAN MACMILLAN